# SHENANDOAH DESTINY

## REBEL SERIES BOOK II

by

Barbara Michel

**Sequel to**

# FORTRESS OF A REBEL

(A trilogy in 1 Volume)

Copyright © 2006 by Barbara D. Michel

*All rights reserved. No part of this book shall be reproduced or transmitted in any form or by any means, electronic, mechanical, magnetic, photographic including photocopying, recording or by any information storage and retrieval system, without prior written permission of the publisher. No patent liability is assumed with respect to the use of the information contained herein. Although every precaution has been taken in the preparation of this book, the publisher and author assume no responsibility for errors or omissions. Neither is any liability assumed for damages resulting from the use of the information contained herein.*

*This is a work of fiction. Names, characters, places, and incidents either are the product of the author's imagination or are used fictitiously. Any resemblance to actual events or locales or persons, living or dead, is entirely coincidental.*

ISBN 0-7414-3485-7

Bible quotations have been taken from the King James Version, unless otherwise noted.

*Published by:*

*1094 New DeHaven Street, Suite 100*
*West Conshohocken, PA 19428-2713*
*Info@buybooksontheweb.com*
*www.buybooksontheweb.com*
*Toll-free (877) BUY BOOK*
*Local Phone (610) 941-9999*
*Fax (610) 941-9959*

*Printed in the United States of America*
*Printed on Recycled Paper*
*Published August 2006*

# DEDICATION

To my husband, Gerald, who has encouraged me to write since I began my first novel. He doesn't complain if I lose track of time while I'm writing at the computer. For this and numerous other reasons, I'm grateful and blessed.

# ACKNOWLEDGMENTS

***Thanks to*** Douglas S. Farnham for the excellent cover picture. His specialty is pencil sketches depicting Amish life and Civil War soldiers. Studio: 814-758-2876

***Appreciation to*** Aaron Weeter, Weeter Photography, Knox, Pennsylvania, for the excellent reproduction of the cover art and for his expertise in choosing the font and design of the title and front cover lettering.

# ABOUT THE AUTHOR

The author lives with her husband, Rev. Gerald W. Michel, in Clarion County, Pennsylvania. She enjoys hearing from her readers. You can write to her in care of:

***Joy Books***, **Box 3, Hawthorn PA 16230**
or
michel@joybooks1.com  *Visit*: www.joybooks1.com

# SHENANDOAH DESTINY

## CHARACTER LIST

### HARRIS FAMILY

Jonathan and Katherine Harris
   Joshua, their eldest son, a lawyer in Richmond
     Melissa Sue, his late wife
     Angela, Joshua's daughter to Melissa Sue
   Breton, second son, missing during the war
     Jo Ellen, his wife
     baby Jonathan, their firstborn
   Tiffany, spied for the Confederacy; married Nathan James.
     Adam, her son to Nathan
   Timothy, youngest Harris son, killed during the war
   Elizabeth Ann, youngest Harris daughter
     Trenton Sherwood, her husband

### HARRIS HIRED HELP

Ellie, housekeeper at Sunny Horizon
   then at Saxon Oaks and Castle Crest
Amos, Ellie's son, was overseer at Sunny Horizon
   then worked at Saxon Oaks and Castle Crest
Jay Michael, Ellie's husband
Cassie & Jonas, housekeeper & field hand at Sunny Horizon
   Children: Priscilla, 17; John, 15; Ben, 13; Naomi, 12;
   Lettie, 10.

### JAMES FAMILY

Nathan, spied during the war; married Tiffany
   Joanna, his late wife
   Trisha, Nathan's daughter to Joanna
   Adam, Nathan's son to Tiffany
Matthew James, Nathan's deceased brother
Emily Rose, Matthew's widow
   Scott & Nat, their five-year-old twins
Mary Burton, Nathan's aunt

# CHARACTER LIST CONTINUED

## HIRED HELP AT CASTLE CREST

Cammy, Nathan's housekeeper
Micah, carriage driver and field hand
Joe Billings, a field hand
Constance Kennan, hired housekeeper
    Alexandra, her three-year-old daughter

## SAXON OAKS

Zachary Saxon, Tiffany's great-uncle
    Darcy Mae, Zachary's housekeeper
    Ruthie Ann, widow of one of the black field hands

## ADDITIONAL CHARACTERS

Luke and Mary Stanford, Jo Ellen's parents
    Luke Junior, their eldest son, killed in the war
    Peter, their second son, married and moved to Indiana
    Hunter, their youngest son, one year younger than Jo
    Alaina, 18, their youngest daughter
David Fisher, mid-twenties, helps rebuild Sunny Horizon
Maggie Travis, displaced during the war; helps at Joshua's home
Sally, black girl at Joshua's, became Jonathan's secretary
Harry Bunsen and Jud Horner, tramps
Bones, Ratford, & Moose, trio of raiders

DeCapendo, Tiffany's black stallion
Quin, Tiffany's Newfoundland
Musket, Nathan's dog
Monarch, Nathan's stallion
Nero, Zachary's dog
Susie, Ellie's cat
Lacy, Jo's Newfoundland puppy

# SHENANDOAH DESTINY

## SCRIPTURES

*"May the God of hope fill you with all joy and peace as you trust in him, so that you may overflow with hope by the power of the Holy Spirit."* **Romans 15:13** (NIV)

*"Wait on the Lord: be of good courage, and he shall strengthen thine heart: wait, I say, upon the Lord."* **Psalm 27: 14**

*"The Lord is my strength and my shield; my heart trusteth in him, and I am helped: therefore my heart greatly rejoiceth; and with my song will I praise him."* **Psalm 28:7**

*"My God shall supply all your need according to his riches in glory by Christ Jesus."* **Philippians 4:19**

*"In all thy ways acknowledge him, and he shall direct thy paths."* **Proverbs 3:6**

*"The Lord is my light and my salvation; whom shall I fear? the Lord is the strength of my life; of whom shall I be afraid?"* **Psalm 27:1**

*"God is our refuge and strength, a very present help in trouble."* **Psalm 46:1**

*"I will say of the Lord, He is my refuge and my fortress: my God; in him will I trust."* **Psalm 91:2**

*"Seek the Lord and his strength: seek his face evermore."* **Psalm 105:4**

*"He giveth power to the faint; and to them that have no might he increaseth strength. . . . But they that wait upon the Lord shall renew their strength."* **Isaiah 40:29-31**

*"May our Lord Jesus Christ himself and God our Father . . . encourage your hearts and strengthen you in every good deed and word."*

**Thessalonians 2:16-17**

# Prologue

### West of Richmond, 1866.

A gust of March wind tore at Jo Ellen's hood and flapped the end of her scarf in her face. Flame's shoes made sucking sounds in the mud and slush. Jo smiled at Bret, then twisted on the buggy seat in order to see Tiffany and Trisha. They stood waving on the front porch of Castle Crest, their blue capes flapping in the breeze. Jo smiled until their buggy rounded a curve and Castle Crest was out of sight, then she faced forward.

Bret's brown eyes sparkled as he leaned toward her to kiss her cheek.

Reveling in his adoration, she tugged on the front of her woolen cape. It was becoming a challenge to cover her expanding abdomen. Her discomfort was increasing, but giving Breton Harris a son or daughter was worth it. She adjusted her bulk, then the lap robe and sighed.

Worry lines appeared on Bret's forehead. "You all right?"

"I feel like a walrus! Her sigh was partly from misery, partly from joy. "One more month to go. I'll be thankful when wee Harris gets here."

He grinned. "So will I. I'd planned to get part of our house built in the Valley before we started our family, but we won't even get to the homestead."

"Are you sorry?"

"Of course not." His chuckle vibrated cords deep within her. "The expectation of your becoming a mother has turned your eyes to silver, darling, and put roses in your cheeks."

She giggled. She wasn't going to tell him that it was the icy wind that added extra color to her face. The adoration in his brown eyes sent her heart racing. His expression told her that he yearned to hug her, but he needed his only hand to gripped the reins. She often thought of the arm Bret had left on a battlefield during the War Between the States, even though he'd adapted well and rarely complained.

A thundering noise drew her attention. She peered ahead. "What's that?" She pointed to a rapidly moving conveyance that was mostly obscured by the trees.

Breton shook his head, making his dark wavy hair move over his ears. The muscle of his squared chin tightened. "Some brute must be whipping his horses."

Jo heard the rattle of a wagon and wheels crashing against the stones on the road. "Give him more room, Bret!"

"I can't get over any farther!" His brows knit with concern as he halted Flame, the buggy dangerously close to the edge of a downward rocky slope.

A lathered team galloped around the bend, the attached wagon on two of its wheels. The horses' nostrils were flaring and their manes flying. Eight large hooves thundered closer, splashing clumps of melting ice and red mud as high as the wagon seat.

"Whoa! Whoa!" George, a young man Zachary had hired recently, bounced on the wagon seat and nearly toppled from his perch. He continued to yell and yank on the reins as he futilely struggled to slow the runaways. The blood had drained from the lad's face, and terror flashed in his widened eyes.

"Jump!" Jo Ellen cried, but there wasn't time.

The team avoided the buggy, but before Jo could draw a relieved breath, the wagon slid sideways, and one of the back wheels locked with their buggy wheel. Metal scraped and wood shattered. Jo Ellen screamed. The impact hurled her body into the air. She landed with a thud and tumbled down the hillside, Flame's wild whinnying echoing in her ears. Small trees tore at her skirt. Her right ankle hit a sharp stone, then her left knee slammed against a protruding root. The jagged edge of a clump of ice ripped across her cheek. Her left arm twisted under her and she heard a bone snap. She screamed again, but the sound died as her head struck a rock and she was sucked into nothingness.

Dazed, Breton groaned. His head throbbed. Blood trickled down his face, stung his eyes and blurred his vision. Excruciating pain ripped through his right leg. He expected to hear another cannon blast and the sound of artillery fire. Instead, silence reigned. The vision of battle slowly vanished as his mind cleared.

"No," he rasped as the recollection of the accident shocked him into clarity of thought. Where was his wife? "Jo?"

There was no answer. He sliced his arm on a piece of sharp metal as he struggled to disentangle himself from the wreckage. More pain seared through the leg that had been wounded in the war. Clawing with his gloved hand, he pushed with his good leg and strained to crawl forward on his belly. Muddy slush clung to his jacket, and blood was smeared on his sleeve. "Jo!" *Where is she?* "Jo!"

Small drifts remained from the last snow and ice particles clung to rocks. He shivered as a blast of wind funneled up the legs of his pants and snatched the knit cap from his head. At the edge of the embankment, he peered down. "Jo!"

She lay so still. Her body was twisted at an odd angle, her arm under her back. Anguish racked his heart. *Is she breathing?* Her cape was open. *She'll freeze!*

"God is our refuge and strength, a very present help in trouble," he whispered, recalling a verse from Psalm 46.

Disregarding his own pain, he grasped a rotting log and tried to maneuver around it. Loose bark peeled off. He lost his grip. Dislodging, the log rolled down the rocky hillside.

Breton tumbled after it. *God, be my strength! I'm in trouble and Jo needs me!*

Bruised and bleeding, he clambered to his wife's side. "Jo!" He jerked his hand free of his muddy glove and reached out to touch her arm. She didn't move.

"Sweetheart?" There was no response. A knife of agony twisted in his gut. How long would it be until someone at Castle Crest realized their predicament and came to help? He tried to call out, but only a garbled sound issued from his throat. If he yelled, who would hear him?

He fought panic as his focus darted over the surrounding fields. Seeing no one, his attention went back to his wife.

"Jo, darling. Please answer me." He tugged on her cape, trying to cover her, but there didn't seem to be enough material. "Jo!"

Her eyes remained closed. Her complexion was pale. Blood trickled from a gash on her temple and soaked into her black ringlets. Another horror slammed him when he noticed the growing bloodstain that darkened her skirt. The baby! It was too early! If they lost their first little one, Jo would be devastated, and so would he. Right now, his darling wife was his first concern. He tugged his own coat off and draped it over her. "Jo!" His voice sounded curdled. "Jo!"

# One

"Mama! Mama, come quick!"

Tiffany hurried from her two-year-old son's nursery and paused to look over the upstairs balustrade at Trisha. The nine-year-old delighted in excitement, but this time her azure eyes were wide and fright seemed branded on her face.

"Horses are coming! Too fast!" She flipped a blond curl over her shoulder, whirled, and ran to the front of the house.

Gripping the banister, Tiffany held up her dark-blue wool skirt with her other hand and rushed down the stairs. In her seventh month of pregnancy, she seemed larger and more awkward than she had been when she carried Adam.

"Papa!" Trisha shrieked, thudding a fist on Nathan's office door. "Runaways!"

Quin, Tiffany's 140 pound Newfoundland, barked and ran circles in the foyer, then whined at the door, his feet dancing on the oak parquet.

The sound of galloping hooves and a rattling wagon came closer. Tiffany hurried to a window. One of Uncle Zachary's teams left the lane and headed across the front yard, the wagon barely missing a stone pillar. George, the fifteen-year-old driver, tumbled from the seat, thumped on the ground and rolled into the shrubbery. Melting snow flipped from the spindly branches and sifted down on him. Tiffany cried out as a back wagon wheel rolled within inches of the boy's head.

"Nathan!" Tiffany grasped Quin's collar as she yanked the door open. Her husband raced down the hall and through the doorway. Trisha skipped after him, her blue skirt wrapping around her ankles.

"Trisha! Wait!" Tiffany's words sounded harsh, but she didn't want the child to get trampled or kicked.

Trisha stopped with a jolt and grasped her face. "Oh no!"

Tiffany tugged Quin's collar. "You stay!"

Crossing the porch, Nathan hesitated on the top step. The team trampled the rose bushes and the wagon barely missed the porch steps. The heaving team finally stopped at the corner of the house.

"They're going to bolt!"

Nathan leaped down the stairs and grasped the bridle of the nearest horse. Stroking the animal, he spoke softly. Their eyes rolled. Sweat lathered their coats. They whinnied, stomped, and shook their tousled manes. Quin pranced back-and-forth, but obediently remained on the porch. Trisha, barely breathing, clasped her small hands. Tiffany's attention was back on George. The boy hauled himself to his feet. His soiled jacket was twisted. Blood trickled from a cut on his chin. He swiped at the mud and snow on his face.

"Wow!" The word rushed through George's lips as though it were a prayer. He blinked and swallowed hard.

Tiffany's focus darted to the boy's arms and legs, then to his face. "Are you hurt?"

He shrugged as though the experience hadn't yet registered in his mind. "A bear! She scared the team. They might've trampled one of her cubs." He choked and spit. "Hit the buggy! Bret and Jo Ellen!"

"No!" Tiffany clutched her throat. She didn't want to hear the young man state what she feared, yet she had to know. "Are they hurt?"

"Our wheels locked. The buggy . . ." Tears filled George's eyes and ran down his freckled cheeks. "It's bad, Mrs. James."

Nathan turned to face the boy. The color had drained from his face. "Where are they?"

"About a half mile toward Zachary's." George drew a quavering breath. "The buggy went over the hill."

Tiffany felt faint, and her hope wavered.

Ellie, the elderly black woman who had been with the Harris family since Tiffany had been a baby, appeared with outdoor wraps over one arm. She handed Trisha a cape and tossed Nathan's jacket to him.

"Thanks, Ellie." Nathan rammed his arms into the sleeves as he peered at George. "Can you handle these horses, now?" Not waiting for an answer, he ran toward the stables.

Ellie cloaked Tiffany with the remaining cape. "You gits into the house, Miss Trisha."

The girl fastened her cape and headed for the steps. "I'm going with Papa."

Tiffany grasped her arm. "You're staying here."

"But Aunt Jo and Uncle Bret need me!"

"I know how you feel, honey." Tiffany yearned to leap on a horse and gallop to her brother and his wife, too. But in her condition, a rough ride was out of the question. Besides, she had to spare Trisha the horror of what Nathan might discover. Had Breton survived the war only to be . . . She refused to complete the thought. And sweet Jo and their expected little one. *Dear Lord, don't let them be hurt badly.*

A shiver, not from the chilly air, traveled across her shoulders, and anxiety tightened her stomach. "Trisha, sweetheart, please make sure the yellow room is ready for your Aunt Jo and Uncle Bret."

Ellie guided the little girl through the door and into the foyer. "Ah's gonna help you."

Following them inside, Tiffany headed back the hall. "I'll tell Amos to take the carriage for Jo and Bret."

Reluctantly, Trisha headed up the stairway. "I'll nurse Aunt Jo when Papa brings her home."

Tiffany hurried through the house, out the back door, and across the veranda, Quin at her heels. Nathan emerged from the stables on DeCapendo and galloped toward the accident. *Again, my dear husband chose the fastest horse instead of his Monarch.* Monarch was an excellent horse, too, but in her estimation, DeCapendo surpassed him. Musket, Nathan's huge gray dog, raced after him.

Evidently Nathan had given the men instructions. Micah galloped a chestnut mare from the barn and headed toward town. Tiffany assumed he was going for Dr. Peters.

By the time Tiffany reached the shed, Amos was rapidly harnessing a team to the carriage. "Take a stretcher with you, Amos."

The huge black man nodded. "And Ah put a heavy hap on the seat."

"Good." She backed against a wall to give the animals more room. She stared at the carriage door. The thought of riding to the accident scene blazed through her mind.

"Yo hain't gonna go." Amos gave her a stern glance. "The ride be too rough."

The man had been with the family so long he could practically read Tiffany's mind. She knew he was right, but the fear that cramped her gut was urging her to do something that wouldn't be wise. Sighing, she conceded.

Climbing to the seat, Amos signaled to the animals, and the conveyance bumped over ruts as the team headed across the fields in the direction Nathan had gone.

Quin pranced by Tiffany's side as though struggling with a decision of whether to follow them or stay with his mistress.

"Go ahead, Quin."

Yipping, the dog tore off after the carriage, ice and mud flying from his back feet. Fighting tears and struggling not to worry, Tiffany headed back to the veranda. It had been sunny the week before, but last night they'd had an unexpected snow storm. The ice was melting and the ground was becoming spongy underfoot. Tiffany stepped gingerly around muddy sections in the yard. For March, the wind was cooler than usual, but it would probably warm up this afternoon. As she stepped onto the veranda, Ellie opened the kitchen door.

"The yellow room be ready. Trisha be dustin' the green room. Ah figures Massa Breton or sweet Jo might be needin' a bed of they's own."

Tiffany shuddered. "I pray neither of them are hurt badly." She refused to consider that either of them could be injured beyond help.

"Ah's gonna be ready just in case they both needs nursin'." Ellie looked into the distance as though she expected to see the carriage coming.

Tiffany smiled at the faithful black woman. She would insist on helping with the new little one as she had with Adam, even though she was slowing down from age.

"Ah be helpin' Miss Trisha." Back inside, Ellie grasped the banister to aid her climb up the back stairway.

Cammy, the black woman who had been housekeeper for Nathan for several years, stepped onto the veranda. "Ah put water on to heat. Is there anything else you want me to do before Mister James returns with Mister Breton and Jo Ellen?"

"No, Cammy. I pray there won't be need for anything more."

"Then Ah'll go ahead with mixin' the cookie dough." She vanished back into the kitchen.

Tiffany wrapped her cape tighter, leaned against a roof support, and pressed a hand against her aching back. Her baby wouldn't be born for another six weeks. Her mind drifted. Would she have another boy that looked like Nathan? A slight smile tugged at the corners of her mouth. *Will it be an auburn-haired little girl? Or will she look like Trisha?* Picturing Nathan's firstborn, she smiled. *Since I married Nathan, Trisha is my daughter, too.*

Quin's bark snapped her back to reality and she turned to face the pasture. No one was in sight. Why was it taking so long to bring her brother and his wife to Castle Crest?

Breton hadn't cried since his childhood--even during the anguish of war. Now, embracing the still form of his wife, tears streamed down his face. "Jo," he murmured. Her pulse was weak, her breathing shallow, and she remained unconscious. The fact that she was still alive gave him hope, but it afforded little comfort. He looked at the blood that soaked her skirt and spilled onto the pasture. Was there any chance of saving their unborn child? Was Jo hemorrhaging? If so, could the bleeding be stopped? He thought about the wife of a friend who had died recently during childbirth when the doctor failed to stop the hemorrhaging. Breton's heart twisted in agony. *Am I losing my firstborn and the only woman I've ever loved?*

Flame stomped nearby. Blood ran down the horse's leg from a gash on her left flank. Otherwise, the animal seemed all right.

A black stallion thundered across the field. Bret glanced up and saw Nathan coming. *Thank God.*

Halting DeCapendo, Nathan leaped to the ground. Yanking his jacket off, he tossed it over Breton, then knelt in the icy mud and felt for Jo's pulse. "I sent Micah for Dr. Peters. He'll be here shortly."

"We can't wait!" Bret looked at the blood on his jeans and wondered if the surgery he'd had during the war had been undone. If so, would he walk again? Would he lose his right leg this time? His questions floated away as his attention went back to Jo Ellen. "She's getting chilled."

"Is there a woolen hap in the buggy?" Nathan glanced in the direction of the wreckage and shuddered.

"There was, but . . ."

Nathan climbed up the embankment, shoved pieces of buggy parts aside, and scrambled back with the hap. "We'll put your coat under her and cover her with this." He gasped when he lifted the jacket and noticed the blood on Jo's skirt. The horror in his expression spoke volumes. She moaned.

Bret clasped her hand. "She's coming to."

Nathan grasped her wrist as though taking her pulse, a frown furrowing his brow.

Jo Ellen blinked. "I . . . hurt," she whimpered.

"Oh my darling," Breton murmured. "You're going to be all right."

She turned her head slightly and gazed at him. "Who . . . are you?"

Shock jangled Breton's bones. "I'm Breton."

She blinked. "Breton?"

"The accident has confused her." Nathan had probably meant his statement to be consoling, but the undertones of worry that punctuated his words created horror within Bret. "She'll be all right once we get her to Castle Crest."

"Castle . . . Crest?" Tears rolled from the corners of her eyes, and she lowered her dark lashes. "It hurts."

Bret didn't want to tell her that she was losing their baby. "Where do you hurt."

"My arm. My head. But mostly . . ." she rested her unbroken arm on her belly and cried out.

Breton clutched her fingers. She groaned, then slipped into unconsciousness. A fear he had never experienced wrapped around him and tightened to squeeze him in a vice-like grip.

Amos drew the carriage close. Compassion brimmed in the huge black man's eyes. He climbed from the seat. "Ah can put her in the carriage."

"I don't think her back is injured." Nathan ran a hand down Jo's spine. Her right arm is broken. Take care when you move her.

Amos seized the heavy hap and spread it over the carriage seat. Joe Billings, one of Nathan's hired men, brought a stretcher and helped Amos gently place Jo on it. When both she and Breton were inside the conveyance, Amos turned the team and headed for Castle Crest. Mounting Monarch, Nathan galloped for home. Musket and Quin, as though worried about the occupants, followed the carriage.

Pain yanked her from unconsciousness. *Where am I?* A child's chattering drifted across the room and vibrated in her aching head. She blinked. Light stabbed her eyes.

"Mama! Aunt Jo is getting awake."

Blinking to clear her blurred vision, she tried to focus on the little girl's face that loomed above her. *Aunt Joe?*

A woman in a dark skirt and sweater approached the bed. "How do you feel?"

She looked up at the stranger. Kind deep-blue eyes shimmered from an oval face that was surrounded by bright auburn curls. "Where . . . am I?"

"We brought you to Castle Crest."

There was that name again. Confusion threatened to capsize her spirit. "Should I know you?"

"Oh, my dear Jo." Concern registered on the woman's face. "I'm Tiffany. You've been in an accident, but you're going to be all right." The hint of a smile brought dimples to life in her rosy cheeks. "I just came from Bret's room. I sutured a gash on his forehead and bandaged his leg. He needs to recuperate, but he's going to be all right, too."

Why did this woman think she cared about someone named Bret? *She called me Jo.* What kind of name was that for a woman? Shock vibrated her core. *I am a woman, aren't I?* She tried to reach to touch her hair to examine its length and discovered her right arm was secured to a splint. She lifted her other arm and bumped a breast. *Yes*, she thought. *I'm a woman.* She would accept the name this person called Tiffany had given her, at least for now. *Who am I?* Over and over, the question ricocheted through her throbbing head. Otherwise, her brain seemed empty and refused to cooperate. She rested a hand on her aching abdomen and wondered why it hurt. She felt as though she'd been kicked by a horse. Is that what had happened?

"The baby is tiny and weak from being early, but Ellie and Cammy are caring for him." The woman smiled. "He's going to be all right."

All these strange names added to the confusion. Jo figured she should ask what baby, but right now she just wanted to sleep. Unconsciousness seemed to be her only comfort. She closed her eyes. She would be able to think more clearly after she had some sleep.

"Mama, why doesn't Aunt Jo remember us."

"She has amnesia from hitting her head. The doctor thinks it might take a few days for her mind to clear."

"Remember when Deardra threw me and I pretended to forget?"

"Yes I do, young lady, and so does your papa." A soft laugh trickled from Tiffany. She shoved another log into the fireplace and poked at the flaming chunks. "Let's leave Aunt Jo Ellen rest now. The doctor will be coming again this afternoon. Maybe she'll feel better by then."

Footsteps left the room. The door clicked shut. Tears flooded Jo's eyes. If it wasn't for the pain, maybe she could remember. Her world seemed blank. *Where am I from? How did I get here? Who are these people that call me aunt? Who is Bret?* Tears rolled down her temples and into her hair. Drums pounded inside her head. The pain in her arm was excruciating, her abdomen ached, her legs seemed numb, and her back throbbed, but it was the misery of not knowing who she was that brought agony to her soul.

Tiffany stood in the hall, pondering. Jo had regained consciousness after two days, but still remembered nothing.

"Aunt Jo is going to be all right, isn't she?"

"She needs time, sweetheart." For Trisha's sake, Tiffany smiled. "Have you finished reviewing your spelling words?"

"Almost." She headed for her room. "I'll learn them quick so I can help Uncle Bret with baby Jonathan."

"I'm going to check on them now." She forced a smile that wrestled to be a frown and entered the green room where Bret convalesced.

He lay on his back cradling the baby with his arm. He looked up, his brow furrowed. "How's Jo?"

"She's going to be all right, but . . ."

"She'll want to see our baby."

"Brother dear, I know it's hard for you to be patient. It would be for me if Nathan had been the one injured." She took a deep breath. "Jo still doesn't remember you, and she doesn't want a man in her room."

"What about the baby?"

"Jo doesn't remember being pregnant." Tiffany fought the tears that threatened. "She thinks I'm a stranger."

Moisture pooled in Bret's brown eyes. "My poor sweet Jo."

"You try to relax and let your leg heal. Baby Jonathan is going to keep you busy for a few days."

Bret's gaze caressed his tiny son. "I'm going to need help."

"Trisha has already assigned herself as Jonathan's nurse. We'll all help." She paused, not knowing how her brother would receive her next statement. "Nathan is looking into more hired help."

"I don't want a stranger to . . ."

"Look, Bret, Jo is going to need assistance, even after her memory returns. And Jonathan will need extra care." When her brother's frown deepened, she quickly added. "The extra hired help will be temporary."

Bret sighed. "I realize it's necessary. It's just hard to accept. Jo and I were through so much during the war. We were just getting started. Our life together looked so promising."

"It still is. You'll both be on your feet in a few days." She smiled to reassure her brother, although her cheerful countenance didn't alleviate her own concern. "Take advantage of the pampering while it lasts."

"I pray you're right, Tiff, but I'm worried about Jo. Does she remember anything?"

"It's going to take time, Bret. She waited for three years for you to come home from the war. The rest of the family assumed you were dead, but Jo never gave up hope. You can wait a few days for her."

"I'll wait forever if I have to." He sighed. "Dr. Peters said there wasn't much known about amnesia. He said a specialist in Boston had been studying the condition, but when the war broke out, he put aside his research to treat the wounded."

"We have to trust that God will work this out, and Jo will recover her memory soon." Tiffany glanced at the flaming logs in the fireplace. "Are you warm enough?"

"When I stay under the covers."

The baby began to fuss, then cry. Tiffany picked him up. I'll bring him back when he's ready to sleep. She quickly left the room before tears ran down her cheeks. Her face hurt from forcing a smile.

Cammy came from Jo's room and hurried down the hall toward Tiffany. "Ah heard wee Jonathan's cry. Ah'll take care of him if you like."

Surrendering the infant, Tiffany went to the bedroom that she and Nathan shared. She pushed the door to, fed the hungry fireplace, and knelt by the blue velvet settee to pray. Life had been difficult during the war and still was, but that had been expected. She and Nathan were happy, in spite of the hardships, because at last they were together. Now she didn't know what to expect. Would her brother's baby die? He was so fragile. Her thoughts centered on her brother. The accident had reinjured his war wound. Would Bret be able to walk when his leg healed? What if gangrene set in? *And what about dear Jo?* "Oh, Lord, please help our dear Jo Ellen. Bring her mind back. And bless and keep her little one."

"Mama?" Two-year-old Adam rapped on the door with a tiny fist, then swung the portal inward. Moving to her side, he looked into her face.

Tiffany read his distress and hugged him. "What's wrong?"

"Auntie Jo cry."

Tiffany noticed that the door of the yellow room stood ajar. "Were you in to see Auntie Jo?"

He nodded, making his blond curls bounce. Moisture formed in his azure eyes. "She cry. I gived her Pup."

"I'm sure that will help." Tiffany pictured the tan and brown stuffed dog and thought about Elizabeth Ann. Her sister had made the toy for Adam before the end of the war when the family still believed that Tiffany's husband had been killed. That had been before Nathan knew who she really was. What torment. She didn't want to think about that time in her life.

"Pup is your favorite toy, Adam."

He grinned, flashing his dimples. "Pup help Auntie Jo?"

"I'm sure he will." Tiffany hugged her little boy. Pup was worn in spots. She'd stitched one ear back on several times and its tail at least twice. She longed to return to comfort Jo, but she didn't want to subject Adam to any more of the woman's suffering. "Let's go downstairs. Cammy's baking sugar cookies, and I'm sure she'll give you one."

A smile brightened the little boy's face, deepened his dimples, and chased away a lingering shadow of concern. He lifted his arms expectantly. "Up."

Tiffany hadn't been carrying Adam for over a month because of her advancing pregnancy, and it was sometimes difficult for him to understand. "Take Mama's hand. You can go down the stairs like a big boy."

"Adam big boy." He held tightly to two of her fingers as he swung one foot out over the first step.

Tiffany wrapped her other fingers and thumb around the little boy's wrist as an extra precaution. With her other hand, she gripped the banister. She felt awkward, and she wasn't going to take the chance of a tumble. At the foot of the steps, she released her son. He ran back the hall toward the kitchen to cash in on the promised cookie. Tiffany turned to follow him, but the sound of an approaching buggy drew her to a front window.

Nathan's office door opened. "Who's coming?"

"I don't know. I don't recognize the buggy."

Glancing out a window, Nathan frowned. "It looks as though it's about ready to fall apart."

"And that swayback mare is close to collapse." Grabbing the cape she had flung over a chair in the foyer, she flipped it around her shoulders and jerked the door open.

A woman wearing a faded brown cape climbed from the conveyance. She slipped on a patch of ice, lost her balance, and nearly toppled under the horse's legs. The animal shied. The woman screamed.

For the second time within two days, Nathan leaped down the porch steps to seize a horse's bridal.

The woman straightened and gripped the buggy with one hand. "Is this Castle Crest?"

"Yes. And you are?"

"Constance Kennan." The bottom of her faded dress showed from under her cape. Had it once been purple?

"Won't you come in?" Tiffany headed for the steps, but changed her mind about descending. The banister had been removed for repair, and small patches of ice and snow dappled the stones. She placed a hand against a porch roof pillar. When the woman turned, Tiffany was glad for the support. Constance appeared ghostly! Large amber eyes, a bit sunken, peered at her from a pale face.

"You the wife?"

"Yes."

"I must speak with the two of you." The woman turned and lifted her arms toward the buggy, but stepped sideways and nearly fell.

A small child appeared from behind the seat. The hood of her red cape was trimmed in white fur and golden curls surrounded her tiny face. "Mama? Want down." She climbed onto the seat and stood precariously near the edge.

Nathan moved quickly and lifted the child to safety. Her hood flopped to her back. Longer curls were tied back with a red ribbon. The bottom of a spotless white lace dress peeped from under the hem of her long cape. Tiffany wondered how she had remained so pristine. Nathan looked as mystified as she felt as he ushered the two onto the porch. Tiffany opened the door and invited them inside.

With timid steps, Constance moved into the foyer, then stopped and drew the little girl to the forefront. "This is Alexandra."

"Hello, sweetheart." Tiffany touched the child's ringlets.

"She's three." Constance waved a hand nervously. "I changed her into her best dress and brushed her curls a short ways back."

Tiffany wondered what had kept the child from getting a chill during the disrobing process. Adam scampered down the corridor from the kitchen, a cookie in each hand. Stopping in front of the little girl, he grinned, looked her over, then offered one of the treats.

"Thank you." The child's green eyes sparkled.

"Adam is nearly two and a half," Tiffany said.

"I know. They look like twins." Constance blinked and a tear formed at the corner of one amber eye. "Maybe folks will come to think they are."

"I beg your pardon?" Tiffany stared at the woman. "Why would people think that?"

"Maybe this will help you understand." Constance shoved a hand into her pocket and withdrew a tattered envelope. Instead of proffering it, she clutched it close to her heart. "This is extremely hard for me. It will be for Alexandra, too, but she'll come to accept it. She's an adorable child and very well behaved."

Tiffany didn't doubt that from what little she had seen, but was this woman losing her mind?

"I'm going to die." A sob caught in Constance's throat. She swallowed and took a deep breath. "I want what's best for my little girl. I know you'll care for her as you do your other children."

The words *your other children* pierced Tiffany's brain.

"You're . . . planning to leave her here?" Nathan's astonishment was evident in his voice.

Tiffany blinked. "Why would you . . ."

"I have no other choice."

"What about your family?"

Shaking her head made the woman's hood slip from her head. Straight honey-colored hair that needed trimmed hung down her back. "I want what's best for her."

"You think leaving her with strangers is what's best?"

She pointed at Nathan. "*You* are not a stranger. She's you're flesh and blood."

A squeak forced its way through Tiffany's constricted throat. What was this woman inferring?

Nathan looked startled. "You claiming . . . to be related?"

"My little girl is."

Tiffany gasped, and bile rose into her throat. *Should I pity this pathetic creature or pull her straggly hair?* In shock, she stared at the woman, then turned to peer at Nathan.

# Two

Tiffany's stomach churned and her brain whirled. "Nathan, what's she saying?"

His brow furrowed. "I'm not sure."

Straightening her shoulders, she eyed Constance. "Just how is your daughter related to my husband?"

"By blood." Constance staggered, then leaned against the wall as though her legs were threatening to buckle.

"By . . . blood?" Tiffany felt like pouncing, but the frailty of this woman held her back. She took a deep breath. "Please explain what you're inferring."

"I was lied to during the war by a man I shouldn't have trusted." Constance sniffed and held a handkerchief to her eyes. "My little girl is the daughter of the late Colonel Alexander Wordsworth Wellington."

*Alex's child!* Tiffany's senses reeled. Feeling faint, she grasped the marble-top flower stand that stood in the foyer. She was relieved that the woman wasn't trying to pin her offspring on Nathan, but why was she here?

Nathan looked as though someone had kicked him in the stomach. "Can you prove this is Alexander's little girl?"

Constance proffered the tattered envelope. "This is a record of her baptism. Reverend Matson signed it. There were witnesses."

Nathan studied the document. "There's nothing in here that proves my cousin fathered your child."

"Look at her, Mr. James!" A tear rolled down the woman's ashen face. "Could anyone who knew Alex deny that he was this girl's father?"

Tiffany examined Alexandra's features, wondering why she hadn't noticed the child's resemblance to Alex. This beautiful little girl was the female image of the man. There was no doubt who had fathered her. The colonel was more of a beast than she had thought, and that took some doing! While Alexander was endeavoring to sweep Victoria off her feet, he was making love to Constance. Had there been any integrity in the man at all? She cringed. In some war proceedings, while she was disguised as Victoria, she had distorted the truth, too. Spying for the Confederacy had made it mandatory. It still bothered her to ponder about the wartime deceit. Most of the time, she wrestled to block it from her mind.

"Please say you'll take my baby and care for her." Constance began to weep. Her shoulders shook.

Stepping forward, Tiffany put her arms around the woman. The War Between the States had been over for nearly a year, but the aftermath was, and would continue to be for many years to come, affecting families throughout both North and South. "We'll do anything we can to help you. You can stay here and care for Alexandra."

Constance shook her head. "I don't want her to see me die."

Tiffany controlled a shudder. "At least stay a few days." Her mind felt like a gyroscope. "Give Alexandra time to adjust." Had she just promised this woman to raise her little girl? How could she agree to such a thing without first talking it over with Nathan. She turned toward him.

He looked dubious as he gazed into her upturned face. "Do you think you can handle this, darling? Especially with our new little one coming soon?"

"Well, we planned to hire more help, and we can count on Ellie. Besides, how could we turn our back on Alex's child."

"We can't, but . . ." He rubbed his temples. "Right now we have Jo Ellen's baby to care for, too."

"Trisha is helping with baby Jonathan, and Jo will be well enough in a few days to care for him herself."

The crease between Nathan's brows deepened. "I pray you're right, but . . ."

"Besides, Bret will mend fast."

Nathan sighed. "He injured his old war wound. What if he can't walk after it heals?"

Tiffany swallowed. "He has to!"

"Tiffany, darling, we have to be realistic. Jo's baby may need our care for weeks, maybe months. Who knows if she'll ever be able to care for him."

"I refuse to consider that. Jo Ellen took care of Adam while you and I were serving our country. Now it's time for me to reciprocate." She smiled, hoping to encourage him. "Besides, even though Bret is flat on his back, he's already taking some responsibility for baby Jonathan." Saying the name brought excess moisture to her eyes. Her father, Jonathan, was going to be proud of his namesake. That was if the baby lived. Tiffany's stomach tightened. *Dear God, bless my brother and Jo. Please don't let their baby die.*

Constance sniffed, and Tiffany looked back at the visitors. The woman looked as though she might faint. Alexandra's attention was on Adam. He giggled. Grinning back, she took another bite of her cookie.

Nathan cleared his throat. "You must consider remaining here for a time, Mrs. Kennan. Maybe you could regain your strength."

"It's Miss." She drew a long labored breath. "I'll stay a few days. Then I must go."

Tiffany reached out to the woman. "To where?"

"It doesn't matter."

The desperateness in the woman's tone tore at Tiffany's heart. Maybe they could convince her to see a doctor in Richmond. He might be able to further diagnose her condition and prescribe something that would improve her health. "It's cold here in the foyer. Please come into the living room and sit by the fire. I'll have Cammy bring tea."

"Thank you." Constance unbuttoned her cape.

Nathan hurried to the living room fireplace, grabbed the poker, and stabbed at the blazing logs. After adding wood, he stood staring at the flames. Adam crossed the room and stood beside him, then sat on the hearth.

Constance shucked out of her cape and flung it over a chair just inside the living room doorway. Her purple dress was more worn than Tiffany had first thought. The woman seemed somewhat relieved, but a tear trickled unchecked down her pale cheek. Tiffany guided her to the sofa nearest the hearth. Slumping to the cushion, Constance grappled in her pocket for a handkerchief, then blew her nose.

"Mama?" Alexandra had quietly followed. She rested tiny hands on her mother's knee and looked into her face. Big tears formed in the child's green eyes. "Mama sick?"

"Yes, sweetie." Removing the little girl's cape, she drew her close.

The side door slammed. Tiffany stepped into the hallway to see who had entered the house. Trisha had taken food to the dogs. She removed her cape and hung it in the closet, then headed toward the kitchen. Checking her stride, she whirled and hurried forward. Apparently she'd heard voices and was drawn to investigate. She followed Tiffany into the living room and stood silently listening to the conversation, then moved forward to grasp Alexandra's hand. "Come with me. We'll get some milk and cookies."

Adam jumped to his feet. "Me, too." He grinned at the expectation of another treat.

The little girl glanced at her mother for approval. Constance nodded. Trisha took Adam's hand, too, and led the children back the hall to the kitchen. Living through the war had matured Trisha beyond her nine years. It hadn't taken her long to assess the situation and conclude that Constance's daughter would be better off out of earshot. Tiffany figured the child had already heard too much. Did she understand what was about to transpire? How could one so young possibly perceive the present circumstances?

The swinging doors between the kitchen and dining room flapped back and forth a second time. Tiffany heard Ellie's footsteps approach and went to meet her in the hall.

"Miss Trisha be sayin' I needs to fix another room. Ah's gonna fix the cream room, if that be fine."

"Perfect. The morning sun brightens that room. Use the yellow bedspread."

Nodding, the black woman ascended the stairs. "Come on, old bones. You don't be lettin' old Ellie down." Her voice lowered to muttering. "Humph. This place be gettin' more offspring to be lookin' after than my old Susie has kittens!"

Ellie's comment made Tiffany smile, even though the events of the day lay heavy on her heart. Pondering Constance's problem, she pushed through the swinging doors and went into the kitchen. "Cammy, I'd like you to fix a tea tray and bring it to the living room."

The woman nodded. "The water in the kettle is hot." Bending, she removed the last tray of steaming sugar cookies from the oven.

Tiffany waited for Cammy to scoop the animal shapes onto a towel, then she chose a cat-shaped one and cautiously nibbled an ear. "Even as a child, I preferred cookies directly from the oven."

"Me, too, Mama." Adam reached toward her.

"I think you've had more than enough, young man."

"One more?" His grin flashed the dimples that reminded her of Timothy, and it made him difficult to resist.

"I'll share mine." Breaking off a section she proffered it.

"Yum." He looked at Alexandra, then back to his mother. "Ally some, too?"

Tiffany broke off another chunk of her cookie, surrendered it, and wished she could slip one into her pocket without her son catching her.

Trisha poured some milk into the glasses she had given the children. "When you two are finished, we'll take Ally out to meet Quin and Musket."

The little boy nodded, spilling some crumbs onto the floor. "Ally like Adam's puppies."

The little girl grinned. "Puppies!"

Trisha giggled. "We have two big dogs, but they act like puppies." She patted the child's head. "They'll love you."

Since everything seemed under control, Tiffany headed back to the living room and the trouble that faced them. A twinge gripped her back. She gasped and leaned against the wall. The muscles across her abdomen cramped. *No!* It was too early. Tears smarted her eyes. "Oh, dear Jesus, please don't let me lose this baby."

Cammy came through the swinging doors, took one look at Tiffany, and set the tea tray on the dining room table. "You all right?"

"The baby. It isn't time."

Moving forward, Cammy placed a hand on Tiffany's abdomen, closed her eyes, and waited. In a few seconds, she nodded. "Could be a preparation contraction. Didn't you have them a month or so before Adam was born?"

Chewing her lip, Tiffany thought back. So much had been going on then. She'd been so involved with the war. The memory of Adam's birth drifted back. She shivered. She wasn't looking forward to going through that again, but Ellie had said the second baby wouldn't be as bad.

"You should sit." Cammy adjusted the teapot, then picked up the tray. "If you have more pains, tell Ellie or me."

Tiffany was relieved, but assumed it would be wise to try to relax. Taking a deep breath, she headed for the living room. Cammy followed and served the tea.

Another twinge tightened Tiffany's abdomen. As soon as she got Constance settled, she would inform Ellie about what was happening. The old woman would know what to do.

Constance sniffed and dabbed her eyes with her wet handkerchief. "I hate to leave my baby, but I don't know what else to do."

"You'll be staying with us for a time, so don't think about leaving her." Tiffany passed the cookie plate.

Constance chose a small round treat, then sat holding it. "Alexandra's reaction to my death is all that I think about. She's all that matters."

Tiffany studied the woman's grief-stricken face. She would've been pretty in the past, but sickness and sorrow had robbed her of youth and beauty, leaving her frail and peaked. The skin on her face had a blue cast. "How much endowment did Alexander leave his daughter?"

"He left her nothing! He denied she was his." Constance drew a shuddering breath. "I thought that after the war he might change his mind, but he only swore at me." She coughed. "Then he died."

Nathan sighed. "Alexandra will be taken care of. My parents raised Alex from the time he was twelve. For a time, before he slipped into resentment and jealousy, we were more like brothers than cousins."

"I told Alexandra that I was taking her to visit her Uncle Nathan." A tear rolled down her face. "I thought it would be easier for her to understand my deserting her if I left her with kin."

"We'll do all we can to help her adjust to any new circumstances. Your room will--" A cry from baby Jonathan halted Tiffany's words. His cry sounded weak. Anguish squeezed her heart, and anxiety stirred her nerves. In spite of all they were trying to do, would baby Jonathan succumb?

Ellie appeared at the door with the infant in her arms. "The room be ready. I be takin' Constance up, if it be all right."

"That would be good." Nathan stood. "Do you have luggage?"

Constance nodded. "It's in the buggy. I don't have much."

Tiffany presumed what the woman did have would be in poor condition. She's probably put on her best dress for the visit. Tiffany figured some of her dresses would fit Constance, and she made a mental note to look in her closet.

Nathan headed for the door. "I'll get your things, then take care of your horse. Ellie will get you settled."

The worry lines on Ellie's wrinkled face created havoc within Tiffany. The old woman summoned with her eyes, drawing Tiffany into the hall.

Ellie handed over the fussing baby. "Missy Jo gots to nurse her child. He hain't gonna make it if she don't."

A band tightened around Tiffany's heart. "You take care of Constance and see if she needs anything. I'll take Jonathan to Jo." She had planned to discuss the pains she was experiencing with Ellie, but her brother's son had an immediate need. Her lips moving in prayer, she went up the stairway. As her foot touched the top step, she heard voices drifting from Jo's room.

"I told you to get out!" Jo's words weren't very loud, but they resounded sharply.

"But Jo, darling," Bret pleaded.

Tiffany hurried to join her brother. He gripped the bedpost, his brown eyes coaxing his wife. Tiffany's heart cramped. Bret turned to peer at the infant in her arms.

"What's the matter with him?"

"He's hungry, and he isn't doing well on gruel." She sighed. "I asked you to remain in your room until Jo was ready to see you."

"I tried, but . . ." As he turned, his weak leg buckled under his weight. He crashed to one knee and yelped in pain. Sitting on the floor, he gripped his injury and closed his eyes.

"What happened?" Nathan, clutching two battered carpetbags, hurried into the room, then stopped to stare at Bret. "Let me help you back to your room." Dropping the bags, he helped his brother-in-law to his feet.

Bret reluctantly permitted Nathan's aid. At the door, he glanced back. Excess moisture brimmed in his eyes, revealing emotional misery as well as physical pain.

When Tiffany's attention moved back to Jo Ellen, the woman lay with the sheet to her neck, her eyes blank. "Your baby needs you."

She shook her head. "I don't have any children." She frowned and bit her lip as though she doubted the truth of her statement.

Nathan appeared and grabbed the worn luggage, then strode from the room and down the hall toward Constance's room. Ellie thanked him. His footsteps quickened, and

Tiffany heard him descending the back stairway. The kitchen door banged. She assumed he was going to take care of their visitor's carriage horse. The animal looked as though it were in as bad a health as Constance. If anything could be done to help the horse, Amos or Micah would do it.

Tiffany's attention was drawn back to Jo. She struggled not to sigh as she approached the bed. "Under most circumstances, I wouldn't press you until you were stronger, but your baby needs you."

"My . . . baby?"

"He came early. You need to nurse him. If you don't . . ." Tiffany's tongue felt thick, making it impossible to finish the statement.

"I can't!"

"Please try."

She weakly shook her head. "I'm hurting now. I don't think I could stand to have someone's baby nurse. My breasts are so swollen, I feel like I'm going to burst!"

"Your engorgement has made you sore. That's what happens after a woman gives birth. It's God's way of preparing you to feed your baby."

Jo blinked and a tear rolled down her cheek. "You say that infant is mine?"

Tiffany nodded.

Jo swallowed. "Who's the baby's father?"

"Bret."

"I'm . . . married?" Her puzzlement was replaced with horror. "To the man called Bret?"

"Yes."

A sob caught in Jo's throat. "I don't even know him."

"You did, dear heart. You waited so long for him to come home from the war. Everyone else believed him dead. You wouldn't. Don't give up now." She studied the anguish in Jo's expression. "Look at the gold band on the third finger of your left hand."

Jo lifted her hand, stared in amazement at her ring, then blinked. "How could I not know my own husband? Or my own child?"

Tiffany took advantage of Jo's confusion and held Jonathan out to her. "I'll help you. Just try to nurse your little one."

"No."

"You have to!" Exasperation and concern made Tiffany's words sound harsh.

"I won't!"

"You will!"

Her sister-in-law's eyes widened. "I'm not going to let a stranger tell me what to do. And with who's baby?"

The infant squirmed and his pathetic whimper spurred Tiffany to action. "You're going to nurse your baby." Lifting the blanket, she placed the tiny boy beside his mother. "Or you're going to watch him die!" Hurrying from the room, she closed the door. Sudden tears ran down her face. She longed to go back in to help Jo, but she didn't want to prolong the argument. Praying she was doing the right thing, she forced herself to walk away.

Searing pain seized her back, then traveled across her abdomen. She cried out, staggered, and gripped the stand in the hall. "No. Please no."

"Tiffany!" Nathan raced up the front stairway and stopped near her. "What's wrong?"

She gasped for air that didn't seem to fill her lungs. "Pain."

Alarm etched lines in his face. "The baby?"

"Yes." A sob made the word catch in her throat.

"There's been too much going on around here." Slipping an arm around her, he guided her to their bedroom and across the carpet. "You relax on the settee. I'll get Ellie."

Tiffany watched him go. Another twinge made her gasp. Yesterday, she'd been frightened that Jo would die, then that her brother's infant wouldn't live through the night. She was still concerned, for the infant could die if Jo didn't nurse him. Resting her hands on her abdomen, she fought tears. *Now am I going to lose my own baby?*

## Three

Ellie hurried into the bedroom. "You be gettin' into bed."

Tiffany closed her eyes and waited for another pain to subside. The worry that deepened the lines on the old black woman's face caused panic to bubble into Tiffany's throat.

Ellie flipped the quilt back, unnecessarily fluffed the feather pillows, then guided Tiffany to the bed. "You's gonna be fine, honey."

If that were the case, why did doubt reverberate in Ellie's tone. She paused to stare at the woman. "What about my baby?"

Ellie turned away. "The good Lord gonna be lookin' after the wee one, too. How long you be havin' pains?"

"The first one was about an hour ago. Since, I had two, but none were as severe as the last." She took a deep breath. "Cammy said she thought they were preparatory pains."

"Ah thinks they's more than that."

"It can't be!" Fear gripped Tiffany's heart. "It's too early! I can't have this baby for at least another month!"

"If the babe be determined to come, we hain't gonna be able to stop it."

"I feel so helpless!" Tiffany swiped at a tear that rolled down her face. "There has to be something we can do!"

"Ah's gonna fix you somethin'." She fussed with the edge of the quilt, then crossed the room and shoved more wood into the blazing fireplace. "Cammy be needin' to know what's goin' on." She headed for the door. "Ah be back."

"Don't leave me, Ellie."

The old woman paused. "You gots another pain?"

"Not yet, but . . ."

"You rest." She hurried away.

Nathan's footsteps resounded in the hallway. "Ellie, should we send for Dr. Peters?"

"Ah don't know. The pains maybe stop and be nothin'."

"And if they don't?"

The silence that followed her husband's question made a tidal wave of apprehension wash over Tiffany. She tried to pray, but her throat constricted and choked off her words. *My faith should be strong enough to bring me comfort.* She wished she had more. "God help me. I know you know what's best, but please don't let my baby die."

She'd always been able to put herself in God's hands before. Why not now? Struggling to calm her anxiety, she pondered the baby names she and Nathan had discussed. If a boy, he would be Timothy Andrew, named for her youngest brother who had been killed during the war. If a girl, Cassandra. That was Victoria's middle name. The least she could do for her Aunt Martha, after using her daughter's identity in order to spy for the Confederacy, was to name her first baby girl for her. She and Nathan had continued to vacillate between two second names. Tiffany liked Sue, after Melissa Sue, her eldest brother's deceased wife. She and Nathan also liked Jo for a second name. Would a name be necessary?

"I won't answer that." A sudden gripping pain made her cry out.

Nathan raced into the room, the color draining from his face. At the bedside, he peered down at her. "What can I do?"

"Rub my back, please." When the contraction eased, she struggled to roll onto her side, thankful to have her face to the wall. If Nathan read the worry she knew was in her expression, his alarm would mushroom. She tried to suffocate a moan, but she gritted her teeth as another pain tightened a band around her abdomen. Tears filled her eyes, seeped from the corners, and soaked into her pillow. She wanted this baby so badly. They both did. Had she done too much to help Jo Ellen? Had she tried too hard to make Constance feel welcome? Had she worried too much over the health of Jo's infant? Was losing her baby her own fault? But how could she have ignored her brother and sister-in-law's needs? Constance looked like walking death and had such grief in her eyes. *How could I have ignored the woman's desperation?* She muffled a sob in her pillow. Jesus always had compassion on those in need. She wanted to be like him. Would God expect her to pay for her compassion with the life of her own child? She gasped. That's what God had done! Jesus, even though he was perfect, had died on the Cross to pay for the sins of man.

*And that includes me, but I want my baby.* "Oh, please, God."

"Darling, everything is going to be all right." Nathan bent to kiss her wet cheek.

"This is my fault." A hiccup separated her last two words.

"No, Tiffany. So much beyond our control has been happening." He brushed an auburn curl from her face. Kneeling, he placed his hand on her side and began to pray.

Jo Ellen stared at the door panels, wondering what was going on in Tiffany and Nathan's room. From what her aching head could decipher, she assumed that Tiffany was losing her baby. Even though she didn't know the woman, she could imagine the anguish in her heart. What would it be like to lose a baby? The infant by her side continued to squirm. She tried to ignore him. His cries sounded like mews. Was he getting weaker?

Turning, she gazed at him. His tiny fists rested near his chin. His lips moved in a sucking motion. Reaching out, she touched his delicate cheek. His eyes opened. She gasped. "Hello, baby."

His mouth opened, then closed. She knew he was hungry. A sudden thought shocked her. What if Tiffany was right? What if this tiny creature was her very own little boy? What if the swelling in her sore chest was because she had

had a baby? How could that be? How could a woman give birth and not know it? Her focus caressed the infant's features. His eyes were again closed. Whether this was her little one or not, how could she let him die if she had the means to help him? Opening her nightgown, she guided the baby to her breast. He didn't seem to understand. What should she do now?

"God, help me know what to do. Or send someone to show me?"

The baby opened his mouth to cry. Jo held him closer and put a nipple into his mouth. His hand opened as he touched her. It was amazing how tiny his fingers were. *Almost as small as toothpicks.* She squeezed a droplet into his mouth. His eyes opened as though he were surprised. He began sucking. At first, she could hardly feel it, but he must have realized what was happening, for he began to suckle with more intent.

After nursing for several minutes, he fell asleep. Was he all right? Should she wake him and try to get him to eat more? He needed to gain strength. Did that mean she should let him sleep? She smiled. Her pain had diminished as her concern for this baby superseded her dismay over her own predicament. Still, not remembering who she was made her miserable. Should she trust the woman called Tiffany? Should she believe her? What else could she do? *Does that mean that the man called Bret is really my husband!* She gasped. Her sudden motion woke the infant, and he began to cry.

"Hush, little one. Are you still hungry?" Again she put the baby into position. Again he nursed, then fell asleep. Her heart seemed to swell and love overwhelmed her. *Is this what it's like to be a mother?*

A knock on her door startled her. If she answered, would her voice wake the baby?

"Jo?"

The voice was low, but she could tell it belonged to Bret. Her heart cramped. She tugged the fabric of her nightgown to cover her breast. The door slowly opened. A man, his steps cautious, entered the room. She opened her mouth to yell at him to get out, but that would alarm the infant in her arm. She glared at the intruder, rebuking him with her eyes.

A white cat streaked into the room and leaped onto the bed. Jo gasped. She didn't want it close to the baby. Lifting her leg made the quilt slant steeply. The feline landed on the floor with a plop.

Bret gripped the bedpost and peered at the cat. "Susie, Ellie's going to put you in a cage."

Jo glared at him. "*You* weren't invited in here either."

"Jo, please listen a minute." His gaze traveled to the infant. A smile softened the worry lines on his handsome face. His soft brown eyes glistened with pleasure as they found hers. "You nursed our son?"

She intended to refute the statement, then wondered if it could be true. She wasn't going to give this man the pleasure of thinking he'd been right. She shrugged with one shoulder. "Someone has to take care of him."

"Oh, Jo, darling, life is going to be so wonderful."

A denial started up her throat, but she forced it back. For some reason, she didn't want to disappoint this man. Still, she wasn't ready to let him claim her as his wife. "I need more time, Bret."

"As long as you let me talk to you, I'll be patient." He limped to the door and put the cat in the hall, then returned to the bed and gripped the post for support.

"You were injured badly?"

"Not too. My leg was reinjured, so I'll have to be careful. I thank God I'm still able to walk." He took one step nearer.

"That's close enough."

He sighed, but remained where he was. "My leg is weak. May I sit on the edge of your bed?"

"No. That's getting too familiar."

He closed his eyes. "All right, Jo. But I'm warning you that I'll be courting you all over again once you get back on your feet. Jonathan needs us both."

"Jonathan?"

"Our baby, Jo." He staggered and nearly lost his footing. He gripped the bedpost, but his injured leg buckled and he sat on the mattress. "I'm sorry."

"It's all right. Under the circumstances."

Another pain ripped through Tiffany, and she cried out. Nathan looked helpless.

Ellie rushed into the room with a cup in her hand. "Drink this."

"Wait!" Tiffany held her abdomen.

"You drink it now!" She glanced at Nathan. "You be supportin' her head."

Tiffany felt him lift her into position. Ellie held the cup to her lips. Opening her mouth, she took a swallow and gagged. "That's horrid!"

"Ah didn't say you was gonna like it. You drinks it all."

A bitter liquid trickled down Tiffany's throat. She knew better than to refuse to swallow. She had never been able to tell Ellie no when the woman wore her determined expression. Besides, in the past, the old black woman had known what was best. Making a face, she gulped down the liquid, then shuddered.

"That be good."

"No it wasn't. Will it help?" Tiffany tried to ignore the aftertaste in her mouth.

Instead of answering, Ellie turned to stare out a window. It was the way she gripped the empty cup that created a spasm in Tiffany's heart.

"Well?" Nathan asked. When Ellie didn't answer, he took a step toward her. "What did you give her?"

"It be one of Ellie's herb brews." She shrugged one bony shoulder. "We's gonna have to wait. The rest be up to the good Lord."

Another contraction began to tighten Tiffany's abdomen. Tears burned her eyes. "Please, God," she whispered.

Nathan rushed to her side. "How bad is it this time?"

# Four

"It's bad." A sob caught in Tiffany's throat. Unable to hold back her tears, she began to cry.

Nathan sat on the edge of the bed and took her in his arms. "It's all right, darling. We'll have other babies."

"I want this one!"

"So do I, but if the Lord has other plans, we'll accept it."

"Don't you say that he needs another little one in heaven. I need it here!"

Nathan kissed her forehead. "I love you, Tiffany. I'm here for you, no matter what happens."

"Mama sick?" Adam came in and stopped beside the bed, worry shadowing his little face.

Nathan turned to his son. "Mama's going to be fine."

"Adam help." He tried to climb onto the bed.

Nathan swept him up in his arms. "Mama needs her rest. Trisha will take you out to play."

He shook his head, making his ringlets bounce. "Did play. Want Mama."

Trisha appeared in the doorway. Her smile faded and concern filled her azure eyes. "What's wrong?"

"Take Adam downstairs and keep him occupied."

"Ally's wondering where you went," Trisha told the little boy. "She wants to play with you."

"Ally wait. Want Mama."

"You can see Mama later." Taking the little boy's hand, she tried to urge him into the hall. He pulled back. She whispered something in his ear that brought a smile. Nodding, he accompanied her.

Tiffany was grateful, even if it meant that Adam was getting another cookie. This wasn't the time for him to be asking questions or worrying over her condition. He hadn't been told of the new baby. She was thankful for that. If she lost the baby, it would be too difficult to explain the circumstances to the little boy.

"Your pain subsiding?" Nathan gazed lovingly at her.

She nodded. "I pray there's no more." She had barely said the words when another contraction began. She wanted to scream at God, then she felt ashamed.

When the pain subsided, Ellie sighed. "That one didn't seem as long. Did it be as bad?"

"I don't think so."

Nathan drew a long breath. "Does that mean . . ."

"It be too early to tell." She pointed a crooked finger at Tiffany. "You needs to be stayin' in bed for awhile."

Tiffany nodded consent. It was the first thing the old woman had said that was in any way consoling. She hoped it meant that Ellie had hope. She gasped. Her own problem had kept her so occupied that she'd forgotten about leaving the baby with Jo. "Ellie, please go and see if Jo needs anything."

"Humph. That girl be needin' a talkin' to."

"She doesn't remember anything, Ellie. Even us. She refused to nurse Jonathan. I left him with her."

The wrinkles deepened on the old woman's face. "Ah hasn't heard him cry." She hurried from the room.

"Tiffany," Nathan said softly, "was anyone else with Jo when you left the baby with her?"

"No. I was exasperated and didn't know what to do. I told her she would either have to nurse him or watch him die."

Surprise lifted Nathan's blond brows, then he drew them together. "Nothing else has worked. I suppose it was time to do something drastic."

"What you be doin' in here?" Ellie's voice resounded from the hall, her tone filled with sarcasm.

"I'm just visiting."

"Bret's in Jo's room again." Tiffany sighed. "Why won't he listen?"

"Because he loves her, Tiffany."

"I understand that, but . . ." She closed her eyes as another cramp seized her. Nathan silently waited. The pain gradually eased. "That one wasn't near as bad."

"Thank God." He hugged her.

"Please go and help Bret back to his room. He shouldn't be on his leg this soon."

"I don't want to leave you." Meeting her gaze, and apparently realizing her concern for her brother, he stood. "I'll be back."

Alone, Tiffany stared at her abdomen. "You rest, baby. Mama wants you to grow some more before you face the world." The infant kicked so hard it made Tiffany gasp. A moment later, it punched her on the other side. "You're an active little one." She bit her lower lip. Did the activity mean the unborn was in stress—or still all right?

Ellie returned, a smile making the creases around her mouth fold into each other. "Jo be nursin' her wee one. He gonna be fine."

"Thank God. Now if my baby is all right . . ."

"You rest and not be fussin'." She studied Tiffany's face. "You be havin' any more pains?"

"Not for awhile."

"That be good. Misa James be helpin' Breton back to his room." She straightened the quilt again. "He be comin' in to see you. I be tellin' him to let you rest, but nobody be listenin' to old Ellie."

Tiffany smiled. "We all listen to you."

"Humph. That'd be the day."

Susie, the old woman's white cat, scampered into the room and leaped to a windowsill. She stretched out in the late afternoon sun and licked a front paw.

Ellie huffed. "You better be stayin' where you belong, you naughty thing, or I'll be sendin' you to the barn."

Eyeing her, the cat's tail swished.

"And don't you be trying old Ellie's patience." She huffed again as she swept the feline into one arm. "You be havin' little ones again, too!" Grumbling, she left the room.

In spite of Tiffany's dire circumstance, she smiled.

Daylight slowly faded and shadows crept into the bedroom. Tiffany had slept, now she felt restless. Nathan had been in frequently to check on her, but she'd drifted into sleep. What time was it?

Nathan returned shortly after dark. He lit the candle on her nightstand and withdrew an envelope. "You received a letter from Jenna Leigh Cristen."

She envisioned the strawberry-blond friend that she'd known since childhood. Jenna Leigh was barely five-foot-one. By the time Tiffany was twelve years old, she was five-foot-six. Neither girl had gotten any taller. Back then Jenna had made her feel gangly. "I haven't heard from her since part way through the war." They'd been close. How could she have neglected a good friend for so long? *The horrid war!* But the war has been over for nearly a year. She sighed. "Read the letter to me, Nathan."

He pulled two sheets of paper from the envelope, unfolded them, and bent so he could read in the candlelight.

"Dear Tiffany, I've thought of you so often. I heard you were spying during the war, and I prayed for your safety. I cried when I learned of Timothy's death. He was so sweet. My brother returned with a scar from only a small wound, but the conflict and devastation he witnessed has affected him mentally. He's still wonderful, but the light has gone from his eyes. I pray it will return.

"I lost my brother-in-law at Bull Run. Katy grieved until she got sick. In her weakened condition, and having lost the desire to live, she died, too."

"Oh no. I'd learned that Patrick Hollis was killed at Bull Run." Tiffany bit her lower lip. "But I didn't know Jenna's sister had died." What about their little boy? He'd be five or six now."

"That's in the next paragraph. She says, 'I've had Robby since Katy's death. He's like my very own little boy. I haven't married. I guess the Lord's taking his time finding someone for me."

Tiffany drew a long breath. "Jenna thought the world of Kenneth Long. I thought they'd marry." She frowned. "He left for the war and didn't come home. Jenna assumed he'd been killed and his body lost like so many others. Elizabeth Ann said a friend had told her that last year someone discovered that he was working on a ranch somewhere in Nevada. No one knew if he'd deserted or gone west after the war without telling anyone."

Nathan pursed his lips. "Seems to me, if he'd gone after the fighting, he would've returned home first or at least notified his family of his whereabouts."

"I don't like to surmise that, but I thought the same thing. I wouldn't reveal my suspicions to Jenna, though."

"Probably no one will. She's been hurt enough."

"And now she's raising Robby alone."

Bending, Nathan kissed her cheek. "She'll find someone. Look at what we were through before we married. And for a time afterward." He studied her face. "Have you had any more pains?"

"No." A smile curved her lips. "God and Ellie are at work."

"You have to do your part, too, darling. I want you to stay in bed until Ellie says you can get up—no matter what."

"I intend to. Now finish Jenna's letter."

"Mr. James!" Cammy raced down the hall and into the bedroom, her eyes wide. "One of the cabins is on fire!"

"Who's?"

"Ah think it's Joe Billings's place."

Tiffany sat up with a start. Nathan gently pressed her back against the pillows. "You stay put!"

"But someone could be hurt!"

"I'll handle it." He released the sheets of paper he'd been reading. They fluttered to Tiffany's quilt like dead leaves. Whirling, he hurried to the bedroom door, but paused to glare at his wife. "I mean it, Tiffany. Don't get up!"

She listened to his footsteps as he ran down the hall and descended the steps. Curiosity flared within her. She was tempted just to get up to look out the window, but that wouldn't help. She'd have to go out onto the balcony to see Joe's cabin. She wished the lace curtains were open.

Reaching, she grasped the candle and blew the flame out. Usually moonlight filtered through the lacy pattern. Now there was a flickering red glow. Something was burning. What had Joe been doing to start his place on fire?

Nathan's heart pounded as he hurried through the house, out the back door, and across the yard. He saw light, smelled smoke, and heard snapping and crackling before he skirted the rhododendron and saw the flames. The field hands had formed a bucket brigade and were dousing the fire. It didn't help. Flames burst through the roof. Tongues of fire licked out the windows and up the sides of Joe Billings's dwelling.

"Men on horseback!" Joe called as he tossed another bucket of water on the inferno.

Nathan rapidly concluded that the cabin was a loss. Within minutes, the men gave up and stood to watch it burn. Nathan moved to where Joe sat on a stump. "Did you recognize any of the riders?"

Joe shook his head. "They wore masks and hoods."

"And white sheets?"

"Yes."

*The Klu Klux Klan*, Nathan thought. He'd heard there was a group in Tennessee calling themselves that and galloping around at night scaring people, but as far as he knew, there hadn't been much violence other than a fight or two. Even if a group formed in Virginia, he'd assumed his property wouldn't be vandalized because he'd freed his black workers right after he'd purchased them. But then, maybe that was the reason for the attack. "Up to now, there hasn't been any Klan activity around here." He peered at Joe. "You're white. Why your place?"

"Teddy wanted to speak with me about something, so he was sitting on my porch waiting for me to come from the barn. The horsemen galloped up, and I guess they thought my place belonged to Teddy."

"Either that or that you were sympathetic and aiding him." Concern gripped Nathan as his eyes spanned the milling field hands. "Did anyone harm him?"

"Some fellow grabbed him by the neck and warned him to move on. He fled into the shadows."

"Did you recognize his voice?"

Joe sighed. "His tone sounded familiar, but I can't put any name to it."

Nathan's hands clenched into fists. "Post a guard tonight. I'll try to get to the bottom of this attack."

"Be careful, Mr. James. Those men acted crazed, and I'm sure they meant their threats."

Nathan figured they did. Who were they? Why here? Why now? Who had started a group in this area? He assumed that most of the men in the Klan were good men who allowed their minds to be corrupted by someone radical, then became excited at their meetings and got carried away by hatred, anger, and group excitement.

He sighed. The way the carpetbaggers were descending on the South was difficult for any Southern gentleman to accept. And some of the politicians sent from the Freedmen's Bureau weren't any better. In some ways they were worse because they had the Federal government behind them.

When the situation was under control and there was nothing more Nathan could do, he headed back to the house. He was nearly to the veranda when Musket's yelping a hundred yards to his left caught his attention. What had riled his dog? Quin's barking joined Musket's. Seizing the lantern that he kept near the back door, he lit it and hurried across the field.

He hadn't gone far when he noticed a horse silhouetted against the night sky. The dogs wouldn't be barking unless the animal was unknown to them. *The rider must be nearby.*

Curiosity hummed within Nathan, but his suspicion was screaming. As he approached, Musket and Quin quieted, but remained near to guard their prisoner.

While he was still several feet away, a man clothed in a sheet sat up and turned to face him. His white hood with its eyeholes shadowed made him look ghostly. Nathan set his lantern on the ground. "You hurt?"

"I think I broke my leg."

The familiar voice stunned him. "Glen! How could you be part of what just happened?"

"I don't know." He groaned. "I guess I'm sick of the Yankees coming down here and telling me I can't vote, but my freed darkies can. They can't even read!" A sigh seemed to come from his boots. "I'm not just disturbed, I'm fed up!"

"I understand, Glen, but this isn't the way to solve the problem."

"I suppose you're going to tell me to love my enemies and let the North trample all over us."

"I'm not going to preach at you, but violence is no way to solve a problem. Didn't the war teach you anything?"

Glen scoffed. "There's a lot at stake, Nathan. I don't have enough field hands left to cultivate my acreage, and my taxes are so high, I'm going to lose my plantation!"

"A group of us are trying to get laws passed to protect the farmer, but it's going to take time."

"My time's running out! A number of my friends have already lost their properties and have moved on!"

"I sympathize with that. I'll do my best to help, but why did your group strike my place? My men have been freed for years! Besides, my taxes are high, too."

"The leader said you had the means to pay your taxes. We don't. A carpetbagger has his eye on my place, and he's determined to gobble up six other plantations as well!"

"I understand your frustration, but not your violent reaction. I hadn't heard that the Klan was active around here. Who started it?"

Glen groaned. "Our leader came from Tennessee. He said he was anxious to change our situation, and the men in his group were dragging their feet."

"Get your men together, Glen. I'll come and talk to them."

"Sure!" Glen laughed. "You think they're going to let you know who they are?"

"I have a pretty good idea, and I know you."

"That's just it. My voice gave me away. The members of my Klan won't speak to you for fear you'll identify them."

Nathan sighed. "Get out of the Klan before someone gets hurt or killed by one of your irate members. You could be blamed. At best, you'd be part of it."

"I won't harm anyone."

"You already have! You've been galloping around in the dark scaring the wits out of folks and starting fires that destroy the homes of innocent people! That isn't harmless. You burned Joe Billings's place. He's white, and having to struggle, too!"

"There was a black man on the porch of the dwelling we burned."

"He was waiting for Joe. Besides, if it had been Teddy's place, I'd be just as angry. Teddy has a family!" Nathan propped a hand on his hip. "I won't turn you over to the authorities if you promise to leave the Klan and get some of your friends to bring lumber and rebuild Joe's cabin."

"That's ridiculous!"

"That's my offer. Take it or face the sheriff."

"I'll do what I can."

"You'll replace what you destroyed. I'll except nothing less."

"The members of my Klan will be incensed over my getting caught."

"If you give up your night rides, I'll try to help you."

"How?"

"Can you work at a lumber mill?"

"I can learn."

"You've been a good man. I'm assuming that at a weak moment, you left yourself be drawn into something that you don't really believe in."

"My back was to the wall!"

"Nevertheless, I expect you to cooperate. Bret Harris is the foreman at my Karn's Ben mill. He's going to be leaving to return to the Shenandoah Valley before long. He was injured, but he'll be back to work in a week or so. He'll train you to replace him—if you're willing."

A rattle resounded in the man's throat. "I'm not the type to grovel."

"I don't expect you to beg. I'm offering you a position."

"I'll take it."

"I don't want any more violence from you or the members of your group."

"I can only speak for myself."

"You can pass the word along to your friends."

"I'll . . . try." He shuddered. "They'll be irate if I say I'm turning my back on the group. I know too much, Nathan. I can identify most of them."

"Glen, my offer is good only if you give up your night raids. Take that hood off. I'll tell one of my men to hitch up a buggy. Amos will drive you to see Dr. Peters."

Jerking the hood from his head, Glen rolled up the sheet that had cloaked him and handed them to Nathan. "Get rid of these. I don't want any of your men to see them. It's going to be difficult enough to explain my presence here."

"I won't announce what you were part of, but I won't lie to protect your honor, tarnished though it is."

Nathan headed back to the barn. A glance over his shoulder revealed Glen with his face in his hands. After he'd removed his hood, the dogs gave a satisfied wag of their tails and romped toward the veranda. Maybe things would quiet down around here for a change.

Before Nathan reached his milling field hands, he halted and peered down his darkened lane. A horse was coming at a gallop. At first he didn't see a rider, then he made out the shadowy shape of a small girl bouncing on the animal's back.

"Misa Nathan! Misa Nathan! They's hangin' my Papa!"

# Five

"Misa Nathan!" The child frantically reigned in. The horse reared. The girl flipped from the saddle and landed on the ground on her backside.

Nathan set his lantern aside, tossed the rolled sheet under a bush, and raced forward to lift her to her feet. She was tiny, probably weighing barely forty pounds.

She lifted her black face up to him. "Ah's Dolly." Tears made her cheeks shiny. "You be Misa Nathan?"

"Yes. What can I do for you?"

"They's gonna hang my Papa."

"Who is?"

"Bad men with bags over they's head." She gasped and a sob caught in her throat. "Mama said come for you."

"Where are you from?"

Teddy approached with Monarch. "I saddled him for yo, Massa James." He glanced at the little girl, then looked back at Nathan. "Her papa be Zebadiah. He be kin of my Minnie. Zachary hired him last month." He shook his head and swiped at excess moisture in his dark eyes. "Ah suppose what Dolly be sayin' be true. It probably be the same riders who be burnin' Joe's place."

"I'm going over there. I pray I'm not too late."

"Ah be goin' with yo."

"You stay here. Someone in that bunch may harm you."

The black man nodded. "Dat child be only five." Turning, he lifted Dolly to her saddle. "Yo be takin' Massa James to se yo mama. Uncle Teddy and Aunt Minnie be comin' to visit yo tomorrow."

Nathan mounted. "Tell Cammy what happened and let her know where I went."

"Yes-um." He headed for the veranda.

Speaking softly to Dolly, Nathan clicked to Monarch, and the two animals trotted down the lane toward Zachary's. Nathan knew what to expect, but prayed things weren't as bad as they seemed. Zachary was an old man. He hoped this excitement wouldn't throw him into a collapse. Of course, knowing the old man, even in his eighties, he'd probably wield his rifle and put fear into the hearts of the raiders.

*Glen would've been part of that, and if a man had been hung, Glen would be guilty in part for murder.* Nathan sighed. The man could thank God for his broken leg.

Nathan longed to gallop to Saxon Oaks, but Dolly looked as though she were about to topple from her saddle. "Would you like to ride with me?"

She nodded. In the moonlight, a tear sparkled at the corner of her eye, then running down her face, it left a trail that shimmered like silver in the glow. Nathan scooped her up and sat her in front of him. The child seemed undernourished. She would be getting enough to eat now that her family was living on Zachary's plantation, but what had this little one been through? Even during the war, Trisha had been taken care of. She hadn't had the variety of food she'd been used to, but she'd been nourished and had good care at Aunt Mary's. The thought of what Dolly's family had endured made him shudder. And it probably wasn't over, yet!

He guided his mount up Zachary Saxon's lane and halted him near the glowing embers of a cabin. A woman lay crumpled on the ground sobbing. Three children hovered around her. The nearby oak that had sheltered the dwelling from the sun now looked as though it were standing at attention, waiting to be sentenced. The silhouette of a man, hanging from a rope tied around his neck, swung in the night breeze. "Dear Lord," Nathan breathed.

"Papa." The strained syllables issued from the child in his lap and her body convulsed with sobs.

Darcy Mae hurried to meet him. Reaching up, she took Dolly and cradled her in her arms. "Twas the Klan what do this, Massa James."

He dismounted. "Did they hurt you or anyone else?"

"No. But what they did be too much for sweet Ruthie Ann to bear." Darcy May shook her gray head. "And now she be alone with four chillen to feed."

"How's Zachary?"

"He be doin' okay. When those men galloped up, he grabbed his rifle. I be scared nearly to my death! Massa Saxon be yellin' and shootin' in the midst of it all." She cooed to the whimpering child and rocked her in her arms, then turned back to Nathan. "If it not be for Massa Saxon, there be more destroyin'. When the men rode away, Ah gots the old man to go to bed."

"Is he sleeping?"

"Humph. He be fussin' as usual."

"Is there anything I can do for Ruthie Ann?"

"There be nothin' to console that dear girl right now, 'cept the good Lord take her to glory, too." Darcy sighed. "She be needin' lots of help." She grumbled something under her breath, then said, "As if the horror of war wasn't bad enough! Now we has our neighbors killin' folks."

Nathan rubbed his chin. "The leader came from Tennessee. I'm hoping to talk sense into the members of the group."

"From what Ah knows, that hain't gonna be easy."

Nathan strode to the swinging figure, severed the rope and dropped the dead man to the ground. Ruthie Ann screamed and ran to him. On her knees, she buried her face in the man's chest. Her shoulders shook with her spasmodic wailing.

"Darcy, take these children into the house and see what you can do. I'll speak with the Saxon Oaks hired men, make arrangements for Zeb, then I'll be in to see Zachary."

"Dat be good." One by one, she collected the stunned children of the dead man and took them to the kitchen.

Nathan strode to the hand's cabins and looked around. The place seemed deserted. He called out the names he knew and knocked on doors. No one answered. In the barn, he found the fifteen-year-old Zachary had hired recently to drive the buckboard. "George, where is everyone?"

"Hiding in the woods. When those men came thundering in with torches, the hired men and their families scattered like chickens being attacked by a hawk. Zeb couldn't find his two-year-old son. He yelled at Ruthie Ann to take the other children and flee. Before he found Ricky, the horsemen seized him, beat him around, and tied a rope around his neck. Ruthie raced back, screaming to the top of her lungs. One of the men knocked her down and hung Zeb. After torching his cabin, they galloped off yelling like crazed idiots."

"Weren't you frightened?"

"I was terrified!"

"Where was Ricky?"

"Here in the barn. I found him after the men hung Zeb."

"Did you know any of the men?"

George shook his head. "They all wore hoods."

"Did you recognize anyone's voice?"

The boy shrugged. "I don't think so. I was too scared by what they were doing to think about who they could be."

"I understand. If you remember anything, come and tell me. I'm going in to see Zachary. Go to the woods and inform the field hands that I want to talk with them. Some of the wives need to help Ruthie Ann."

Nodding, George took off across the field toward the stand of pine. Nathan watched until the young man vanished into the darkness, then he headed toward the house. Before he reached the veranda, he heard the children crying. "Dear God," he whispered. "When the war ended, I thought this type of conflict would be over." But had the Klan violence just begun? Taking a deep breath, he entered the kitchen.

Darcy Mae looked up. Her black face was wet from tears. She cradled the two youngest children of Ruthie and Zeb. Dolly and her four-year-old brother stood at the woman's knee. Tears continued to run down Dolly's tiny face. Her brother looked stiff, his expression gaunt. He stared straight ahead as though he were trying to figure out what had transpired. All the children acted frightened. Their mother's wailing had confused and upset the younger three. Dolly was old enough to grasp what had happened. Shock and grief registered in her eyes.

A plate of cookies and four glasses of milk remained untouched on the table. Of the four chicken sandwiches, only one had a tiny bite out of it. These children probably were hungry, but what they'd just been through had stolen their ability to eat.

"Nathan." Zachary appeared at the hallway door. "Thanks for coming over."

"There wasn't much I could do." He sighed. "My place was hit, too. They burned Joe Billing's cabin and beat up Teddy. Joe said for a time, he thought they were going to kill him."

Zachary leaned heavy on his cane. "If I find out who did this, I'll shoot him myself."

"There's going to be more violence before this is settled. The Federal Agent will be getting a posse together. There's going to be more bloodshed on both sides."

"Oh dear Lordie, have mercy." Darcy Mae clucked her tongue. "Will the war never be really over?"

"I'm afraid that in the hearts and minds of some, it's going to continue for awhile." He sighed. "At least until the Freedmen's Bureau either gets a grip on the situation or gives up."

"These poor chillen gonna be feelin' it for the rest of their born days."

"They need you to comfort them now, Darcy Mae."

"Ah's gonna be here 'till Ah die." She glanced at the old man. "Or 'til Massa Saxon kicks me out."

The old man grinned. "Now what would I do without you?" He turned serious eyes to Nathan. "Will the Klan strike again?"

"Probably, but who knows where."

Zachary shook his gray head, making his beard swing. "Or when."

"Do you have enough help here?"

"I hired a new man to take care of the horses, but he won't be here until next month."

"Do you want me to send Micah over until your new man arrives?"

The old man scratched his beard as he thought. "Maybe it would be a good idea to have him here after dark."

The thought of Micah being attacked where he couldn't come to his aid bothered Nathan, but Zachary's health was at stake, too. He thought about the grieving family. "Is there a place for Ruthie Ann and her children to live?"

"There are two unoccupied cabins. I'll give them one."

"They both need fixin', and they hain't got no furniture." Darcy rocked from side to side and hugged the two little ones in her arms.

A light knock resounded on the kitchen door. Nathan opened it.

George stepped across the threshold. Fear made the freckles stand out on his pale face. "I told them to come back, Mr. James. They're in their cabins."

"Thank you. Choose the best of the vacant cabins and ask some of the ladies to help you clean it up for Zeb's family. I'll send some furniture over in a wagon with Amos."

With a nod that was becoming familiar, George raced out the door and across the yard.

Nathan thought about Tiffany and concern filled him. "I'm going to speak briefly with your field hands, then I'm leaving for Castle Crest." He studied Zachary. The old man looked weary and more worn. He wondered if he should tell him about Tiffany's condition.

"What's going on, Nathan?"

As usual, no one kept anything from the wise old man for long. Nathan quickly explained Bret and Jo's accident, then sighed. "Tiffany had a scare this afternoon. The baby threatened to come."

Darcy's eyes widened, then she pursed her lips. "If anyone can get things under control, it be Ellie."

"She gave Tiffany something she called her herb brew, and the pains stopped."

The old man sighed. "You'd better be getting back to her. Babies sometimes have a mind of their own. If things start to happen, she'll want you near."

"If you need me tonight, send George. I'll get some furniture together as soon as I can, and Micah will be over."

"He'll be needing the other cabin, and it needs repair."

"Micah will make do in the barn. Let's hope this arrangement is temporary." His attention was drawn back to Darcy Mae. "If Tiffany discovers what happened, she'll want to come over here and help out."

"Don't you be tellin' her about this. She has her comin' little one to be concerned about."

Zachary nodded. "There'll be time for her to aid Ruthie after the baby comes."

Nathan agreed. After speaking with the workers and arranging for Zeb's body to be handled properly, he mounted and kicked Monarch into a gallop. *Please, Lord, let Tiffany be all right.* He longed to take the shortcut through the woods, but it was so dark tonight. Crossing a field would cut several minutes from his ride; however, there were groundhog holes in the pasture, and his horse might break a leg.

Tiffany stirred and blinked. She'd fallen asleep, again. What had wakened her? What time was it? The new candle had burned down nearly to the holder. Where was Nathan? She looked around. Where was Ellie? Was everyone asleep?

She peered at the pillow beside hers. It hadn't been slept on. Nathan wouldn't sleep elsewhere even if he was concerned over disturbing her rest. "Nathan," she called softly. No one answered.

The way Nathan fled from the bedroom and raced down the stairway when Joe Billings's cabin was burning, flashed into her recall. That had been hours ago! "Ellie," she called.

Again there was silence. Had Nathan returned to find her asleep? Her eyes widened. *Or isn't he back yet?*

Concern for her unborn encouraged her to lean back against her pillows, but worry over Nathan's absence made her heart pound. Sitting up, she called for Ellie, then for Cammy.

"Can I help you?" Constance, wearing a long white nightgown and robe that Tiffany recognized as one of her own, came in. In the candle glow, the woman looked ghostly. Her pale complexion nearly matched her night garb.

"I was wondering where everyone had gone."

"Well, Jo Ellen is nursing her little one. Bret is asleep, although he seems restless. He's been tossing and mumbling. Ellie is sleeping in the room beside the nursery, and Cammy went to her quarters."

"Where's Nathan?"

"I don't know. I went to the balcony when Joe's cabin was burning, but I was too frightened to go any farther."

There was something Constance wasn't saying that alarmed Tiffany, especially when she discerned fright on the woman's face. "What caused Joes's place to catch on fire?"

Constance turned to peer out a window into the night. Her hands trembled. She tried to hide them in the folds of her robe.

"Constance, I have to know what's going on. Has something happened to Nathan?"

Taking a deep breath, the woman described what she'd witnessed.

An icy chill settled over Tiffany. She'd never dreamed the Klan would strike here. Why? Nathan was admired by everyone she knew. "Was anyone hurt?"

"I don't think so, although I thought for a few terrifying minutes the hooded men were going to harm a black man who was sitting on Joe's porch."

"Did you see Nathan at the fire?"

"Yes. He couldn't do anything to help. The place was destroyed. He was coming into the house, then he took a lantern and hurried across a field."

"Why?"

"I haven't any idea. He was only gone a short time. When I noticed him coming back to the house, I came inside."

"Then where is he?" Tiffany felt panic bubble into her throat.

"Ellie told me not to say anything, but a small child galloped a horse into the yard. Nathan spoke to her, mounted a horse that one of his men had saddled, and the two galloped down the lane."

Tiffany's alarm turned into horror. "Where'd he go?"

Constance shrugged. "One of the hands said he went to Zachary's—wherever that is, because the man's place was under attack."

Tiffany swung her legs over the edge of her bed. "I have to find out what happened to him and see if Uncle Zachary is all right."

"You must stay in bed!"

Tiffany swallowed. Concern for her baby churned within her, but horror over what could have happened to her husband drove her to her feet. "Get me a robe."

"Please don't do this. You might lose your baby!"

"I don't know what to do."

Constance fled from the room.

Moments later Ellie rushed in. "Ah warned you 'bout gettin' up. You gonna be gettin' back in bed."

"Where's Nathan?"

"He hain't come back from Saxon Oaks."

"I have to know what happened over there! Uncle Zachary could have been harmed!"

"You gets back in bed. Ah's gonna get someone to ride out to fetch Mr. James." Grasping Tiffany's arm, she propelled her back to bed.

Reluctantly, Tiffany obeyed, but tears stung her eyes.

She settled herself against the pillows, then a pain seized her abdomen. She clamped her mouth shut on an outcry. Had just standing up caused this? She shook her head. The way her heart was pounding and her blood was surging through her veins had her system riled. Was it enough to cause a premature birthing? Now her worry had increased over the well-being of her baby as well as her husband. Taking deep breaths, she prayed and tried to relax.

Nearly an hour passed before Ellie came back. The look on the old woman's face screamed through the silence.

Tiffany stared at her. "Where's Nathan?"

"Amos be bringin' him in."

Tiffany sat up. "Is he hurt?"

"Ah's sure he gonna be fine. Ah gots the purple room ready."

"I want him with me."

"You both needs rest."

Tiffany didn't like the sound of that. She sat up and flipped the quilt aside.

The old woman pointed a finger at her. "You stay put."

"I have to see him!"

"You can't do nothin' and you can't be trampin' around all fussed."

A commotion on the stairway made Tiffany's pulse throb in her temples. Against Ellie's orders, she got up and went to the hall door. "Nathan!"

Amos and Joe, gripping the handles of a makeshift stretcher bearing Nathan, ascended the stairs. He looked dead! "What happened?" The time she'd been at Nathan's North Fork lumber camp, when an explosion had sent hundreds of logs careening down the mountainside toward him, seared through her mind. Nathan had barely escaped death. He'd looked in bad shape that time, and she'd thought he was dead. This time, he looked worse! "What happened?" Her question was a scream.

Joe paused at the top of the stairs and gave her a side glance that betrayed his worry. "He was shot."

Tiffany gasped. "Shot!"

## Six

"Shot!" Tiffany repeated, staring incredulously at the bloodstain that darkened the front and side of Nathan's shirt. "By whom? Why?"

Joe shook his head. "We don't know, but we have our suspicions."

Tiffany stepped aside for the men to pass. Tears sprung to life and raced down her cheeks. "Nathan!" She reached toward him.

Ellie pulled her away. "You gots to wait 'til Amos and Joe gets Misa James in bed." She turned to Amos. "You be puttin' him in the purple room."

"I want him with me!" Tiffany jerked from the old woman's grasp.

"He be needin' nursin', and you be needin' rest and quiet."

A sob jerked Tiffany's throat. If Nathan needed to be nursed, he was alive. Thank God. She'd been too afraid of what she might find to check his pulse or to see if he was still breathing. She felt like crumbling to the hall carpet, but she followed the men to the purple bedroom and waited until they put Nathan on the bed.

Amos pulled off Nathan's boots, then with questions in his eyes, he looked at Tiffany. "Yo gonna undress him?"

"No." Huffing, Ellie pushed forward. "She gots to be in bed, too."

Tiffany glared at the black woman. "It wouldn't be proper for you to undress Nathan. That would strip him of his dignity as well as his clothes!"

Joe stepped forward. "Ellie's right, Mrs. James. You go back to bed and protect your little one. Amos and I will undress Mr. James and make sure he's as comfortable as possible."

"Thank you." Instead of retreating to her bedroom, Tiffany slumped to an armchair and stared at her husband, prayers flowing from her heart. Ellie had placed an oilcloth on the bed and covered it with an old thick hap. If Nathan bled, the featherbed wouldn't be stained. The woman must have known Nathan had been shot and had avoided informing her. "Joe, did you send someone for Dr. Peters?"

"Yes." Amos lifted Nathan so Joe could slip the shirt from his arms. "Jack Hall went for him. I felt it was better to send a white man, due to the Klan activity."

She didn't know Jack, but she'd visited with his wife and six children. "Has anyone else been hurt?"

Joe hesitated. Taking a short breath, he averted his gaze. "Not here."

Tiffany's heart jolted. "Uncle Zachary?"

Amos unfastened Nathan's belt. "Yo uncle be fine."

Tiffany drummed her fingers on her knees. "What's keeping the doctor?"

"He was setting Glen Allen's leg."

"How'd he break it."

"He said he was on his way to help put out the fire at my cabin, and his horse stumbled. He said he was thrown from the saddle and his leg twisted under him and he landed on it."

"You don't believe him?"

"How he broke his leg, yes, but not why he was in the field."

The reason Glen was crossing their property didn't concern Tiffany. She struggled to calm her frazzled nerves. Nathan's condition had her agitated as well as worried. The longer the bullet was in her husband, the more chance of it poisoning him. "Removing that bullet is more important than setting a broken leg!" She struck the arm of her chair with a fist. "Where was Nathan when you found him?"

"At the side of the road between here and Zachary's. Apparently, whoever shot him was hiding in a nearby thicket."

"I can't imagine anyone wanting him dead." Tiffany sniffed. "Where did the bullet lodge?"

"I'm not sure. He's bleeding from his left side. The blood has soaked his shirt at the side and back."

"Was he unconscious when you found him?"

"Yes. When he was hit, he must've fallen from his horse. There's a bump on his head. It looks like he struck it on a rock when he landed in the ditch."

She eyed Joe. "You said you had suspicions. You mean about who'd do this and why?"

"Well." He seemed to be pondering as though he were evaluating whether to share his thoughts, then he sighed. "We think he knew too much."

"About what?"

"Glen could have been part of the group that descended on us like a band of banshees from Hades."

Tiffany's mouth dropped open. "Glen Allen? Part of a Klan?"

A shrug lifted one of Joe's shoulders. "Nathan found him. He had Kent take Glen to see doctor Peters. I think Glen was lying when he told us he was coming to help."

"You think Nathan realized the truth?"

Joe nodded. "It's possible. Nathan could've discovered Glen still wearing his hood."

"And covered for him?"

Joe shrugged. "If so, I'm sure he had a good reason. The other men in the group might think that Glen, to save his own hide, had revealed the identities of the men who were with him. Maybe they wanted to silence Nathan."

Tiffany bit her lower lip. "If that were true, then Glen's in danger, too."

"He's probably aware of that and protecting his neck."

A sudden pain across Tiffany's abdomen made her gasp. It was instantly followed by another.

Amos peered quizzically at her. "Yo be all right?"

"The baby," Tiffany whispered.

Amos strode rapidly from the room. "Mama Ellie! Come quick."

The old woman appeared at the door, saw Tiffany, and raced to her side. "Amos, you gets her to her bed. This time, Ah don't thinks Ah can stop things from happenin'."

"No," Tiffany wailed. "God please don't let me lose my little one or my dear Nathan!"

The huge black man lifted her as though she were a doll and carried her to her bedroom. Ellie instructed him to set her on the settee until she could prepare the bed for birthing. Tiffany's rested her hands on her abdomen. Tears flowed down her face. Had her disobedience caused this? *Is losing my baby my own fault?* But Nathan had been hurt. She'd had to go to him. She tried to pray, but the only words that issued between her lips were, "Dear Lord, oh please, dear Lord."

When she was in bed, Ellie hovered over her, her hands resting on Tiffany's belly. Another contraction ripped across her middle. She cried out.

"It be time, child, whether we wants it to be or not."

The statement was like a pronouncement of doom. "Ellie, you'll need help."

Cammy rushed in from the hall. "Constance came for me. She said it was Tiffany's time. Ah sent Amos to fetch Alice."

Within minutes a middle-aged black woman entered the room. She was the midwife who aided the other black women with birthing. Elizabeth Ann and Jo Ellen had helped when Adam was born. But Adam had been full-term and healthy. *What will I do if I have to cradle my stillborn? No! God please don't let my baby die!*

The night wore on. Tiffany's pains got worse. Sweat poured from her face. Cammy sponged her, but it didn't help. *Is it really my physical agony? Or is it the overwhelming expectation of loss that grips me?*

Dr. Peters strode into the room to examine Tiffany. She eyed him. "How's Nathan?"

"The bullet wasn't in too deep. I removed it, but the healing part will be up to him. He's going to need a lot of nursing."

"Did he say who shot him?"

"He hasn't regained consciousness."

"Why?"

The doctor straightened. "I suspect a concussion, but I don't know how bad."

*Jo Ellen hit her head, and now she doesn't remember anything!* Tiffany prayed Nathan's mind would be clear when he woke. She gasped when another contraction seared through her. She gritted her teeth to keep from screaming.

"Try to relax." Dr. Peters watched closely until the pain subsided.

Was the man mad? "How can a woman relax during birth?"

"Breathe shallowly like your panting. Tensing your muscles makes this process more difficult. It's a cycle that only multiplies."

Tiffany gasped for a needed breath. "Where did you hear such a fool thing?"

"From a woman who has had eleven babies."

She scoffed. "How many babies have *you* had?" Tiffany knew her question was sarcastic, but the man's chuckle irritated her. How could he come in here and tell her to do the impossible? He knew how to deliver an infant, but he couldn't know how to bear the misery of birthing.

As the next contraction began, Dr. Peters coached her on how to breathe. She was amazed. It really did help! Still, the expectation of what was to come pinched her heart. "I can't have a dead baby," she whimpered.

Ellie wiped a cloth across Tiffany's forehead. "You gots to have faith, girl." When the pain subsided, the old woman massaged Tiffany's back. "The good Lord be doin' miracles every day."

Tiffany prayed, but wondered if a premature baby could be normal and healthy. "It's coming!" she cried as another contraction gripped her.

"Push," the doctor commanded. "Push!"

In another moment, Tiffany felt the infant leave her body. She stared at the doctor. The baby hadn't cried. What had she expected.

"It's a girl." Dr. Peters lay the baby across Tiffany's abdomen, then cut and tied the cord. "I think we made some wrong calculations." He glanced at Tiffany. "This infant is early, but she has hair and nails."

Tiffany stifled a sob. "She isn't crying."

"She doesn't need to squall. She's breathing normally."

Tiffany's eyes widened. "She's all right?"

"From what I can see quickly, she's perfect." He grinned. "She has some red in her hair like you." Wrapping the baby in a small blanket, he laid her beside her mother.

Joy fountained within Tiffany. "Hello my little Cassandra Jo." She had admired her newborn only minutes when a pain seized her that made her gasp. She hadn't remembered the afterbirth creating such a violent contraction after Adam was born.

"Take the baby!" Dr. Peters said, his tone sounding like a bark.

Ellie lifted the infant and stepped back, her eyes wide. The doctor examined Tiffany and frowned, then he shook his head. "With your next pain, push."

Confused, Tiffany followed instructions. Whatever was coming was huge! She felt like her insides were being expelled. *God help me!* Oh, why did Nathan have to get hurt? She needed him desperately. What was happening to her? Something wasn't right. This hadn't happened when Adam was born. "What's wrong?" she whimpered through a pain.

The doctor didn't answer.

"Please tell me what's wrong!"

# Seven

Tiffany's alarm mushroomed. "What's happening!"

Dr. Peter's ignored her question. "Push!"

Tiffany tried, but she was exhausted and knew something was different. "Nathan," she mumbled, wishing he was with her.

"I said push!"

Tiffany tried. Feeling something else being expelled, she gasped with relief, although she was confused and puzzled.

"It's another girl," Dr. Peters said.

"What!" Tiffany's eyes widened when she saw the man lift another baby. This one began to scream and kick.

"She's all right, too." The doctor chuckled. After examining the infant and tying the cord, he wrapped her and gave her to Tiffany.

"Hello, baby." She thought about the name she and Nathan had chosen, should the baby be a boy. Smiling, she touched the infant's cheek. "You can't be Timothy Andrew. Your name will be Andrea Sue." She studied her second daughter's face. "They look the same! How will I ever tell them apart?"

"A lot of babies look alike." Dr. Peters chuckled. "But these two are identical twins."

"Praise the Lord!" Tiffany's exultation was a whisper, although her heart was shouting her praise and thanksgiving. Now if Nathan got well, life would again be a little bit of heaven. She sighed and closed her eyes. "I feel as though I've been working a week without rest."

"You've done a great job." Dr. Peters chuckled. "Tomorrow you'll feel like you've been trampled by a herd of buffalo."

The doctor was doing what he was supposed to do. Tiffany no longer cared. "I just want to sleep." Her eyes closed on their own accord, and she didn't try to open them.

Alice lifted the baby. "Ah's gonna take this wee one downstairs for her first bath. Ellie be bathin' Cassandra Jo."

"These infants might be a bit premature. You ladies make sure the kitchen is warm enough."

Alice gave a little snort. "Ah's been bathin' newborns since Ah been ten years old. You don't need to be tellin' Alice how to do it proper, Misa Docta."

He straightened. "I didn't mean to infer that you didn't have enough wits to know not to chill a newborn." He sighed. "You ladies be sure and mark those little girls with different color clothing or ribbons. For a time, that's the only way you're going to tell them apart."

Ellie patted Tiffany's hand and laughed, her voice cracking. "You better not be talkin' about my old Susie's litters no more. Now you's havin' babies two at a time." She headed for the door, Alice at her heels. "We's gonna be back, Missy Tiffany. You git your rest while you can. Lord knows there gonna be little time for sleepin' around here for months to come."

The doctor left. Cammy sponged Tiffany and changed the bedding. Tiffany wondered when the woman would stop fussing and leave her sleep, although she knew Cammy was only doing what was necessary and trying to make her comfortable.

Finally, Cammy straightened. "You sleep now. The good Lord knows you deserve a good rest. It's almost daylight."

Tiffany closed her eyes. She couldn't tell what her lips were doing, but inside, she was smiling. As she drifted into slumber, she pictured Trisha's surprise and delight over finding out she had two babies to play with. But what about

Adam? He'd been the baby all his life. How was he going to take to being the big boy? *And what about my dear Nathan?*

Rays of dawn were piercing the darkness when Ellie brought one of the babies to Tiffany to nurse. She slipped in and out of sleep and wasn't sure which infant was suckling. How was she ever going to tell the girls apart? They had her hair color. Did they look like her as well? How long would she need to mark them with ribbons or bows?

Her hand rested on her abdomen. It was a lot smaller, but felt puffy. "I'm not going to fit in any of my dresses."

"You's gonna shrink." A smile crinkled Ellie's face. "But it gonna be takin' longer this time."

Tiffany moaned. "I'm so sore."

"It gonna be takin' you longer to git back to racin' around like you likes to do, too."

When the babies were sleeping, Tiffany stretched and yawned. She yearned to see Nathan, but both Ellie and Cammy had warned her to remain in bed. Taking a deep breath, she closed her eyes.

Jo gazed at her son's sweet face. His dark lashes lay against his now rosy cheeks. How thankful she was for him.

Constance came in. The rest she was getting seemed to be refreshing her, although she still looked pale. "Do you want me to take Jonathan to the nursery for you?"

"Thank you." Jo yawned. "I'd like to rest." A smile tugged on the corners of her mouth. "Then I want to see those twins."

"They're darlings."

"Are they blond like Trisha and Adam?"

"No. They have auburn hair like Tiffany's." She gingerly lifted Jonathan and headed for the nursery.

Jo watched her go, then sighed. *All this talk about hair, and I don't even know the color of my own!* Reaching up, she tugged on a curl. It was too short in front to pull forward far enough to see it. The long part in back was tied at her nape with a ribbon and she was resting on it. Right now, she felt too weak to sit up and free the curly mass.

Lifting her hand, she studied her skin tone. *My complexion is light, so I must be a blond like Trisha.*

Constance returned. "Jonathan is sleeping peacefully. Can I get you anything before I go downstairs?"

"Is there a small mirror handy?"

"I was wondering when you would ask. Trisha said you hadn't seen yourself since the accident." She smiled. "I put one of Tiffany's mirror's on your washstand." Retrieving an ivory handled glass, she proffered it.

Jo turned the glass side down on her quilt. Mixed emotions swirled through her. She couldn't summon even a fraction of memory of her appearance. *I don't want this woman to read shock on my face if I'm ugly.*

Constance laughed. "Don't worry, Jo. You're pretty." As though she understood Jo's reluctance, she hurried away.

After freeing her hair, Jo slowly lifted the mirror. She suppressed a scream. Her heart-shaped face was pretty, but large unfamiliar gray eyes stared back at her. And her hair! It was a mass of curls and as black as coal!

It took a few minutes to regain her composure. She had delicate features and a clear complexion. Constance was right. "I am fetching." She bit her lip. Was that thought haughty?

Shrugging, she clattered the mirror to her bedside stand. *How long will it take me to get used to my own face?* She wound a long curl around a finger and studied the shiny strand as she pondered.

Hearing a noise, Tiffany turned her head and peered into two identical five-year-old faces. "Nat? Scott?"

Giggling, they looked at each other, then one turned back to Tiffany. "You had two babies, just like Mama."

Emily Rose, Nathan's sister-in-law, swept into the room, a bright smile on her face. Tiffany had thought that by this time Joshua, her eldest brother, and Emily would be married. They seemed to care deeply for each other, practically from their first meeting. Maybe Emily needed more time after

Matthew's being killed in the war. *One of these days, I'm going to talk to them about it.*

Emily's smile lit up her pretty face. "You-all really did it right this time, Tiffany." The woman's elation seemed to make her Georgian accent more acute. Gold highlights shimmered in her brown hair and her turquoise eyes sparkled. Laughter bubbled from her. "I'm going to delight in watching our dear Nathan chase those girls around when they're two or three."

"Nat and me, too, Aunt Tiffany!"

"Now Scott. You boys go out and play. Mama wants to talk with your Aunt Tiffany." She watched the boys scamper through the door and down the stairs, then she turned back to Tiffany. "Joe rode over last night to tell me about Nathan. I arrived early this morning to check on him, and I found your family considerably larger."

"Did you see Nathan? How is he?"

"Doing as well as one could expect. He's pale and hasn't regained consciousness, but he's breathing normally, and there's no sign of fever. Thank the Lord." She sighed. "Poor Jo Ellen is so confused. She didn't even know me!"

Tiffany nodded. "At first, she refused to nurse her baby."

"She accepts him now and seems delighted with him." Emily waved a hand. No woman, whether or not she knows she's a mother, could refuse for long to take care of a newborn."

"Jo's getting stronger, and Bret is healin' fast. I shudder to think of how easily they could have been killed."

Emily nodded. "It's a miracle that they weren't. When I saw the demolished buggy, I expected Bret and Jo Ellen to both be worse off than they are." She studied Tiffany's face. "Having twins takes a lot out of you. I told Ellie that I'd stay for a few days until you were up and around." She grinned, bringing her few freckles to life. "I have a lot of experience caring for two babies at once. I'll give you some pointers"

"I'll appreciate any advice you have to offer." She gazed across the room at the bassinet and thought of how rambunctious Emily's boys were and hoped Cassandra and Andréa would be easier to control.

"I can't wait to dress your little ones in pink bows and lace dresses." Emily sighed. "Boys are so active and don't care what they wear."

Tiffany was still exhausted, but she would never be too tired to inquire about her brother's love life. "Have you seen Joshua lately?"

Emily giggled, telling Tiffany that the woman still adored Joshua. "I sent him a message about Nathan. I think he'll be coming to Castle Crest today."

"Will Mama be with him?"

"I can't imagine dear Joshua coming to Castle Crest without both Catherine and Jonathan. Especially when they discover that our sweet Nathan has been hurt." Another giggle bubbled from her. "I can't wait to see your Mama's face when she peeks into the baby basket!"

"She'll be ecstatic that she won't have to share one infant with Papa."

Trisha seemed to float into the room. "I overslept." She glanced at the bassinet, then back to Tiffany, a wide grin stretching her lips. "Ellie said the baby is here." She hurried to the bassinet, looked in, gasped and stared wide-eyed. "Mama! There's two!"

Emily laughed. "I guess Ellie and Cammy kept that part a secret."

Trisha glanced at her mother, then her attention was back on the infants. "This is better than great!"

"I wanna see a baby." Adam came in, looked around, then joined Trisha. Standing on tiptoes, he peered over the rim of the basket. "Oh no!" He looked at his mother. "Doctor left two!" He held up two fingers and blinked at Emily. "One baby yours?"

"No, darlin'. They're both your new little sisters."

He shook his head. "Don't need a sister. Got Trish."

Crossing the room, Emily lifted the little boy and held him where he could look straight into the basket. "Their names are Cassandra and Andréa."

He stared at the infants, at Emily, then looked across the room at his mother. "Cass and Andie?"

"Cassandra Jo and Andrea Sue."

He shook his head until his curls bounced. "Cass and Andie."

Trisha gazed in awe at the babies. She reached out and touched first one, then the other. "Which one is which?"

"I'm not sure. You'll have to ask Ellie." Emily set Adam on his feet and took his hand. "We're going to go downstairs and let Mama sleep. She needs her rest."

"Why?" Adam peered up at her. "It's light out." A frown shadowed his little face as he faced Tiffany. "Mama sick?"

"No. I'm just tired." She was grateful to Emily for taking Adam downstairs.

Trisha remained behind. When she was sure the little boy couldn't hear her, she smiled. "Can I hold one?"

"Ellie will show you how to pick them up."

"I know how. Papa taught me how to handle a baby when Nat and Scott were born. Aunt Emily needed help—at first." Carefully, she lifted one of the baby girls and cradled her in her arms. The other one began to cry. Gently lowering the first baby, she picked up the other one. It quieted, but the first one began to cry. She faced Tiffany. "Oh brother! I guess this is what it's going to be like raising these two."

Tiffany struggled not to sigh. "Bring me one, and you rock the other one."

Cammy hurried into the room. Apparently she'd heard the cries. "Ah see that all be well."

"Which baby is this one?" Trisha asked.

"That be Cassandra Jo. She has one pink bow on her gown. Andrea Sue was born second. She has two pink bows." Cammy approached the bed and looked at the infant in Tiffany's arm. "They sure look alike." She straightened the quilt. "If you need anything, send Trisha for me."

When the babies had nursed and were asleep, Trisha left Tiffany to nap. A shuffling noise woke her. She blinked.

Was Nathan really there, or was this a dream? He looked pale and clung to the bedpost. "Nathan?"

He knelt beside the bed and placed a hand on her belly. His eyes widened, then his face creased in regret. "Oh, darling, I'm so sorry. I wanted to be here for you."

"Thank God you're all right."

"I feel like I've been trampled by a herd of buffalo. But what about you?"

"I'm doing all right, now, but I had a rough night."

Moisture formed in his azure eyes. "We'll have other babies, darling."

"Oh please! Don't say another baby!"

One of the babies made a mewing sound. Nathan's head jerked toward the bassinet, then he turned back to Tiffany. "The baby is all right?"

She smiled. "Go take a look." She anxiously waited to see the surprise on her husband's face. Apparently he'd thought she'd lost the baby. Now he expected to see one infant.

Nathan groped his way across the room, braced himself against the wall, and peered into the basket. His eyes widened. His lips moved, but no words issued forth. Finally, he voiced one syllable. "Oh."

Tiffany laughed, then grasped her abdomen. She was a lot more tender than she'd been with Adam, but Ellie had said that was to be expected with a second pregnancy. "Cassandra Jo and Andrea Sue."

The smile that brightened Nathan's face gave the sun competition. "I'd pick them up, but I'm still wobbly." He looked puzzled. "I think I was shot."

"You were. The doctor removed the bullet. You hit your head, too, and you were unconscious all night." She took a deep breath. "Thank God you didn't lose your memory like our dear Jo Ellen."

One of the babies began to cry. Within seconds, the second one's wails joined her sister's. "I guess this is what we can expect for a time." He chuckled. "Nat and Scott did the same."

Jo Ellen stumbled into the room. "My baby." She gripped the dresser, then slumped to the floor.

"Jo!" Tiffany cried.

Nathan looked distressed. "I can't help her! I can barely stand up."

"Ellie!" Tiffany cried. "Cammy! Alice! Someone please come."

# Eight

"Ellie!" Tiffany called again. She felt so helpless. Even if she got out of bed, there was no way she and Nathan could lift Jo Ellen.

Bret hobbled into the room, glanced at his wife's crumpled body, and knelt beside her, an expression of horror on his face. "Jo! Darling. Oh, Jo."

Ellie stopped at the door. Her dark eyes widened, then she turned and hurried away. Tiffany knew the old woman was going for help.

Constance hurried in, stopped with a jolt and stared. "Oh no." Her focus darted to Tiffany. "What happened?"

"I think she fainted. At least, I hope that's all that happened." Tiffany sighed. This woman wouldn't be able to help either. *What a crew we are!*

"She's breathing normally, but . . ." Bret glanced toward the crying babies. "She must've thought she heard Jonathan, and was coming to get him."

"That's a good sign." Constance hurried to the door. "I'll get Joe Billings to carry her back to bed."

*Why Billings?* Tiffany wondered.

Ellie came in with Amos in tow. "You be watchin'" her broken arm."

"Yes-um, Mama Ellie." The huge black man bent to lift Jo Ellen. "Yo be supportin' her arm while Ah lift her."

Ellie gently laid Jo Ellen's broken arm across her stomach, then held it in place as Amos picked her up. She lay limp in his arms, her long curly hair tousled. She looked like a rag doll with a pretty china face.

Bret's worry lines deepened. "Take her back to her bedroom." He stepped aside to let Amos lead the way.

Nathan slumped into the settee and sighed. "I haven't felt so useless since I was wounded in the war."

"I remember a helpless Yankee who lay rotting in Maggie's stable until I came along to nurse him."

He chuckled. "My darling rebel. Even on the flat of your back you're feisty."

"One has to be around here with all that's been happening."

"It's a good thing we have several bedrooms."

"Humph." Ellie swept through the doorway. "They's just about full. Next thing Ah knows, Ah's gonna be sleepin' on the hearth with my old Susie."

Tiffany smiled. "You'll always have your room, Ellie."

The woman crossed the carpet to the basket of whimpering infants. "We needs another nursery. Adam hain't gonna be puttin' up with three squallin' babies. 'Sides, you and Jo Ellen both be runnin' in there all times of the night. If the wailin' don't wake dear Adam, you fussin' mamas will." Lifting Andréa, she changed her and handed her to Nathan. After changing Cassandra, she took her to Tiffany. When one baby was nursing, the old woman sat with a plop to the bedside chair. "All these offspring gonna be the death of old Ellie."

"Nathan's going to hire more help."

"You hain't gonna need to replace old Ellie. Ah hain't dead yet." Getting up, she dug in the baby's dresser for a clean sheet and exchanged it for the wet one in the basket. "All be well here, so Ah's gonna help Cammy with dinner.".

A half hour later, Trisha came in. "Papa." She hugged him. "Constance told me you were awake. You all right?" Not waiting for an answer, she took Andréa from her father. "She's wet, Papa. I'll change her."

Surrendering the little one, Nathan let his arms drop. "I think I'd better get to bed before I pass out like Jo did." Instead of returning to the purple room, he staggered around the bed and collapsed on the mattress beside Tiffany. "Love you," he muttered with a sigh. His head dropped to the pillow like a sack of chicken feed.

"Welcome home." Tiffany smiled. She was weak, weary, and worn, but happy. "Did something happen at Uncle Zachary's?"

Nathan opened his eyes to gaze at her. "Oh, darling, let's let that rest until tomorrow." He drew a deep breath, then pressed a hand to his side. "Feels like a war wound."

"That's sort of what it is." She eyed him. "I want you to tell me what happened at Saxon Oaks."

He sighed. "I know you, my lady. You won't let me sleep until I explain everything."

"Well? Is Uncle Zachary all right ?"

"Yes." He groaned. "He's the same as always. Darcy Mae has her hands full, attending to him as well as Ruthie Ann's distressed children."

Tiffany sat up, but a cramp in her abdomen encouraged her to lean back against her pillows. Trisha brought Andrea and took Cassandra. Tiffany waited until the second infant was nursing. "Did something happen to Ruthie Ann?"

"No. It was Zeb. Tiffany, the Klan hung him."

"Oh no. Poor Ruthie Ann. How's she going to raise her four children without Zeb?" She wished she hadn't ask for a report, but she'd had to know. "As soon as I get on my feet, I'll go over to visit her."

"Emily Rose left Adam and Ally in Alice's care and went to Zachary's this afternoon." He yawned. "Now, my lady, let me sleep." His eyes closed, then flashed open. A gasp made him cringe in pain.

"What's wrong?" Ellie came in, but Tiffany's attention remained glued to Nathan.

He frowned. "I just remembered that when I was shot, I was on my way home to get a wagon with some furniture for Ruthie and her children. They were counting on me for a bed to sleep in last night." He struggled to get up.

"Wait." Tiffany cradled Andrea in one arm. With the other, she reached out to restrain her husband. "You need your rest. I'll take care of it."

"After all you've been through, you're still trying to be all things to all people?"

"I learned that from you."

"No you didn't." He grinned. "You were acting like some sort of mighty woman the first time I met you."

She giggled. "I had to. You were the wounded enemy, and I needed to glean priceless information from you."

He laughed, then gently touched his side. "You're torturing me, my lady."

Ellie sat on the blue settee. "Amos will get a wagon. You tell me what furniture you wants him to take. He'll make sure Ruthie be havin' what she need."

Trisha came to the bedside and took Andréa to the basket. "They're both asleep, Mama."

"You're a wonderful little nurse, Trisha."

"It's going to take Adam awhile to get used to having two tiny sisters. I've been telling him stories about what it will be like when they are big enough to play with." She giggled. "He's considering letting them stay."

Tiffany gave Ellie a list of furniture and told her where it could be found. The woman hurried away. Tiffany was nearly asleep when Trisha tiptoed toward the door.

"Good night, honey."

"It's afternoon." The girl giggled. "But I guess you old folks need your rest. Emily is back and watching Adam. Joshua is on his way with Grandma and Grandpa Harris."

"Wake me up when they get here, honey. I look a fright!"

"I'll get you a basin of water if you want to wash your face and comb your messy hair."

"Thank you, sweetheart, but I'm too tired to bathe right now."

"I'll come back when Grandma gets here." After checking the twins, again, Trisha left and shut the door.

Tiffany yawned. What a hectic, tumultuous, but perfectly wonderful day.

"Jo." Kneeling by the bed, Bret rubbed his unconscious wife's hands. Then ramming his hand into his pocket, he withdrew her diamond ring and slipped it onto her finger with her wedding band. *That's where it belonged.* "Jo, darling." Overwhelmed by his love for her, he kissed her cheek, then rested his lips lightly on hers. They were warm and pliable as always. His kiss was long and tender. His heart throbbed and his spirit was in ecstasy. He had longed to kiss Jo like this since the accident. His dear, sweet Jo. *When she comes to, will she remember me?*

It was difficult to end the kiss. He wanted to go on like this forever—at least until Jonathan demanded his mother's attention.

She stirred. Bret straightened to look at her face. She blinked. Had his kiss wakened her? He wasn't going to confess his actions until she was ready to hear his tender words of love. Right now, she may accuse him of taking advantage of her helplessness.

Instead of the smile he'd prayed for, Jo glared at him, her eyes accusing. "What are you doing in here?"

"You fainted. Amos carried you back to bed. I waited to make sure you were all right."

"Well I am. Now go to your own room."

"Jo, I thought that maybe we could . . ."

"Don't. Please." She frowned. "Where's Jonathan?"

"Cammy rocked him until he fell asleep. He'll be awake and wanting to nurse soon."

"Tell her to bring him to me."

"I'll get him."

"You're leg is still weak. Don't you drop my baby."

He smiled. "He's my baby, too, darling." He watched her face, but there wasn't a flicker of recognition. Heart heavy, he headed for the nursery.

"Tiffany." Emily touched her shoulder. "Your parents have arrived."

"Oh?" Tiffany yawned. "Where are they?"

"Cammy is giving them tea. It's almost time for supper. Trisha said that you-all had ask her to waken you so you could get freshened up a bit before visiting."

"Thank you." Tiffany sat up and rubbed her temples. "Having twins was harder on me than the retreat from Gettysburg with General Lee, and it was raining that night."

Emily laughed. "I brought you a basin of water and a clean towel and washcloth."

Tiffany glanced around. "Where's Nathan?"

"He welcomed your parents, and he's filling them in on what happened last night."

"He's telling them that I had twins?"

Emily held her grin. "He told me he was going to let the baby surprise up to you."

"My dear thoughtful husband." Tiffany smiled. "He's proud of the girls, too."

"He's bursting at the seams." As usual, excitement emphasized her Southern accent. "I don't know how much longer he'll be able to hold himself back."

"What about Trisha?"

"She keeps grinning. Your mama asked her what she was so happy about, but dear Trisha just told her that she'd find out in a little while."

"My sweetheart daughter."

"Well, Nathan and Trisha might be able to contain themselves, but I'm so excited! You'd better get ready pretty quick, or I'm not going to be able to stop myself, and I'll tell them." Wetting the facecloth, she proffered it.

"The cool water feels so good."

"I'll get the brush and fix your auburn locks. Pardon me, Tiffany dear, but you-all look a fright." Laughing, she crossed to the dresser. "I looked worse after the boys were born. I thought I'd never get my figure back. And I felt so haggard."

Tiffany wondered if that was when Matthew strayed and made Olivia his mistress. That was over now. Matthew got his comeuppance on a battlefield; and Nathan had hired Jonathan to take the case against Olivia and made sure the woman returned to Emily what she had fraudulently taken from her. Joshua would love Emily forever. Tiffany sighed. *He'd better marry her soon, or I'm going to demand to know why.* There was no sense in their waiting to marry.

She was tying her robe when she heard her parents on the stairs. When they came in, Tiffany stood, but sidestepped and grasped the bedpost.

"Darling, what's wrong?" Kathryn rushed across the room to hug her. "Are you ill?"

"I'm fine." She hugged her mother, amazed at how slender she still was. The woman had a few gray hairs, but for the most part, her honey-colored locks were the same as they'd been for years.

Jonathan followed the sound of their voices and stood patiently, waiting for his hug. When he'd been blinded in the war, it had taken him time to adjust. Now, one could hardly tell he couldn't see, unless he was in a place that was strange to him. He limped slightly because of his prosthesis. Tiffany noticed that there was more gray at his temples, and his dark hair was thinning more on top. The war had been hard on him, but thank God he'd returned.

"My turn, Kate." Stepping forward, he wrapped his arms around Tiffany, then gasped. "Oh! You had your baby!"

"We have a new addition, Papa."

Kathryn laughed. "So that's what Trisha was grinning about. And Nathan, too." Her laugh tinkled again. "And to think that I hugged you and didn't take notice! Your father wasn't fooled. Where is our new little darling?"

Tiffany grinned at her mother and waved a hand toward the bassinet.

"A girl?"

"No."

"Oh, darling, you had another boy."

"No."

"What else is there?" Puzzled, Kathryn went to the basket. "Oh, Jonathan! They're twins!"

Emily smiled as though the babies were hers. "Identical girls. Nat and Scott are so excited." Her Georgian accent drew out the syllables.

Tiffany wouldn't have wanted to miss the expression that crossed her mother's face for anything in the world.

"I know they're sleeping, but I can't help myself." Scooping up one baby, Kathryn handed her to Jonathan, then lifted the other in her arms.

"That's Cassandra Jo, Papa. Mama has Andrea Sue."

Jonathan's smile distorted the war scar that zigzagged down his cheek. "Chair still in the same place?"

"Yes." Tiffany didn't move. Her father preferred doing things for himself.

Crossing the room, he touched the chair with his good shin, then turned, sat, and cradled the baby. Wonder crossed his face as he took a tiny hand and touched each finger. "God's wonderful creation."

"And it's been duplicated!" Kathryn marveled over the baby she held, then faced her daughter. "Your father and I had decided to spend a few days with you." She laughed. "Now I'm staying longer. Nathan took our luggage to the purple room. Emily said she was staying, too. She'll work." Joy tinkled in her laughter. "But as for me, dear, I plan to play with my grandbabies. All three of them!"

"You always help, too, Mama." She glanced at Emily. "Where are you and the boys planning to sleep?"

"Nathan's such a dear. He had Cammy change the sitting room into a bedroom. We'll be fine." Her smile brightened. "If my dear Joshua accomplishes what he says he's going to, Bret and Jo Ellen may be in the same room soon. That will free another bedroom."

Kathryn continued to peer at baby Andrea as she spoke. "How is Jo?"

"Physically she's improving, but her memory hasn't come back yet."

Kathryn glanced at Emily. "Nathan explained her condition to us. Joshua thinks maybe he can help. He said he'd stay the night and speak with her in the morning."

Tiffany watched the glow on Emily's face as Kathryn spoke of Joshua, then she turned back to her mother. "Bret is trying so hard. He could use some encouragement from Joshua."

"That was the reason we came, darling. That and baby Jonathan. Now you'd better go back to bed. You look a bit pale and seem shaky on your feet." She smiled. "You have an excellent excuse to rest. Take it while you can, dear."

"She's right, Tiffany." Emily folded back the quilt. "If your babies are anything like Scott and Nat, you're going to be exhausted for the next two years!"

Tiffany's legs were beginning to wobble, and she was glad to take the advice. "I don't remember being this weak after having Adam."

"Each new baby takes a bit more out of a woman than the one before." A warm glow brightened Kathryn's cheeks. "And after having five, I should know." She gazed at the babe in her arms. "I never had twins, though. Emily's right. You'd better take your rest while you can."

Tiffany flipped a sheet over herself and yawned. "I'm going to do just that."

Jo pictured the hurt look on Bret's face when she'd driven him from her room, and tears pooled in her eyes. Had she loved this man? She must have or she wouldn't have married him. She frowned. Could she had married for security? Or maybe companionship? What about baby Jonathan? Could it be that? *No!* She knew that much about herself. Or did she? *Why can't I remember the man I loved?* She drew a long breath as she thought. It must be possible, because she didn't remember being pregnant or giving birth.

The late afternoon sun streamed through the window and across her quilt. She put her hand through a warming beam. Light struck the gold band on her finger. Another ring had joined the first. A diamond flashed at her. She gasped. She had seen the wedding band, but how had the second ring got onto her finger? Had Bret slipped it on before she'd come to after her faint? Should she take it off and throw it at him or give him a chance to prove his love for her? Should she try to love him in return?

"Here's our son. He's hungry again."

Jo tried to smile as Bret made his way across the room, baby Jonathan cradled in his right arm. Jo didn't like looking at his left shoulder where the empty sleeve had been pulled inside his shirt. Had she gotten used to living with a one-armed man? She could feel his pain. Was that a good sign? A giggle nearly burst forth when she glanced at her cast. She, too, had to get along with one arm. It was the knowledge that she would be getting her right arm out of the sling and would be whole again that gave her courage. Bret would never be completely whole. As she accepted her baby from this man who claimed to be her husband, something stirred within her. Pity? No. She didn't think it was just compassion, but defining the sensation was difficult. Maybe in time she could learn to care for Bret. "I noticed a diamond ring on my finger. How'd it get there, Bret?"

Apprehension flashed across his features. He shrugged. "It's your ring. How it got on your finger doesn't matter."

That solidified her suspicion. She would decide later what she should do about it.

Bret stood gazing at the baby and a smile spread across his handsome face. "The moment I gave him to you, his mouth started to move. He's a smart little guy. He knows where his meals are coming from."

Jonathan began to squirm in Jo's arm and whimper. She looked at him, then eyed Bret. "If you think I'm going to nurse a baby with you standing over me like a turkey buzzard, you're crazy." The hurt that replaced his smile touched her. "I'm sorry, Bret, but you can't expect me to nurse my baby in front of a stranger."

"Stranger?" He sighed. "I'm the one who's sorry, Jo. Maybe I'm expecting too much too fast. When your memory returns, we can pick up our lives from where we left them." Turning, he left and closed the door.

Standing in the hallway, Bret battled depression. It was almost like a living death to have Jo and yet not have her. He felt as though he were existing in a dark cloud. The accident hadn't been his fault, but could he have done something to prevent it?

He shook his head. Jo was the one who had wanted to visit Tiffany before they headed for the Shenandoah Valley. There was no way he could have avoided the runaway's wagon. There had been that steep downward slope to their right. To the left, the bank rose sharply and had trees. Still, if he would have thought fast enough, could he have helped Jo out of the buggy and had her safely behind a tree on the hill? *I didn't know the team were runaways.* He sighed. If only he'd known. However, there had been only a few seconds. If he'd taken his wife from the buggy, they could have both been directly in the path of the oncoming team and been trampled to death. A team usually tries to avoid running over people, but there was no place for them to go, either.

He continued to ponder as he made his way to his room. Sitting on a chair beside a window, he gazed toward the workers' cabins. The spot where Joe Billings's cabin had stood was now a chard and blackened ruin. Bret watched tiny streams of smoke slowly curl upward from a few smoldering timbers. Life seemed like that. One moment you had a firm grip on your dream, and the next it was ripped from your grasp. "Up in smoke," Bret mumbled.

Movement in the yard below drew his attention. Constance sat on the bench under the apple tree. He recognized her pink dress as one of Tiffany's. Joe Billings stood near her. She said something that made him laugh. A smile brightened her pale face. The woman had looked like walking death yesterday. Visiting with Joe seemed to breathe life into her. Bret chuckled to himself. Was Constance flirting with the man? Whatever it was, Joe seemed to be enjoying it. He rubbed his chin. Hadn't Nathan told him that the woman was dying?

Micah called from the barn. Joe excused himself and headed across the yard. Constance's focus followed him.

When he was out of sight, her smile remained. With one hand, she smoothed her honey-colored hair. It looked like one of the ladies had trimmed and washed it. Smiling, Constance cuddled in her cape.

"Well, well." Bret grinned. "There was no doubt that Constance was attracted to Joe. That was probably why she had hurried to fetch him instead of Amos to aid Jo Ellen. Ellie had beat her and brought Amos instead. It had given Constance an excuse to search for Billings. "Any excuse will do when a woman is out to catch a man," he whispered. But why would she want to attract a man when she was dying? Had she lied? Or was this just one last fling before the grave?

Bret sighed. He needed an excuse to get Jo Ellen back in his arms. Waiting, even though it was sheer torture, was what he intended to do. Patience was the problem. He wanted to hug and kiss her now!

As he sat meditating, an idea began to form. Maybe he should leave for the Shenandoah Valley as soon as Jo had regained her strength and was on her feet. He could begin to collect the lumber and supplies he would need to rebuild Sunny Horizon. Jo could join him later. The thought made his heart cramp. *What if Jo's memory doesn't return? What if she refuses to come to the Valley? Maybe it would be wise to try to convince her to accompany me.*

Since Jo wouldn't remember where Staunton or Harrisonburg were, he retrieved a map, then cautiously knocked on her door.

"Yes?"

"Are you finished nursing Jonathan?"

"Yes. And you can come in."

He smiled. If she was permitting him to visit her in her room, he had cleared the first hurdle. Opening the door, he went in. "Is he sleeping?"

She nodded. "But I want to hold him for awhile."

"Jo, when you get strong enough to travel, will you accompany me to the Shenandoah Valley as we planned?"

She stared blankly at him. "Is that nearby?"

"No, darling." He opened the map and pointed to where Castle Crest was located. "We're here." He traced his index finger to Richmond, then northwestward to Staunton, then Harrisonburg. "Sunny Horizon was about here." He pointed to approximately midway between the towns. "The house and barn were burned. We're going to rebuild them."

"That's so far!" The color had drained from her face, then bright pink spots appeared on her cheekbones. "I can't go away with you Bret. I won't! How could you suggest such a thing? I don't even know you."

He felt as though a horse had kicked him in the stomach. "Jo, darling, we can start again."

"No one would expect me to go gallivanting off to the ends of the earth with a stranger."

"But you're my wife. We have a son."

"No, Bret!" Anger created silver sparks in her gray eyes. "Get out of my room!"

He hesitated. There was no sense in arguing with her, but maybe a little gentle coaxing was in order. "Jo, sweetheart I --"

"Out! Now!" Jonathan began to cry. "See what you've done."

Jo Ellen's heart pounded. She pointed to the door. Bret, his shoulders slumped, left. Guilt squiggled within her. She shouldn't have been so harsh with the man. He loved her. That was evident. Tiffany had told her that during the war Bret was missing. She frowned. *What war?*

Hushing her baby, Jo pondered what Tiffany had told her. *If I hadn't loved Bret, why would I have waited for him and refused to believe he'd been killed?* Apparently everyone else had accepted his death. *The woman also said that even after I'd considered Bret's never returning, I'd refused to see any other man.* Shock knocked her against her pillows. *If Tiffany isn't lying, and she has no reason to, I really must be married to Bret!* She swallowed. Did she owe the man an audience? Should she consider his request? If she loved him, and she must have, should she try to love him again?

She gasped. *Does my concern mean I still love him and just don't know it?*

# Nine

Jo Ellen shook her head. The thought of her loving Bret and being unaware of it was so absurd that she nearly laughed. Then another thought sobered her. What if Bret left without her to go to that valley? He seemed determined to rebuild some building. What if he didn't return? What if he met an enticing woman? *Would she eventually make him forget me?*

Staring out the window at the early sunset, she wondered if she was the one being stubborn. What would she do if Bret left and didn't come back? Did she intend to raise Jonathan alone? What if she lost Bret, then her memory returned and she discovered she really did love him and it was too late to win him back? Tiffany and Nathan had been so gracious, but she couldn't continue to stay here after her strength returned. Where would she go? *I don't know Bret, but I don't know anyone else, either!*

Trisha stepped through the open door from the hall. "Are you all right, Aunt Jo?"

Jo looked at her. The child seemed perceptive. "I've been thinking about something."

"You look tired. I see that Jonathan is asleep. Do you want me to put him in the nursery?"

"Thank you."

The girl gently lifted Jonathan and put him in the crook of her arm without waking him. "Mama's two babies are asleep, too." She rolled her azure eyes. "To have all three little ones sleeping at the same time is a miracle." She smiled. "Now you can rest."

*No sleep yet.* She wasn't sure about what she was going to do, or if it was right, but she couldn't just ignore her circumstances. *Or my gut feeling, if that's what it is.*

This time, when she got up, she stood slowly and gripped the back of the wooden chair beside her bed. If she could shove the chair ahead as she went, it would offer support, and if she felt woozy, she would have something to sit on. A tug revealed that the piece of furniture was too heavy in her weakened state. She planned to walk slowly and pause if she got dizzy. If she felt faint and there wasn't a chair handy, she'd supposed she could slowly lower herself to the floor.

"I could call someone to help me," she whispered, then decided against it. She preferred that no one knew of this venture. Creating false hope in Bret would be bad enough. *Is that what I'm doing?*

Crossing the room, she braced a hand on the door frame and hesitated to reconsider her actions. *What choice do I have?* A frown tugged on her brows. Was it wise to make a decision out of desperation? *My place is with Bret.* Desperate or not, even if she couldn't remember the man, she was his wife.

Taking a shaky breath, she made her way down the corridor and stopped in Bret's doorway. He sat staring out the window, his brow furrowed. Entering the room, she leaned against the dresser. "Bret?"

His head jerked to face her, and his eyes widened. "Jo!" Standing, he limped toward her.

She raised a hand to stop his approach. "Don't rush me. I just came to talk."

"You better sit. You look pale." He dragged the wooden chair he'd been sitting on to the front of the dresser and held it secure until she was sitting. He rubbed his leg injury as though it still hurt. "You remember something?"

"No," she whispered. "I want you to tell me about the valley you mentioned and what you want to do there."

He sat on the edge of his bed. "We were going back to rebuild the homestead that was burned during the war."

"If you wait until I'm stronger, I'll go with you."

"Jo!" He jumped to his feet. His injured leg gave way. Seizing the bedpost, he grinned. "I guess I should get a bit stronger, too." He took a step toward her.

"Sit and listen. There will be stipulations to my accompanying you."

"Oh, darling Jo, I'll do anything you say."

"You must promise not to expect too much too fast."

"I promise."

"We will have separate bedrooms."

"Jo! You're my wife!"

"Please Bret. Living as your wife is going to take me time."

He drew a long breath. "I'll do whatever you say and wait as long as I have to. You've accepted that you're Jonathan's mother. I thank God for that. I pray you'll let me be his father."

"Of course. The child needs us both." She swallowed, wondering if she was being foolish. "That's one of the reasons I'm willing to go with you."

"I yearn to hold you, Jo. I love you, and I want to kiss you so desperately, that it's driving me mad, but I'll wait until you're ready."

"I appreciate your affection and patience. Until I remember you, we can live as brother and sister." She stood. "Now I must go back to bed before I collapse."

Ellie stopped in the doorway. "You two be together?"

"Not quite, Ellie, but I have more hope." Bret stood. "Please get someone to help Jo back to her room. I don't want her to fall again."

The old lady eyed Jo Ellen. "You stay put. Ah's gonna fetch Joshua."

Jo peered at Ellie. Who was Joshua? She didn't feel like asking. Every time she ask someone, she could read sympathy on their face. She would wait and find out who the man was. Sitting there in Bret's bedroom seemed awkward. Bret continued to grin, but Jo Ellen didn't see anything to smile at. She'd made concessions that she'd thought were impossible only yesterday. Trying to pull the top of her robe completely shut failed. She must be getting bigger, unless this robe belonged to someone else. Tiffany had said that after giving birth, in preparation for feeding the infant, engorgement increased the size of a woman's breasts. Again, she endeavored to cover her exposed neckline. Still, some flesh was exposed! Sitting in Bret's bedroom, even though he claimed to be her husband, was embarrassing. Should she wait and possibly flash a bit of skin in front of another man or stagger to her room? Feeling dizzy, she sat still.

A chuckle vibrated Bret's throat as he retrieved a man's handkerchief from a dresser drawer and proffered it. Grateful, she tucked it under the front of her robe. Could the man read her mind—or did he feel guilty for admiring her exposure? However, if she was his wife, he was used to seeing her. There was a sparkle in his brown eyes that she hadn't noticed before. It chased any lingering doubt that this man loved her dearly. She'd probably made the proper choice. Whether it was right for her or not, she didn't know. Living in the same house with Bret would be good for their baby. *I'll pray to love Bret. Surely if I adored him once, I can learn to again.*

"When do you think you'll be well enough to travel?"

The question startled her. She'd given her consent to accompany him, still putting a date on their departure seemed premature. "I don't know."

"We should be clearing the foundation by now. I hope we won't have to put off beginning to build much longer."

"Where will we live while we're rebuilding?"

"There are cabins where the hired hands used to live. As far as I know, Jonas and Cammy and their five children are the only ones still living on the property. Dad is counting on them to look after the place. We'll need their help during the building process, and Priscilla can help you with Jonathan."

She sighed. "And who is Priscilla?"

"Their seventeen-year-old daughter. A band of raiders nearly hung Jonas during the war."

"They black?"

"Yes. Dad purchased them, then gave them their papers. He's paying Jonas to oversee the place. They are living off of the land and they're free to sell the extra crops they grow."

While he spoke, she studied his face. "But you're not sure there'll be a house for us to live in, are you?"

He seemed to squirm under her surveillance. "I can't promise that it will be comfortable the first few days, but I'll take care of you, Jo."

She knew he meant it. What was the unrest that twisted her insides? Should she accompany Bret or wait until he had a place for them to live, then join him.

"I thank God you agreed to go with me, darling. A wife's place is by her husband's side."

"Bret, I told you . . ."

"I know," he broke in. "I'm just dreaming out loud." His grin softened his slightly squared chin. "I'm trying to be patient. You may have to remind me from time to time."

"If you get out of line, Mr. Harris, I promise you I'll put you back in your place."

He chuckled. "You don't remember what you were like, darling, but believe me, your personality hasn't changed."

She gasped. "Was I a shrew?"

"Oh no." He burst into laughter. "You just knew what you wanted, and in your sweet way, you usually got it."

"Was I selfish and demanding?"

"You were and are the sweetest, most wonderful woman I've ever known. I understand your reaction now, and I'll try hard to abide by your stipulations."

That didn't sound too bad. Maybe she could handle this.

A white cat stepped into the room and paused to look around. Jo Ellen's focus met the feline's green eyes. "And who are you?"

"That's Susie, Ellie's cat. Ellie tries to keep her downstairs, but Susie thinks she's queen around here."

Jo smiled. "You walk like a queen."

Meowing, the cat leaped into her lap. Jo stroked her and was rewarded with a loud purr. "I think she's going to have kittens."

Bret chuckled. "That's been a semiannual occurrence for years."

She eyed Bret. "Do we have a cat?"

"No."

He didn't sound too enthusiastic, but he had just said that she usually got her way. Not that it mattered, but she thought she'd give it a try. She grinned at him. "You think we could keep one of the kittens?"

"Sure. Ellie would be delighted to give you all of them."

"One will be enough. She can grow up with Jonathan."

A good-looking man, a few years older than Bret, stepped into the room with Ellie. Sandy hair waved away from his friendly face. The compassion that shimmered in his brown eyes told her that they must have known each other. He grinned at Bret. "Hello, Brother."

"Good to see you, Joshua. Jo needs supported to get back to her room, and I'm crippled again."

A chuckle that spread warmth through the room issued from the man, and he gripped Bret's shoulder. "You'll be fit before long."

Ellie spotted the cat and frowned. "You be gettin' downstairs if you be wantin' dinner."

The cat jumped to the floor, avoided the old woman's hands, and swept through the doorway. Joshua chuckled.

Jo clutched at the front of her robe. It had been bad enough to expose a bit of skin to a man who was supposed to be her husband, but the thought of not being completely covered in front of this stranger made her cheeks burn. She was thankful to note that the handkerchief was still in place, but she vowed not to leave her room again without a garment that properly covered her.

Joshua stepped forward. "Let's go."

Before she could protest, he swept her up in his arms and carried her down the hall. She closed her eyes in horror.

"Don't be embarrassed, Jo. We're good friends. Even before you were my sister-in-law, I loved you like a sister. During the war, you and Elizabeth Ann stayed at my home and worked at the hospitals in Richmond."

More names and places that she didn't know! *Dear Lord, when will this confusion end?*

Apparently, Joshua interpreted her dilemma. "I'm Tiffany and Bret's eldest brother. Elizabeth Ann is our sister."

"Then Bret has three siblings?"

"There were five of us. Timothy, our youngest brother, was killed during the war. We thought for quite a time that we'd lost Bret, too."

She would have to ask about the stupid war, but she was too weary and confused this evening to care.

Bret followed Joshua to Jo Ellen's room. He longed to sit by her bed and continue their discussion, but that would probably press his luck. This new development couldn't be luck. It was an answer to prayer. *Except I want to be her husband, not her brother.*

Placing Jo on her bed, Joshua straightened. "I know you're tired this evening, but tomorrow, we'll have a long talk." Smiling, he left.

Ellie fussed with Jo's quilt, then studied her face. "You needs anything?"

"I'd appreciate a drink of water."

"Ah be back." She hesitated in the center of the room and glanced back. "You be wantin' apple juice, too?"

"That sounds good. Thank you." When the woman left the room, Jo eyed Bret. "I'm tired. Please let me sleep."

He longed to climb in beside her, but knew better than to suggest it. The way things were going, it may be quite awhile before she permitted that. *Unless her memory returns.* He would pray for that. He wondered how a man could be elated and disappointed at the same time. He sat on a chair beside her door. "I'll write to Cassie and ask her to make sure a cabin is ready. I think Ellie's is still in adequate condition."

Was that true? He pictured the old woman's place and drew a long breath. It needed repair during the war. *By now, could it be beyond help? Jonas would make sure it was ready for occupancy, wouldn't he?*

"How many rooms does Ellie's place have, Bret?"

"Two, I think. There was a living area and a bedroom."

Her eyes widened. "Only one bedroom?"

"Yes, but you and the baby can have it. I'll manage on a couch or cot in the main room." He prayed that wouldn't be for long. With the work of building Sunny Horizon, there wouldn't be much time to court his lovely wife, but somehow he'd manage. He would ask Jonas what he would need to repair Ellie's old cabin, then ship the supplies by rail. Nathan's North Fork lumber camp would be the closest to the Valley. By the time Jo could travel, they would at least have a temporary home.

"I'll see you after your nap, darling."

"Please shut my door on your way out."

He nodded, but paused at the door and turned. "Have a good rest, sweetheart."

On his way to his room, he thanked and praised God, then he petitioned the Lord to create a situation where he could be near Jo more. He frowned. Was that wrong? He shook his head. *She's my wife. We belong together.*

Tiffany yawned. Dawn's glow filtered through the curtains, making the embroidered yellow roses stand out on the bedspread. She lay quietly, listening to Nathan's even breathing. He was nearly back to his old self. She turned her head to gaze at him. As usual, the blond curl dangled across his forehead. Oh, how she loved this man. *What if the rifleman had killed him?* She refused to dwell on that morbid thought.

Andrea began to whimper. Tiffany got up slowly, as not to waken her husband. Before she reached the bassinet, Cassandra began to fuss, and Andréa's plea turned into a wail.

"Again?" Nathan mumbled.

Tiffany laughed softly. "We'll be moving them to the new nursery soon." She scooped up Andrea in one arm and Cassandra with the other.

"The nursery isn't ready."

"It's almost. Micah painted the walls pink. Cammy scrubbed the floor and Amos painted it white. Emily Rose sent over a braided rug that she made with light colors."

"Which baby are you going to feed first?"

"Both, although Andrea was the first to get awake. She usually is. At least she's the first one to cry."

"How can you know which one yells first if you're not beside them?"

"I can tell them apart by their cry."

"They sound the same to me." Yawning, he sat up. "I'll try to shush Cassandra Jo while you nurse Andrea."

"You get a bit more sleep. Emily showed me how to take care of both babies at the same time." She placed one baby behind the other on the dressing table. After changing Andrea, she switched and changed Cassandra. Lifting them both, she went to the large armchair. Nathan watched. His expression made Tiffany giggle. She hadn't found a way to nurse them both at the same time and still appear demure. Exposing both breasts, she put a baby to each nipple.

Nathan shook his head. "I don't want to say what just went through my mind."

"You might as well say it. I know what you're thinking." She grinned at him. "Just like old Susie."

He laughed. "Well, we have two very special little kittens."

"You called Trisha your kitten. You'll have to think of another endearment for these two."

He stretched. "I'm working on it." Getting up, he dressed. Instead of going downstairs, he stood gazing at his wife. "That chair is soft, but our babies need rocked."

"The rocker I used with Adam is in the nursery. He claims it, and I won't move it to the new nursery."

"That one won't do anyway." He grinned. "I hired Clay to make you a wider one to accommodate both babies." He pursed his lips. "Is it time to start calling the first nursery Adam's room?"

"That's a good idea, since we're telling him he's a big boy now."

Nathan studied his infant daughters. "They're sleeping." He came to Tiffany and gently lifted one. "Which one is this?"

"Cassandra."

"I would've guessed otherwise." He sighed. "I guess I'm going to be fooled a lot in the future."

"They'll be pulling tricks on their papa." She laughed. "And probably getting away with it."

"You think that's funny. Why? Just so Emily Rose can gloat?"

"She will. In her own sweet way."

"Maybe she doesn't have enough to occupy her time. What's slowing Joshua down? I thought he and Emily would be married by now."

"I thought so, too. Maybe I'll have a talk with him."

"You behave. You tried to match him up with Jo Ellen before Bret returned from the war."

"That was because our dear Jo was so miserable. We all thought Bret had been killed."

"Nevertheless, my lady, that would've been a disaster."

"Well, it's different with Emily."

He chuckled. "Of course it is."

Tiffany stood and took Andrea to the bassinet.

Nathan laid Cassandra beside her. "We need another basket, too."

"I don't think so. They're so used to being together that when they're separated, they cry. I think we need a larger one, though."

"I'll see if Clay can make a double-wide cradle."

"That would be wonderful! If we had a cradle, Adam could rock the babies."

"He'll have to accept them first." Nathan sighed. "Our son has a mind of his own. Right now, he insists the twins are just visiting."

"He'll adjust in time."

At that moment, Adam entered their room and frowned. "Too many babies." He eyed his mother. "Can we give one away?"

Nathan picked him up and held him over the basket. "Which one do you suggest we give away?"

The little boy looked at one, then the other and shrugged. "Both of 'em."

"God gave them to us. They're your little sisters."

"Why'd God do that?" He wiggled to get down. "Don't want more girls." He headed for the door, then stopped with a jerk and turned to his mother. "We trade Aunt Jo. Boys are better!" He ran from the room and back the hall.

Tiffany looked at her husband. "I think we have a problem."

While they were still discussing what to do, Adam came back. He had both fists full of blanket. Baby Jonathan was hanging as though in a hammock. "Here him is."

With a cry, Tiffany hurried forward and took the baby. "Adam, you can't just take Aunt Jo's baby."

"Why. Aunt Jo won't 'member. She don't 'member nothing."

"God gave Jonathan to Jo and the girls to us."

He blinked his long blond lashes and turned big blue eyes to Tiffany. "God made a mistake."

"Young man, I think you and Papa better have a talk." Nathan picked the little boy up and headed downstairs.

Tiffany bit her lip. She knew Nathan wouldn't be too harsh with Adam. The little boy's reaction was to be expected. She blamed herself. She should have prepared her son for a new baby. Having two instead of the expected one would have been surprise enough. She'd tried to protect Adam. *Instead, have I made it more difficult for him?*

A shriek from down the hall startled Tiffany. Whirling, Jonathan in her arms, she hurried toward the old nursery.

# Ten

"Where's my baby?" Jo stood in the center of the nursery, her eyes wide and her hands splaying.

Tiffany rushed to her. "I have him."

Jo pressed a hand to her chest. "I was frightened that something had happened to him." Her gray eyes were accusing. "I told you I wanted to care for him myself. I told everyone else, too. If they heard him cry and I didn't, they were to come and tell me."

"I know. I'm sorry." Tiffany had no intention of telling her what Adam had done. Jo would probably faint—even though she was nearly back to health. She handed Jonathan over. "I'll have Nathan move this crib into your room. It will be easier, now that you're regaining your strength."

"I'd appreciate having him beside me."

Tiffany eyed Jo's pale face. "How are you feeling this morning?"

"Disgusted with myself. I'm regaining strength, but it seems to be taking me so long." She peered at the babe in her arm and sighed. "My broken arm doesn't help. I could better manage caring for my son if I had the use of both arms." Her eyes found Tiffany's. "That was such a selfish thought. Bret will never again experience having both arms." She looked contemplative. "And with twins, you could use four!"

"It might be handy sometimes, but it would be impossible to buy a dress, and extremely difficult to make one that fit."

Jo chuckled. It was the first time since the accident that Tiffany had heard her laugh. It was a good sign. "Adam isn't accepting the girls."

"He will. It must be a shock to have two new sisters at once."

"Adam isn't the only one who was surprised." A giggle bubbled from Tiffany. "I was surprised, but Nathan was in shock. He still can't tell them apart."

"Neither can I, but a mother bear knows her own cubs." With a chuckle, Jo headed for her room. "I'll bet Nathan and Bret wouldn't be able to tell the difference between Jonathan and the girls. It might be interesting to put the three babies together and see if the papas can tell."

"Don't be surprised if Adam suggests a switch."

Jo half turned to look at her. "He already has. He offered me both of yours for Jonathan." She held her smile. "You and Nathan have a bit of a problem, but I'm sure Adam will accept the twins in time."

One of the twins began to cry. "That's Cassandra Jo."

"Wait a minute." Jo studied Tiffany's face. "Jo?"

"Her second name is for you. Andrea Sue's second name was for Melissa Sue."

"Who's she?"

"Joshua's late wife."

"Late wife? Then he isn't married?"

"Not yet, but if he pays attention to the lecture I'm going to give him, he will be married soon."

"To whom?"

"Emily. They adore each other, and I can't think of any reason why they should wait any longer to be together."

"I like Emily. She has such a darling accent. I think I like Joshua, too."

"You and Joshua were very good friends in the past. For a time, I thought you two would be getting together."

Jo gasped. "You mean we were . . . involved?"

"No. You were in love with Bret, and Joshua insisted that he loved you like a sister."

"He told me that when he was here visiting." She drew a long breath. "He talked to me until he was about to turn green, but I can only agree to accept a little at a time."

"What did he want you to do?"

"Be Bret's wife. Tiffany, I'm trying by just going to the Valley with Bret. I so appreciate your understanding. I just pray that Bret will be patient."

Tiffany followed Jo to her room. "Joshua thinks we should invite people in to visit who know you. He says some face that should be familiar to you may strike a cord that may help you remember."

"Thanks, but I don't feel like entertaining company yet. I'm still trying to get used to Bret and your family."

"I understand. Let me know when you're ready. It would be nice to have a party before you and Bret leave for the Shenandoah Valley. It's so far away, and I don't know when we'll see each other again."

Jo shook her head, making her black curls sway. "Bret promised that we'll come back to visit before winter sets in."

"The family tries to get together for Thanksgiving. The last two years, we've gathered at Uncle Zachary's. I pray you and Bret will be able to come home to visit at that time."

"We'll try." Sitting, Jo began to nurse Jonathan.

Tiffany perched on the edge of the bed. "My parents will be here for another week. That will give you a chance to get to know them again."

"They seem a lot like you. Kathryn is so gracious." Jo laughed softly. "Except she can't keep her hands off of the babies."

Tiffany smiled. "She seems to have one of them every time I see her. Having three grandbabies at the same time has her exuberant." She listened, then giggled. "Cassandra isn't crying, so I assume Mama has her."

"I can't believe how your father runs around through the house without seeing! Emily said he and Joshua have a law practice. How can he do that?"

"For one thing, he has a fantastic memory. He uses Braille to write his notes and to mark his files. Sally reads his mail to him, takes dictation, and helps to keep the printed material in order."

"Sally?" Jo frowned. "There's probably someone else I should know."

"Sally is the black girl who used to help in Joshua's house. You and Elizabeth Ann taught her how to read and write, even though it was against regulations."

"She must have learned her lessons well."

"She's very bright. And she loves being Papa's secretary. They keep her working there quiet. A lot of whites get angry if black women do much else than domestic help."

"That doesn't seem fair." She shook her head as though confused. "I suppose Bret has told you that we'll be leaving soon."

"I hate to see you go, but I'm happy for you."

"Don't forget to pray for me. I'm going to need it."

A baby began to cry. Tiffany stood. "There goes Andrea again. Cassandra didn't cry when she was born. Andrea came into the world kicking and screaming."

"Their identical in looks, Tiffany, but their personalities are different."

Tiffany headed for the hall door. "Nat and Scott seem to think the same way."

Jo giggled. "Don't all men? It must begin when they are quite young."

Halting mid-step, Tiffany whirled to face Jo. "Think about what you last said. How would you know something about men?"

Jo looked back, her expression blank. "I don't know."

Tiffany smiled. "At least a tiny part of your memory must have slipped back. We can have hope."

A smile curved Jo's mouth. "Maybe before too much longer. It's difficult for me to not recognize people I should know well, but not knowing who I am is the most devastating."

"We know you, Jo. I've loved you like a sister practically from the time we met." Tiffany smiled. "Everyone loves you."

By the time Tiffany had the twins asleep, there was barely time to dress for supper. She'd bathed earlier and donned a robe. Getting into a pretty dress would make her feel human again. Choosing one of the frocks she hadn't been able to wear for several months, she smiled. She flounced the skirt over her head, pulled the fabric into place, and gasped. The dress was too tight across the bust. She could hardly breathe! It was difficult for her to wiggle out of the garment. One by one, she went over the items in her closet. "This is the largest thing I own," she mumbled, staring at a purple and white dress she abhorred and seldom wore.

Slowly, she tried the dress on. It spanned taut across the bodice, but wasn't too restricting. She reached to button the back and moaned.

Ellie stopped in the doorway. "You be feelin' all right?"

"Oh Ellie! I'm so fat! I can't fit into anything!"

The woman came in and assessed the situation. "You can't be expectin' to fit into those little things after havin' two babies."

"I fit after having Adam."

Ellie shook her head. "You just don't remember." The old woman laughed. "Ah can remember the day you cried 'cause you was too fat."

"I want to dress for supper. What can I do?"

"Let's me see." She circled Tiffany and nodded. "Ah'll fix you somethin' tomorrow. For tonight you gonna have to make do."

"I can't go downstairs half naked!"

"You hain't gonna be naked, girl." She tugged on the fabric and buttoned the top button. She grabbed a shawl from the closet and draped it over Tiffany's shoulders. "There. You be lookin' fine."

"My back is covered, but this is horrid." Tiffany felt like crying. "At least before the girls were born, I had an excuse to be fat."

Ellie laughed. "You gonna be little again. You just have to work at it more the second time." She surveyed the effect of the shawl. "You looks good, honey. The lavender flowers on the shawl be good with the dress."

By the time Tiffany entered the dining room, the evening meal was on the table. Alice carried trays to Jo and Bret, but everyone else was present, except for Nathan. The next moment, he breezed through the swinging doors from the kitchen and stopped to look at Tiffany.

"You look great. I've always liked that dress." Smiling, he pulled out her chair, then took his place at the table.

There wasn't much conversation while they filled their plates. Tiffany glanced across the table at Constance. The woman seemed happier, but the dark shadows under her eyes were a deeper blue, and her pale complexion made her appear ghostly. Her light-blue dress didn't help. *This evening I'll go through my closet and pick out a few more dresses for her. Ones with more color will be better.*

Kathryn, who was sitting to Tiffany's left, touched her arm. "Constance has finally agreed to accompany us back to Richmond to see a doctor."

"I've seen a doctor before." Constance shrugged. "He couldn't do anything to help, but Joshua said there was a new man in Richmond who had advanced treatments."

"That's wonderful." Tiffany sipped her milk. "Alexandra will be fine here until you return."

"No." The child straightened, apparently catching the meaning of the conversation. "I wanna go with Mama."

"I won't be able to be with you, sweetie." Constance blinked as though she were fighting tears. "I'll come back as soon as I can."

The girl pushed her plate away and a tear rolled down her tiny face.

As usual, Kathryn came to the rescue. "She can come with you, Constance. Maggie is there to watch her."

"I'm gonna go, too." Adam waved his spoon and flipped a blob of mashed potatoes onto the tablecloth. "Them babies haffa stay here."

"Your papa and I can't part with you," Tiffany said.

He shook his blond curls. "Uncle Joshua don't have babies. I'm gonna be with him."

Tiffany sighed

Trisha giggled. "When Uncle Joshua marries Aunt Emily, they'll have two children, too."

Tiffany didn't miss the bright pink spots that suddenly appeared on Emily's cheeks. Not smiling, the woman lowered her eyes to her plate.

Adam considered his sister's comment, then nodded. "Aunt Emily has all boys." He grinned. "We kin do lots of things."

"I'll bet." Trisha eyed him. "Don't forget you're a big boy, and you have to help take care of our twins."

He shook his head. "Mama takes care of 'em."

"Mama and Papa would cry if you left."

Shoving a bite of muffin into his mouth, he looked ponderingly at her. "Adam stay. But no baby sisters."

Tiffany knew the problem with Adam's adjustment had just begun.

The rest of the meal was relaxed. Sometimes, everyone seemed to be talking at once. Emily had taken to encouraging Constance. Kathryn mothered them all. It was the woman's loving way.

After supper, Nathan excused himself and went to his office. Tiffany took her coffee and went to the library. It had been some time since she'd relaxed with a good book. Would she have more than a couple of minutes before one of the girls demanded to nurse? Sighing, she scanned the titles, then strolled to a window and looked across the fields. The sky was a brilliant crimson with pink and gold streaks. As she watched, the blue deepened and shadows formed under the bushes. Eventually, they crawled outward like living things. She lit an oil lamp and sat on the arm of a chair.

A familiar but unpleasant feeling began to stir within her, then magnified. Something was about to happen. Concern for the twins drove her upstairs. They were sound asleep in their basket.

She found Adam in his room with Emily's boys. Nat was helping him build a tower out of the wooden blocks Nathan had made for him. Scott was loading a small wooden wagon that Joshua had given Adam last Christmas. Jo was rocking baby Jonathan in her room. Bret was pondering over maps. Everyone else seemed all right, too.

Going to the office, she peeked in at Nathan. He was pouring over his ledgers in the oil lamp's light. The golden curl she adored dangled on his forehead. Slipping back upstairs, she went to their bedroom and stood peering into the basket at her girls. *How truly blessed we are.*

The feeling within her was still so strong it seemed to vibrate. "Something's wrong," she whispered. Disturbed, she knelt by her bedside to pray.

Nathan wrote a few more figures in a ledger, then rubbed the back of his neck. His Karn's Bend lumber mill was doing all right, but without Bret's expertise, problems could be developing. Sales were good, but the number of customers who were charging what they ordered had doubled. Glen was willing to learn how to manage, but now that Bret had been injured, there was no one to train a new man. He hoped he wouldn't have to spend too much time at the mill himself.

Swiveling his chair, he looked out a window at the moon. He'd been slaving over the books for hours. Tiffany would wonder what was going on.

Standing, he yawned and stretched, then frowned. The sutures had been removed, but his side was extremely tender. He supposed it would take a few more days to feel normal again.

A horse galloped to the front of the house, drawing him to a window. He recognized the rider as Cole, one of the men from the mill.

Leaping from the animal's back, the man raced for the porch. "Mr. James!"

"Now what." Nathan clenched his teeth. Had there been another accident at the mill? He hurried to open the door. "Cole, what's wrong?"

Breathless, the man stepped into the foyer. "The mill's under attack!"

"By whom?"

"Don't know." The sweat that poured from the man's face soaked into his collar. "There was rifle fire!" He swiped a dirty hand across his brow, leaving black streaks. "Glen was hit!"

"Go to the barn and tell Amos and Joe what happened. Tell someone to saddle Monarch for me. I'll be right with you." Nathan raced up the stairs two at a time, ignoring the pain in his side, and rushed into the bedroom.

"What's wrong?" Tiffany looked up from the babies she was holding.

"Trouble at the mill. A man's been injured. I'm going over there now. Don't know when I'll get back."

"Nathan, wait."

"There isn't time. I'll see you when I get back." He didn't want to explain things further. Tiffany would get upset, and his being agitated and alarmed was bad enough. Had the Klan struck again? Why? There were only two black workers at the mill, and he had ordered them both to remain at their homes until the ones who had hung Zeb were caught and it would be safe for them to return to work.

"I'm jumping to conclusions," he muttered as he ran toward the stables. Amos had Monarch ready. Mounting, Nathan galloped his roan down the lane. A sudden thought struck him. *Had the attack been to draw me out so I'd be a target?* He prayed for God's protection. Both men kept their mounts in the shadows, yet they tried to make as much speed as possible. Neither Nathan nor Cole spoke.

As They approached the lumber mill, Nathan slowed his horse to look around. All was silent. Nothing moved.

"You wait here, Cole." Dismounting, Nathan slipped through the dark and entered the building from the back.

"It's James," he announced, not wanting to get shot by one of his own men.

Hal Cullen stepped from a darkened corner. "Glen's over here." He held a lantern so the light revealed a man on the floor.

Nathan didn't like the way Glen sprawled over a board, his head bent back. "Is he hurt badly?"

# Eleven

Hurrying forward, Nathan knelt and felt for Glen's pulse. The man was dead. "Hal, who did this?"

The man shrugged one massive shoulder. "The shots came from the dark."

"Was anyone else hit?"

"No." Hal glanced at Glen's body, then turned away. "Looks to me like someone was gunning for him."

"Why were the three of you here so late?"

"Harry Schooner rode in just before dark and ordered two wagonloads of lumber. He said he wanted them delivered early in the morning and suggested we load the wagons tonight. That way I'd be able to make the delivery at dawn."

Nathan frowned. "Do you suppose Harry is a member of the *Klan*? Could he have given the order late knowing it would keep Glen here until after dark?"

"I wondered that, too, after the attack."

"I told you about Glen's past involvement, because I wanted you to know what was going on."

"I appreciated knowing." Hal eyed him in the lantern's glow. "Do you suppose some of the K*lan* members were afraid Glen would identify them?"

Nathan ran his fingers through his wavy hair to put his truant lock back in place. "That's what I suspect."

"You'd better watch your back on your way home." If one of the *Klan* silenced Glen, they will probably attempt to muzzle you as well."

"They've already tried! My side is still tender from someone's bullet."

Hal sighed. "I'd hoped that they weren't aware of your speaking with Glen the night of the raid."

"Someone must have been watching from cover." Nathan knew he was in danger. He turned as Cole joined them. "Cole, please see that Glen's family is notified. Take someone with you when you escort Glen's body into town."

Cole looked worried. "You better be on guard on your way home, Mr. James."

Nathan nodded. He intended to ride north first and approach Castle Crest from the opposite direction, hoping to foil any would-be attacker. "You men keep alert, too." Mounting, Nathan kicked Monarch into a gallop and leaned forward, his head protected by his horse's neck. *This is like being back in the war!*

Tiffany glanced at the clock. Where was Nathan? He should've been home by now. Wondering what problem had developed at the lumber mill, she wandered out onto the second-story balcony and peered into the darkness. Had a shadow moved near the barn? She gasped. The silhouette of a man appeared near the stables, then vanished into the night. What was going on? Where was Nathan? Was he in danger?

Racing to the bedroom, she dug in the top dresser drawer. Nathan's revolver was gone! Had he expected trouble when he rode out? Heart pounding, she hurried through the dark hallway, down the stairs, and into the office. She'd kept Timothy's pistol in Nathan's bottom desk drawer. She grappled on a high shelf for the key, unlocked the drawer, yanked it open, and ran her hand to the back. "There it is!"

The cool metal felt hot in her hand, and her fingers trembled as she shoved a bullet into place. Climbing the stairs hurt. Her abdomen cramped as she tried to hurry. She wished she was back to normal. Nathan needed her.

Again on the balcony, she squinted to see into the night. Where was the man who had been slinking around the stables? Her breath caught when she noticed two figures near the barn. Sweeping behind the verdure, she watched and waited. *If my heart wasn't beating so loudly, I might be able to hear more.* What did those men intend to do? Were they lying in wait for Nathan? Where was Amos? Was Micah asleep? Tense, she waited.

A horse galloped across a distant field toward the barn. She squinted. The rider leaned forward, as though to protect himself behind the animal's neck. Nathan? The horse looked like Monarch. Could someone be planning to do Nathan harm? She must warn him. If she shouted, he wouldn't hear her. There was no way he could see her waving. Besides, that could get her shot. Pointing the pistol into the air, she fired, then streaked across the balcony to the cover of the vines on that side. Staying in the spot from where she'd fired would give a marksman a target.

No one returned her fire, but the horseman flattened himself against his mount. Apparently he thought he'd been shot at. When he disappeared behind the barn, a spasm jerked Tiffany's stomach. Her temples throbbed, and her palms sweat until the pistol felt slippery. *What can I do now?*

Amos ran from one of the cabins and entered the barn. Thank God he'd returned from helping Zachary. He must be on guard. The other two shadows entered the barn as well. Alert, Tiffany waited, her breath coming in spasmodic gasps.

When a man left the barn and hurried toward the house, relief flooded her. She recognized the figure as Nathan. When he stepped onto the veranda below, she could no longer see him. Back inside, she unloaded the pistol and shoved it into her middle dresser drawer under her sweaters. She intended to have it handy, should she need it again.

Nathan burst into the room and grabbed her in a fierce hug. "Amos and Joe said that gunshot came from the house."

She giggled. "I wanted to warn you that there were two men sneaking around the barn and stables."

He chuckled. "Darling, that was Joe and Teddy. They were watching for someone who might want me dead."

"I wasn't going to shoot them." She grinned. "Unless I identified them as the enemy."

"I thought whoever shot Glen was in the house."

She gasped. "Glen Allen? Shot?" She studied his face in the candle's golden glow .

Nathan nodded. "He's dead."

As he described the raid on Castle Crest, then what had happened at the lumber mill, her alarm grew. "And now they're after you. Did Glen tell you anything?"

"No. He tried to deny his connection with the Klan."

"Then he was killed for nothing."

"Sweetheart, being a member of the Klan is asking for trouble." He sighed. "Had he not busted his leg, he would've been in on hanging Zeb."

"How far is this going to go?"

"Who knows. There's a lot of unrest by men who risk their lives to fight for the Confederacy. They felt they were being loyal to their country. Now any man who served as an officer isn't permitted to vote or hold a political office."

"Including you." Her fingers formed fists. "It's so aggravating! I can understand the Klan's anger and frustration."

"But not the destruction and killing, Tiffany."

"How long will this go on?"

"Probably until this government situation is solved and the men of the South who fought for their country are permitted to take their place as leaders."

"That's going to take awhile. And women need the right to vote and be free to hold a political office as well as men!"

"That, my lady, is going to take even longer."

"When I get back on my feet, I'm going to fight for women's rights."

He chuckled. "My darling rebel."

"Well! That's what it's going to take. We ladies are going to have a war on our hands." She yawned. "But for now, I'm exhausted. I was tired to begin with, then the turmoil around here had me on edge. I'm going to bed."

Andrea began to whimper, then Cassandra joined her. "Oh no."

Nathan's grin broadened. "Isn't this what women call the joys of motherhood?"

The morning sun shimmered on Bret's dark hair. He held his breath as Jo Ellen climbed into Nathan's landau. He thanked God for her willingness, but at the same time, he prayed she wouldn't change her mind. Tiffany had told him that Jo was questioning her decision. When they were seated, he handed her their baby.

Micah closed the door and climbed to the driver's seat. He clicked to the team, and the carriage jerked into motion. Bret glanced at Jo and tried to read her expression. What else, other than doubt, could he interpret?

"Thank you for coming, darling."

She eyed him. "I only promised to go as far as Saxon Oaks. You said all my clothing was in a bedroom there."

"Our bedroom."

"Breton." Her gray eyes warned him.

"Don't worry. I'll sleep in another room."

"Will your Uncle Zachary and the others who live there understand?"

"I imagine so, but it doesn't matter."

A frown creased her brow. "Who all are living at Zachary's?"

"He has a room downstairs. Darcy Mae is always fussing about somewhere. Elizabeth Ann is staying there until Trenton finishes building their house in Charleston."

"Where's Charleston?"

"South Carolina." He explained where it was.

"Why are they moving so far away?"

"Trenton is rebuilding his father's shipping business. The company isn't doing too well right now, but along with constructing new buildings, he thinks he can infuse some new ideas that will enhance productivity."

Jo sat staring at the toes of her shoes that showed beneath the hem of her green skirt, then she faced him. "If the business isn't doing well, why can't he move it closer."

Bret shrugged. "Maybe he never thought of it."

"He has to rebuild anyway. You'd better wise him up."

Bret chuckled. "I'll write to him."

"You could send a wire quicker. I'll talk with Elizabeth Ann." She turned to peer out a window. "After the trouble at the Karn's Bend Mill, are you going back to work there?"

"Yes. After Glen Allen was murdered, I promised Nathan I'd give him two more weeks. That will be long enough to train Hal Cullen to take my place."

"You think he'll do a good job?"

"Nathan said he'd give him a try. I think the man will do all right." He noticed Jo's focus search one side of the road, then the other. "What's bothering you, darling?"

"Where did our accident take place?"

"About a hundred yards ahead."

"Tell Micah to stop and let me see the spot."

*Will studying the place where we were hurt bring back any memories?* He was afraid to hope, yet he found himself doing so.

When they were at the accident site, he bumped on the landau's roof. Micah halted the team.

"Do you want to get out of the carriage?"

"No." She shivered as she gazed down the embankment. "Where did I land?"

The log that had rolled with Bret lay at an odd angle, it's bark nearly gone. "There's a large rock by that log. You hit your head on it and were unconscious beside it when I reached you."

"I don't remember falling. Emily said the buggy was demolished. Was the carriage horse killed?"

"No, thank God. Flame was Tiffany's favorite carriage horse. Tess, her saddle horse was Flame's sister."

"Tiffany told me about DeCapendo, her black stallion, but she didn't mention Tess."

"Tess was killed during the war." He had no intention of telling her that the mare had been shot by Colonel Alexander Wellington to try to frighten Tiffany into marrying him.

Jo sighed. "I'm getting sick of people referring to some war. What war?"

"The War Between the States. It lasted four years, and ended only a year ago. I'll tell you about it during our evenings at Zachary's."

"I'm not so sure I want to remember the war. Tiffany's comments tell me that it would be good for everyone to try to forget those four years."

"You're right. The healing of hearts won't be complete as long as there are resentments and an unwillingness to forgive."

Within fifteen minutes, Micah pulled the landau to a stop at Zachary's back door. Darcy Mae stepped onto the porch, a big grin on her face. She waved both arms. Nero, the black and white collie, bounded through the yard and waited for them to alight.

"Is that dog friendly?"

"Yes, and he loves you."

Jo wanted to go back to Castle Crest. At least there, she now knew the members of the family.

The black woman on the porch had to be Darcy Mae. She rushed to the carriage, her arms extended. "Let me see dat wee boy." Cradling Jonathan, she fussed over him. "Your Great Uncle Zachary will be a stompin' his cane if Ah don't hurry in with you, little man." She scuttled away.

Alarm blasted Jo. She didn't want her baby to be out of her sight. Feeling Bret's hand on her arm, she faced him.

"It's all right, darling. Darcy is like family. She'll love our son as though he were her own grandchild."

Nero bounced at her feet, then ran circles around her. Reaching out, she gave him a pat. "Good boy."

Movement just inside the door drew Jo's attention. A slender young woman in a pink dress pushed open the door and stepped forward. Her long blond hair flowed over one shoulder. Smiling hazel eyes surveyed Jo from a pretty oval face. As Jo stepped onto the porch, the woman flung her arms around her. "I'm so sorry about your accident."

She ushered Jo through the open door. "It's so good to have you home. I wanted to visit, but Tiffany told me to be patient. That was hard." Her soft laughter seemed to sift around them. "Oh, I just have to see that baby! Uncle Zachary insisted on seeing him. I can't wait any longer. See you more later." She gave Jo's hand a gentle squeeze, then hurried down the hall toward the back of the house.

Jo smiled. "That, without a doubt, has to be Elizabeth Ann, your bubbly sister."

"Right." Bret set the box of baby items by the stairway. "She'll be near to aid you with Jonathan." He chuckled. "At times, she may be a delightful nuisance."

"That short trip exhausted me." She drew a long breath. "I don't know how soon I'll be ready for the longer journey to what you call *the Valley*."

"It may be wise for me to go up there and get a place ready, then return for you."

That had been her idea from the beginning. Now she was skeptical. How could she remain here among strangers? She was getting to know Bret, and she liked him. He'd proven himself trustworthy. She sighed. "Give me a few days. I may be ready for the trip by then."

A smile lit up his features and put a sparkle in his brown eyes. "I've been longing for you to say that, darling. I'll wait." He reached toward her. "Are you too exhausted, or shall we go back to see Uncle Zachary?"

She thought about the baby and nodded. Her stomach in a knot, she accompanied him to the old man's room.

He sat in a padded rocker holding Jonathan. The baby clutched one of Zachary's gnarled fingers. The old man's smile was worth a thousand words. He looked up, his sagacious blue-gray eyes shimmering with excess moisture. "My second grand-grandnephew."

Elizabeth Ann hovered around the old man's rocker. "Tiffany had the first." She giggled. "And the second and third grand-grandnieces!" She waved a hand. "Angela was the first. Of course there's Trisha. She's Tiffany's now, too."

"I'm so blessed." Zachary's voice cracked with emotion.

Swooping down, Elizabeth Ann lifted the infant from his arms. "I get a chance to see him now, Uncle. I'm Jonathan's aunt. You can have another turn holding him later."

Bret watched, a grin stretching his lips. He turned to Jo. "Everything's under control here, darling. Let me help you to our room where you can rest."

Jo nodded. Behind her smile, she clenched her teeth. Was Bret going to press her to be his wife before she was ready? Did being in the old man's home give him courage to rush her?

On the way up the stairs, Bret kept his arm behind her. Was it to support her, or was he beginning to take liberties?

Darcy Mae stood at the top of the stairs. "Ah gots your room ready. You be lettin' me know if you need anything."

Once Jo and Bret were inside the room, she shut the door and glared at Bret. "Just what are you trying to pull?"

"Nothing." He sighed. "I haven't told Zachary or Elizabeth Ann that we aren't sharing a room. Darcy took it for granted that we were using the same accommodations."

"Well, you'll just have to inform them differently!"

Again, he sighed. "Jo, I promised you I'd give you time, and I will." He rubbed his chin. "Tonight, I'll sleep in the sitting room. Tomorrow, I'll explain our situation to Uncle Zachary and Elizabeth Ann."

She felt ashamed for not trusting Bret, but she was well aware of what he wanted. How could she blame him for trying to make their marriage work?

"You look tired." He folded down the quilt. "Why don't you rest a while. I'll bring Jonathan's things up to the nursery. Darcy will have it ready."

"Is there a crib or cradle?"

His eyes flashed to her face, then he seemed to remember. "Yes. We got everything we would need and fixed up the nursery. Darcy Mae has it in order and ready for the baby."

"She seems quite efficient." She remembered Tiffany's telling her that the black woman would make sure she had everything she needed. "Maybe we should head for the Valley soon."

"I want to make sure you're ready to travel."

"We'll manage." Yawning, she stretched out on the bed.

Bret covered her with a quilt, then went to sit near a window. Gazing at the sky, he seemed to be deep in thought. Closing her eyes, Jo tried to relax. What new surprises lay in wait around the next bend? If only she could remember something. Anything. Her past remained a black hole. She felt as though, if she weren't careful, she would tumble into it and vanish. Would praying help? She'd prayed a lot lately, but she couldn't remember how she'd talked to God. Tiffany had said that Jesus was her friend, so Jo had talked to him as though he were her friend, too. "I'm waiting to remember something, God, but being patient is hard."

A light rap resounded on the door. "Jo? Jonathan is beginning to fuss. I think he's hungry."

Sighing, she sat up. "Bring him in."

When the door opened, a black dog rushed in and put its front paws up on the bed. Jo frowned.

Bret stepped forward and gripped the dog's collar. It shook itself, scurried around the bed and yipped at her.

Jo shook her head. "You're a bad boy."

"She's a girl."

The dog barked again.

"Lacy. Quiet."

"Lacy?" She studied the canine.

"That's what you called her."

"I'm sorry, Jo." Elizabeth Ann handed her the baby. "She was so anxious to see her mistress, I took pity on her and left her come with me."

A ripple of dismay pinched Jo's insides. She didn't even recognize her own dog. The poor thing must be confused, too. "She's a bit naughty!"

"She'll learn, if you teach her." Bret laughed. "She's only ten weeks old. You loved Quin and insisted that a Newfoundland puppy was all you wanted for your birthday."

"She's big already! I must've been crazy." She chuckled. "I like her, though. But why did I name her Lacy?"

"You do a lot of tatting. You were stitching the lace on pillowcases and left your sewing basket on the floor. The puppy got into it and got tangled in the lace. She stumbled into the hall to meet you, pink tatting draped over her body and over one eye. You hadn't named her, so Lacy she became."

"So Lacy she'll be." She eyed Bret. "I need to nurse Jonathan."

Nodding, he scooped up the puppy and strode to the door. "I want to talk to Uncle Zachary, so I'll see you ladies later." Going out, he closed the door.

Jo drew a satisfied breath. Her husband had understood and done what she'd wanted him to without her reminding him. *Yes. I can trust this man.*

As Jonathan nursed, Jo noticed Elizabeth Ann watching with misty eyes. Slowly, a frown replaced her smile. *Could the woman perceive the strained relationship between Bret and me?* Sudden tears began to sparkle at the corners of Elizabeth Ann's eyes. Jo realized there was more to this than her brother's marital problems. "What's wrong?"

Elizabeth Ann sniffed, then turned to stare absently out a window.

Compassion welled up in Jo as she interpreted Elizabeth Ann's heartache. Was she having trouble with Trenton? Had he really left to investigate his father's shipping business? Or was he and Elizabeth Ann experiencing less than marital bliss? "Tell me what's troubling you."

Swiping a hand across her eyes, Elizabeth Ann drew a shuddering breath. "You've been through so much. I don't want to burden you with my problems."

"I want to help."

"You can't."

"I can try."

A vacant look crept across Elizabeth Ann's face. "No one can help."

"Nothing can be that bad."

"Yes it can." She sniffed again and reached for her handkerchief.

Suddenly Jo's predicament didn't seem so terrible. "Elizabeth Ann, please tell me what's bothering you."

# Twelve

Jo, concerned for her sister-in-law, got up slowly and laid the sleeping baby in the center of the bed.

Elizabeth Ann gazed at him. "He's so beautiful." Her admiration issued forth in a whisper. A tear raced unchecked down her face.

Jo's right arm was still in a sling. She put her left around Elizabeth Ann's shoulder and hugged her. "What could be so bad?"

"For months, I've been hoping and praying for a baby. It just doesn't happen."

Jo read torment in Elizabeth Ann's eyes, and her heart reached out to her. "You haven't been married for a year yet. You have lots of time."

"You got pregnant right away." Elizabeth Ann sniffed and blew her nose. "Tiffany spent one night with Nathan before he had to leave during the war. She conceived Adam."

"Some of us are like that. Others take a while." Was she right? She searched in her mind, but couldn't bring up one memory to back up her statement. "Does Tiffany know how you feel?"

"No. She's been through so much lately. I won't burden her with my unfulfilled desires."

"God knows what's best. Maybe he wants you to wait until your house is built and you have a place for a baby."

"You didn't have to wait! Trenton is going to start building our house soon. You and Bret have to travel to the

Valley and stay in Ellie's old cabin while you build. By this time, that ancient place could be falling down!"

"I'm sure it's adequate, or Bret wouldn't be taking us there."

"At best, it isn't a good place to raise a baby. Until I have my own home, I'll be here, and Darcy Mae would help me with a little one." She hiccupped. "Oh, I wish Trenton wasn't so far away. Our separation is almost as bad as it was during the war."

*God help me.* Jo took a long breath. "Bret said Trenton had to completely rebuild his father's business. I don't want to interfere, but has Trenton given any thought to moving the business closer? Maybe he could rebuild in Virginia instead of South Carolina."

Elizabeth Ann pursed her lips. "I never thought about it."

"Well, maybe Trenton hasn't considered it either. You'd be nearer your family, and you could visit more often. He has to build the business as well as your house. Would it make a difference if he moved it farther north?"

A slight smile tugged at Elizabeth Ann's lips. "That's a great idea. Trenton's mother died before the war began, and his father was killed at the Battle of Gettysburg, so other than owning the property, Trenton has no ties in Charleston."

"Does he have siblings?"

"Two married sisters, but one lives in Kentucky and the other in Richmond."

"Well, he'd at least be closer to one sister."

Elizabeth Ann nodded. "He could sell the land and buy some in Virginia." She sighed. "I must stop feeling sorry for myself. I'll write to Trenton tonight." She hugged Jo. "You've been through so much, yet you're still reaching out to help others. That part of you hasn't been altered by your inability to remember. I'm going to miss you so when you and Bret leave for the Valley."

Elation welled within Jo. Apparently she'd helped this delightful girl. "I'll add your request to my prayer list. I'm going to believe that God will soon bless you with a little one."

"Thank you." She kissed Jo's cheek. "You've always been more like a sister to me than a brother's wife." She moved to the door, then paused to look back. "Since Mama moved to Richmond with Joshua, I've been lonely for female conversation." She pressed a finger against her cheek. "My parents are looking for a house in Richmond, so I'd be close to them. I don't know where they're going to live after Joshua marries Emily."

"Is that a sure thing?"

"If it isn't, I don't know what is!"

"According to Tiffany, Joshua hasn't asked Emily to marry him."

"He's slow, but I know they dearly love each other." She sighed. "If my sweet brother doesn't propose shortly, I think Tiffany or I will do it for him."

Jo laughed. "I don't doubt that. I noticed how they look at each other. Wedding bells can't be far away."

Elizabeth Ann rolled her hazel eyes. "I pray you're right."

A week flew by. Jo was feeling stronger, but trembled inside at the thought of heading somewhere strange with a husband she didn't know. He'd kept his word and slept in the sitting room. But would his patience continue when he was far away from family and friends? How long should she hold him at bay? *Should I agree to be his wife and hope for the best? Or should I make him wait until I remember him?*

She pondered over how she felt about him now. He was a wonderful and patient man. Maybe she would fall in love with him again. *What if I don't!*

He stopped in her doorway. "The rain has stopped, darling. Are you ready to go?" Concern shadowed his face. He seemed to be struggling to analyze her emotional response.

Elizabeth Ann had helped her let out the seams of a blue dress. She felt thick, but looked presentable. She hoped her smile didn't look as forced as it felt. "I'm packed."

"Good. Elizabeth Ann has everything that we're leaving in Richmond crated. We'll take what we need for the first two weeks with us to Sunny Horizon. Joshua said he would ship the rest of our things."

"What about Lacy?" She was getting attached to the pup.

Bret chuckled. "She's prancing beside our luggage, determined not to be left behind."

"Will we have trouble with her on the train?"

"She won't be able to join us in a passenger car, so she'll have a fit, but she'll do all right."

Elizabeth Ann appeared in the hallway. "I'll carry the baby downstairs, Jo, so you'll be able to use the banister. We don't want any more mishaps." Moisture pooled in her hazel eyes. "Besides, it will be the last time I get to hold him for months!"

"Time will pass quickly." Jo smiled. "Especially if Trenton decides to place his business in Virginia. You'll be so busy you won't have time to think."

When they were settled in the carriage and ready to head for Richmond, a fast approaching buggy drew Jo's attention. Amos clutched the reins with one hand and wildly waved the other. He halted the horse behind Zachary's carriage. Ellie climbed from the conveyance, skirted a mud puddle, and approached.

Bret opened the door and stepped to the ground. "Is something wrong at Castle Crest?"

"Everything be fine." A grin stretched the old woman's face. "Misa Nathan hired two more to be helpin' Missy Tiffany, so she be havin' more help than she be needin'. Missy Jo be needin' help at Sunny Horizon. Ah's goin' with you." Smiling, she climbed into the landau.

Amos carted Ellie's trunk from the buggy, then retrieved his mother's carpetbag and a small crate containing Susie. "You have a safe trip, Mama Ellie."

She grinned. "Ah feels like Ah's goin' home."

Jo returned the old woman's smile. She wouldn't have asked Ellie to accompany them, but the woman's presence gave Jo courage. "Thank you, Ellie."

Reaching out, the old woman patted Jo's knee. "We's gonna be doin' fine, honey." She nodded. "And you's gonna be gettin' your memory back once we's home."

Lacy yipped at the crate. Susie hissed. Lacy barked as though telling the feline to keep her place.

Ellie patted the crate. "You be settlin' down. You's gots a long trip. Humph. And don't you be havin' them kittens 'till we's home."

Bret studied Ellie's face. "What about Michael Jay? How can you leave your husband to return to Sunny Horizon? You've only been back together for a year."

The old woman's grin broadened. "He gonna be comin', too. Ah's gonna go first to get the place ready. He bein' tottery and all." She nodded. "He be comin' when the weather gets warmer."

"Good. I wouldn't want to see you two separated again."

"Don't you be forgettin' he wants you to be callin' him Jay."

Jo frowned. "Why, if his name's Michael?"

"Darling," Bret touched her hand. "Michael Jay was cruelly treated by an owner who called him Michael. He wants to forget that part of his past. He requested that we refer to him as Jay. We were happy to do so. He and Ellie began their life again last year when Joshua located Jay in Georgia and brought him to Saxon Oaks."

Jo smiled. "We'll get Sunny Horizon in shape quickly so they can be together."

Darcy Mae waved farewell from the porch. Zachary leaned on his cane, looking as though it were a struggle to keep smiling. Elizabeth Ann smiled and waved, but tears were swimming in her eyes. Jo was glad when they were out of sight. Parting was difficult for her, too, especially when she didn't know when she would be back for a visit. It might not be so bad if she knew where she was going or who the people were that she would have to face at the end of their journey. Of course, Kathryn and Jonathan would be in Richmond with Joshua.

Ellie took the baby and rocked him in her arms. The trip would be taxing on her, but taking care of Jonathan would be easier than caring for Tiffany's twins while chasing after Adam and Alexandra. Constance had said she was dying. From what? When would the woman die? How would little Alexandra face losing her mama?

When Jo could no longer see Saxon Oaks, she straightened her shoulders and looked ahead. *Into the unknown I go.*

Bret rubbed his injured leg. "Sunny Horizon isn't too far from Winchester, and the train is running through the Valley again."

She looked blankly at him. Why did he think that bit of information would interest her?

"I'm sorry, Jo." Bret looked pained. "I assumed that Tiffany had told you that your parents lived in Winchester."

"Oh." Jo fought tears. Somehow the thought of having parents hadn't occurred to her. What was her mama like? Had Papa fought in the war everyone was always referring to? *Do I have siblings?* "My . . . parents?" she whispered.

"Their wonderful and caring. Tiffany thought it would be better to wait to inform them about the accident after you got your memory back."

"But I haven't!"

Bret sighed. "It isn't like my sister to forget something so important."

"Oh, Bret, she's had so much lately."

"I know. It was my responsibility. I should've notified your folks within a few days, whether or not you'd regained your memory."

A vacancy seemed to widen within Jo. She absently studied the gold rings on her finger. She was getting used to seeing her own face, but not knowing her own family was emotionally devastating. "What are they like?"

"You look a lot like Mary, your mother. She is sweet and thoughtful, like you, and she has the same personality. Her eyes are also gray, but her hair is brown and not as curly. You have your father's black curly hair. Luke has been a wonderful father. He has light-brown eyes like your little sister."

Gasping, Jo faced him. "I have a sister?"

"Her name is Alaina. She would be about eighteen now. She looks like your father." Bret grinned. "Of course she's feminine and your father is masculine."

"What's Alaina like?"

"She's much like you, but more bubbly like Elizabeth Ann." He shrugged. "She's probably acting more grownup now. I haven't seen her since she was about fourteen." He smiled. "You two always got along great. She said in one of her letters that she planned to come to Sunny Horizon to help after the baby comes."

Jo straightened to look at him. "They don't know that Jonathan is already here?"

Bret looked abashed. "I'm so sorry, darling. I've been so preoccupied with your condition and involved in praying for your recovery, but there's no excuse. I've been lax in fulfilling many responsibilities. We'll write to your family as soon as we get settled."

Anxiety swirled inside Jo as though threatening to pull her into a vortex of confusing emotions. She took a deep breath. "Do I have brothers?"

He nodded. "Three. Luke, your eldest brother, was a major during the war. He didn't make it back. His wife and two daughters live with your parents. Peter is two years older than you. He was married last summer and moved to Indiana with his bride. Hunter is a year younger than you. He plans to come to the Valley to help us rebuild."

Her eyes widened. "And you didn't tell me?"

"Sweetheart, I'm so sorry. Can you forgive me?"

"Of course. Under the circumstances, I wouldn't expect you to remember everything. After all, I can't remember anything!" Love shimmered from the depths of his warm brown eyes. An urge to kiss him washed over her, and heat rose to her cheeks. Could she be falling for this wonderful man who claimed to be her husband? *Does my heart know things that my mind fails to recall?*

Bret studied Jo and smiled to put her at ease. What they were doing had to be difficult for her, yet she was putting up a gallant front—like the good soldier she'd always been. He vowed to make her life as easy as he possibly could. It was evident that she was struggling with the unknown, and he had to fight to keep from hugging her. "We'll spend two nights in Richmond at Joshua's home, before we head for the Shenandoah."

Ellie had been listening intently. She nodded. "Dat be good, Misa Bret. Missy Jo be there for three years durin' the war. Maybe somethin' there be helpin' her remember."

He touched Jo's arm. A thrill surged through him when she didn't pull away from his fingers. "Angela is anxious to see you, darling."

She looked blankly at him. The expression was becoming too familiar. His stomach cramped. "She's Joshua's daughter. She was missing and presumed dead for nearly four years. Nathan discovered her in Charleston. He and Tiffany went for her and brought her back to Joshua."

"How old is she?"

"Nine, same as Trisha. She was only four years old when she vanished. Amos and Nathan found her shoe in the mud by the swamp near Sunny Horizon, and the family assumed she'd been sucked under."

"What really happened to her?"

"She was kidnapped, mistreated, then sold to a couple who loved her dearly. They still come to visit her twice a year. Joshua promised that when she's twelve, she can spend a month with them each summer. Angela called them Mama and Papa. Now she refers to them as Aunt and Uncle."

Jo turned her attention to Jonathan. "I pray nothing so horrifying ever happens to our baby."

"So do I." The way she'd said our baby made his heart pound. Oh, my sweetheart Jo, if only you knew how much I love you.

As the carriage neared Richmond, Bret sucked in his breath. The number of blacks encamped around the outskirts of the city was growing. Because of poverty, the stench of excretion and sickness was suffocating.

Jo's eyes were wide and the color drained from her face as she took in the tents and dilapidated shacks that crowded the road. "What are they doing?"

"Most are looking for work, but they're uneducated and have few skills—other than farming and domestic."

"Where did they come from?"

"Mostly from large plantations. When they were freed, they just took their families and left. There isn't enough work around here that they can do."

"Is someone helping them?"

"The Freedmen's Bureau is trying, darling, but some of the men the government sends are in the South to acquire financial empires and to advance their political careers."

"That's terrible! Is that what Trisha means when she makes remarks about carpetbaggers and scallywags?"

"No. The officials the Bureau sends are supposed to analyze the situation to aid the freed slaves and to make sure the laws set up by the Freedmen's Bureau are not breached. Carpetbaggers are men of the North who travel into the South in hopes of making it rich by buying land cheap from Southern farmers who can't afford to pay their taxes."

"How horrid!"

"Scallywags are men of the South who cooperate with the Federal government against the Southern states in the hope of getting rich quick."

"That's even worse!" Jo shook her head. "I still don't understand why these people are here. Would slavery be worse than this?"

"There's very little that's worse than not being free, darling. Slavery wasn't good."

She blinked. "There are black men at Castle Crest who work for Nathan. And Zachary had black men working for him."

"Zachary and Nathan, as well as my father, bought slaves, freed them, then paid them just like their white hired hands."

"Then what could be wrong with it? Wouldn't it be better to work and do something you didn't really enjoy to support your family than to hope for something better and drag them into starvation and death?"

"Some masters were very cruel." Jo was so innocent she appeared angelic. He knew she wouldn't understand the deploring conditions at some plantations or even imagine the inhuman treatments and beatings some of the slaves had had to endure. He reached out and took her hand. "We'll talk more about this later. We just turned onto Clay Street. Joshua's home is only a few blocks away."

She nodded, but her eyes scanned the streets. "What are those soldiers doing here?"

"They're Federals. Northern troops have been occupying Richmond since the end of the war."

Her eyes grew wide. "Why?"

"We lost the war." He studied her changing expressions. Since she didn't remember the horrors of war, it was difficult for her to analyze the situation. He didn't like the occupation any better than other Southerners did, but there was nothing they could do about it. Most of the Federal soldiers were cordial, but some seemed to enjoy lording it over the vanquished. Most didn't seem to want to be in the South any more than the South wanted them to be here. He supposed the situation was difficult for both sides.

Jo grew quiet. Bret figured she was pondering the poverty of the blacks she'd seen. It was difficult for him to understand the harsh treatment that some slave owners had been guilty of. He had no intention of trying to explain the mutilation that some runaways had suffered or the whippings some of the slaves had endured because of some small displeasure they'd caused their owner. Few things in life could be worse than being the slave of a harsh master.

Micah halted the team and leaped from the driver's seat to open the carriage door. Bret stepped down first, then turned to aid Jo Ellen. Ellie handed Bret the baby and Micah took the old woman's arm as she descended the step.

Jo appeared to be trying to smile, but Bret could tell this wasn't easy for her. "You know Mama and my father. You're now reacquainted with Joshua."

She nodded. "There's Angela and the hired help."

"I'll give you clues, darling. You'll do fine."

Lacy leaped from the conveyance and scampered to the porch. Bret ushered Jo to the front door.

Kathryn hurried to meet them as they stepped into the hallway. "Hello, Bret. Dear Jo, it's so good to have you back in Richmond." She studied Jo's face. "Do you recognize anything yet?"

Jo shook her head.

"Mama, if Jo remembers anything, she'll tell us." Bret hugged her.

Lacy raced toward the kitchen, apparently following the aroma of baking ham that wafted down the hallway.

Kathryn smiled at the dog, then kissed Jo's cheek. Turning, she lifted baby Jonathan from Ellie's arms. "Your grandpa is anxious to see you, little man." She swept through the doorway into the office.

"You look tired." Bret touched Jo's arm. "Are you all right?"

She nodded, her curls swaying, but yawned.

"You be needin' rest." Ellie ushered Jo toward the stairway. "Ah's gonna take you to you's room."

At the top of the stairs, Jo turned to glance down. Her eyes met Bret's. He smiled to reassure her. He intended to give her privacy, no matter how it anguished him.

The next morning, Bret woke a bit later than usual, dressed and headed for the dining room. Before he reached the doorway, he heard voices and paused to listen.

"Bret loves you so much, Jo." Joshua's cup rattled on his saucer. "Why don't you just try to be his wife?"

"I'm trying one step at a time."

"It must be difficult for you not to remember anyone or anything. Still, if you gave Bret a chance to be your husband, maybe you'd remember him quicker."

"You're one to talk about marital bliss." Jo laughed softly. "You encourage me to be a wife to Bret when you should be considering being a husband to Emily."

"That's different. We aren't married yet."

"Why not?"

"Well, I . . ."

"Tiffany told me that you were attracted to Emily from the first time you met her. Those boys need a father. And Angela needs a mother. What's holding you back?"

"Well, I . . ."

Bret chuckled. Jo was turning the tables on Joshua and backing him into a corner, just like always. It was enjoyable to witness. He strode into the dining room and bent to kiss the top of her head. Joshua seemed relieved, but not for long.

Jo eyed him. "Just when do you intend to propose?"

A grin spread across Joshua's face. "Soon."

Jo waved a hand. "There's no time like the present. I think you should have a summer wedding."

He laughed. "Bret, you'd better take your wife in hand. She's giving me a difficult time." His brown eyes glistened.

"As usual, she's right, Brother." Moving to the sideboard, Bret loaded his plate with scrambled eggs, sausage, and pancakes.

Angela, followed by Lacy, skipped through the swinging doors from the kitchen. The girl's long blond hair, much like Trisha's, waved to her waist. She gave it a toss as her blue eyes swept the room. She grinned. "Hi, Aunt Jo. It's good to see that you're getting better. Baby Jonathan is beautiful! Grandma let me rock him."

The family visit seemed short. Joshua's carriage driver waited to take them to the train station. Kathryn smiled and waved, but there were tears in her hazel eyes. "I'm looking forward to seeing Sunny Horizon again in all it's glory."

Jonathan gave Bret a manly hug. "Don't try to do it all this year, Son. You can build the house in stages. By the time the weather gets cold, you'll have five or six livable rooms. I built the right half the first year, then added the left side the next summer." He shrugged. "The large porches and balconies can be added later."

"That's my plan." Bret returned his father's hug, then guided Jo Ellen toward the waiting landau.

Jo fought tears as they entered the train station in Richmond. Nothing at Joshua's had been familiar to her. She'd hoped that something would click in her brain. Leaving everyone she knew behind made her stomach spasm. She was thankful that Ellie was accompanying them. Jo held the baby in her good arm and boarded the train with the old woman. Bret took care of Lacy and Old Susie. Jo saw him approach as the engine hissed, whistled, and slowly chugged forward.

Ellie glared at the open window and frowned. "You best be puttin' the window shut, if you don't wants baby Jonathan to be gettin' soot on him."

Bret closed the window. "I hope it doesn't get too warm."

Jo sighed. "Even so, I don't want Jonathan sprinkled with coal dust."

They took turns holding the baby. Bret accepted the bundle from Ellie. The clacking rhythm of the wheels became monotonous. Jo closed her eyes and nearly fell asleep. Maybe she had, for Jonathan's whimpering brought her out of a stupor.

"He's hungry."

Alarm flooded Jo. "What can I do about it here?"

Ellie grappled in her bag and proffered a blue knitted shawl. "If you wants to feed the babe, this be coverin' you."

Accepting the garment, Jo draped it over her shoulder and was amazed at how effective it was. Jonathan nursed, not caring about being under the wrap.

The man in the seat ahead of them opened his window. The breeze was refreshing, but each time the smokestack belched, some soot drifted through the opening. Jo protected the baby's face, but black dots sifted onto his white blanket. She figured her cheeks were freckled with soot, just like Bret's. Soot didn't show much on Ellie's dark face, but her light-green dress looked peppered.

The trip became tedious. Jo sighed for the tenth time. Her blue skirt was wrinkled. She glanced through her streaked window and felt as grungy as the glass looked. She'd seen a picture of miners covered with coal dust. She imagined herself nearly as grimy, although she knew better.

"This is Staunton, darling," Bret said as the train screeched to a halt and hissed spouts of steam. "This station was used for a hospital for soldiers during the war. So was the blind and deaf school. You, along with Tiffany and Mama, helped to nurse the wounded."

The place looked strange. She felt as though she'd been dropped into another world. Did she really care? Her back ached. "How much farther do we have to go?"

"Sunny Horizon is a few more miles. I'll get Lacy, Susie, and my horse. We'll rent a buggy."

Ellie took a labored breath. "Ah be glad when we be at my cabin."

Jo studied the old woman. The trip had been taxing on her. Her own fatigue didn't matter. Tonight, she would make sure that the black woman slept in her own bed. *I'm exhausted enough to sleep under a tree!*

Bret collected the animals, gave Jo the handle of Lacy's leash and put the crate containing old Susie in the back of the buggy. The cat meowed her complaints. Ellie ignored her. The old woman was too fatigued to hold Jonathan. Jo put him in his basket, because she still didn't have the use of her right arm, and she needed to hang on to make sure she didn't topple from the seat. The doctor had said that she could remove her sling in a few more days. She was anxious, although her arm felt too weak to be of much use. The conveyance bumped in and out of ruts in the road. Lacy lost her footing and flopped to the floor.

The buggy crested a small hill. Bret pointed. "There it is."

Jo straightened. Her eyes widened as she took in the scene. She swallowed and her heart began to pound.

"Jo, darling, what's wrong?"

## Thirteen

Surprise had registered on Jo's face, then she looked horrified. She blinked at the excess moisture that turned her gray eyes to silver.

"Jo, darling." Her reaction made his throat tighten.

"Bret! There's nothing here!"

"There's Ellie's cabin. Amos's cabin is beside it. It looks like Cammy and Jonas are living in the third dwelling."

"One cabin might be livable, but the two you mentioned look in sad shape, two more are worse, and the last two are beyond help! Take me back home!"

"Darling, we can take lumber from the last cabin and repair the first two."

"Before nightfall?"

Ellie patted Jo's arm. "My cabin be home. Ah's gonna be takin' care of you. We's gonna be fine."

Bret's focus traveled over the foundation stones of the once majestic house. "We have a lot of work to do."

Jo shook her head. "It's impossible to do all you say."

"Not impossible, darling. We'll manage."

"The mornings are still chilly, and it gets cold at night." She chewed her lower lip. "We might have to burn the wood of the last cabin to keep the baby warm."

"There's a wood lot, and I can cut firewood."

"Sure. And fix Ellie's cabin, build the house, care for the animals, and probably plant the fields, too."

He understood Jo's sarcasm. She didn't remember what the house had been like. What she saw from here was a fallow field, a shed built from charred wood, the remains of a once large barn and the stained foundation stones of the Harris family dwelling. Of the seven worker's cabins, two looked to be in good condition, and that was thanks to Jonas.

*Bringing Jo could have been a mistake.* Their remaining here would challenge them both. He sighed. This was the first week in May. He had a year's work to do before winter, and he would have to accomplish it with one arm. No wonder Jo was discouraged. *God help us.*

Jo drew a shuddering breath. "Tomorrow, I want you to take Jonathan and me back to Virginia Station."

Anguish ripped through Bret. "Jo, darling, you used to be so positive. One of the Scriptures you frequently recited was, 'But my God shall supply all your need according to his riches in glory by Christ Jesus."

"Maybe so, but that was before."

"We's home." Emotion caused Ellie's voice to falter, and tears collected in the corners of her dark eyes. She cleared her throat and straightened her skirt.

Cassie came out of the third cabin. Moving to the porch railing, she shielded her eyes to peer at the buggy. A broad smile indicated that she recognized them. "Master Breton," she called. "And Miss Jo! Welcome home!"

Jo looked puzzled. "Doesn't she know we're married?"

"Yes, sweetheart, but she called you Miss Jo for a long time, and old habits are difficult to break." He glanced at the sky. "Looks like it might rain. I'll get the luggage."

Jo watched Cassie as she approached the buggy. How much did this black woman know about the accident? *Does she know I don't recognize her?* Bret hadn't told her family about the accident, so why would he inform this woman?

Cassie grinned, crinkling the corners of her dark eyes. "I wasn't expectin' you, Ellie. Ah cleaned your place for Mister Bret and Missy Jo. Jonas stuffed the tick with new straw. Priscilla fixed a pot of stew. It's bubblin' on your stove. Ah figured the folks would be just about starvin'." Coming near, she peered into the buggy at the baby basket. "Ah's been anxious to see baby Harris."

Ellie picked him up and handed him to Cassie.

The woman's black pupils dilated as she gazed at the tiny face. "He's perfect! Oh, it's gonna be wonderful havin' some of the Harris family home."

A black girl about seventeen came onto the porch. Two boys and two more girls approached from other directions like baby chicks gathering around a mama hen. A man came out of the shed and headed toward the buggy.

"The eldest daughter is Priscilla," Bret whispered, apparently not wanting Cassie to hear him. "John's fifteen, Ben's thirteen, Naomi twelve and Lettie ten." Climbing from the buggy, he turned to aid Jo.

She figured introductions would have been easier had Cassie been informed of her memory loss. She wanted to scream. What next?

Bret lifted Lacy to the ground. The puppy raced to greet the children, wiggling spasmodically when they made a fuss over her. Bret spoke to each individually, using their names. Jo realized it was for her benefit. Priscilla nodded a welcome. The other children grinned.

The black man stopped near Bret. "Welcome home."

"Jonas, good to see you." Bret reached to shake the man's hand. "It's good to be back. I'll want to discuss the condition of the land, buildings and animals."

Jonas nodded. "There hain't much new to report."

Bret studied the henhouse. "How many hens?"

"Twenty-four. Only half are laying'."

"Then we'll roast some of them." He glanced around. "You built the shed?"

"There was some usable timber after the burnin'. Ah saved what Ah could. The building hain't much, but it protects the animals and the winter supply of feed." He shrugged. "Any extra that don't fit, Ah store in the cave."

"What livestock is there?"

"There are four plow horses, Amos's mule, one carriage mare, and one cow. There are two pigs to be butchered this fall and one old sow that's about to drop her litter. Ah's been plantin' what Ah could to feed them."

"You've done a good job, Jonas."

The man grinned. "Cassie plants a big garden. She always dries loads of all kinds of beans and some peas for the comin' winter. Ah grows corn and takes it and wheat to the mill for grindin'. The fruit trees be producin' plenty."

"Sheridan burned a lot of fruit trees, but some of ours don't seem to be badly damaged. Looks like they're recovering."

"Yep. Not much black left from the burnin'. God brought new green to the Valley." Jonas pointed. "Ah planted corn in yonder field." He waved in another direction. "Ah have wheat and oats planted, too."

John retrieved Susie's crate, then followed Ellie as she hurried to her cabin and vanished inside.

Cassie turned to Jo. "You need to rest. There's a couch. Ah scrubbed it and stuffed the cushions with fresh straw."

"That will do fine, Cassie." Jo tried to smile. "We weren't expecting hotel accommodations right away."

Jonas eyed Amos's cabin. "That place be needin a heap of repair." He pursed his lips. "Ah could take lumber from the last cabin to fix it for you and Mrs. Harris."

Bret studied the cabins in question and nodded. "Amos's place is about twelve feet from Ellie's. There's enough lumber to join them into one structure. That will provide four rooms and will make adequate accommodations for us and Ellie while we're rebuilding the house." He sighed. "I want to get as much rebuilt as possible before winter."

"Ah'll be helping. And my boys are anxious to help."

"I know you'll do what you can, but your first responsibility will be to continue caring for the animals and seeing to the crops."

"Ah'll take care of your carriage horse."

"He's my saddle horse. I trained him for the buggy, too. He's good breeding stock and gentle."

"That's good. Ah'll brush him down and turn him into the corral with the carriage mare. She be ready for breedin'."

He eyed Ben. "You and John tote this luggage into Ellie's place and put it where she says."

Cassie cradled Jonathan in one arm and put her other one around Jo. "You look tired. Let's go inside."

Thankful to leave the men and their livestock evaluation, she accompanied the woman. A seat on a soft couch would seem like a little bit of heaven. "Come on, Lacy." She fought a yawn as they crossed the porch and entered the cabin. The delightful aroma of meat simmering with vegetables wafted to greet her. "Oh, Cassie, that stew smells good."

Lacy scampered into the kitchen, went to the stove and sniffed the air.

Cassie laughed. "Ah guess she thinks so, too."

The puppy caught sight of Susie, barked, and took chase. The cat streaked behind the couch. Lacy wiggled between the wall and the piece of furniture after the feline. Susie came out the other end and raced into Ellie's bedroom. The old woman shut the door before Lacy could scamper through the opening.

Jo called the puppy and fastened the leash to her collar. "You can't chase Susie. She's going to be a mama soon." Bending, Jo hooked the leash handle around the leg of the couch, then surveyed the kitchen.

The room was adequate size, and had room for more items. The couch seemed long enough to accommodate Bret. Jo glanced across the room at the wood cookstove, a sink, a cupboard and a wooden hutch. A small kitchen table with a red and white checkered tablecloth and four chairs set in the center of the room. The fireplace was in the middle of the right wall. If Bret joined Amos's cabin to Ellie's, the door would have to be toward the front corner.

John and Ben made two trips to the buggy and carried the luggage inside. Ellie pointed to where they should put it.

*Where will I sleep tonight?* Jo wouldn't take Ellie's bed, and she intended to give Bret the couch. She shrugged. The floor was old bare wood, but it was clean. It would do if she used a thick hap under her.

Ellie came from the bedroom and moved to the stove. Lifting the lid from the pot, she stirred the contents. "This be ready for eatin'."

Priscilla came in the back door, collected plates and cups from the cupboard, and set the table for three. The china didn't match, neither did the tableware.

"Ah have coffee brewing at my place," Cassie said as She glanced out the open doorway. "John! Come in here."

When he stepped into the kitchen, she opened the bedroom door and flipped a hand. "You be draggin' that out here beside Missy Jo."

Nodding, John slipped into the bedroom.

Cassie grinned. "Ah fixed my old cradle for your wee one."

"Thank you. I was wondering what I was going to do about a place for the baby to sleep until our things arrived."

"Ah's happy to see mine in use again." Cassie rolled her dark eyes. "Ah hope Ah won't be needin' it no more."

The wooden rockers screeched on the floorboards as John pulled the cradle closer to the couch. Cassie put the sleeping infant in it and rocked him gently. She eyed her eldest son. "You fetch Lettie to watch Jonathan while the folks eat."

He grinned. "She's been anxious to get her hands on the baby." He followed Cassie outside.

The stew, probably venison, was delicious, and Cassie's fresh bread with butter was tasty and filling. The coffee seemed a bit old, but it was hot. Jo finished her meal, then sipped a steaming cup of tea and relaxed.

Ellie put a kettle of water on to heat and took the dirty dishes to the sink. Most cabins didn't have a drain for water, and the women had to carry their dishpans outside to dump them. Amos had dug drains and connected pipes so Ellie and Cassie could dump dirty water down their sink.

John appeared in the doorway. "Need me to fetch water?" At Ellie's nod, he snatched both pails from the sideboard. On the porch, he handed Ben one of the pails. The well was thirty yards away and shared by the occupants of the cabins.

A few minutes later, the boys returned with the pails filled. Ellie thanked them. Grinning, they set them in place and left. It had been sprinkling, but it suddenly began to pour. Yelling, they raced for their cabin.

Bret rushed inside and sat on a kitchen chair to catch his breath. "Darling, I've been thinking about sleeping arrangements. I think Ellie should sleep in her own bed."

"Of course." Smiling, Jo got up and handed him a towel to dry the raindrops on his face. "And you use the couch."

"The couch is yours. I'm tired enough to sleep on a cement slab."

Ellie poured boiling water into the dishpan. She mumbled under her breath, but Jo couldn't tell what she was saying.

Bret looked at Jo. "You'll be sleeping here in the kitchen. Would you mind me snoring in the same room?"

"Under the circumstances, there's nothing else we can do."

"If you would rather, I'll bunk in the shed with the horses."

"And keep them awake with your snoring?" She giggled. "I won't hear of it. Those poor animals have to work tomorrow." She sighed. "Besides, Cassie doesn't seem to be aware of my memory loss, and she wouldn't understand."

"I should've explained the situation to her, but I assumed it would be easier to do after we arrived." He studied her face. "I think you should take a rest."

Ellie propped her fists on her hips. "Ah's been listenin' to you givin' orders. Now Ah's gonna tell you how it's gonna be." She huffed. "Ah's gonna use the couch. Jo gonna be usin' the bedroom. She be needin' a bed. You can sleep in the corner of whatever room you wants."

"Now, Ellie," Jo began.

The old woman shook her head. "Don't you 'Now Ellie' me. This be my house, and Ah says where folks is gonna sleep. Dat be final." She huffed and returned to washing the dishes. "Cept for Lacy," the old woman mumbled. "That pup be havin' a mind of her own."

"Well, I guess the decision has been made." Bret chuckled. "What about Susie? She isn't taking too well to Lacy."

"Humph. Ah's gonna shut her in the closet for tonight. Tomorrow, she's gonna be learnin' to fend for herself."

Jo smiled. "If she shows Lacy her claws, the puppy will learn a thing or two as well."

"Jonas and I were looking things over." Bret stretched, then rubbed his face with his hands. "Tomorrow, we'll connect the cabins. We can use the connecting room as a living room and Amos's one-room place as our bedroom." He quickly added, "For you and Jonathan."

Jo smiled at him. He understood and was taking her feelings into account. "When I get stronger, I can help you build."

"You're a carpenter?"

"Since I don't remember, I suppose I can be anything I desire."

"Right. You'd make a very pretty carpenter."

Jonathan began to fuss. "He's hungry." Jo picked him up and went to the couch. "Our traveling has probably upset his schedule." She unbuttoned the top two buttons of her blue dress, then paused to look at Bret.

"Looks like the rain has slowed. I'm going out to appraise the livestock. Jonas fixed a wagon, two plows and a harrow. He's been doing the planting by hand." Bret shook his head. "The man must work from dawn until dark."

"The boys are old enough to help out."

"And they do. Priscilla milks Polly. There's a pregnant sow in a pen in the woods along with two pigs that will be butchered this fall. Naomi slops them. Lettie feeds the chickens." He drew a long breath. "They've been tending the garden and the boys help Jonas plant the fields." He went to the door, but paused to tell Lacy to stay inside. He went out quickly, crossed the porch and strode across the yard.

Jo felt overwhelmed. Going to a window, she watched Bret stride through the rain toward the shed. He was taking on a tremendous responsibility, too. *I have to do my part.*

A rifle resounded and dirt kicked up at Bret's feet. He leaped to take cover behind a tree. Jo stared in shock. "Ellie! Someone shot at Bret!"

The old woman stared at her in disbelief.

"Ellie, who would shoot at Breton? And why?"

## Fourteen

Ellie's eyes were wide. Dishwater dripped from her fingertips. The droplets dappled the floor as she rushed to look out a window. "You sure someone be shootin' at Misa Breton?"

"The bullet plowed into the ground a few feet from him! A hunter would be more careful."

"Where'd the bullet be comin' from?"

Jo pointed to a forested area about two hundred feet to their right. "Someone must be hiding among those trees."

"Ah hears a horse. Whoever be shootin' be gettin' away in a hurry."

Jo chewed her lower lip. "If he's fleeing, he must have fired on purpose."

A frown deepened the creases between Ellie's brows. "Ah thank the dear Lord that the fellow's aim be off."

"So do I." Jonathan had been fussing, now he began to cry in earnest. Jo put him to a breast, but continued to stare out a window at her husband. His focus searched the grove of trees, then shaking his head, he turned and hurried to the shed. Jo was thankful when he was inside the structure. What would she do if something happened to him? She'd treated him with respect, but hadn't returned his love. The last few days she'd come to realize that her feelings for him had been growing. *My heart indeed has a memory.*

She moved to the sofa. Lacy was licking the droplets from the floorboards that had dripped from Ellie's fingers. "The puppy needs a drink. Do you have an old pan we can use for her water dish?"

"All my pans be old, girl." Ellie laughed. "Ah guess Ah can spare one for pup." She dug in the cupboard and found one that was missing a handle. "Amos promised to fix this, but Ah thinks the time be past for expectin' that." With a dipper, she scooped water from the pail on the sideboard, dumped it into the container, then set it beside the back door. Lacy began lapping and splashing water onto the floorboards. Ellie threw up her hands. "You gots two babies to be takin' care of, Missy Jo."

"I can handle that. It's Bret's safety that worries me."

"Your brother and sister be comin' 'fore long. There be safety in numbers."

Jo turned to Ellie. "Will it be safer, or will they be in danger, too?"

The old woman shrugged a bony shoulder. "It might be safer for Misa Bret if there be more men here."

"I can't figure out who would be after Bret. Did he do something during the war that would make someone hate him?"

"Ah can't be knowin' about that." Ellie returned to the dishpan. "What Ah do knows is that durin' the war, a band of bummers kept showin' up and givin' Missy Harris problems. When they attacked Miss Tiffany, she shot one. Ah got one in the ribs with a knife. The next time, Miss Tiffany and Miss Elizabeth Ann shot one or two." Ellie turned to face Jo and grinned. "You killed one, too."

Jo gasped. She didn't know she had it in her to shoot a man. "That horrid war must have done a lot to warp folks thinking."

The old woman nodded. "And it still be causin' trouble."

There was a lot Jo didn't know. She quickly concluded that she didn't want enlightened about the violence that had disrupted lives during the war. She hoped Ellie was right about there being safety in numbers, but the thought of a brother and sister appearing on the scene made her heart spasm. They didn't know about her memory loss. How would her family accept it? *They'll have to*!

The next morning, Jo woke early. Her eyes traveled to the mat in the corner where Bret had slept. He was gone. She got up and put on a floral-print dress. She didn't have many dresses that buttoned down the front, and she needed access to nurse the baby. She grappled for a pin to secure the top button. There were a couple blouses and two skirts, but they were uncomfortable, too. *I need more changes of clothing.* It wouldn't help much when their trunks arrived. The clothing hers contained was also too tight. She chewed her lower lip.

*I could make some dresses.* She sighed. Even if she knew how to sew, there wasn't a sewing machine here. Doing much altering would be a mistake. When she stopped nursing, she'd be wearing smaller garments, and she didn't have more than she needed.

The sun was shining, and sawing and pounding began shortly after breakfast. The noise kept Jonathan awake. Jo rocked him until she felt dizzy and exhausted. She knew Ellie was still tired from their journey, and she didn't want to depend on her to take care of the baby. Lacy always asked to go out to relieve herself at the times she was most occupied with the baby. Maybe having Alaina here would be a big help. That is if the girl didn't get hurt.

Getting up, Jo paced. She wanted to go for a walk, but where was the assailant that shot at Breton yesterday? She didn't want to take Jonathan out until they knew who had fired and why. She even stayed away from the windows.

By evening, Amos's cabin had been attached to Ellie's. The roof needed shingles, but Bret put a front and a back door in place, then cut a doorway into Ellie's cabin. Jo stood in the opening to watch him work.

Jonas was out of sight in Amos's cabin, but his hammer or saw kept busy. Cassie was chasing sawdust and wood chips with her broom.

John carted several boards inside and stacked them in a pile. "These will do for flooring, Mr. Harris. I think I'll find enough straight planks. We can light a lantern and finish the floor after dark." He hurried away.

Twelve-year-old Naomi smiled as she came into the addition, stepped over the joist, and joined Jo in Ellie's living room. "You look tired. Would you like me to watch the baby for awhile?"

"Thank you." Jo handed Jonathan to the girl and massaged her aching left arm. Cassie's children spoke fairly good English. Jo wondered why. Had Kathryn Harris given them lessons?

"I would've been here sooner, but I had my chores." Naomi sighed. "The old sow is about to have her litter, and I have to keep an eye on her. The last time, the fat old thing rolled on some of her babies and smothered them."

Jo shivered.

Ellie called everyone for supper. She'd cooked enough ham with cabbage and potatoes for Cassie's family, too. Since there wasn't room at Ellie's table to set ten places, she divided the food and took the largest portion to the other cabin. The place reeked of steaming cabbage, but the meal tasted good. Jo's plate had faded pink flowers, her cup blue ones. Bret's china had a gray pattern, the plate cracked. Ellie ate from a matching plate and cup, but they were both chipped, their green pattern faded. Ellie surprised them with pudding for dessert.

Bret covered his mouth to hide a burp. "I finished putting in the flooring joist this afternoon. With John's help, I'll get the flooring down before bedtime."

Jo studied him. "Cassie said that The Yankees burned the mills during the war and lumber is still difficult to get."

"That's right. I'll be building my sawmill in the spring and we'll have all the lumber we need and plenty to sell. For now, Nathan is shipping it to us. I ordered it from him and paid for it in advance with my work at the Karn's Bend mill. We'll be receiving the first wagon load from his North Fork mill next week." Bret yawned. "I want to get the foundation for the house ready by then."

"You can't do everything at once!"

"I'll have help." He seemed to be fighting another yawn. "Nathan's shipping the wood by rail. I hired a man with a wagon to deliver it from Staunton."

"Bret, who shot at you this morning?"

He rubbed his chin. "I wish I knew." Standing, he pushed in his chair. "I need to stay alert. I have no intention of cheating Jonathan out of a father." He grinned. "Or my lovely wife out of a husband."

Within two days, the cabins were joined and the floor and roof finished. Cassie and her girls cleaned Amos's cabin. After scrubbing the old bed, they stuffed new straw into a freshly laundered tick. It wasn't a featherbed, but it looked comfortable. Bret and Jonas moved the couch and rocker into the new living room. Their trunks and boxes arrived, and Jo placed the braided rugs in front of the furniture.

Bret stretched. "This place isn't a palace, but it's livable." He sat on the couch and stretched his long legs out in front of him.

Lacy leaped to the cushion beside him, flopped to her stomach and looked at Jo with laughing dark eyes.

"On the floor, Lacy." Jo eyed the puppy and pointed to the rug. The dog looked pleadingly up at her. She nearly gave in, but when Lacy was a full-grown 130 pound adult, her being on the couch would be a problem. Now was the time to teach her the boundaries. Lifting the pup, she placed her on the floor. One jump took her back onto the couch. Bret laughed. Jo glared at him. "Get the leash, Mr. Harris. You are going to be the mean one tonight."

Jo grinned as her husband coaxed the puppy to the floor and held on until she seemed to understand her place. Jo sat in the rocker with the baby. "Have you contacted Alaina and Hunter?"

He nodded. "We haven't received a letter notifying us of their arrival time, but I assume it will be in a few days."

She massaged her right arm. It felt good to have the cast off, but the flesh looked pale, and her muscles were weak. "I wish I knew more about them. Should they come to the door when you aren't here, I wouldn't know who they were!"

"Don't worry about that, darling. Alaina would fling herself into your arms and squeal with delight. You'd know who she was within seconds."

"I still wish you would've told them about the accident so they'd know my condition when they arrived."

"It won't make that much difference." He smiled at her. "You're the same as you've always been, you just don't know it."

"Where are they going to stay?"

"Jonas has been looking over the remaining cabins. He said the dwelling next to his place would be the easiest to repair. He suggested that we fix it with the remainder of the wood from the last cabin." He surveyed her face. "If we were sleeping in the same bedroom, Alaina could use the couch."

"Soon, Bret. I hope." She watched his face. A light from inside seemed to make his brown eyes glisten. He was so wonderful. How could she treat him as coldly as she had? She owed him more than that. If she'd loved him once, she knew she would again. *Actually, I'm starting to care for him now.* The thought surprised her. She didn't want to build his hopes, then dash them, so she didn't say anything. However, her heart had began to pound at the thought of sharing his bed. Heat cruised across her face, and she lowered her gaze.

Bret snatched the pillow on the couch beside him and shoved it behind his neck.

"If you stand up, I'll fix your bed." Jo crossed the room and handed him the baby. She spread the quilt on the couch for her husband, then turned to take Jonathan.

Handing her the infant, Bret grasped her shoulder and pulled her toward him. She didn't resist. He put his arm around her and pulled her close. She rested her head against his shoulder. His lips brushed her forehead, then he kissed her cheek. "I love you so much, Jo."

She reveled in his embrace for another moment, then gently pulled away. "I'll see you in the morning."

"Will Jonathan sleep the night through?"

"No. He usually begins to fuss between two and three o'clock. He nurses, then goes back to sleep."

"If I can help you, just call."

"I'll be fine."

Ellie appeared in the doorway. "No good night yet. The puppy be at the door wantin' out."

"Oh." Bret snatched the leash. "I'm glad she asked. I forgot to take her out for her evening walk." He paused to smile at Jo. "I'll see you in the morning, darling."

"Good night." She entered the bedroom and lowered Jonathan into the cradle, then dressed for bed in a darkened corner. This time, she didn't close the door. When she stretched out on the bed, she peered through the shadowy doorway. Bret brought the puppy back inside and unclipped the leash. Lacy scampered into the bedroom and put her paws on the mattress. Jo gave her a pat. It was easy to understand the puppy's request to sleep on the bed. "You sleep on the rug," Jo whispered, giving the animal a gentle push. With a sigh, the pup flopped to the rug. She was smart. Training her was going to be easier than Jo had expected. The puppy loved Jonathan already and understood not to wake him. When he began to toddle all over the place, Lacy would protect him like Quin did Adam. Jo thanked God for the puppy.

Before closing her eyes, Jo glanced through the doorway. Bret sat in a beam of moonlight on the couch. He ran his fingers through his thick black hair and yawned. After a heavy sigh, he stretched out. Jo reached to touch the extra pillow, then she ran her fingers over the sheet beside her. What had it been like to share a bed with Bret? The thought sent a rush of heat up her neck. She smiled into the night.

The aroma of brewing coffee seemed to float into the bedroom and tantalized Jo. She yawned and stretched, then her focus drifted to the couch. Bret was gone. The quilt he'd used was folded and draped over the back of the piece of furniture. His pillow, now fluffed, rested where his head had been. A vacancy widened within Jo. If anything happened to that man, she'd miss him more than she'd realized just a few days ago. She listened intently, but heard nothing. She glanced at Jonathan's cradle. The baby dozed peacefully, his tiny fist tucked under his chin. Jo noticed how the boy's forehead and eyebrows were a miniature of Breton's. She drew a contented breath and got up.

After rooting through her clothing, she decided to wear her pink blouse and navy skirt. The skirt was a bit too tight, but if she left the button of the waistband unfastened, the garment would be satisfactory.

She fumbled her pink blouse. As it landed, Lacy sprang to life, seized the garment, and raced from the room, the fabric trailing after her. Jo opened her mouth to yell at the puppy, but her sharp tone would waken the baby. She raced after the dog, wondering how to discipline her. "No!" She grabbed the blouse. Lacy jerked it from her fingers and scampered around a chair. "Lacy, come here."

The puppy dropped the blouse and looked at Jo with shining eyes and wagging tail. Jo lunged for the blouse. Lacy grabbed it again. This time, Jo gripped the puppy's collar and rescued the garment.

Ellie had watched, a grin stretching her lips. "You gots to get that pup somethin' to play with."

"You're right. I'll find something later." When she tried to fasten her blouse, she muffled a cry of alarm. "There's no way I'm going to button this!"

"Nursin' a baby be addin' extra inches."

Whirling, Jo fled to the bedroom. Rummaging, she found a yellow flowered shirt that looked bigger. She managed to fasten the front, but if she took a deep breath, she would probably pop a button.

Ellie appeared in the doorway. "You find one what fits?"

Jo sighed. "Sort of. I have two blouses I can get into, and one skirt!" She sighed. "There are two dresses that will do, but I can't be washing my clothing every day."

The old woman grinned. "You would be gettin' back into your clothes in a few weeks, but as long as you be nursin' the wee one, your blouses hain't gonna button."

"What am I going to do?"

"The best you can, girl." Turning, she headed for the kitchen. "Breakfast be ready."

Jo followed her. "Where's Bret?"

"He ate two hours ago. Now he be cleanin' ashes and soot from them foundation stones."

Gasping, Jo looked at her watch. "It's still early! What time did he get up?"

"'fore dawn."

Jo took a place at the table. Ellie set a bowl of steaming oatmeal in front of her and scooped sliced peaches from a can into a small dish. While Jo ate, she pondered. *If Naomi would watch Jonathan, I could help Bret.* The idea of working side-by-side with her husband created a warmth within her that she didn't understand. It was a new and pleasant feeling.

Lacy barked. Jo glanced down. "You don't get food from the table while we're eating, bad dog." She ripped the crust from her bread and got up to drop the morsel in Lacy's dish.

One gobble and it was gone.

Ellie chuckled. "She be an empty pit. What's you gonna do when she's big like Quin?"

Jo shrugged. "We'll have to fill her up with something. Maybe she'll take to hunting her own dinner."

"Humph. That girl gonna be too spoiled to hunt!"

"I'm trying to train her." Jo sighed. "The baby's things need laundered this morning, Ellie. Put on a bucket of water to boil."

"Ah's already gots a tub of hot water on the back porch and have them soiled things soakin'. You gets your blue dress and the flowered one, and old Ellie be washin' them, too."

Jo intended to take more cleaning responsibilities. Apparently, Ellie was used to taking care of the Harris family, but she was getting too old to labor from dawn until dark. "I'll finish the washing, Ellie."

"You be needin' more strength in that right arm 'fore you be scrubbin' on a board."

"Is that a carriage coming?" Jo went to a window. A team and landau came to a stop in front of the building site.

Ellie came to peer out a window. "Looks like we's gettin' company. Ah don't have time to be entertainin'. Ah gots work to do." With a huff, the old woman grabbed her stirring stick, shuffled to the back porch, and began sloshing clothes in a tub of water.

Jo ran her fingers through her curls, wishing she had time to pin the mass on top of her head. She wanted to run into the bedroom and hide, but curiosity held her in place. The door of the landau swung open. A tall man with dark hair and a short beard jumped to the ground. Broad shoulders made his blue-barred shirt taut across his back. He pulled out the step, then reached to assist a female passenger.

A young woman grasped his fingers and stepped to the ground, her movements graceful. The early morning sun created red highlights in the waves of her dark-brown hair. A smile lit up her oval face. The pink in her cheeks matched the embroidered roses on her light pink dress.

*She's lovely. And slender!*

Bret left his work and hurried to greet the couple. He shook hands with the man, then turned to hug the woman. She returned his hug and kissed his cheek. A strange twinge twisted inside Jo. Was it jealousy? She fought tears. She didn't feel attractive enough to compete with this vibrant young woman. What did the creature want? When the trio headed for Ellie's cabin, Jo gasped and fled to the bedroom. Snatching the brush, she raked it through her curls. If only she had had something nice to wear!

Lacy pranced inside the kitchen door as though anxious to greet the company. The door opened. Lacy woofed.

"Oh, you adorable thing," a sweet voice resounded. Light laughter tinkled like delicate wind chimes. "I didn't expect a welcome from a sweet puppy."

Jo's stomach tightened.

"Jo," Bret called. "Where are you, darling?"

She swallowed and wrestled a desire to hide. *Or slip out the back door and vanish into the woods*! Her heart pounded and her mouth went dry as footsteps came through the living room and approached the bedroom door.

## Fifteen

Jo's pulse drummed in her temples. She swallowed. The back door was close, but that was a coward's way. Had she been a coward? *No.* She couldn't imagine that. Taking a deep breath, she squared her shoulders.

Bret appeared in the open doorway. A smile lit up his face. "Alaina and Hunter are here."

"Oh!" Strangers would've been bad, but meeting her family seemed worse. She wasn't prepared! A glance in the small mirror underscored her apprehension. She seized a brush and tried to coax her curly locks into order. There wasn't time. Her face was pale. "My blouse won't button properly! Oh, Bret, what can I do?"

"Just smile, darling. Everything will be all right."

"What does a man know."

"You look adorable to me." He chuckled. "All Alaina will notice is your sweet face."

"Jo?" a cheerful feminine voice summoned.

"I'm in the bedroom." Jo tried to sound delighted, but her voice quavered.

Bret stepped out of the way as the young woman breezed through the doorway. Alaina's pink skirt swished as she raced across the room. Jo braced herself as the woman grabbed her in a fierce hug.

"Oh Jo! You had the baby!" Alaina's focus darted around the room and came to rest on the cradle. "Boy or girl?"

"Boy. His name is Jonathan Breton."

"He's adorable. And you haven't changed at bit!" A giggle bubbled from her. "Except you're a bit fatter than you were." She wrinkled her nose. "Mama says girls always look thick for a while after giving birth." Her attention went back to the baby. "Can I pick him up?" Not waiting for an answer, she tossed her long hair over her shoulder, bent over the cradle, and lifted the baby. "Oh, Jo, he's so precious! His hair is black." She touched above his tiny ear with an index finger. "And it's going to be curly like yours." She giggled. "He looks like Bret, though. He's wet. I'll change him." She glanced around the room. "Where are his things?"

Jo grinned. Alaina's personality was indeed like Elizabeth Ann. She was more refreshing that a drink of cool water. Jo pointed. "His belongings are in that trunk. We don't have much furniture yet."

"I'll use the bed." Alaina fumbled in the box and chose a few items of clothing. "Mama collected a few things and is sending them on a wagon. They should arrive by tomorrow."

"Things?"

"We figured you wouldn't have much furniture, since the house here and everything in it had burned."

"We don't have a place to put furniture, yet."

Alaina shrugged. "You can put the bedroom suit in here. There's a rocker that would fit in that corner." She flipped a hand in that direction. "And on these bare floors, you need the braided rugs Mama sent."

"I appreciate your effort to make this cabin more comfortable, Alaina." Jo sighed. "I can hardly wait until the house is completed."

Alaina giggled. "A lot of folks don't have as nice a home as this cabin." She looked puzzled. "This place seems larger than any of the workers cabins I remember."

"Bret and Jonas connected two cabins, and it made an extra room where they were joined."

"That was clever." She grinned. "I was wondering why you had a cookstove and sink in your bedroom!" She giggled. "You always were one to want a cup of coffee early in the morning. I thought maybe you'd decided to keep the pot handy."

Jo laughed. It truly was easy to talk with this girl. Still, she would have to explain the accident and the results before someone said something awkward and was embarrassed.

Alaina put Jonathan on the bed and began to remove his soiled diaper.

"Hey, Sis." A tall good-looking man swept into the room and grasped Jo in a bear hug. "It's so good to see you."

Lacy followed at the man's heels, bouncing and yipping.

Jo returned the man's hug. *This has to be Hunter*. She'd hoped that seeing two members of her family would bring back some memory. It hadn't, but there wasn't time to permit her disappointment to linger.

Hunter looked at the baby. "So this is your new little man." A big grin stretched Hunter's lips. "He's so tiny." Reaching out, he touched the baby's cheek. Jonathan grasped the man's finger. "Hey, Jo, look at this. He likes his Uncle Hunter."

Bret scooped up the puppy, apparently to get her out from under everyone's feet. The dog wiggled, and her tail slapped against Bret's arm. She climbed his shirt to kiss his chin. He chuckled and leaned against the door frame. "We were going to repair a cabin for you two, but we haven't had a chance."

Hunter straightened. "Don't worry about us. We can bunk almost anywhere. Is Jonas still living on the property?"

"Yes. His family is in the next cabin. He's the only field hand who remained after the war." Bret sighed. "There wasn't much here to encourage them to stay, and there isn't enough happening yet to draw any of them back."

"We're here to get things started." Hunter grinned. "I have Alaina's trunk and some other things in the landau." He glanced around. "Where can I put our luggage?"

Alaina flipped a small blanket around Jonathan and picked him up. "Bring the trunks in here. You can put our carpetbags in the living room." She smiled. "I can use the couch tonight."

Jo's heart did a flip. She looked at Bret, but he avoided her gaze. He had some tall old explaining to do before nightfall. What if he didn't tell them? She drew a long breath. It looked like it was going to be up to her to inform Alaina.

Hunter carted one trunk into the room. The driver of the landau brought another. Jo wondered how long Alaina intended to remain. The girl wouldn't need more than one trunk of clothing for a short visit. Hunter had only one small trunk and one suitcase. Alaina also had a large suitcase and a carpetbag. A laugh issued from the girl, drawing Jo's attention.

"You think I'm moving in?" Her warm light-brown eyes studied Jo. "We brought you a number of things. And of course, Mama made a lot of items for the baby." She sighed. "We knew you'd want to make some things, too, so Mama sent some yard goods."

"I appreciate that, but I don't have a sewing machine."

"You will. Papa got you one. It's on the wagon that's coming tomorrow."

"Oh!" Joy bubbled like sarsaparilla within Jo. Alaina's smile seemed contagious. The girl was more than a wonderful sister. She was a delightful whirlwind. Hunter seemed genuine, too. She was anxious to know them better.

Alaina went to a window and watched the landau head back toward Winchester. "Floyd seemed anxious to get started home. That's why Hunter was in a hurry to help unload our things."

It took over an hour to go through the items in one of the trunks. Her mother had sent several dresses that fit Jo.

"Mama said that you'd be bigger for a time, and she figured you wouldn't be able to fit into your clothes. The way these are made, you'll be able to easily take them in when you get your shape back."

Jo picked out a lilac dress and changed into it. "I like how they button in the front."

Alaina giggled. "Mama said that when a woman nurses a baby, it's necessary to have ready access to the source. All these dresses and blouses fasten in front. There are extra buttons on the skirts, so when you lose weight, you'll be able to fasten them tighter, then eventually, take the seams in."

"She thought of everything!"

Alaina shrugged. "She had five of us. I guess experience is a good teacher." She glanced out a window. "Bret and Hunter are already busy. The way they're working, the foundation will be ready by tomorrow!"

Jo brushed her hair to the top of her head and pinned it, except for two curls that she let dangle on her left shoulder. "Bret has a difficult time doing some of the heavy work with one arm. I so appreciate you and Hunter coming to help."

"What else would we do?"

Jo didn't know what to expect from any of the members of her family. She struggled to keep her tears back, but her vision blurred with excess moisture.

Alaina studied her, then took a step forward. "There's something wrong, Jo. What's bothering you?"

"There's something you don't know." She sniffed.

A frown rapidly replaced Alaina's smile. "Jo! What on earth could be so bad?" She peered at the infant in her arms. "The baby's all right, isn't he?"

"Yes. And Bret is fine." Jo took a deep breath. "There was an accident. I just got my arm out of a sling." She swallowed. "And there's a lot more. Let's sit on the couch."

For the next hour, Jo explained the accident, her physical recovery, then her memory loss. When she told her sister that she didn't remember Bret or being pregnant, the girl's lips parted in astonishment.

"You don't remember me?"

"I'm sorry, Alaina." Jo sniffed and swiped at a persistent tear. "It's horrid! She ended her story by confessing that she and Bret hadn't been living as man and wife.

Alaina's eyes were wide. "Are you ever going to be his wife again?"

"Bret has been so understanding. I was praying I'd remember something. I don't." A slight smile tugged at her lips. "But I'm falling in love with him all over again. I think my heart knows things I can't remember."

"You can trust your heart, dear Jo." Alaina pursed her lips. "It might be better if Hunter and I stay in one of the other cabins. At least you'll feel more comfortable."

Jo shook her head. "I want you here. Besides, we don't have the other cabin ready."

"There's a bed on the wagon, and cots for Hunter and me. We'll make do." Leaning forward, she kissed Jo's cheek. "I love you so much, Sister. I've always looked up to you. What you're going through like a soldier only makes me admire you more. You have my full support."

Jo sighed. "My arm is so weak. I get frustrated." She flipped a stray curl from her temple. "It must be terribly difficult for Bret to live with one arm, but he never complains."

"I love him like a brother, Jo. You indeed are fortunate." She sighed. "I don't have anyone. I thought for a while that I'd marry Calvin Larson, but that sort of fell through."

"What happened?"

"During the war, he got involved with a girl from Tennessee. He said he was sorry and wanted me back, but somehow I couldn't handle it. I figure if a man is unfaithful once, he could be again."

"What if you'd been married?"

"If I'd taken vows, I would've probably tried. Forgiving him, because of the war, was easy. Getting over his unfaithfulness was the difficult part." She shrugged. "Maybe I didn't love him as much as I thought."

"You were very young."

Alaina gasped. "How'd you know that, if you don't remember anything?"

"Oh!" Jo covered her lips with the tips of her fingers. "I don't know." A tingle ran down her spine. "Oh, Alaina, do you think my memory's coming back?"

"What else do you know?"

Massaging her temples, Jo struggled to think. Nothing came. "I wish I could remember what Mama and Papa looked like. Bret said we have a brother named Peter and one who was killed in the war."

"Yes. When Papa and our three brothers went away to war, Mama and I felt so alone. When we heard that Luke had been killed, I was devastated, and Mama grieved so. She was worried that Papa or one of the other boys wouldn't come home either. We found comfort in Scriptures such as, 'God is our refuge and strength, a very present help in trouble."

Jo nodded. "I read the Bible to find guidance. One verse that helps me is from Proverbs. 'In all thy ways acknowledge him, and he shall direct thy paths'. I don't remember the war, of course, but everyone says it was so horrid."

"That's one part of your life that you probably would be better off not to remember. Most of us are trying to forget."

Lacy yipped, raced to the door, then back. Looking into Alaina's face, she barked.

"You adorable pup! I haven't paid enough attention to you." Her eyes followed Lacy back to the door. "Oh, I get it." She stood and handed the baby to Jo. "Where do you keep her leash?"

"I don't think you'll need it."

Alaina scooped up the puppy, breezed out the door and across the yard. Within minutes, she was back. "Lacy must weigh fifteen pounds! You called her a puppy. How old is she?"

"About three months."

"What is she? Part horse?"

"A Newfoundland. They are rare in these parts. Bret said he'd looked for her for over a year before he found her."

"That's the kind of dog Tiffany has. I love Quin, so I know I'll adore Lacy." Alaina's brown eyes sparkled with gold flecks. "Maybe when Lacy is grown, she and Quin can have a family."

Jo laughed. "You mean you'd like to have six or seven one hundred and thirty pound canines bounding through your house and yard?"

"No, but I'd like one. I'm putting in an order for Lacy's first baby."

"That will be awhile. Besides, if Quin is involved, Tiffany gets first pick."

Ellie came into the room. "You be ready for dinner? Ah's fixin' fried potatoes with bacon. There's buttered carrots, and Cassie be sendin' over another can of peaches."

Alaina stood. "I'll call the men in." She hurried away.

Ellie eyed Jo. "Ah guess you two be gettin' along fine." She grinned. "Ah knew you would. You see, you been worrin' about nothin'."

There was still Hunter's reaction. Would he be as understanding and compassionate as Alaina? Had Bret had time to inform her brother or had they been too busy with the foundation?

At dinner, Jo realized that Hunter didn't know she didn't remember him. Bret filled in when there was a question she couldn't answer. When did the man plan on telling Hunter?

Alaina got up to slice more bread. She clattered the plate to the sideboard near the stove and seemed to be listening to something Jo didn't hear. A slow smile spread across her face, and she eyed Jo. "All right, Sister, where are you hiding the other babies."

Both men stared at her as though she'd lost her mind, and Jo wondered if the girl was dreaming.

Ellie hurried across the kitchen and peered behind the stove. "Ah was wonderin' when you was gonna be a mama again." A grin deepened the old woman's wrinkles. "Ah put a box back there for my old Susie. She done had her kittens."

Alaina's eyes shimmered. "How many are there?"

"Ah see three."

"Can I have one?"

Ellie laughed. "You gonna have to wait 'til Susie be ready to give them up."

Jo was on her feet. "What color are they?"

Pressing her face against the wall, Alaina squinted. "I can't tell."

"I want a white one like Susie." Jo wanted a peek at the kittens, but Alaina didn't move aside.

Lacy became interested as well and tried to squeeze behind the stove. Ellie had shoved the box with chunks of wood at one end and a box of kindling at the other as a barricade to keep Lacy away from the new feline family.

"You hain't gittin back there pup." Ellie watched the dog and grinned.

Racing around the other side of the stove, Lacy tried again, then looked under, but she was too big to wiggle through the opening.

Bret watched. "This evening, I'll fix something more substantial to keep Lacy from the kittens. Susie can get to them by slipping under the cookstove." He shoved the last bite of his potato into his mouth and stood. "I'm going to get back to work."

"Well, that was a filling meal." Hunter stood and pushed in his chair. "By nightfall, I think we'll have the foundation ready for the right side of the house."

"We're limiting the summer's building to the right half, Hunter." Bret stretched, then pushed his chair under the table.

Hunter nodded. "That makes sense. Completing the whole structure in a few months would be a monumental effort for the two of us."

Bret spoke over his shoulder as he made his way to the door. "I plan to start a lumber mill in the valley, but that probably won't be until next summer, although I already have acquired a saw. Nathan James is my supplier for the lumber for this year's building project."

"I expected that. His North Fork lumber mill isn't too distant by rail to be out of the question."

"Right. But we need a sawmill in this part of the Valley. A lot of folks need building materials. Jonas said he'd be finished hoeing the corn and would give us a hand. Maybe we can get some work done on your cabin this evening."

Jo rested a hand on Hunter's arm. "You don't have to do it all in a day. We have all summer to build the house."

He chuckled. "A lot of women would be cracking the whip to get us to work harder."

They left and Jo went back to the trunk. At the bottom, she discovered a set of china with a wild rose pattern.

Ellie's eyes widened when she saw the set. Gently lifting a plate, she ran her fingers over it, then admired the matching pieces. "There be cups, saucers and small plates!"

Jo counted them. "There's service for twelve!"

Alaina giggled. "They were part of your hope chest. Mama sent a tea set with the same pattern. You'll be fixed for entertaining when you get your house." She straightened. "Is that someone coming?" She raced outside. A moment later, she hurried back in. "Jo! The wagon's coming! They got here a day early. Hunter and I will have cots for tonight." She smiled. "God took care of everything."

The men stopped working on the extra cabin to help unload the wagon. They brought several boxes in first and lined them up along the wall in the connecting living room. Everything had to come into Ellie's place. They couldn't leave anything exposed to the weather, and there was no where else to put it.

"Don't look so worried, Ellie." Jo smiled, trying to put the old woman at ease. "We'll use what we can, including the new china."

Ellie's eyes widened. "Ah don't wants to be breakin' your things."

"You won't."

Jonas and Hunter moved Ellie's small kitchen table to the corner beside the sink, then lugged in Jo's oak table and six wooden chairs. Ellie ran a hand over the table's smooth surface and made a humming sound.

Jo eyed the cherry rocker that Hunter toted in, then watched the men carry in a light-walnut bedroom suit. Jo admired the finish and style. When her brother brought in a large mirror she gasped. "This bedroom suite is one of the most beautiful I've ever seen!"

He spun to face her. "Jo! What's wrong with you? This is your own furniture from home!"

She closed her eyes. Her hand went to her throat, and she swallowed hard. Feeling dizzy, she sidestepped and gripped the back of a chair.

"Jo?" Hunter stepped toward her. "What's wrong? Jo?"

## Sixteen

Jo blinked to keep her tears from spilling over.

Hunter rested a hand on her arm. "Are you all right?"

Bret put his arm around her. "She's going to be fine." He pulled Jo closer. "I'm sorry, darling. We were so busy. I didn't explain your condition to your brother."

"Condition?" Worry lines appeared in his forehead. "Are you ill?"

"Here we go again," Jo mumbled.

Bret and Alaina filled Hunter in. The compassion in his brown eyes soothed Jo's spirit. His beard tickled as he kissed her cheek. "Don't concern yourself, sweet Jo, everything is going to work out for the best. We'll get the house built and before you know it, everything will be back to normal." Smiling, he gave her arm a pat and headed for the wagon for the last few items.

Jo sighed. "That's over with. Now we can get on with living."

Night fell softly. Bret sat on the couch beside Jo. "Hunter, I'm sorry we didn't get a chance to do more repair on the cabin you'll be using."

Alaina smiled. "I'll fix your cot in a corner of the kitchen."

"Well, that way I'd be sure not to miss breakfast." He chuckled. "But I can stay in the old cabin. It isn't going to rain, and it isn't cold."

Alaina sighed. "If that's what you want, but I'm going to fix the couch for myself."

Jo had the featherbed, so Jonas helped Hunter carry the bed she'd been sleeping in to the other cabin.

Alaina giggled. "If it rain's tonight, Hunter can sleep and bathe at the same time."

"Not a chance." Bret tugged on a strand of Alaina's long hair. "Jonas repaired the roof this afternoon."

Hunter laughed. "Two windows are missing, and the door doesn't close, so I might have a raccoon or squirrel join me."

A giggle bubbled from Alaina. "Maybe a bird will roost on the head of your bed."

He grinned. "I won't mind--as long as it doesn't roost directly over my head."

Alaina pursed her lips. "I don't think I'd like sleeping without a secure door. I'd be afraid some wild thing would crawl into bed with me in the middle of the night."

Hunter waved a hand. "I'll be more comfortable than I would be camping out under a pine, and I've done that often enough. Will you join me, Lacy?"

"He stays in the house." Alaina tapped a toe on the floorboards. "I know you, Brother. You'd invite her to sleep in your bed."

"What's wrong with that?"

"Jo is training her to stay off of the furniture."

A teasing grin toyed with Hunter's mouth. "You ladies are too fussy." He rumpled Lacy's ears. "You think so, too?"

She woofed and grabbed the cuff of his pants.

"I don't think my sister would approve of that, either, girl." He yanked one of his socks off. "I wore a hole in this today. It will make a good tug-toy."

"That smelly thing needs washed!"

He flipped one end of it on the floor. Lacy seized it and growled. Hunter held on.

Alaina rolled her eyes. "She has more nerve than I do."

The game lasted ten minutes. Lacy seemed to be just getting started, but Hunter collapsed onto a kitchen chair. "More tomorrow," he promised.

Bret collected towels and soap. "I'm going to bathe in the stream behind the pine, Hunter. It comes from a spring in the mountains, and it hasn't warmed much yet. You want to try it?"

"You promise I won't get pneumonia?"

Bret chuckled. "You're tougher than that. Don't forget a towel."

The men hurried out. Within ten minutes, they were back dressed in clean clothing. Hunter whistled. "That was the coldest bath I've ever been subjected to!"

Bret's teeth were chattering. "The water will warm up this summer and bathing in it will be comfortable. Until then, I'll bathe quickly."

A giggle bubbled from Alaina. "I'm not that brave! I'll heat water on the cookstove and use the tub."

Bret and Hunter moved the dresser and chest of drawers to form a divider in the bedroom and set up a cot in the far corner. Jo noticed Lacy sprawled on the rug beside the couch, her chin on Hunter's old sock. Alaina's hand rested on the puppy's head. Both seemed contented. Jo's heart did a flip as she quietly closed the bedroom door.

This would be the first time since their accident that she and Bret had spent a night in the same room. She wanted to invite him to join her in the big bed, but shyness overwhelmed her, and the words stuck in her throat.

She sat on the bed and waited until Bret began to snore, then she undressed and slipped into her nightgown. Crawling into bed, she pulled the quilt to her neck. Loneliness shrouded her and a longing she didn't understand gripped her heart. She closed her eyes. The featherbed made it seem as though she were floating on a cloud. Still she didn't sleep.

At two o'clock, Jonathan began to fuss. Jo got up, changed his wet clothing, and took him to the rocker. She hadn't realized until after the baby was nursing that she was in a beam of moonlight, and Bret would be able to see her, should he get awake.

Before five minutes had lapsed, Bret stirred. Jo's heart leaped into her throat when he opened his eyes and looked her way.

"You all right?"

"I'm . . . feeding the baby."

"Oh." He turned to face the wall. "I'm sorry if I caused you any distress."

When the baby was asleep, Jo got up and put him in his cradle. She longed to go to Bret. Her arms ached to embrace him. What was she waiting for? Slowly approaching the cot, she reached out to touch his shoulder. He was breathing deeply. Disappointment washed over her when she discovered he'd gone back to sleep. He was working so hard to make a home for her. Bending, she kissed the side of his face. There would be other nights. *If I don't lose my nerve.*

As though sensing her presence, Bret opened his eyes. He blinked. "Jo?" His voice was a soft whisper, as though he doubted what he thought he was seeing.

She straightened. Her insides quavered. Her fingers trembled. She opened her mouth, but no words came.

He sat up. "Darling, are you all right?"

She took a breath that didn't satisfy. "You're working so hard. That cot must be terribly uncomfortable."

He yawned. "I'm so exhausted that I could sleep on a pile of rocks."

"But I . . ." She cleared her throat. "I . . . feel so selfish taking the featherbed."

He chuckled. "Sweetheart, there isn't a selfish fiber in your body."

"Well, I'd feel better if you . . ." her voice faltered, and she tried again. "I think it would be best if you slept in the bed."

He shook his head. "You need a good night's rest. I won't let you sleep on this cot. You have to get up in the middle of the night to care for Jonathan, and he keeps you busy during the day." He yawned again. "Besides, Ellie tells me you've been helping out with the dishes and sweeping."

"That's what a woman is supposed to do!" She emphasized her words, although they continued to converse in whispers.

"You assume that, or did you remember the Bible reference in Proverbs about the virtuous woman."

"I . . . don't know."

"You'd better go back to bed, darling. We both have a lot to do tomorrow."

"Well, I'll go back to bed if you . . ." She choked, then went on. "If you accept a place on the other side of the bed."

His eyes, visible in the moonlight, grew wide. "What did you say?"

"Of course, you'll have to promise to stay on your own side." She wished she hadn't said that when she interpreted the disappointment that shadowed his face.

"It might be wise for me to stay right where I am."

She shook her head. "I won't go back to bed until you agree to sleep in comfort beside me."

Bret's heart throbbed. He longed to sleep beside Jo. But how could he join her and not put his arm around her and draw her close? It would be a big mistake to believe he could live up to the promise to stay on his own side. Nevertheless, desire won the conflict in his mind.

Getting up, he followed her around the partition. According to her stipulations, he crawled into bed and stretched out on his back. If he could tie his arm behind his back he'd feel more confident. He sighed. Taking a deep breath, he closed his eyes. He was fatigued beyond measure, but how could he sleep with Jo so close?

As though trusting him, she gingerly climbed into the other side of the bed. He longed to turn his head to face her. *I can't do this!* He gritted his teeth and struggled to remain still. His fingers tingled with yearning. He swallowed. *If I could get to sleep, I'd be all right.*

Listening to Jo's breathing didn't help. Love for her overwhelmed him. Minutes ticked by. He was wide awake. This was one of the most foolish things he'd ever agreed to.

When he figured Jo was asleep, he slowly turned his face toward her. Her eyes were wide open. She blinked. He swallowed. "Jo." The syllable issued forth in a caressing wave.

"Hello."

Her voice was so soft he hardly heard her. As though his hand had a will of its own, he reached to touch her cheek. When she rested her fingers on the back of his hand, it was nearly his undoing. When she kissed his thumb, his insides quivered with desire. "Jo, I love you so."

She turned her face slightly and pressed her lips against the palm of his hand.

"Jo, darling, please don't, if you don't want me to . . ."

"I . . . want to be your wife."

It seemed as though Bret hadn't moved, but he had his arm around Jo. Their kiss was long and wonderful. It was like a wedding night all over again. He knew that this was another night he would never forget.

Jo woke. The light of a misty dawn filtered into the room. Her head rested on Bret's shoulder. Their fingers had remained entwined through the night. How she loved this man. What would happen when she got her memory back? Would she forget the night before? *Never!* A smile of contentment curved her mouth. How could complete surrender be so wonderful?

Bret stirred, then gasped. "Jo!"

She lifted her head and gazed into his lustrous brown eyes. "Hum?"

"Last night wasn't just a delightful dream?"

She shook her head. A curl rolled onto her cheek. "Not unless I dreamed it, too." She smiled. "I love you, Bret."

Reaching up, he brushed the ringlet from her cheek. "You're my wife again, Jo. Will it be like this for always?"

"For always." The promise was easy. She kissed the stubble on his cheek.

He pulled her close. "I know Hunter is going to be banging on our door, or I'd stay here with you for a time longer."

She grinned. "Well, he may knock, but he won't open the door."

"Oh, Jo. My sweet Jo." Pulling her close, he kissed her.

Jonathan began to fuss. Jo giggled. "I guess Hunter isn't the only possible interruption."

"Our little man is sometimes demanding, but I have no intention of trading him in."

The infant began to kick and cry. Jo untangled herself and got up.

Stretching, Bret yawned. "Do I get to watch him eat?"

"If you like."

After changing Jonathan, she took him to the rocker and unfastened the front of her nightgown. She expected to be shy or embarrassed, but pleasure trickled over her as she watched amazement cross Bret's face. She smiled. What was happening between herself and her husband was beyond description.

Bret sat transfixed until Jonathan went back to sleep and Jo put him in his cradle.

Standing, he stretched. "I wish I didn't have anything to do but spend time with you and our son. I'd better dress and grab a bite of breakfast. The sun will be up, and there's a ton of work to be done before dark."

While Jo dressed, she watched him from the corner of her eye. It seemed so natural. Why had she waited so long to give in to what she knew was right? From now on, their life would be different. *We're together again.*

It was encouraging to see Bret don his clothing, button his shirt, and fasten his belt buckle. Was there anything this man of hers couldn't do with one hand?

He grinned at her. "You ready for breakfast?"

"Yes." Snatching her green dress, she flipped it on over her head. It smelled fresh from Ellie's laundering. "The coffee smells good."

He grinned. "Along with a couple of cups, I think I could eat six eggs, three slices of toast, and a pound of crispy bacon."

"Would you like some pancakes and sausage with that order, sir?"

"Maybe a few."

"With you here, it's a good thing Jonas had extra hams and slabs of bacon in the smokehouse!"

"Yes and that Cassie rendered extra lard and preserved more sausage last fall." He chuckled. Stepping forward, he put his arm around Jo, drew her close, and kissed her.

She felt ecstatic within his embrace, and his lips on hers made her heart race. Life was going to be so wonderful—whether or not she regained her memory.

Near noon, Jo heard a horse coming at a mad gallop and hurried to a window. Both Bret and Hunter labored within the foundation of the new house. They straightened to look toward the pine that screened the rider. A large white horse came into view, but Jo's attention was riveted to the broad-shouldered rider with dark curly hair. He galloped to Bret and jerked back on the reins. The horse reared and whinnied. Leaping to the ground, the visitor approached the men. As he spoke, his expression revealed anxiety. Jo wished she could hear what he was saying. He was good looking and appeared a bit boyish, although he looked to be in his mid-twenties. As the man spoke, surprise registered on Bret's face, then anger. Hunter clenched his fists and looked southward.

"What's going on?" Alaina joined Jo at the window, her yellow dress bright in the sunshine. The matching ribbon in her hair resembled a halo, making her look innocent as well as fetching. Her attention remained riveted to the newcomer.

"Who is he, Jo?"

"I don't know, but his actions ignite my curiosity."

"Mine, too." Alaina brushed the curtain aside. "He has a gorgeous deep tan. And look at that shiny dark hair. He's so tall and handsome."

Jo muffled a laugh. "Behave yourself, little sister. He's probably married and has several children." Alaina was right, though. The man was muscular and his handsome face clean-shaven.

Bret hurried toward the cabin. Jo raced to open the door.

He swept into the kitchen. "Jo! The wagon delivering our lumber was attacked!"

## Seventeen

Jo stared in disbelief at Bret. "Who would attack? Why?"

"I have no idea."

"Did they take the lumber? Was anyone hurt?"

"The men didn't take anything, but they shot the driver in the leg. David Fisher sent him back to Staunton with the wagon."

Jo could hardly breathe. "Who's Fisher?"

"The man who rode in here. He was helping the driver we hired to deliver the lumber. Dave said there were three men on horseback who galloped up and attacked."

Alaina listened, her mouth agape. "Did he know them?"

Bret shook his head. "He said one was quite heavy, one skinny, and one was tall and muscular. They had their faces covered."

Horror smote Jo. "The Klan?"

"No. The men each had tied a bandanna around the bottom half of their face and wore a hat low to hide their eyes. David said one man held a rifle on him and the driver while the other two scattered the lumber. It was a big load, so it took time. They started several fires in an effort to burn the lumber, but since they'd scattered the boards, the destruction was limited. After a warning not to deliver any more wood to Sunny Horizon, they galloped away."

"It doesn't make sense." Jo flipped a black curl over her shoulder. "Was David able to put out the fires before much lumber burned?"

Bret nodded. "He said that a number of boards were singed, but they can be salvaged."

Hunter stood listening in the doorway. "They're not getting away with this!"

Jo studied her husband's face. The determination in his expression alarmed her. "What are you going to do?"

"We're going after our wood."

"That's dangerous!"

"Darling, we can't lose that load of lumber. Besides, we have to find out who is creating this trouble and why."

"But it might be the same ones who were shooting at you the other day."

"That's all the more reason why we have to get to the bottom of this. If we don't, they will probably attack the next wagon load. The next time, someone could get killed!"

Her eyes widened. "Bret!"

Hunter nodded. "I'll get my rifle and help Jonas harness a team to the wagon."

David had remained on the porch. Hunter invited him into the kitchen. He combed his dark curls with his fingers, then stepped through the doorway and smiled. His jeans and blue barred shirt had collected a bit of pink dust, but they appeared clean.

Bret introduced him to the ladies. David acknowledged them with a nod of his head. His warm indigo eyes met Alaina's.

She smiled, her complexion a bit flushed. "Hello, Mr. Fisher. I'm thankful you weren't hurt." Her voice resounded in a purr.

Lacy ran circles around the stranger, demanding to be noticed. He bent, spoke softly, and rubbed her ears. Lacy licked the back of his hand. He chuckled. "I guess your pup accepts me."

Bret turned to him. "Have a seat." He motioned to a kitchen chair. "You have a rifle?"

"I have a revolver in my saddlebags."

Jo swallowed. This was a nightmare, but she was sure she was awake. She rested a hand on Bret's arm, but he averted his gaze.

Alaina bustled around the kitchen. Dipping into the crock on the sideboard near the stove, she retrieved molasses cookies and raisin-filled tarts, arranged them on a plate, and set it on the table in front of David. "Help yourself."

A smile filled out his wholesome face. "Thank you." He chose one of the raisin treat. The man was muscular, but it wouldn't hurt him to gain a little weight.

Alaina held her smile, but she appeared a bit apprehensive. "Would you like a cup of coffee, Mr. Fisher?"

"If there's some made. Bret is anxious to get started."

"The dinner coffee is still hot." Filling a cup, she thudded it onto the table in front of him.

Jo watched. Alaina was trying not to stare at the man, but she continued to study him from the corner of her eye. It was evident that she was striving to make a good impression.

Bret hurried into their bedroom. Jo followed. Her heart nearly stopped when he yanked the bottom dresser drawer open and pulled out his revolver. "Bret! No!"

"Don't worry, darling. Hunter and I will be careful."

"Is Jonas going with you?"

"No. I want him here to protect you ladies. He has a rifle."

"So do I. I can protect myself! And I'll take care of Alaina, too." She planted her feet in determination. "Ellie told me that I shot one of the bummers to protect the Harris women. I'm capable of doing so again."

A grin spread across his face. "I don't doubt that for a minute." He pulled her into an embrace. "I love you, Jo." He kissed her. "Dave will be an extra set of eyes to watch for the gang. He offered to help us reload our wagon."

"You know him?"

"No, but he seems genuine."

She frowned. "What if he conspired with the gang and is planning to lead you into an ambush?"

"You worry too much." He chuckled. "Maybe you should write novels." He hugged her. "We'll bring the lumber home, and we can get started with the framing this afternoon."

Bret and Hunter hurried toward the wagon and team that Jonas had ready. David mounted his white stallion. Lacy raced across the porch to join the horsemen.

"Come back here, you naughty puppy." Alaina chased the dog across the yard, her yellow skirt billowing behind her.

David dismounted, picked up the dancing canine at his feet and proffered her to Alaina. Their eyes met. David smiled and said something. Alaina blushed. Jo wondered if this was the beginning of something between him and Alaina. *If so, David better be genuine--or he'll have me to contend with.*

Cuddling Lacy, Alaina made her way to the porch. Instead of coming into the house, she watched the men proceed southward.

Jo watched them until they were out of sight around a stand of pine, then she turned to the door as Alaina came in. "If anything happens to either one of them, I don't know what I'll do."

"We'll pray, Jo. That's the only thing we can do." She lowered the puppy to the floor, brushed black dog hair from her dress, and grinned. "You and Bret are living as man and wife now, aren't you?"

Sudden spots of heat burned Jo's cheeks. "He's . . . my baby's father."

"Is that all?" Alaina touched the heated flesh on Jo's cheekbones and giggled. "I think it's wonderful. Someday, I hope to find a man like Bret."

"You deserve a good man." Her sister turned to the window. The way she stared at the settling dust left behind by the men's retreating horses made Jo wonder. Was the girl thinking about the handsome stranger? Jo hugged her. "Be careful, little Sister."

Alaina sighed. "The best thing to do to keep from worrying is to work. Is there something we can do to aid the men with their building? We could surprise them with having something done when they returned."

Jo laughed. "We'd surprise them all right! I'd put in something crooked—or maybe upside-down."

"Why don't you try out your new sewing machine. You could make Bret a new shirt. Isn't his birthday coming up next week?"

Jo stared at her sister. "I have no idea!" Turning, she hurried out the back door to where Ellie was washing clothes. The woman had her arms into the bubbles up to her elbows. "Ellie, when is Bret's birthday?"

"It be next Thursday."

"You should have told me."

The old woman straightened, suds flipping from her hands. "Girl, Ah can't always remember that you hain't rememberin' nothin'."

"I know. It's just that I would've let his birthday go by without a word or a present."

Ellie grinned. "You be gettin' him a present?"

"My sister suggested that I make him a shirt." She chewed her lower lip. "Do I know how to sew?"

"You sews more than fine."

Alaina had followed to the open doorway. "I'll help. Let's get started." She led the way to the living room. "I think Mama sent a piece of green material and some blue. Either would do." She shrugged. "There are other pieces you may prefer." Kneeling, she opened the trunk and began flipping different colored pieces of folded material onto the couch. "What's your husband's favorite color." She put a hand over her mouth. "I'm sorry, Jo. Just pick out a manly color."

"That blue would make an outfit for Jonathan." Jo eyed the other cloth. "I like the green for church. The brown would be better for building. It wouldn't show the stains as much."

"Well." Her sister sat back on her heels. "You going to church or building a house?"

"Both. I'll use the green."

Alaina gobbled up the other material. Lacy jumped to grab a piece. "Oh no you don't!" Alaina flopped the material back into the trunk. "No time like right now to begin sewing."

Instead of starting to cut out the pattern, Jo went to a window and looked southward. "How long do you think it will take the men to get back?"

"Oh, Jo, they have to gather up an entire load of lumber and put it back on the wagon. It will take longer than usual because one of them will have to keep a sharp lookout for the criminals who made the attack."

"That's what worries me." She stared at her sister. "What do you think of my riding out there to help Bret and Hunter?"

"That would be crazy! I won't let you do it." Alaina shrugged. "Besides, Jonathan would get hungry and scream to high heaven before you got back. Your first responsibility is to him." Standing, she hugged Jo. "The men will do just fine without your aid and advice. Even with one arm, Bret is a good marksman."

"I pray he isn't put to the test." She peered at the green material and frowned. "I can't remember what to do first."

"Get a shirt that fits Bret. We'll use it for a pattern."

An hour later, Jo leaned back in her chair. "I have the shoulder and side seams done and the right sleeve ready to set in."

"That's the only one you need. I cut a circle of material to sew in the other sleeve opening."

Jo swallowed. Her heart cramped as she pictured her husband. The way he'd adjusted, one wouldn't pity him; yet having two arms would make his life less complicated. She glanced at the clock. "I think I'll go out and look down the road."

"That won't hurry the men any." Alaina moved to a window. "Priscilla's coming." She opened the door. "Come on in. Is there something we can do for you?"

Priscilla shook her head. "John was up in a tree. He says he can see half the world." She grinned. "Anyway, I thought you would like to know that the men are in sight, and the wagon is piled high with lumber."

"Thank God." Jo dropped her arms to her sides. She'd tried not to worry, but hadn't been able to stop herself.

"There's another reason I stopped in." The seventeen-year-old looked at Jo. "Before you and Miss Elizabeth Ann left for Richmond, you were teaching us how to read and do figures. Mama wondered if you would start the lessons again."

"I'd love to continue teaching you, but I can't promise too much with all the building going on."

"Mama meant in the fall. Right now, there's the crops, and the boys are trying to help with the new house."

"Maybe your papa can build a schoolroom with the lumber that's left."

Priscilla's smile made her dark eyes sparkle. "Mama will be glad to hear that. So will my sisters." She giggled. "I can't promise John and Ben will be happy though."

The sound of a rumbling wagon made Jo's heart rejoice. What would happen with the next lumber delivery? Would there be a man brave enough to accept the delivery job? Or would Bret and Hunter decide to go to Staunton after it? She stepped onto the porch as the wagon came into view. Hunter was driving the team. Bret smiled and waved.

Alaina joined her. The radiance emanating from the girl's face wasn't for Bret or her brother. Her brown eyes sparkled as she gazed at the man on the white stallion. He waved. Jo noticed that his attention was glued to her sister.

Bret climbed from the seat and strode toward the cabin. "That was a lot of work, but the thugs didn't cause any trouble." Stepping onto the porch, he kissed Jo's cheek. "Dave has agreed to stay and help us build the house."

Jo figured the job was the least of the reasons David was willing to stay. "How are we going to pay the man?"

"He said he'd work for food and lodging." He glanced at Alaina. "He'll be bunking out with Hunter, so you'll have to stay here at Ellie's cabin and sleep on the couch."

"I don't mind. The more hands nailing boards together will mean you have your house sooner."

The music in her tone was undeniable. Jo wondered if having David around would be an asset or a detriment. *Will Alaina fall for him and get hurt again?*

"Hey, dreamer." Bret touched Jo's chin with his index finger. "You haven't heard a word I said."

"Of course I did. You said David was going to help you build our house."

He chuckled. "I said that I was starving. When do men eat around here?"

"I'll fix something right away." Alaina hurried into the cabin.

Bret stared after her. "What's going on with your sister?"

Jo giggled. It was like a man not to notice a budding romance. She wasn't going to enlighten him, at least not yet. "I'll help Alaina." Before entering the cabin, she turned to look at the stranger. He was busy stacking boards near the foundation. He looked up and his eyes met Jo's. She read questions in their depth. Or was it something else? How far could they trust this man? Still pondering, she went inside. Bret followed her.

Ellie stirred a pot of something she had simmering on the stove. "This be hot and ready." She sighed. "The pup be askin' out again."

Jo snatched the leash from its nail. She didn't want to chase the black ball of fur to David's feet. "I'll take her out back."

Alaina counted out plates. "We have to use your china, Jo. We don't have enough old dishes."

Jo figured Alaina was happy she had an excuse to use the good dishes. Lacy cooperated and the trip to the back yard was speedy. As she came in the back door, she thought about the shirt she'd been working on for Bret and gasped. It was a surprise, so she didn't want him to see it. If she went into the room, maybe Bret would follow her. She hurried to her sister. "The thing we were working on," she whispered. "Please hide it."

Grinning, Alaina rushed away. Jo stepped in front of Bret to distract him.

"Jo!" Alaina's voice rang through the small cabin. "The baby's choking! He's turning blue!"

# Eighteen

Shrieking, Jo raced toward the bedroom. Bret followed.

Alaina met them in the living room, her face pale. She had Jonathan in her arms. "He isn't breathing!"

Jo took the baby. His body was limp. Tears ran down her face. "Bret! Do something!"

David, apparently hearing her scream, suddenly appeared by her side. "Give him to me." Not waiting, he snatched the baby. Using his little finger, he searched the infant's mouth, then flipping him over, he gently thumped his back. Nothing happened.

Jo wailed. The color had drained from Bret's complexion. Alaina stared, fright branded on her face.

David turned Jonathan facedown over his knee and pressed on his back.

Jo couldn't watch her baby die. Was he already gone? She closed her eyes, but tears pressed between her lashes. At first she'd refused to nurse this baby, not believing it was hers. Now her entire life revolved around his needs. How could she stand to lose him. A sob jerked her frame.

Jonathan let out a piercing cry. Jo's lashes flashed upward, and she stared at him, then at David.

The man smiled, but the look in his eyes remained serious. He handed the crying infant to her. "He's going to be all right."

"What happened to him?"

David opened his hand. A tiny button lay in the center of his palm.

Jo cried out in dismay.

"Make sure the buttons or hooks on his clothing are fastened securely."

"I thought they were! I've been so careful. I promise to be more so." She hugged her baby. Tears ran down her face. "I can't thank you enough. I had no idea what to do!"

Alaina eyed David. "How'd you know what was wrong?"

A frown made creases between his brows. "I don't know. Checking his throat for an obstruction seemed to be an automatic reaction." He smiled, relaxing his tense features. "I think he wants to eat. Maybe that was why he was sucking on a button."

A thick strand of Alaina's dark hair draped over her left shoulder and waved to her breasts. Admiration was stamped on her face, and gold flecks sparkled in her light brown eyes.

David returned her smile. "Now that everything is under control, I say we get a bite of dinner and get back to work."

Heart still pounding from her scare, Jo went to the bedroom rocker. Jonathan wanted to nurse. She just wanted to continue hugging him.

When the baby fell asleep, Jo wasn't ready to put him back in the cradle. Carrying him in the crook of her arm, she joined the family in the kitchen. Bret looked up, but said nothing. The remnants of fright were still on his face, too.

Alaina lowered her fork to her plate. "We'll go over every article of Jonathan's clothing this afternoon, Jo. We'll make sure he's safe."

Apparently anxious to get back to building, Hunter shoved huge bites into his mouth, chomped a few times, and swallowed. Bret was shoveling chunks of potatoes, too. David ate slower, methodically chewing each bite. Was the man eating slower out of habit, or was he trying to get out of work?

Jo chewed a bite of carrot, but could hardly swallow. She was still quavering inside. Her fingers trembled, and it was difficult to sip her coffee without spilling it. She didn't want to become paranoid, but anxiety flooded her at the thought of leaving the baby alone in the bedroom.

Bret and Hunter gulped down their cooling coffee and stood to leave. David thanked Ellie for a delicious meal, smiled at Alaina, then followed the others outside. A twinge of guilt pinched Jo's insides. David hadn't eaten as much as her husband and brother. Did the man have enough?

"I didn't get Bret's shirt hidden, Jo." Alaina sighed. "I don't think he noticed. We were all watching David with Jonathan." Her expression looked dreamy. "David knew just what to do. He saved Jonathan's life."

"I'm more than grateful." Jo shook her head. "And to think I doubted him. I was concerned about his remaining here. Now, if you'll stop watching him, we can get back to our sewing."

Alaina giggled. "He went to his horse, and he's looking in his saddlebags. Oh, here he comes." She hurried to the door and flung it wide. "Is something wrong?"

Lacy streaked through the opening, scrambled down the steps and headed for David. He slapped his leg and coaxed her to follow him back to the porch. "I nearly forgot. There was mail for you folks." He handed a packet to Alaina. "I'm glad those rowdies didn't find your letters." He smiled at her, then turned and went back to the lumber pile.

Alaina grabbed Lacy's collar and pulled her back inside. Her fingers fumbled the string as she untied the packet and tossed the paper covering aside. "The first one is from Kathryn Harris. There's one from Mr. and Mrs. Nathan James and one from Mr. and Mrs. Trenton Sherwood."

"Open Tiffany's and hand it to me please." Accepting the pages, Jo sat back down at the table. "She says the girls are gaining weight and doing fine."

"Girls? Nathan had Trisha, and I thought they had a son called Adam."

"Oh. Tiffany had twin girls right after Jonathan was born." She glanced up to see her sister's face brighten, then she returned to her letter. "She says Andrea Sue is still the first one to wake up in the morning. She wails, Cassandra Jo just fusses. Other than that, they're identical."

Alaina clasped her hands. "I think twins would be wonderful!"

"I suppose, but one baby keeps me busy." Jo continued to read. "Adam is tolerating the babies, but he still insists that he doesn't need any more sisters." Jo chuckled. "He tried to talk me into trading my boy for Tiffany's two girls."

Alaina laughed. "Two for one is usually a good deal."

"Jonathan is worth more than a dozen other babies." Jo's focus dropped to the last page. Tiffany explained that it had been Randel Dixon, the man from Tennessee, who had shot Glen Allen in an effort to keep his identity a secret. He was also the one responsible for hanging Zeb. Since Dixon had been arrested, Klan activity had quieted in their area. Drawing a long breath, Jo set the papers aside. Bret would want to read his sister's letter.

Alaina glanced over her shoulder. "What does Elizabeth Ann have to say?"

Jo broke the seal and withdrew the letter. Unfolding the paper, Jo scanned the hand writing. "Oh, wonderful! She says that Trenton likes the idea of moving his shipping business to Virginia. Elizabeth Ann sounds ecstatic." Jo sighed. "She wants a baby, and it hasn't happened. I told her I'd pray for God to bless her with a little one." Jo read on. The doctor that Kathryn had taken Constance to had discovered the woman's problem. Among other things she had severe anemia. It would take her time to get back on her feet, but with proper nourishment and medication, she was going to be all right. Jo grinned. If what Bret had said about Joe Billings having an eye for Constance was true, he was going to be a happy man. Sweet little Alexandra would be delighted that she wasn't going to lose her mama.

Jo looked up and noticed that Alaina was at the window again. Had she heard the letter or was the girl's mind on David Fisher? Need she ask? Before her sister became too involved with the man, Jo intended to find out who he was, where he was from, and what he'd been doing of late. He acted like a man without a home. Why? She intended to discretely question him. Getting up, she joined her sister at the window. "Alaina, please keep a rein on your heart. We don't even know this David Fisher." She shrugged. "He could be an escaped convict for all we know."

A light laugh tinkled from Alaina. "You have quite an imagination, dear Sister." Her focus lowered to the baby in Jo's arms. "He's awake. Hi, there. You have such pretty blue eyes." She offered a finger. Jonathan grabbed it and made cooing sounds. "You talking to Aunt Lainy?"

Alaina made light of Jo's warning. Jo underscored her determination to investigate the man. She wasn't going to make it easy for him to break her sister's heart.

Alaina turned. "I'll help Ellie with the dishes." Glancing down, she squealed. "Lacy! You naughty girl!" Bending, she scooped up the remainder of Tiffany's letter. "I'm sorry Jo. I hope you read all of it."

"I did, thank goodness."

Ellie huffed. "You didn't give her dinner. No wonder she be eatin' the mail."

Alaina knelt on the floor and rolled the puppy to her back. Lacy growled as though she were going to attack and grabbed one of Alaina's fingers. "You have big teeth for a baby." She laughed. "I'm glad you're not as ferocious as you sound." Standing, she scraped tidbits of leftover food into the dog's dish. Lacy gobbled it and looked for more.

Retrieving the leash, Alaina tied the dog to the doorknob, then crossed to the stove. "I want to play with the kittens, and I don't want Lacy getting too rough."

Jo glanced at her puppy. "She'll have to learn to be gentle."

Ellie grinned. "Susie be teachin' that pup a thing or two with her claws if she be gettin' too close to her babies."

"She's already given her a couple of swats." Jo hoped the puppy would learn before the cat's claws swiped too close to her eyes.

Alaina came across the room with a kitten is each hand. "There's one white one. I suppose it's yours, Jo." She lifted her right hand to give Jo a better look, then showed her the second kitten. "This one has such cute yellow markings. I think he's the one I want, but the calico is cute, too."

Susie came around the stove, her tail swishing as she eyed Lacy. Apparently realizing the dog was tied, she strolled closer and hissed, her tail accentuating her remark. Lacy growled, then took a playful leap toward the cat. Susie whirled and raced back under the stove.

Nearly a week went by. Jo hadn't had a chance to question David. Her determination was mounting along with her sister's attraction toward the stranger. She straightened her shoulders. Today, she would press David Fisher into a corner and get some answers.

Ellie prepared scalloped potatoes with wild garlic and shoved the pan into the oven. She had dressed two of the hens that hadn't been laying. Dredging the pieces in flour, she dropped them into the skillet. The hot grease snapped and sizzled. "Hungry men be like a bottomless pit." She sighed. "The carrots from the root cellar be withered."

Jo smiled. "They'll be fine with butter and herbs, Ellie."

The old woman looked wistfully out the back window. "Ah can't wait for Cassie's fresh carrots to be comin' on."

When the men came in for dinner, they were exhausted, but eyed the fried chicken and brightened. They bantered some, but for the most part, they stuffed food into their mouths. Jo kept sneaking glances at David. His expression seemed so innocent. Instead of putting her at ease, it made her suspicious. "Where are you from, Mr. Fisher?"

"Just call me David." He smiled at her, crinkling the corners of his dark-blue eyes. "I've been living in Staunton."

"How long have you lived there?"

"About a month." He picked up his coffee cup and took a long swallow.

She eyed him boldly. "Where did you live before that?"

"Well, I've been traveling."

Jo noticed her sister's disapproving glare, but pressed on. "Where all have you been?"

Grinning, he turned to face her. "You just curious or do you suspect me of being a criminal?"

"Are you?"

Chuckling, he clattered his cup to the saucer. "After the war, I drifted from job to job. Lately, I worked at the freight yard in Staunton." He shrugged. "Maybe it's time I consider settling down."

Jo noticed that he hadn't denied being a criminal. Her suspicion about his past soared. She opened her mouth to ask about the man's family, but Bret interrupted her.

"Do you think we can get part of the frame up tomorrow?"

"Sure." Hunter drained his cup.

Alaina got up and refilled it, then offered coffee to everyone.

David held his cup to where she could easily fill it, but his attention shifted to Bret. "I was out looking at the garden. Cassie is doing a great job, and there will be plenty for her family. I was calculating, and I figure, if you're going to eat this winter, the garden should be doubled in size."

Hunter nodded. "I hadn't even thought about that."

"It's time we plow and plant. If we put it off too long, the harvest could be late enough to get nipped with the frost."

Alaina nodded. "The potatoes won't grow as large if we wait much longer. I took care of Mama's garden last year, so I can plant most of ours." She tossed her long hair back over her shoulder. "That is if someone does the plowing and gives me the seeds."

Bret looked contemplative. "I know you're right about the garden, David, but I hate to take the time from building."

"I'd be glad to do the plowing. Do you have a harrow?"

"There used to be two, but you'll have to ask Jonas. I was away at the war when the Yankees burned the barn. Our hired men managed to salvaged some of the equipment."

"Ah been listenin' to you." Ellie poured boiling water over the tea leaves in the pot. "My Jay be comin' soon. His black thumbs be green. If Miss Alaina does the plantin', the weeding' be Jay's job."

"Wonderful, Ellie." Alaina grinned. "I love planting and watching vegetables grow, but I hate hoeing!"

"I'll talk with Jonas tonight." David stood, thanked Ellie for the good meal, and went out the back door.

Watching him go, Jo bit her lower lip. Was he that anxious to get to tilling the ground? *Or is he using it as an excuse to escape my interrogation.* She shrugged. Tomorrow was another day, and there were more questions she wanted answered. Alaina's emotional well-being was at stake.

Bret and Hunter went to work on the house. Jo and Alaina washed the dishes. Since Jonathan was sleeping, Jo decided to do a bit of handwork on Bret's new shirt.

After an hour, Jo folded her sewing, stood, and massaged her back. On her way to the kitchen for a cup of tea, she passed a back window. Her fingers curled into fists. David and Alaina were walking over the area David planned to plow. He was pointing and talking. Why wouldn't her sister listen to reason? When they faced each other and laughed, Jo's concern mushroomed. Alaina was lovely. The evening sun played in the waves of her thick dark hair and kissed the ridges with reddish highlights all the way to her slender waist. The bottom ruffle on her pale blue dress played around her ankles. She appeared angelic. Did David intend to take advantage of her innocence? *What can I do to stop him?*

When the couple headed for the stand of pine, Jo whirled and headed for the door. It was at that moment that Jonathan began to fuss. Jo stepped back-and-forth between the cradle and the door, indecision tormenting her.

The baby began to cry and was kicking his blanket off. Swooping him up, she went back to the window. Alaina was sitting on a log with David. They were only a hundred feet from the cabin, but it was what he might be saying to her that disturbed Jo. She had to go out there. Jonathan had been a bit patient, but now he began to scream and demand. Sighing, she unbuttoned her blouse. "God, please protect my naive little sister."

David reached out to touch Alaina. Jo's heart jolted. *What shall I do?*

## Nineteen

David touched Alaina's fingers, then withdrew his hand. She was so lovely, and he assumed pure. It was a struggle to wrench his gaze from hers. He forced his focus to the tree line. It was crucial that he fight his attraction to her until he could figure out where his life had been and where he was headed.

"Do you think we should plant squash?"

David's mind snapped back to the topic of discussion. "That would be a good idea, since it can be kept in a root cellar for months." He glanced around. "Is there one here?"

"Yes." She pointed over her shoulder to a door in the hillside not far away. "Jo said that the Harris women hid runaway slaves in that root cellar during the war. The family was part of the underground railroad."

He nodded. "That figured, if the rest of the family is anything like Bret. Now about the garden. I think we should plant several kinds of beans. Cassie and Ellie will dry them. And I assume we should store a lot of potatoes. They should keep until spring in a root cellar."

"They will. We're eating the last of last years crop of potatoes as well as carrots. Cassie buried the carrots in sand to help preserve them." Alaina sighed. "During the war food was so scarce. Many people nearly starved. What much of the South did have was destroyed by the Federals."

"War is a horrid waste."

"Were you in the war?"

He shrugged. "Weren't most men?"

She appeared intrigued. "What side did you fight for?"

He hesitated. What would be safe to say? Since the conflict was over, whatever he said would probably be all right, still . . .

"David?"

He drew a long breath. "The war is over, Lainy. We'd better talk about this garden." He yawned. "Then I want to help Bret and Hunter before dark."

"You're right. I don't like to discuss the conflict anyway." She shook her head. "In Winchester, we never knew which side was winning! The Yankees would storm in, then the Confederates would show up and take over. The next day, Yankees would stomp up and down the streets. It was horrifying!" She eyed him. "Were you there?"

"No." This time, he covered her hand with his. A desire to protect her rose within him. He had to get his life straightened out. *And soon!*

"Alaina!" Jo's voice echoed.

He looked up. Jo stood on the back porch with Jonathan in her arms. She appeared irritated. *Does she think I'll harm her sister?*

"Jo may need help." Alaina smiled. "I'll see you later."

He stood. "I've got to get back to work, too. Bret and Hunter will accuse me of shirking."

She laughed. The tinkling sound made something strange happen within him. He couldn't let the attraction between them blossom further. *At least not yet.* He watched her graceful movements as she strolled toward the cabin. The sun kissed the waist-length hair that swayed against her back and made red highlights dance on the dark silky strands. What would it be like to run his fingers through it? Or to kiss her pink cheeks? Or better, her rosy lips. Were they as soft and smooth as they looked? Or as warm as her personality?

*Stop it, man!* He gritted his teeth. Since leaving the island, he'd avoided an emotional involvement. It hadn't been difficult—until he'd met Alaina. What this delightful girl was doing to him was frightening. Taking a deep breath, he hurried toward the new house foundation. He had to fight to ignore how her radiance warmed his insides.

"One of you fellows need my assistance?"

Bret looked up. "Either of us could use you."

Smiling, David headed toward Bret. The man braced a support with his shoulder and gripped a hammer with his one hand. He'd never seen such determination. A man with one arm could just give up. Not Breton Harris. "You want me to hold or pound?"

"Either."

"Then I'll take the hammer." How this man pounded a nail with one hand amazed David. He'd press the nail into the wood, tap it slightly to get it started, then pound it on in. David couldn't help admire him, but who wouldn't?

For the next week, the men worked diligently on the framework. David marveled at the size of the house. Bret had told him he was just building the right half this summer. That made sense. According to the architect's drawings, there would be a center stairway with a hallway on each side. Bret intended to include both halls and cover the door openings that would eventually lead into rooms in the left half of the house. Since the roof slanted toward the front and back, it could easily be expanded next spring.

David wondered if he would still be here to watch the house rise to completion. He loved working with lumber. It was thrilling to watch the framework grow like the bone structure of a huge animal. Hunter was the one who climbed over the frame like a monkey. David scampered up the tall ladders, carting boards to him. Even on the third story, Hunter strolled from joist to joist as though he were hiking through the woods. That part made David jittery. He'd be more comfortable when the flooring was down.

The sun slipped behind the mountains to the west. Gradually, the upright supports cast shadows across the flooring joist. Hunter straightened. "I think it's time to quit. I need a bath, something to eat, and a good night's rest."

Bret clattered his square to a foundation stone. "I second the motion."

David collected the tools and put them in a canvas sack, then headed for the cabin with the men. He knew it would be wise to bathe and go to bed instead of going into Ellie's cabin. He figured Alaina would be waiting with a coffee pot and a plate stacked with sandwiches. He sighed, knowing it was more than hunger that lured him across the porch and into the kitchen.

Taking a place at the table, he fought to keep from looking at the young lady who filled the coffee cups; however, when her fingers rested lightly on his shoulder, he met her gaze. In the lantern's glow, gold flecks shimmered in her light-brown eyes. He swallowed. Smiling, she handed him the plate of sliced ham.

"Thank you." He made his sandwich, but her nearness made it difficult to swallow. If he felt like this only two weeks after he'd met Alaina, what would it be like by the end of summer? Should he remain or leave? He needed the job. *Come winter, I'll have to move on, regardless.*

Jo watched her sister. The girl wasn't throwing herself at David, but she was making it clear that she was available. She prayed David wouldn't misinterpret Alaina's attraction to him and take advantage of her innocence. She thought of Constance Kennan. Tiffany had said Alexander Wellington had used the woman during the war. Jo studied David. He didn't seem to be another Colonel Wellington; however, questions concerning him buzzed through her brain like a hive of inebriated bees.

"Where do your parents live, David?"

He put another bite of food into his mouth and avoided her gaze.

His silence made her more suspicious. "You have siblings?"

Bret eyed Jo. "Isn't it time you get ready for bed, darling?"

The amorous relationship they had shared last night flashed through her recall. Heat splashed against her face, and she knew her burning cheeks had turned scarlet. Getting up quickly, she fled to the bedroom. When she got that husband of hers alone, she intended to give him a tongue lashing that he wouldn't easily forget.

David sat sipping coffee and wondering what Jo was up to. Her distrust was evident. Had she known him in the past? Was there something in his background that made her suspicious? What?

Bret and Hunter grabbed a towel and headed out the back door. David supposed he'd better leave as well. He stood.

"You have something to dry with, David?" Smiling, Alaina approached, a blue towel, the same shade as her dress, draped over one arm.

"I do now." He grinned at her. Then a vision of her using the towel after taking a dip in the stream invaded his mind. He forced it away. What was getting into him? He'd been wearing a gold cross on a chain around his neck when he'd came to on the island. Was his Christian heritage being tested? Was he up to the challenge? "Thank you," he whispered, then turned and hurried out. He longed to look back, but fought the urge. Again he wondered if he should move on.

Screened by a row of thick bushes, he stripped, stepped into the water, and gasped. "The sun was warm this afternoon. How can this stream be this frigid in May?"

Bret chuckled. "It's fed by rivulets from up the mountain. It's usually July before it warms up." His teeth chattered. "Sometimes I wonder if it would be better to stink!"

David chuckled. His hands were shaking. He dropped the soap and clamped his mouth shut on a word that would be better not uttered. He had to fumble in the water to find the cake. Hunter's chuckle irritated him. The baths he been taking the past two weeks were the worst he'd ever been subjected to. He seized the soap, but it flipped from his grasp. "My hands are so cold I can't hold on to that thing!"

Bret scooped it up and proffered it on his way to where he'd left his clothes. "I'm leaving. You fellows can enjoy the water as long as you like."

Hunter jumped to land and snatched his towel from a bush. "That's enough for me."

David didn't know if he was clean or not, but he'd had enough as well. "I'd prefer to use a tub with a bit of warm water mixed with this frigid."

"That takes too long." Bret yanked on his jeans and worked his arm into his shirt sleeve.

"Nevertheless, tomorrow night I'm going back to using a tub in our cabin." Teeth chattering and arms shaking, David snatched his towel and began buffing his skin. Before he was dry, he grabbed his jeans and shirt. "I'm so awake now, I don't know if I can sleep!"

Hunter dried his hair and beard, then buttoned his shirt. "When we work as long and hard as we've been doing, we could probably sleep on rocks in a snowstorm!"

"I'm looking forward to a soft bed and eager arms." Bret hurried toward his cabin.

"I'm just anxious for a place to rest my head." Hunter glanced at David. "How about you?"

"Right." But was he? David thought warm arms sounded pretty good. *That is if they're Lainy's.* When he realized what he was beginning to picture, he rebuked his thought.

Hunter vanished inside the deteriorating old cabin and lit an oil lamp. Still shivering, David stepped over the threshold. "Isn't much like home yet, is it?"

Hunter laughed. "We just need glass in a couple windows and a new back door."

"Plus!" David spotted a bird on a rafter, eyed droppings on the floor, and was thankful the nest wasn't over the bed. "It hasn't rained since I arrived. Does the roof leak?"

"No, but I can't say much more for the place." He crossed the room to the bed and straightened his hap. "You want to bunk on the other side again, or do you prefer that cot?"

David eyed the cot. He'd used it occasionally and found it uncomfortable. It was in good condition, but so was the straw tick. "If rest is the criteria, I prefer the bed."

Hunter nodded. "I'll take this hap." He tossed the second one across the bed. "You roll up in that one."

"Is this the way we're supposed to exist all summer?"

"Jonas is working on this place. He doesn't have glass for the windows yet, but he fixed the front door today." Hunter yawned. "Once it's repaired, the ladies will scrub and make the place more livable."

"And find another bed?"

Hunter sneezed. "I saw an old bed frame in the shed. I'll dig it out tomorrow and see if it salvageable. Cassie will be glad to stuff another tick with straw." He yawned. "It will be nicer when the weather warms up a bit more."

An image of hot sand under a searing sun blasted David's senses. "I don't relish steaming in the hot sun all day."

"Didn't think of that."

David stretched out and flipped his hap over his body. He punched his pillow until it fit the crook of his neck, then squirmed until the straw in the tick shifted to support his six-foot frame. He preferred a bed of his own, but this beat sleeping on the island with sand working under his clothing.

Thoughts of his weeks on the island crowded his mind. He wished he could forget those days, but the Lord must have had a reason for the experience. He supposed it had strengthened his faith, but how could he know that for sure?

He closed his eyes. A vision of Alaina formed before him. His heart beat increased. It would be so easy to fall in love with her. *I don't dare! It wouldn't be right.*

In a dream, she ran to him. He took her hands in his. She gazed up at him, affection shimmering in her eyes. He swung her in a circle, then pulled her into an embrace. His lips touched hers, then moved slowly back and forth. He woke with a start, his pulse throbbing and his blood surging.

*I can't stand this soaring into ecstasy, then being slammed into reality and misery! Somehow, I have to find answers to my questions!*

He drifted into slumber, wrestling to still the vision of Alaina dancing on the back of his eyelids. As deeper sleep overtook him, the amorous vision was slowly replaced by one not so lovely. Groaning, he coughed. His body screamed at him to remain prone, but a sense of danger probed at him. When he tried to call out, no sound issued from his parched throat. His face pressed against splintering wood. Sand gritted between his teeth. Mustering strength to lift his head, he tried to spit, but his mouth felt as dry as old bones.

*Where am I?* The words ricocheted through his muddled brain, although he hadn't made a sound.

A strange bird whistled from nearby. Another answered.

Wiping the back of a hand across his gritty lips only deposited more sand on his face. *So thirsty.*

He wrestled with ropes, then discovered that his arms were tethered to a wooden raft. It was as though he were caught in a giant spider web. A shiver raked his six-foot length, although the sun scorched his back.

Finally untangled, he rolled to the sandy beach and struggled to a sitting position. Blinking, he peered out across a great expanse of water. A wave broke on the beach and salty water washed over his toes. His navy pants were saturated. One of the legs had been torn off to the center of his right calf, the other hung ragged above his left ankle. The buttons were missing from his blue-barred shirt. The wet garment clung annoyingly to his back.

Another wave rolled in. It washed over his ankles. It was deeper than the first one had been. The next was even higher.

*The tide is coming in!* He longed to rest, but climbing to higher ground was imperative.

Squinting, he spanned the ocean. Nothing was in sight but water and sky. He turned, hoping to see someone coming to his rescue. Only barrenness welcomed him. Rocks lined a hill that slanted upward about a hundred feet. He estimated the top to be about thirty feet above sea level. Under most circumstances, gaining the crest would take minimal energy.

*I don't have the strength.*

The next wave was a foot deep. On its way back to the sea, it yanked sand from under his hips. The raft lifted as though preparing for launch. He couldn't just sit here and allow the ocean to claim him. He must have been unconscious when his raft washed onto this beach. Had an incoming wave brought him to?

"Merciful God, please help me." Gripping the rope that remained tied to the raft, he rolled to his hands and knees and forced himself to inch forward. Groping, he grasped a protruding rock. His hand slipped and he nearly tumbled back the few feet he had gained.

Fatigued, he crumpled to the sand. A wave washed over his head. A warning gong reverberated through his stodgy brain. Retreating, the water yanked on the raft as though determined to rip the ropes from his grasp. He turned in time to see another wave approach. *Should I drag the raft with me? How?*

"Oh, God, you are my refuge and my strength. Please help me." He didn't recognize his own raspy voice.

As another wave rolled up the beach, he forced his arms to lift his broad shoulders from the sand. He'd crawled only two feet when the water hit. The raft dislodged. The force of the wave shoved it forward. The edge of a board knocked his hands from under him. Again he went under, but regained his balance and pulled himself forward. Every few inches, he dragged the raft with him. "I can't make it." A corner of the wood snagged on a protruding rock. He jerked on the rope, but it was to no avail. Shoving his foot under the raft, he pried upward. A splinter jabbed his toe, but the float didn't give.

Rocks hampered his progress. They scraped his hands and bruised his bare knees. Still, with the ocean threatening to engulf him, he clambered upward. Sand shifted under his feet and caused his hands to slip. The incline slanted upward at a thirty-five degree angle, but his weakened condition made it seem as though he were scaling the face of a ninety degree cliff.

As each wave lifted the raft, he struggled to pull it further up the incline. It was becoming more difficult to hang on as the waves receded. The next wave swished under the raft and shoved it forward with a force that knocked him down. On its way back to the ocean, it jerked the rope from his grasp.

Another wave splashed over his feet. Minus the raft, he clawed his way from one rock to another, although he felt as though he had a weight on his back that seemed intent on smashing his face on the rocks.

Finally, he collapsed on the small plateau. He tried to take a deep breath. It hurt his chest. His cough sounded like a dry wheeze. He slowly sat upright, leaned against the trunk of a palm tree, and inspected his right knee. It was bleeding. His hands had brush burns from the climb. The salt water stung his injuries, but he supposed it would aid the healing process.

Dazed, he stared at the sandy shore. Each new wave climbed higher as though threatening to engulf the island and drag him to the depths of the sea. Squinting, he peered out across the water and watched his raft float away.

Something hot burned his chest. He looked at the gold cross that dangled from a chain around his neck. The sun made the metal so hot that it began to sear his flesh. He unfastened the chain, but not wanting to lose the cross, he refastened it around the palm.

Something in his back pocket poked him. Jerking it free, he stared at an oilcloth covered rectangle. He slowly unwrapped the parcel and discovered a book of Psalms. It was wet, but not saturated. He tried to leaf through it, but found it difficult. It would take time to dry the pages, but the thought of reading the word of God was his only comfort.

Within minutes, the foam lapped at his feet. Was his sanctuary temporary? The next wave was higher and fast approaching. The sound roared in his ears.

Gasping woke him. His heart drummed in his head and breathing came in short gasps. He swiped a hand across his moist brow. What could he do about these dreams that robbed him of sleep?

Several minutes of deep breathing calmed his nerves, but his heart continued to pound for another reason. He wondered if he should talk to Alaina. Would she understand if he explained his situation? Dare he? What difference would it make? Telling someone wouldn't, couldn't, change the facts. He was caught in a vice that was tightening, crushing in more every day. There had to be a solution. He had to find it. *How? Where can I begin?*

# Twenty

Alaina lay on the couch, staring at the darkened rafters and listening to distant thunder. Sleep had evaded her for two hours. A cup of tea would relax her, but a noise at the cookstove might disturb Ellie. The old woman slept light. *What about the sound of the coming storm?* Maybe natures noise lulled the woman. Alaina wondered if Ellie slept at all. She seemed to know everything that was going on.

*I wish I could stop dreaming about David.* Whether awake or asleep, it didn't matter. Her feelings for him had been growing since the first time she'd seen him. He seemed attracted to her, but he turned away just when she thought he wouldn't. What was wrong? What was holding him back?

The kittens began to make mewing sounds. Susie was curled up on the rocker cushion, and didn't move. Getting up, Alaina went to the box and picked up all three kittens and went back to the couch. They played with her hair and nibbled on her fingers. It would be another month before they would be drinking from a saucer. She was beginning to favor the female calico, and had named her Patches.

Susie stretched and thumped to the floor. When she slipped under the cookstove, Alaina got up and took the feline's offspring back to her.

Returning to the couch, she leaned her head back, closed her eyes, and drew a long breath. The inactivity generated thoughts of David. What would it be like to feel his arms around her? *What would it be like to feel his lips on mine?* She was falling in love with him. What can I do to stop my heart from making a foolish mistake?

Getting up, she tiptoed to the back door and opened it. Instantly, Lacy was by her feet. She tried to slip out without the dog, but Lacy had other ideas. She began to fidget.

"I'm only going to the porch." Alaina was afraid the puppy would bark and wake the family. Maybe she needed to use a spot of grass. Grabbing the leash, she fastened it to the dog's collar. "You're going to get wet."

The cool night breeze caressed Alaina's heated cheeks as she stepped outside. The darkness that surrounded her made her feel timid. She moved to the banister. Refreshing moisture sprinkled her face as she peered into the black sky. There were no stars twinkling tonight. She felt so small. "Hey, God, I'm down here," she whispered. God knew that. She supposed she had to remind herself that he was on his throne.

Crooked fingers of lightning slashed through the clouds as though angrily grasping for the treetops. Thunder rumbled nearer. The rain increased. Had something moved near the tree line or had the wind caused the bushes to sway? A twig snapped. Alaina's breath caught. She backed against the log side of the cabin and squinted to see into the darkness. Lacy woofed, and the shadow moved again. It might be wise to dash into the cabin, but curiosity held her captive.

In the glimmer from lightning, the being took shape, and the silhouette of a deer moved from the thicket. Lifting her head, the doe sniffed the air and took a few more steps. Lowering her nose, she began to graze. Alaina smiled. Her night venture must be safe enough. If anyone was about, the deer would race for cover.

Lacy pranced as though she were anxious. She didn't bark again, but her attention remained riveted on the doe.

Alaina's eyes moved to the cabin where Hunter and David slept. Cassie's cabin screened most of it, but she could see the back porch and part of one corner. Was David awake? *If so, is he thinking about me?*

"Foolish girl." It was time that she accepted reality. David might be attracted to her, but it was plain that he didn't intend to do anything about it. Jo was right

The puppy pulled on the leash. Alaina stepped forward far enough to let the dog go down the steps and sniff the grass. She circled, squatted for a few seconds, then peered into the night as though she were enjoying the rain. A bolt of lightning seared across the canopy. A loud crack made Lacy jump and scramble onto the porch. Thunder boomed overhead. A sudden downpour drummed on the porch roof. Shivering, Alaina went inside, shut the door, and released the clip on Lacy's leash.

Back on the couch, she envisioned David and a new thought seared across her mind. There were ways a woman could get a man to notice her. She smiled into the dark. *Tomorrow is another day, Mr. David Fisher.*

Allowing her mind to conjure the possibilities seemed peaceful. The smile on her lips relaxed as slumber drifted her into another world where David took her in his arms. They danced in a field of flowers as sunbeams caressed them.

Deep in slumber, David moaned. He tried to spit particles of grit from his mouth. It was futile. He tried to stand, but fatigue gripped him. *How close is the nearest dwelling or fishing village?* He leaned his back against a palm tree. He must rest, then try to resolve this dilemma.

*How can I rest when I don't know where I am?* He folded the square of oilcloth that had covered his book of Psalms and shoved it into a hip pocket, then slipped the book into the pocket of his shirt. He would work on drying the pages later. Gripping the tree, he hauled himself to his feet.

"No!"

Isolation slammed him. Ocean surrounded the island. A few palms, some rocks, and tons of sand composed his oasis. He guessed the island was about five hundred feet long and two hundred feet wide.

"I'm alone." His words were carried aloft by a brisk salty breeze. Except for the sound of waves crashing against the rocks, his world was silent and void of humans.

"Hey, God!" he shouted.

Palm fronds above him rustled and a bird with bright red and yellow plumage squawked and took to wing.

Forcing his emotions to a more even keel, he took a deep breath and followed the bird with his eyes. He squinted. Could he distinguish treetops in the distance? How many miles away? Was it the mainland, a source of help, or just another deserted island? If birds lived there, there must be a fresh water source. The thought of a drink made his thirst more acute. He must get a grip on reality and plan a lifesaving strategy. Was it possible? The distant treetops were too far away to swim, especially in his weakened condition. *Not to mention my thirst.* The possibility of finding fresh water on this tiny oasis was next to nil.

"I must rest a few minutes." He sank to his knees on the sand. The attempt to brush the wet grains from his pants was futile. He noticed that the fabric still covering one knee had been torn during his climb to safety. The sun beat on his head. If he took off his shirt, could he form a shelter large enough to keep the back of his neck from becoming blistered?

Again, he rose slowly to his feet, then saw the scrapes on his bare toes. The salt from the water continued to make his abrasions sting. Ignoring his discomfort, he studied the rising tide and shook his head. His island was shrinking. What if the entire surface became inundated? He tried to swallow. It felt as though he had a mouthful of coffee grounds that scratched his parched throat.

A strange calm settled over him. He was alone, thirsty, hungry and confused, but he knew he was in God's hands.

What was the verse he'd just read from Psalm 91? "I will say of the Lord, He is my refuge and my fortress: my God; in him will I trust."

He glanced upward. A white cloud floated listlessly overhead and peace filled his heart. If he were to meet his Maker today, he was ready.

Sitting propped against the palm, he opened his book of Psalms and began separating the wet pages. The paper was thin. With patience and diligently separating pages the sun would dry them. Frequently, he glanced up, trying to calculate the speed of the rising tide. Each incoming wave brought the froth closer.

When he looked down to pull two more wet pages apart, his focus fell on the Twenty-third Psalm. "The Lord is my Shepherd; I shall not want."

He reached to touch the gold cross that dangled from the chain he'd fastened around the palm. *I am a lamb of God.* He pictured God leading him to green pastures and still waters.

A sigh rasped from his parched throat. "I really need a drink of water, God." Forcing his mind from his thirst, he recited a few more lines of the Psalm, then paused to ponder. *Yea, though I walk through the valley of the shadow of death, I will fear no evil: for thou art with me.*

He raked his fingers through his hair. It was matted and stiff from the saltwater. *All this water, and am I going to thirst to death? The thought made him shudder.*

He paced the width of the island, then sat on the edge of the bank and let his legs drape over the rocks. Froth from an incoming wave tickled his toes before it receded. The next one covered his feet.

Standing, he waited. Another gush sent water above his ankles. Shoving the book of Psalms into his shirt pocket, he climbed to the highest point on the rocks. A larger wave humped like a mountain in the distance and rushed toward him. Just before it hit he took a deep breath.

Gasping, he woke. His heart drummed against his rib cage. *Will this torment ever cease?* His mouth felt pasty, but if he got up for a drink, he would probably waken Hunter. The man needed his sleep. *So do I!* If it weren't for his wretched dreams.

He thought about Alaina and the growing bond between them. He didn't want to hurt her. *I don't want hurt either.* He had no right to hope that they could share a future when he couldn't promise her anything.

The horrid dream had made him thirsty. The rain pounding on the roof made it worse. He wouldn't sleep without wetting his throat. Giving in, he got up and went to the pail of water. Grasping the dipper, he filled a cup. As he sipped the liquid, he moved back to sit on the edge of the bed. His mind scrolled back to another time. A time when thirst and another kind of confusion had gripped him.

*Forget that*! The mere thought of what he'd been through made his stomach spasm. He set the empty cup on the floor and slowly resumed a prone position. Thank the Lord he hadn't disturbed Hunter's rest. Tomorrow he would get another bed if he had to cut down a tree and make it!

If he could get just one night of sleep without being tormented by nightmares or disturbing dreams. Had his experience on the island caused the rest of his life to be ruined?

Although his mind was troubled, his body gradually relaxed. Sleep drew him into a vortex of anxiety that whirled him into an unknown world of anguish and confusion.

Sitting on the sand, David pondered. He'd been on the island about two hours. He shaded his eyes to gaze across the expanse of water to the treetops. Attempting to swim the distance would be foolish, and there wasn't material to build a boat. He probably wasn't going to die by drowning, unless a storm sent a tidal wave that swept him out to sea.

"If only I hadn't lost my raft." The dorsal fin of a shark broke the surface of a nearby wave, magnifying his decision not to try to swim.

His strength slightly renewed, he stood and shoved his right hand into a front pocket. He discovered a pocket knife and a ball of string. Ramming his left hand into the other pocket, he withdrew a tongue depressor. Shaking his head in confusion, he shoved it into a back pocket

He stared at his feet. He would have to be careful of sharp stones and broken sea shells as he investigated the island.

From habit, he supposed, he grappled for his watch chain, but the gold ring that fastened it to his pants was all that remained. He shrugged. After being in the sea, the watch wouldn't be working anyway. His clothes were dry, but the salt water made them stiff and his shirt made his back itch.

The skin covering his entire body was so dry and tight that it felt as though movement might crack open his flesh.

He uttered a guttural sound and raked his long fingers through his hair. A strand caught on a broken nail. The salt water and sun had made his curls resemble twisted wire. Even though his circumstance was far from humorous, a hoarse laugh vibrated his vocal cords. Were isolation and anguish making him crazy?

Forcing a semblance of sanity, he strode across the sand toward the far end of the island and prayed he would find a clue to what had happened to him. The orange-and-scarlet hues on the horizon warned him of the coming night. He wanted to find out what other living creatures may be sharing his abode before darkness shrouded him.

A ray of sun glittered on the neck of a glass bottle and flashed in his eyes. The cork was in place. He hurried forward and dropped to his knees. Ignoring his sore fingers, he scraped at the sand to uncover the rest of his prize. His thirst became more acute at the prospect of an unopened container of ingestible liquid. Yanking the bottle free, he held it up. *Empty!* Grasping the neck, he swung the bottle over his shoulder, intending to hurl it out to sea. At the last second, he changed his mind and lowered his arm.

His eyes spanned the open sea, then jerked back to the right. Had he seen a vessel? Shielding his eyes, he squinted and searched the horizon. His heartbeat quickened. *A ship!*

Jumping and waving his arms, he prayed someone aboard the vessel would notice him. The boat was about three miles away as it glided parallel to David. He needed a flag. Yanking off his shirt he feverishly waved it. Even though he knew no one could hear him, he tried to shout, however, his mouth and throat felt as dry as the sand under his feet. Only a garbled sound issued forth.

He held the bottle up, hoping to catch and magnify the sun's rays to signal the ship, but the sun was at the wrong angle. Discouraged, he helplessly watched the ship pass the island and continue its course. He waved. No one saw him. He yelled. No one heard.

Awakened by his own voice, David suffocated a groan. Taking a deep breath, he closed his eyes and struggled to relax. It was futile, so he permitted himself to daydream. Instantly his thoughts were on Alaina. She was so sweet, so innocent, so precious.

He pictured the overgrown path he'd come across yesterday. By following it about two hundred feet upstream, he'd discovered a wooden bench enclosed in an arbor. An inch of mud and decaying leaves covered the seat. The rose vines had gone wild and straggly protuberances stuck out in all directions and waved in the breeze. He remained a few feet from the entangled mass. One got the impression that to get too close would endanger one of becoming ensnared.

A desire to tame the roses and repair the arbor filled him. In the morning he would ask Jonas if there were hedge trimmers at Sunny Horizon. Envisioning the finished project, he smiled.

*That will be the perfect place to take Alaina to talk.* There were things she should know. He wasn't prepared to reveal his circumstances, but he owed her some sort of explanation.

*Oh, Lainy.* His heart reached out to her through the night. Was she awake and thinking about him? He thought about the circle of metal that he kept in his pocket. His heart contorted. It was only right to explain at least that part of his past to her. How? It would be the most difficult task of his life. Would she understand? Could she understand?

Sleep finally overtook him, but it was a restless slumber.

Bird calls drew David from a foggy mist. He blinked. The first rays of dawn filtered through the east window. Sitting up, he rubbed the back of his neck. How could he do what was expected of him if he didn't get more sleep? Working on the house could endanger more than himself. If he caused injury to either Bret or Hunter, he'd regret the decision to stay here. Maybe he should move on.

*If it weren't for Lainy, I would.* But it was because of her that he definitely should move on. He slammed a fist into his straw tick.

"What's with you, Fisher?" Hunter stretched and groaned. "You tossed all night." He yawned. "Right after breakfast, I'm going to find that extra bed frame and fix it before we begin work on the house."

"Good idea." David eyed him. "I'll help."

"What's bothering you?"

"I suffer from nightmares."

Hunter chuckled. "You must have led quite a life to be tortured every night!"

Jerking his jeans on, David yawned. "I'm hungry."

"Me, too. Ellie and Alaina will have breakfast ready by now." Getting up, he quickly dressed and headed for the door.

Following, David's mind had shifted from food to the sweetheart who would be serving it. He couldn't put off talking with her any longer; although, he wanted to bring the arbor back to its original beauty before taking Alaina there for the discussion. *Will it be the first of many to come? Or will it be the last talk we ever have?*

Hunter headed for the shed. David, heart throbbing, crossed to Ellie's cabin and stepped onto the porch. He reached for the doorknob, but the sound of a horse and buggy made him turn to stare down the lane. Who could be coming before daylight

Drawn by curiosity, he stepped to the edge of the porch to wait. The conveyance became visible through the dawn's gray mist. The slender driver halted the carriage horse in front of the construction site and leaped to the ground. Rounding the buggy, he reached to aid someone's descent. David squinted. A black man, evidently elderly, climbed down, took a step and tottered. He gripped the rim of the wheel. The driver, who was much younger, handed the old man a cane.

*Whoever this is, he needs help*. David rushed around the foundation and a pile of lumber. "Can I assist you, sir?"

The old man looked up. "Ellie be here?"

"Yes. She's in the cabin."

"Ah's come to see her."

David glanced at the driver. The boy was in his late teens. "Do you usually drive your passengers to their destinations this early?"

The boy shrugged. "I wanted him to wait until daylight to leave Staunton, but he wouldn't hear of it. He said Ellie was expecting him and he wasn't going to wait a minute longer than he had to." He thudded a trunk to the ground. "I'll be on my way if you can help him inside."

"I'd be glad to." David offered the old man his arm.

"Ah's slow, but Ah can make it without hanging on."

David obliged, but remained close. If the visitor stumbled, he intended to catch him before his face slammed onto the stones.

Pausing, the man leaned on his cane and looked around. "Which cabin be Ellie's?"

David pointed.

The man's eyes widened. "The big one?" His voice quavered, then cracked.

"Bret made it larger to accommodate his family while he's building the big house."

Nodding, the man took a few more steps, then stumbled. David grabbed him as he went down on one knee. The man went limp. David slowly lowered him to the ground. "Hunter!" He cradled the old man's shoulders and stared at Ellie's door. "Bret!"

The shed door opened and Hunter hurried across the yard. Apparently grasping the situation at a glance, he turned toward Ellie's cabin. "Bret! Jo! Come out here!"

It was Ellie who stepped onto the porch. With a cry, she hurried forward and knelt on the hard ground. "Jay! You all right?" She touched the old man, then lifted her dark eyes to David. "What he be doin' on the ground?"

David swallowed. It was apparent that the old woman cared deeply for this man. He hadn't had time to check him and couldn't answer Ellie's question.

"Jay?" She gasped. Tears filled her eyes. "You's home. You don't be dyin' on old Ellie. You hear me? Jay!"

## Twenty-One

David glanced up at Hunter. "Get the cot. We can use it as a stretcher."

"Bret's bringing it." Hunter rushed to aid him, then helped David put the old man on it.

Ellie was in the way. David gently touched her arm. "I want to examine him."

Nodding, the old woman stepped aside, tears running down her withered face.

David felt for a pulse. "He's alive." He glanced at Ellie. "Who is he?"

She sniffed and seemed to be struggling to regain control. "He be my husband. He be comin' from Castle Crest."

Bret peered curiously at the old man. "Apparently the trip was quite taxing on him."

A moan issued from Jay.

Ellie crowded close. "You's gonna be fine. You's home."

His eyes opened, and a smile deepened the folds around his mouth and eyes. "My dear Ellie. Ah didn't mean to . . . give yo such a scare."

"Let's get him inside." David stood. "I think he's just exhausted. Right now, rest will do him the most good."

Lacy scampered from the cabin. Apparently she wasn't going to be left out of any new and different happening. Alaina called her back, but Lacy insisted on examining the old man on the cot. She sniffed his hand, then kissed one of his gnarled fingers.

"Bless me," the old man wheezed. He lifted a trembling hand to give the puppy a weak pat.

Alaina stepped close, her pink skirt swishing. Snatching the wiggling bundle, she retreated to the porch. David and Hunter carried Jay inside.

When he was on Ellie's bed, he struggled to take a deep breath. "Ah's finally here." He yawned and reached a trembling hand toward Ellie.

She grasped his fingers. "We's gonna do fine." She kissed his sunken cheek and pulled the quilt over him. "You sleep now." Smiling, she patted his arm, then went to the kitchen.

David picked Lacy up. She was standing with her front paws against the side of the mattress, trying to see the old man. Her tail slapped his side as he carried her from the room. He quietly closed the door and released the puppy. Alaina stood at the stove, a pancake turner in her hand. The white ruffles that trimmed her pink sleeves fluttered around her elbows as she turned the pancakes. He grinned at her. "That pup gets bigger every day. It won't be long until you and Jo won't be able to lift her."

Alaina turned to face him. During all the fracas, she had nearly let breakfast burn. "She's an armload now. Jo's trying to train her. She's smart and catches on quickly."

"That's essential. Training makes the difference between a wonderful pet and a nuisance."

Hunter and Bret took their places at the table. Alaina's focus followed David. Her heart reached toward him. She fought to restrain it. She'd had a miserable night and had vowed to ignore the man, unless he proved to be more attentive. But he was, wasn't he? There was something creating an invisible barrier between them, and she was determined to discover what was eating at him. His actions could be the result of a warped personality, but that didn't seem to be the case.

David gripped the back of his chair and met Alaina's gaze. "You look like a ray of sunshine, Lainy."

"It's barely light."

"You could've fooled me." Sitting, he lowered his gaze.

When he looked at her, Alaina thought she could read adoration in his eyes. Other times, he would turn his back on her. Confused by his alternating actions, she was torn between hugging him and slapping the side of his handsome face with her spatula.

Hunter raised his coffee cup. "Hurry, Sister. I need a shot of caffeine." He whistled. "Dave kept me awake all night!"

Her mouth dropped open. "Why?" She turned to flip the pancakes.

"Beats me. Those smell great."

She stacked several on a plate and clattered it to the table, then grabbed the coffee pot. As she poured David's, she tried not to touch him. Could he tell that her hands were trembling?

"Thank you, Lainy." He moved his arm and it touched hers.

She tried not to jerk away, although his touch ignited something within her. Did he know it would? Had he touched her on purpose? Did he care? Was he deliberately trying to tantalize her? Maybe she should dribble a little hot coffee on his leg.

Bret yawned and stretched. His hair, usually neatly in place, looked disheveled. "I could've used a bit more rest."

A chuckle vibrated Hunter's throat. "So could I! Dave likes to tame wild horses in his sleep."

Bret yawned. "I think Jonathan was riding one last night."

"Oh?" Hunter rammed a bite of pancake into his mouth, then licked the syrup from his bottom lip. "And I suppose you took care of him?"

"I rocked him for an hour in the middle of the night."

Sipping his coffee, Hunter eyed him over the brim of his cup. "Isn't that supposed to be the joy of fatherhood?"

"Yes, and I wouldn't have missed it." He reached for his coffee cup. "I like to watch Jo when she feeds him." He grinned and looked a bit sheepish.

"You be wantin' pancakes, Misa Bret, or scrambled eggs with the bacon?"

"Both."

Alaina poured his coffee and served his plate. "Is Jo awake?"

"I think." He yawned. "We should be able to finish the framing for the third-story rooms today."

"I'm going to take an hour off this morning," Hunter said. "David and I are going to scrounge around in the shed for the frame of an old bed I saw. We're going to fix it."

Ellie eyed him. "Jonas be sayin' that he's gonna divide the cabin so you and Misa Fisher be havin' you's own rooms."

"Wonderful." Hunter shook his head. "Dave wrestles angels in his dreams."

David playfully punched Hunter's upper arm. "And you snore!"

When the men left, David hesitated in the doorway and looked back. His deep-blue eyes met Alaina's. Did she read pain in their depths? Why? What was tormenting him? If only he would confide in her.

David went with Hunter to locate the bed frame. The pieces were intact. "I'll clean this up, Hunter. Maybe you should join Bret at the building site. I think he wants to reinforce the roof trusses, and you're the climber."

"Right. John will help you lug this bed inside and set it up."

Jonas was in the cabin, measuring for the dividing wall. "I might not have enough lumber, so I'll start the boards two feet from the bottom. Eventually, we'll have enough scrap pieces to finish the job."

"A wall will be nice, but a separate bed is a must." David peered at the boards that formed the platform for a tick and tried to calculate how hard it would feel under his hap.

Jonas laughed. It was a low throaty sound. "Cassie is stuffing a tick with fresh straw. Ah's sure you'll be comfortable tonight."

"Thank you. I'd better get out there with Bret and Hunter before I get fired."

John tailed after him. "I told Mama I was gonna help. I don't wanna climb to the third floor of the frame, but I know how to nail down floorboards. I'll work on the first floor." He swiped a hand across his face. "Looks like that could be started today."

"We appreciate your help, John."

All morning, the sound of sawing and pounding echoed up the valley. By noon, one room had flooring. Maybe by tomorrow they would be able to place the wall joist on the third floor. Before long, they would be nailing side boards on the structure.

David figured that if the second and third floors weren't completed on the inside before winter, the family could live on the first floor. He shook his head. As determined as Bret was, barring any calamities, half the house would be completed by the first snowfall.

*And I'll be on my way to elsewhere, if not before.* David missed the head of the nail he was pounding and frowned. How could he leave before the right half of the house was completed? Bret had increased his plans to build more of the house because he had the aid of two men. *My leaving would complicate matters.* He sighed. Remaining was going to complicate his life. *No matter what I do, I'll be wrong!*

He glanced toward the cabin when he heard a shoe roll a pebble. Alaina approached with a pail of water. She offered Bret a drink, then Jonas and his sons took a turn. Finally, she stopped near David, but she kept her eyes averted as he drank. Her reaction made it difficult for him to swallow. *Her confusion, or hurt, is my fault.*

She sighed. "Dinner will be ready in fifteen minutes."

Hunter straightened. "What are we having?"

"Chicken soup with vegetables and fresh baked bread."

His hammer clattered to the floorboards. "I vote to get washed up. I'm as ravenous as a voracious wolf."

The next two days, David kept too busy to think. The lumber pile had dwindled. He counted the boards. "Looks like we'll need another load of lumber by tomorrow."

Bret nodded. "Nathan notified us that another load was on it's way. It should be in Staunton by tonight."

"Were you able to hire someone to deliver it?"

"No. But after the threats, I think we should go for it."

Hunter agreed. "You going with us, Dave?"

"Wouldn't miss it. If those malefactors attack again, we'll be ready for them."

They continued to measure, saw boards, and hammer nails until suppertime. David examined the calluses that were building on his hands. The early May sun had burned Hunter and Bret, but David had been exposed on the desert island earlier in the season, thus these harsh rays had little effect on his skin. July might be another story.

After the evening meal, David gathered the tools he needed and headed for the rose arbor. He cropped the twisting vines, then turned the ends inward. They could gradually be trained. Grabbing a shovel, he scraped the mud and decaying debris from the bench, then carried water from the stream to scrub the wood. The boards were in good condition, but had grayed from exposure. He hoped he could locate some paint and a brush. He would ask Jonas.

The light was beginning to fade when he finished trimming the long grass and weeds from around the bench. A sickle lay by his foot. He didn't have time to chop the weeds and high grass at the sides of the path. He would tackle that job later.

*Tomorrow we have to go for lumber and maybe get shot at.* While they were in Staunton, he would pick up the carpetbag he'd left at Virginia Station. He hoped no one had taken it. The first few days at Sunny Horizon, he'd had to wash his only clothing every night and dress in the morning when they were still damp and cold. Hunter had noticed and offered him an extra pair of jeans and a dark-blue barred shirt. He still had to launder them every night, if he wanted to wear clean clothing. But at least they had a full day to dry in the sun. Ellie had offered to wash them, but he figured the old woman had more than enough to do now. Alaina offered, but he refused to take advantage of her kindness.

Back at Hunter's cabin, David filled a large kettle with water and started a fire in the cookstove to heat it. The creek wasn't as cold as it had been, but it still made him shiver. He dragged the tub in from the back porch. A leisurely soak in warm water would soothe his sore muscles. He wished there was an easy remedy for his aching heart.

Jonas had finished the partition to just above eye level and to within a foot of the floor. *A private bath and a comfortable bed. What luxury!* Now if he could get Alaina to listen and understand. Was that too much to hope for?

How could she understand? *I don't understand myself!* He slipped his hand into his pocket, felt the circle of metal that nestled there, and cringed.

Activity had ceased, and Ellie's cabin had been silent for over an hour. Alaina flopped onto her back. The couch was comfortable, but she missed her own bed. No, this restlessness wasn't because she wasn't in a familiar bed. She wanted to be here with Jo. This feeling of desertion was all David Fisher's fault. Her misery was on account of him. She would leave, but she felt Jo needed her. "Oh, David, why did you come here?"

A shudder raked through her as she remembered going into Jo's bedroom and finding Jonathan not breathing. What if they had eaten supper without checking on the infant? That was too horrid to try to imagine. What if David hadn't been there? Had God sent him? If he hadn't been here, would Jonathan have choked to death? Tears smarted Alaina's eyes. Her heartache was slight compared to what her sister would suffer should anything happen to the baby.

Lacy whined. Alaina sighed. The puppy's night walks were becoming a habit. "I took you out just before dark." The pup was on her feet, her tail wagging.

"Oh, all right." She retrieved the leash, fastened it to the pup's collar and quietly opened the door. Picking Lacy up, she carried her several feet from the cabin and lowered her to the grass. Gazing upward, Alaina began to count stars. They seemed to vanish. There must be a lot of clouds. A lone star winked at her, then several seemed to turn on. The moon looked like a big smile in the sky. Was it making fun of her? No wonder. She was acting foolish. How could she be attracted to a man who acted pained every time he came near her? But why? No other man had ever treated her as though she had a plague.

Lacy apparently had done what she intended to, for she headed to the porch. Alaina opened the door, but the dog hesitated at the threshold to stare into the brush. A growl vibrated her throat, then she darted through the opening.

Yawning, Alaina flopped back onto the couch and wished for sleep. Her thoughts traveled back over the evening. She'd seen David strolling along the tree line, then he'd vanished up an old trail. She remembered the path, but had forgotten where it led. What was upstream that interested David? He'd been acting strangely the past few days. Could the man be up to something?

Gasping, Alaina sat up. She'd almost forgotten that Jo had suspected him of being part of the gang that attacked the lumber wagon. The men were going after another load tomorrow. Had David slipped away to meet with the other members of his gang? Did they plan to sabotage the wagon? Or ambush Bret? She shook her head, refusing to believe David capable of such deceit. Nevertheless, she intended to secretly investigate. "In the morning," she whispered. Dropping her hand, she rested her fingers on Lacy's back. The puppy had chosen the braided rug by the couch as her bed. Her even breathing seemed to comfort Alaina.

Morning came quickly. Alaina heard Ellie at the stove and got up to dress. She donned her bright yellow dress, then frowned. Had she chosen the frock because David had called her a ray of sunshine? She seized the fabric of the skirt, intending to rip it off over her head and toss it aside, but Ellie appeared in the doorway.

"Shall Ah fix waffles for breakfast?"

"That sounds good." She smiled as she toyed with the urge to stuff something sour in David's waffle. If he wanted to act like a pickle, maybe she'd could help him accomplish it. Stifling a giggle, she followed the old woman to the kitchen.

Instead of dribbling vinegar in David's waffle, she added a few of the wild strawberries she'd picked yesterday and drenched them with maple syrup. So much for plans.

After breakfast, Hunter harnessed the team to the wagon, and the men headed southward. Alaina stood on the porch and watched the wagon rumble away. Bret and Hunter sat on the seat, facing forward. David sat at the rear, facing backwards. He'd told her that he intended to keep an eye on their back trail so he could catch anyone who might try to sneak up on them from behind or from the side. Was that true, or was he pretending so his gang members could catch up without Hunter or Bret noticing them.

His eyes met hers. She swallowed. Forcing a smile, she waved. His smile sent her heart into spasms. Turning away was impossible. She stood statuesque until the wagon rounded a curve and was out of sight behind a row of pine.

Drawing a shaky breath, she went back inside and stacked the dirty dishes beside the sink. The water was hot, so she shaved soap into the dishpan. Her mind was as busy as her hands. How could she investigate David? What should she do first? What would he do if he became suspicious of her covert activities. The word *covert* made her grin. She had a lot to learn about spying before she would be as good as Tiffany had been during the war.

By late afternoon, the men hadn't returned. Alaina fought anxiety. Going to the porch, she sat on the banister and peered down the lane.

Jo, holding the baby with one arm, buttoned her blue blouse with one hand. "I still think it would have been wise to have Hunter ride out front to scout the road ahead."

Alaina frowned. "In such a case, he'd be a good target."

"I'm afraid they all will be, regardless." Jo sighed. "It was hard to watch them go, not knowing what they might have to face before they return."

"David is along to help."

A crease formed between Jo's brows. "I'm not so sure that his presence is an asset."

That thought had been gyrating through Alaina's mind all day, but she refused to voice it. "We'll pray for their safe trip." Jonathan made a cooing sound, drawing her attention. She smiled at him. "You're getting a double chin, little man." She touched his cheek.

Jo laughed. "He's got a big grin for his Aunt Alaina." She handed her the baby. "Ellie is peeling potatoes for supper. I'll help her, if you'll watch Jonathan."

"Sure. I'd rather play with him than labor at a hot stove."

The child's swing Joshua had put up for Angela still hung from an oak limb a few feet from the big house's veranda. Hunter had tested the ropes and said the swing was safe. Alaina loved to sit there to do the mending. She probably wouldn't admit it, but if no one was watching, she would swing high and feel as giddy as she had as a child. Would Jonathan enjoy swinging? He was becoming more alert and seemed bright and inquisitive.

"Would you like to swing with Aunt Alaina?" He waved his tiny fist. "I'll take that as a yes." Chuckling, she crossed the yard, Lacy running circles around her feet. The puppy was learning that getting too close was apt to trip someone, but she was still misjudging distance and needed watched.

At the swing, Alaina positioned herself on the small seat.

"Okay, little man, hang on." She wouldn't swing much with the baby, but as they swept back-and-forth a couple of feet, the baby seemed to study the overhead branches. A bird landed not far away. Eyeing it, Jonathan made a grunting noise. His reaction was probably coincidental, but Alaina preferred to think her nephew was brilliant.

Her focus drifted to the beginning of the path. She wanted to see what had drawn David. Jo wouldn't mind if she took the baby for a walk. Getting up, she strolled in that direction. Stopping beside the stream, she watched the water gurgle over rocks. Lacy lapped at it, then slopped across the stream and back, her belly hair getting soaked. She shook, then sniffed the rocks and weeds.

Curiosity lured Alaina to the path. "It looks a bit overgrown, Jonathan." He didn't seem to care. Shrugging, she headed into the trees. If the trail became obscured or rough, she would turn back.

Minutes later, she stopped to look around. It was easy to follow the trail. It had curved several times, but that was understandable because it followed within a few feet of the stream.

A shrub partially blocked the path ahead. The trees were becoming more dense and she couldn't see around the bend. Should she be watching for snakes? A shiver traveled down her spine. She could almost smell danger. She stopped when she heard a noise on the trail ahead. Barely breathing, she poised to run. If she did, would some animal chase her?

Lacy barked as a strange man stepped into view. His appearance startled Alaina, but it was the way he peered at her from under hooded eyes that sent rivulets of fear surging through her being. His tall, cadaverous form jerked as he walked. His right hand was missing, and the empty cuff flipped from side to side with his every step. His dark eyes met hers. She stifled a scream. Could she outrun him with Jonathan in her arms? She was going to try.

She whirled, but halted and stared. A second man stood on the center of the path, blocking her retreat. Lacy continued to bark, but her puppy yips wouldn't scare off a rabbit let alone two marauders.

"What have we here?" A chortle rattled in his throat. The rotund man, wearing a faded and tattered Federal uniform, stood balancing on one foot and tapping a peg leg on a rock. His pewter eyes roamed her frame, and he licked his lips.

Alaina looked back. The tall man, also wearing an old army jacket, slowly stepped toward her. *Which man poses the greatest threat?* She had to protect Jonathan! She intended to protect herself, too. Her mind whirled. How could she escape? Her eyes darted to both sides of the trail. *Which way should I run?* What could she use as a weapon? How could she fight with the baby in her arms?

## Twenty-Two

Alaina's heart drummed as both men stepped closer.

*God, please help me.* Jonathan must have sensed her fright, for he began to cry. *What might these ruffians do to the baby to have their way with me?*

"Jonas!" she called. The black man would come running if he heard her summons. Her tone made Jonathan jump and increase his wailing. The heavy man laughed. The flesh of his double chin jiggled. It would've been funny, had this situation not been so dire.

"Jonas!" Alaina yelled.

The skinny man's laugh whistled through his nose. His head bobbing like a pheasant's in tall grass, he stepped forward. At the same time, the obese man thumped a step toward her. Alaina panicked. Her eyes darted into the brush lining both sides of the path. Which way should she go to avoid briers? How could she protect the baby's delicate skin? *The Lord is my light and my salvation; whom shall I fear?* drifted through her mind. *The Lord is the strength of my life; of whom shall I be afraid?*

Footsteps raced down the path. "What's going on!"

*David!* She'd never been so happy to see anyone.

With clumsy movement, the heavy man turned on his peg leg to face David. The effort made him wheeze.

David glared at the man. "What are you doing?"

Alaina had never heard him speak in such an authoritative tone. Jonathan continued to cry. She tried to hush him.

"I asked you a question." David stepped closer to the rotund man.

The taller of the two stepped forward. The fabric of his thin jacket draped over his body, nearly displaying his skeletal structure. The Yankee-blue of his worn uniform had faded to a dull blue-gray, and the brass buttons, all but a tarnished one, were missing. "We just want permission to camp on your land."

"We aren't the owners." Moving to Alaina, David took the crying infant, rested him against his shoulder and patted his back. "You're all right, little man." He swung from side to side and hummed a measure of *Rock of Ages*. Jonathan calmed and began sucking on his fist. David's eyes sought Alaina's. "Did these two harm you?"

She shook her head. "It wasn't what they did. It was their insinuations that frightened me." Her voice quavered, although she struggled to appear brave.

David's attention went back to the men. "Who are you?"

The fat man grinned, showing a space left by a missing incisor. The remaining one was yellow with a tinge of green near the top. "Name's Harry Bunsen. My friend here is Jud Horner."

"You'd better be on your way."

Peg leg waved a thick arm. "Some hospitality. We're tired and hungry. Just wanted to camp here for a few days."

"You'll have to ask the owner."

The skinny man twitched his pointed nose. "And who might that be?"

"Breton Harris."

The obese man swiped a palm across his sweaty forehead, then dug under his missing top shirt button. "Where might we find him?"

David pointed. "Follow this path to the end. Let the women in the cabins alone. Breton Harris and another man will be unloading a wagon of lumber." He narrowed his eyes. "You two get out of line, and you'll answer to me."

"We mean no harm." After one last dig under his grimy collar, the fat man limped away. Jud followed, his pants flopping as though his legs were made of sticks. What was the bulge under his jacket? A revolver?

Alaina watched them until they were out of sight. Jo had told her that someone had shot at Bret their first day here. Had one of these men been the rifleman? Did they have camping gear? What about horses? Might they be planning to do Bret harm? Since she had the baby, did they assume she was Jo? Had they intended to hurt her to spite Bret? Blinking, she tried to stay the tears that threatened to spill over.

"Oh, Lainy." Moving to her, David cradled the baby in one arm and put the other around her shoulders. "You must have had quite a scare, but you're all right now."

Jonathan cooed contentedly. Alaina looked at him, then weakened and rested her head against the front of David's shirt. "I should be more brave."

"You didn't know what they might be up to, and you had the baby to consider." He patted her back.

He was so tall and strong. She felt so secure standing next to him. His head rested on her hair, then his lips moved across her forehead. A thrill she'd never experienced made something strange squiggle within her. She should pull away. Instead, she lifted her face to meet his gaze. His blue eyes shimmered. Did she read compassion on his features— or something else?

"Lainy." His voice was a whisper that caressed her spirit.

"We . . . should go back." Her voice broke, and a tear escaped and trickled down her face.

His lips moved to brush away the moisture. "Lainy. Oh, Lainy." His mouth touched hers, and his embrace tightened.

At first, the pressure of his lips was slight, but their kiss gradually intensified. Alaina's heart soared. One moment melted into another, but she was oblivious to time and space. She'd been kissed before, but never like this! His mouth moved tenderly over hers, igniting a fire within her. She was carried aloft by the passion that created an aura around them. She wanted the kiss to go on forever.

David pulled away slightly, but tightened his embrace and feathered kisses across her forehead. "Lainy . . . Lainy."

She listened to his thudding heart, and felt it against her palms. Her's was pounding, too. It was as though they were beating together, finding their own rhythm.

"Alaina!" Jo's voice rang.

Gasping, Alaina stepped back and covered her mouth with trembling fingers. Her legs weak, she sidestepped. What was she doing? Had her brain turned to sponge? She knew what had happened. *But do I really?*

Lacy raced down the path toward Jo's voice, her ears flopping.

"Alaina!" Jo's voice sounded frantic.

"She's all right!" David called. There was a quaver in his voice, too. "We have Jonathan."

"Where are you!"

Alaina took a deep breath. "We're coming!" She wondered if she could walk. Her legs threatened to buckle. David's kiss had made her lightheaded and she felt gushy inside. But it was more than that.

"Come on, Lainy." David put an arm around her and urged her down the path.

His touch sent tiny arrows of fire coursing through her veins. She longed to turn into his embrace and hold him close. What was the sense of dread that she couldn't define?

Footsteps swished the long grass on the path. David assumed Alaina's sister was coming to join them. "Jo's coming." He let his hand fall away. His fingers tingled from touching this delightful woman, and his lips burned from their kiss. He paused and let her move a few steps ahead of him. What had gotten into him? Why had he permitted his desire to rule his head? Alaina had felt the kiss, too. *It shouldn't have happened. It won't again!* His vow was made in earnest, but his heart rejected it.

They rounded a curve in the path. Jo raced toward them, her expression revealing panic. Her gray eyes traveled over her sister, then met David's. "What are you two doing out here?"

David wondered if passion was visible on his face. To camouflage his emotions, he smiled. "Alaina wasn't at the cabin when we returned. Ellie said she'd seen her walking toward the trees. I heard her call Jonas and came to see what was wrong."

Jo reached toward David for Jonathan, but her focus was on Alaina. "Did those two ruffians harm you?"

"No. They frightened me nearly to death, though. I didn't expect anyone, and they seemed to appear from nowhere." She shivered. "Then David came and took charge."

"Thank God they didn't hurt you." She eyed David. "Who are they?"

He shrugged. "The heavy one said their names were Harry Bunsen and Jud Horner."

"The names seem to fit their personality." Jo tilted her chin and peered at him through narrowed eyes. "They friends of yours?"

He shook his head. "I never saw them before."

Alaina flipped a thick strand of hair back over her shoulder. "I hope I never see them again."

"So do I." Jo turned to leave, then paused to glance back. "You coming, Alaina?" The look she gave her sister spoke volumes. She hesitated until Alaina joined her.

David stood and watched them retreat. His arms felt empty. A cavern formed in his heart, then widened. Was he emotionally tumbling into the expanse? Gripping a small tree, he closed his eyes. *I should've moved on the moment I laid eyes on Alaina.* Was it too late to salvage his feelings? Was it too late for Alaina? He would rather die than hurt her! The way she'd responded told him that if he wasn't careful, he would crush her. What should he do about it?

*What can I do?* He could disappear right now, but Bret was depending on him. He shook his head. If he left, and that was what he had to do when Bret no longer needed him, he would have to explain his problems to Alaina. He owed her at least that much. *Before I depart for lands unknown, I want her to know how much I love her.* He blinked. Nothing he'd so far experienced, and that was a lot, had shook the foundation of his being as much as leaving his sweet Alaina would. *But leave I must.*

He shook his head to try to clear his thoughts. He had to get a hold of his runaway emotions. Bret and Hunter were unloading the lumber. He should be aiding them. Clenching his fists and struggling to bring some semblance out of the chaos in his heart, he headed down the path. It was essential for Alaina to understand his reaction and the circumstances that would keep him from her. He would explain. Maybe tomorrow.

Alaina accompanied Jo to the porch and opened the door for her. Instead of going inside with her sister, she turned to peer at the end of the path. Where was David? Hadn't he been following them? She'd longed to look back, but she hadn't wanted him to see her expression and read her torment. Their kiss had elevated her to a lofty pinnacle that she hadn't known existed, then when he'd pulled away, her spirit had landed with a thud that had knocked the wind from her. What had the anguish in his indigo eyes meant? He'd felt the kiss, she knew he had. What was wrong?

When David came from the trees, he didn't look up. His labored strides displayed his dismay. She opened her mouth to call to him, but no sound came. If he didn't want to look at her, she wasn't going to make him. Was he playing her for a fool, or was he hurting, too. Why? If he cared, why didn't he say so?

Without glancing her way, he approached the men and began hoisting boards. For a time, she watched, her heart a lead weight. Swallowing hard and struggling to get her emotions under control, she entered the kitchen. Ellie stood at the cookstove stirring something in a big pot.

Alaina approached. "What can I do to help?"

The old woman turned. It looked like she was going to ask questions, but she only sighed. "Ah's fixin' dinner. You wants to slice the bread?"

Nodding, Alaina mechanically sawed the knife back and forth through the loaf and piled slices on a plate. "I'll set the table." She fumbled one of Jo's good dishes and nearly dropped it. Clutching the pile of saucers, she moved to the table. She had to get her emotions back on an even keel before she broke something. *Besides my heart.* Jo had been right about David Fisher. *Why didn't I listen?*

As she worked, she pondered. This wasn't over yet. Mr. Fisher had some explaining to do. He couldn't kiss her that passionately, then just turn and walk away as though nothing had happened. She would confront him. If not today, she would tomorrow. Her fingers clenched. *You're not going to get away with this, Sir David!*

The back door opened. Jay tottered into the kitchen. Ellie hurried to pull out a chair for him. "Ah knows you likes a rocker. It now be in the living room."

He grinned at her. "Ah's fine. Ah was just lookin' over the garden spot. It be needin' plowed."

Alaina grabbed a handful of forks. "Cassie said that since David was busy building the house, Jonas would start the plowing tomorrow."

The old man yawned. "That be good. It be gettin' a mite late to be plantin'."

"Humph. You hain't gonna be doin' no plantin'. You's gonna be takin' it easy for a few days."

He chuckled and his voice cracked. "Yo still be as sassy as yo always be."

"Humph. Ah gots to be lookin' after you. You hain't never be lookin' out for you's self."

"Oh my Ellie. Ah be havin' my hands full just lookin' after yo!" He thumped his cane on the floor as though to punctuate his statement, but humor danced in his eyes.

Jo swept into the kitchen. "Jonathan's sleeping. I'll help with the finishing touches." Moving to the stove, she peered into the bubbling pot. "That potato soup smells delicious. Whatever spices and herbs you used are sending delightful aromas through the entire cabin!"

The old woman grinned. "Ellie be havin' secrets. Before

Ah dies, Ah's gonna tell you about herbs."

David grabbed the last board. "That was quite a load." He eyed the structure. "We'll need more though, since we're building half the house."

"I'm determined." Bret leaned against a corner stud and swiped his arm across his face. "I don't know about you fellows, but I'm ready for dinner."

Hunter chuckled. "I've been ready for an hour." He studied David. "How about you?"

"I can always eat." Was that true? His stomach was tied in knots. He couldn't stop thinking about Alaina. How was he going to go into the kitchen and not look at her? How could he face her after the amorous moment they'd shared? She needed an explanation, but it was going to be nearly impossible. He'd yearned for that kiss, and it had sent him soaring into a delightful world of swirling passion and wonder. Instead of it fulfilling him, it only made him desire more than ever to kiss her again. Over and over! *Now and forever!*

Bret and Hunter went to the cabin. Bret stopped on the porch and turned. "Come on, Dave. Those boards can wait until after we eat."

Taking a long breath, David straightened his shoulders and followed the men inside. He sat at the table without glancing at Alaina. He could feel her eyes on him. Being in her presence had always been delightful, but after their passionate exchange, it was difficult to face her. He'd never been so torn. He wanted to jump up and take her in his arms. He longed to press his lips on hers. He yearned to feel her arms around him. He wanted to pound the table with his fist.

When Alaina set the plate of bread on the table, she rested a hand on his shoulder. Her touch sent waves of longing surging through his being. She walked away, but his shoulder felt warm where her fingers had been. Breton said a blessing. David closed his eyes, but his mind was elsewhere. He couldn't seem to help it.

Jo served them steaming bowls of potato soup. Bits of ham floated amid dried green peas and slices of carrot. The mixture smelled like ambrosia. David figured he was more hungry than he felt. Mechanically, he lifted the filled spoon to his mouth. He tried to enjoy the flavors, but his aching heart wouldn't let him concentrate on anything except the lovely girl across the table. Was she looking at him? Slowly, he lifted his eyes and became enveloped in a warm-brown hue that sent his heart spiraling out of control again. He tried to swallow the vegetables in his mouth, but his throat constricted until he thought he was going to choke.

Springing to her feet, Alaina raced from the room. Jo jumped up and followed her.

Bret stared after them. "What's going on with those two?"

"Humph." Ellie grabbed the coffee pot and refilled the cups. "There be somethin' goin' on that you men hain't never gonna understand."

David stared into his cup as the old woman filled it. *Bret and Hunter might not understand, but I sure do!*

Jay dribbled a few drops of soup on the front of his shirt. Grabbing his napkin, he dabbed at the spot and frowned.

"You don't be mindin' that spot." Ellie patted his hand. "Ah's gonna be washing clothes this afternoon."

Jay gave her backside a gentle swat. "Ah's worse than the baby."

Ellie laughed. "You waits till wee Jonathan be at the table. He gonna be makin' lots of messes."

David enjoyed the humorous banter between the old couple. It was easy to interpret their abiding love for each other. Where would he be when he was Jay's age? Where would Alaina be? *And with whom?* The thought pierced through his middle like a hot sword. Finishing his soup, he stood. "I'm going to get back to work. I have a lot to do to catch up on what I wanted to accomplish today."

A scream rent the air.

"That be Cassie!" Ellie headed for the door.

David dashed through the opening ahead of her.

## Twenty-Three

Cassie ran across the yard toward the building site. Fifteen-year-old John stood by the foundation, fright branded on his face.

David raced forward to see what had terrified the woman. When he saw Ben's crumpled body in the cellar of the new house, his heart nearly stopped. "What happened?"

"He slipped." John swallowed. "We just wanted to help."

"Help?" Not waiting for John's explanation, Cassie climbed down to her thirteen-year-old son and knelt beside him in the dirt. "He isn't conscious!"

"Don't move him." David jumped to the dirt and felt for the boy's pulse. "He's alive. We need a stretcher. Tell Hunter to get the cot from our cabin."

Tears streamed down the black woman's face as she eyed John. "Go!"

He ran.

Moments later he returned with Hunter and the cot. The boy looked bewildered as he lowered the cot to David. "Ben is so sure-footed. He never falls."

Hunter joined David. "Where was he when he fell?"

John pointed to a first-floor ceiling beam. "He slipped from up there. He grabbed that two-by-eight, but couldn't hang on. He hit the flooring joist and tried to grab it, but he slipped past it and fell through the open stairway into the cellar." Fright made the boy hiccup.

Bret appeared, glanced at the beam, then looked down at David. "Is he all right?"

"I don't know yet."

"He has to be all right!" John looked like he was going to cry, although he probably hadn't shed tears since he'd been a small child. "I think he hit his head."

David ran a hand along Ben's spine. "His back isn't broken. His neck is all right. Thank God." He continued his examination. "His shoulders are fine. His arms are all right." When he examined the boy's legs, he cringed. "His left leg is fractured in two places."

"Thank God this part of the cellar is dirt, and he landed where there was no building debris." Hunter placed the cot beside Ben and helped David ease the boy onto it.

Ben moaned.

Cassie reached out to touch her son's shoulder. "He's coming to."

"Take it easy, Ben," David said. "We're going to get you out of here and fix your leg."

Jonas appeared. "He okay?"

"He's injured, but we're bringing him up."

The black man reached over the foundation stones. "Ah'll take an end of the cot."

Hunter lifted his end to where Jonas could grasp it, then climbed to ground level and turned. David hoisted his end to meet Hunter's fingers, then climbed out and hurried after the men. They carted the cot to Cassie's porch.

Cassie followed, then rushed ahead to open the door for them. The men strode into the large center room that served as a kitchen and living area. David noticed a bedroom to the left. Cassie directed them to the right. The second bedroom was divided into two. Dresses hung in one, denoting that the three daughters shared the space. In the other, a slingshot, two canteens, a hatchet and a bow and arrow hung on the wall, signifying this was John and Ben's quarters.

David eyed the bunk beds. "Leave him on the cot. I need room to work."

John jumped to the top bunk, apparently to be out of the way. Cassie pressed herself into a corner.

David turned to Jonas. "I need a splint. See what you can find among the lumber scraps." He turned to the boy's mother. "We'll need clean cloths to make bandages." He glanced at Hunter. "You'll have to help me set this break."

Hunter's eyes widened. "I don't know anything about broken bones!"

"Just follow my instructions." David hoped no one asked him how he knew what to do. The knowledge just seemed to be somewhere in the recesses of his brain. No matter. Ben needed him, and he would do his best.

Eyeing John, he sighed. "I think it would be best if you go to help your father."

John shook his head. "If that's not an order, I'm stayin'."

Maybe seeing what the accident had caused would encourage him to be more responsible in the future. He told Hunter what to do. When David straightened Ben's leg, he screamed.

Cassie raced into the room, her face drawn. "What happened?"

"I'm sorry, Cassie. There was no way to set the break without hurting him."

She nodded.

He wrapped the injury and fastened Ben's leg to the boards Jonas brought. "He should use the cot instead of his straw tick. It's important to keep his leg from moving."

Unshed moisture glistened in Ben's dark eyes. "I couldn't move it if I tried!"

Cassie eyed him. "Just what were you doing?"

"Trying to help. We thought maybe we could get one of the braces on the ceiling and surprise Mister Bret."

Cassie sighed. "You surprised more than Mister Bret."

"I slipped! I never slip."

"You shouldn't climb without one of the men present." She glared at John. "You should've known better, John. You're the oldest, and Ah depend on you to have more sense."

"I'm sorry."

"Not as sorry as you're gonna be. Until Ben is back on his feet, you will be doing his chores as well as your own."

"But I won't have any time left to help with the building."

"You heard my decree, young man. Ah'll have no back talk."

"Yes Ma'am." His answer was quiet, but resolute. Slipping from the bed, he moved toward the open door. "I better get started."

David sighed. "We need to get back to work, too."

Cassie followed David and Hunter to the porch. "Thank you so much." She grinned. "I'll bake apple pies for supper."

David smiled at her. "That's what I call a real payment."

"Hey!" Bret stood on a ladder that was propped precariously on a board nailed to two floor supports.

David hurried toward him. "Is something wrong?"

Bret climbed down and held out his hand. "What's this look like to you?"

"I don't see anything." On closer inspection, he noticed moisture on the ends of Bret's fingers. "What is that?"

"That's what I'd like to know."

One swipe across the man's hand deposited the substance on David's fingers. Rubbing them together, he gasped. "It's oily! Where did it come from? How did it get up there?" He craned his neck to look at the beam in question. Puzzled, he climbed the ladder to get a closer look. It wasn't difficult to figure what had happened. He smeared his fingers across the beam. He could smell the substance.

"This isn't oil! It's rancid lard! Someone would've had to deliberately smear it up here, probably to cause one of us to slip and fall." David frowned. "By whom? And why?" He climbed down. "We're going to have to be more cautious."

Hunter scowled. "Do you suppose one of those two who frightened Alaina could've done this?" He looked at Bret. "Do you remember seeing either of them before?"

"No." He wiped the remainder of the grease from his fingers with a rag and tossed it to a foundation stone, then made a fist. "Are we going to have to post a guard?"

"When could someone have slipped in here to do this?" Hunter took his turn at climbing up to examine the beam. "It's lard all right. It smells like it's been around for ages."

David frowned. "It wasn't up here when we went in to eat. Whoever did this is pretty brazen. If one of us would've glanced out a window, we would've seen the culprit."

"We have no choice." Bret slapped his thigh. "We have to take turns guarding this place."

"Ben was fortunate that he only fractured his leg." David shuddered. "He could have been killed."

"That reminds me." Hunter eyed him and shook his head. "You set that break like an old pro. How and where did you learn to do that?"

In an effort to appear nonchalant, David grinned. "During the war, soldiers learned how to do a lot of things."

"Did you work with a doctor?"

"I had to learn it somewhere. A man learns a lot in a hurry when he has to." He picked up a flooring board. "I think we should put flooring down on the first floor and cover the cellar opening before we do anymore climbing." He glanced at Bret. "What about the fireplaces? You know how to repair them?"

"No. And someone needs to inspect the standing chimneys. They look sound, but there was a lot of heat in this place when it burned. I wrote to a man in Harper's Ferry. Hunter knows him and said he was an expert bricklayer and stonemason. He's finishing another job. I expect him to show up in two or three weeks."

During the afternoon, the men worked without a break. Jo brought the pail of drinking water twice. Ellie came once. Alaina didn't show her lovely face. David increased his pace. The harder he worked, the less time he would have to ponder his dilemma. Still his heart ached. The sun beat down on his back. Hunter had been right. The water in the cool stream, although it was warmer than it had been, would feel refreshing tonight.

Jonas came from the shed and stopped at the house. "I'll keep an eye on things while you fellows eat supper."

"Thanks." Bret stretched. "We'll take turns guarding tonight."

"I'll take first watch." Hunter wiped sweat from his brow. "How about you, Dave. You want second watch or third?"

David looked at Bret. "Which would be best for you?"

"Third."

"All right. I'll take second."

Jonas nodded. "And I'll stay out here while you fellows eat meals."

The aroma of baking bread wafted to David. His stomach growled. He wished he had a watch. At least now he had his carpetbag. He'd picked it up when they were in Staunton for the lumber. It would be a joy not to have to wash clothes every night.

When Jo called them in for supper, Jonas came to sit on a foundation beam. He had a cup of coffee in one hand and three cookies in the other.

Anxiety swirled inside David as he stepped onto Ellie's porch. How would Alaina react this evening? The hurt look on her face during dinner had gripped his heart and tore at his soul. He was miserable, too. *My misery is my own doing. Lainy's is my fault.*

He took his usual place at the table. Alaina wasn't in the kitchen. He glanced through the doorway into the living room. She wasn't on the couch. She had to be in the bedroom with Jonathan. Maybe she was rocking him to let Jo and Bret have a relaxed meal together. He hoped the couple enjoyed it. He certainly wasn't. The venison was cooked to perfection, but he couldn't savor the taste. The buttery lima beans seemed to turn to sawdust in his mouth. The whipped potatoes could have been balls of cotton the way they stuck in his throat, although they were as fluffy as a cloud.

Finally mustering courage, he turned to Jo. "Where's Alaina?"

"She wants to finish her sewing before she eats."

That was one of the lamest excuses for missing a meal that he'd ever heard. But if she felt anything like he did, her not eating was understandable. This couldn't go on. He had to resolve this situation. How?

"Another delicious meal, Ellie." Bret stood. "That should hold us until quitting time." He bent to kiss Jo, then headed for the door. "Jonas is waiting to go in for his supper."

Jo picked up some of the dishes and carried them to the dishpan. "Why is he waiting for you to get back to hammering before he goes in to eat?"

"I'll tell you tonight." Bret bent to ruff Lacy's coat, then he stepped onto the porch and took a deep breath. "It will be more comfortable to work this evening."

"Yes, but the sun will set before we finish laying the flooring in the first room if we procrastinate any longer." He playfully poked David. "What's with you? You look like you were forced to eat brambles with the goat."

David forced a smile. "I was wondering what our assailant might try next."

"He's not going to get a chance to try anything!"

Darkness fell before they finished putting the last few flooring boards in place in what would be the kitchen.

David straightened. "If we do much more, we'll have to light a lantern. We'd make a good target, and it would be impossible to see someone taking aim."

"Right." Bret frowned. "A man could get pretty close before we detected him. Let's quit for tonight."

"I'm for that." Hunter rubbed the back of his neck.

As David passed Ellie's cabin, he slowed his pace to see if he could catch a glimpse of Alaina. She was making herself scarce. Other than going to a window and peering in, he evidently wasn't going to see her. Disappointment washed over him.

After a quick bath in the stream, he stretched out on his bed and stared at the rafters, deep in thought. For the hundredth time, he berated himself for remaining here. Leaving was becoming more and more essential, but Bret needed him more than ever. Now that Sunny Horizon could be attacked, Bret needed every man he could get. He sighed. Why was life so complicated? He hoped he would be able to sleep. Second watch would come too soon, even if he could get to sleep. He closed his eyes. Thoughts of Alaina crowded his mind and prevented slumber.

Alaina sat on the couch. What Bret had told them tonight had her nerves on edge. Again, she looked out the window to see if Hunter was all right. He seemed to be hiding near a bush. Why? Had he seen or heard something strange? Her heartbeat quickened. What if something happened to him? It had been difficult getting over Luke's death, and he'd been fighting in the army. What would it be like for a brother to be killed in peacetime by a rotten sniper?

She yawned. She couldn't help Hunter by staying awake. Stretching out, she covered herself with a thin quilt and closed her eyes. She had to get some sleep so she could help Jo tomorrow.

A thought streaked through her mind and she gasped. David was to take second watch. He'd be out there in the middle of the night. She thought about how she'd avoided him at supper by staying in the bedroom. What had she been trying to prove? It hadn't helped. She'd strained to hear every word. David had spoken only when someone had asked him a question. His answers had been short and sounded clipped. Was she making him as miserable as he made her? Did he care the same way she did? What was the problem between them that seemed insurmountable? If only he'd talk to her.

She lay staring out the window at the moon, tormented by her thoughts. Like a foggy ghost, slumber drifted over her. Her rest was punctuated with disturbing dreams, but fatigue finally dragged her into deeper sleep.

A Rebel yell and galloping horses shocked her awake. It was still dark. At first she thought she'd been dreaming, but she was awake, and she could still hear the horses.

Another cry rent the air. David yelled from somewhere out front. Bret raced from the bedroom. Alaina jumped up to follow him, then realized she was wearing her nightgown.

David yelled again. Alaina's pulse drummed in her temples. "Are we under attack?"

## Twenty-Four

Bret raced to the door and jerked it open. Alaina seized the back of his shirt. "Wait!" He yanked free.

"Bret!" Jo hurried from the bedroom, her face white.

David met Bret on the porch. "There was no damage. Three men on horseback galloped their mounts to within a few feet of the new house. One of them shot a flaming arrow. It stuck in an upright support on the second story, but it went out right away. I think it was just a scare tactic."

Bret frowned. "Did you recognize any of them?"

"I think they were the same three who attacked the lumber wagon and wounded the driver."

Alaina stood inside the door in a shadow where David couldn't see her. A longing she had never experienced gripped her. Dressed in her nightgown or not, she had an urge to race across the yard and fling herself into his arms. *I'm not a hussy! What's getting into me?*

Bret glanced toward the third cabin. "Is Hunter awake?"

"I don't think so. When I came out to take second watch, he looked exhausted."

"It's nearly time for third watch, so I'll get dressed and join you."

"I'm wide awake. You get another hour or so of sleep."

Bret yawned. "Well . . . I'd like to."

"If anything suspicious happens, I'll call you." He rounded the foundation and slipped into the night.

Alaina went back to the couch, but sleep evaded her. When she heard Bret's snore, she got up gingerly and put on a dark blue dress. It was after two o'clock, but Mr. Fisher wasn't the only one who was wide awake. *And my not being able to sleep is his fault. He owes me an explanation.*

Lacy jumped up and beat her to the door. Her tail thumped against the door frame, and she pranced, displaying her excitement.

"Not this time, girl," Alaina whispered. "You're not going to get into a habit of going out in the middle of the night."

The puppy's whines softened and she woofed.

"Sh." Alaina was glad she couldn't see her pleading eyes. She opened the door, careful that the puppy didn't slip by her, then closed it quickly. Lacy sniffed the crack at the threshold and scratched the floorboards.

"Be quiet." Her voice was a whisper, but her tone stern. The dog obeyed. She hesitated a moment to make sure that Lacy had gotten the message.

At the banister, her eyes searched the shadows. Nothing moved. Where were the men who staged the attack? Would they return? What might they do if they caught her out here? Peering into the night, she detected a shadow by the trees. Remaining hidden by the darkness, she studied the form. His gait was familiar. She watched him a moment longer, then lifting her skirt above the dew moistened grass, she headed across the yard.

Hearing footsteps, David turned. "Lainy! What are you doing out here?"

Without hesitating, she moved to stand before him. She was like a lovely dream. Had he fallen asleep during his watch? If he reached out, would she vanish? Unable to resist, he lifted his hand and touched her cheek. Her skin was soft and warm. She hadn't answered his question. Did it matter? What had he asked her?

"David, we must talk. There are things I don't understand."

Her voice was as gentle as a summer breeze, and her words caressed him like the velvety petals of a rose. He knew he should encourage her to return to the cabin. Instead, he tenderly clasped her fingers. "Lainy, there's something I must explain."

"I know." She moved nearer.

In another moment, she was in his arms. Her face lifted for his kiss. "Oh, Lainy." His embrace tightened as his lips found hers. This time, not cradling Jonathan, he could hold her with both arms. Was the ecstasy double? How could it be. Their kiss was long and amorous. When they broke away, they were both out of breath. "I love you," he whispered, pressing his face against her sweet scented hair. "I can't love you, but I do. Oh, Lainy, I do."

"I love you, too, David." She rested her face on his chest. "I just wanted you to know that there's nothing we can't solve, if we try."

"Oh my darling. How I wish you were right." He kissed her again. "I want to keep you out here with me all night, but if your brother or sister discover us, you'll be in trouble, and I'll get shot." He continued to hug her. How could he let her go? How could he not?

"I'm old enough to make my own decisions, Sir David."

She kissed his neck, driving him to distraction. "Those men could come back and destroy the entire house and all the cabins and I wouldn't know it." He feathered kisses down the side of her face. "Where were you during supper?"

"Being foolish."

Again, his lips found hers. He yearned for this moment to go on forever, but he couldn't let this happen. Not until he had his life back in order. But was that possible? If only the mountain of frustration and confusion could be dissolved. He fought to shove the past into oblivion, but it pressed in on him from all sides. He pulled away. "Please go back inside. I'll see you in the morning."

"I'll go in if you promise that we can talk tomorrow."

"I'll try."

"That's not good enough. I want you to promise."

A grin tugged on his lips. "I promise to try."

"I guess I'll have to be satisfied with that." She narrowed her eyes in the moonlight. "For now." Turning, she walked away.

He watched her go. His heart followed her. Why would God permit him to have such a deep and abiding love for Alaina if he had to leave her? What kind of destiny was this?

The rest of his watch was quiet. Maybe one ride per night was all their adversaries could handle. He yawned. The first part of the night he hadn't been able to sleep. He needed rest.

The cabin door opened, and Bret stepped onto the porch.

David crossed the yard to join him. "All is well. If you're here to take over, I'll get some sleep."

"I'm here, but I'm not sure I'm awake."

"You'll wake up in a hurry if those ruffians gallop in." Chuckling, David headed for his cabin. He undressed on his side of the partition and tried not to disturb Hunter. The man was sleeping soundly. Once in bed, David took a deep breath and closed his eyes. A vision of Alaina formed before him. He took her in his arms and drifted into sleep, but the unknown reached out, seized him, and dragged him into a quagmire of restlessness and torment.

He stood statuesque as the ship drifted further away. It hadn't mattered how much he'd yelled and waved. He stared until he could no longer see the vessel. *So close*, he thought, yet it was as though it had never been. If only he had a flare or could start a fire. What would he burn? His shirt? The small trees at the end of the island? The few palm fronds were his only protection from the searing sun. If only he'd been able to keep his raft. But would he burn it? Or would he have tried to sail to the treetops in the distance? *And maybe feed the sharks.* The least he could have done was use the raft for a lean-to to shade himself from the sun.

His arms hung limp by his sides. His shirt dangled from one hand, and his eyes smarted from strain. If only he could devise a distress signal that would attract attention, should another ship pass his island.

Frustration pressed heavily on his heart as he trudged across the sand toward the far point. He slung his shirt over one shoulder and clutched his empty bottle. Were ships a rare sight in these parts--or had the Lord shown him that there was a chance of a rescue? Would there be another vessel tomorrow?

Hope began to bud. He'd only been on this island for two hours. One ship had passed him by. It was gone, but his thirst was more acute. His tongue was swelling, and it felt as though it were going to stick to the roof of his mouth.

"I need to scout the entire island." How many poisonous snakes or insects were here to torment him? He looked carefully as he neared the clump of bushes and small palms.

Rounding a large gray rock, he stopped and stared, his mouth agape. A tiny spring bubbled from between the smaller rocks, pooled in a three-foot shallow basin, then trickled over the rim and tumbled down a rocky incline to the sea. He wrestled with the urge to fling himself onto his stomach and gulp. He must test to see if the water was salt or fresh.

His bruised knees being tender, he crouched and dipped his hand into the clear water. Ripples trailed his fingers. Cupping his hand, he brought a tablespoon of liquid to his cracked lips. His tongue sampled the moisture and found it sweet. Closing his eyes, he permitted a mouthful to trickle down his throat. Stretching onto his stomach, he lowered his face to the pool and drank, slowly at first, then he gulped several mouthfuls.

He shook his head, but his brain felt like mud. In an effort to clear his thinking, he lowered his face into the water and held it there until he needed air. He lifted his head, refreshed, but no closer to a solution. Droplets ran down his face. His tongue lapped the ones that touched his lips.

He pushed himself into a sitting position, bent his legs, propped his elbows on his knees, and braced his chin on his hands. A large piece of driftwood lay nearby. *Firewood*, he thought. He could start a fire by using the thick bottom on his bottle to magnify the sun's rays, but he couldn't keep feeding a blaze without soon depleting his fuel supply. If he spotted a ship, could he get wood burning in time for the blaze or smoke to be detected? He inspected the driftwood. It was too wet to burn.

A hope for escape began to form as he thought about using the log to help him sail to the trees on the horizon. Trying it, he discovered the log was too water-soaked to float. *Besides, what about the sharks?*

Rounding a huge rock near the crest, he noticed a recess under it. The opening was about three feet high, four feet wide, and it extended back in about eight feet. "My humble abode," he mused. Bending, he examined the area for snakes or biting insects. There was nothing alive that he could see. "No wonder!" If a creature had a choice of a habitat, why would it choose this deserted island?

As night fell, David lugged the log closer to the cave opening and hollowed a shallow depression in the sand that would serve as his bed. He spread his shirt so it would be under his back and head. The sand was soft to walk in, but he didn't want it in his hair. He rested his head and prayed that sleep would come quickly and blot out his torment. On the lee side of the island he was protected from the wind, and the log close by his side afforded a sense of protection. Hunger gnawed at his insides. Tomorrow, he would have to devise a way to fish. He had a ball of string. Could he fashion a fishhook with his pocketknife? Maybe he could carve one out of the tongue depressor in his pocket. A vision of a fish sizzling over a fire crept into his thoughts. His stomach growled. Closing his eyes, he prayed.

Words from a Psalm nestled in his heart, as soothing as a pleasant breeze. *Wait on the Lord: be of good courage, and he shall strengthen thine heart: wait, I say, on the Lord.*

Each new morning, David took his pocketknife and carved another nick in the palm near his cave. Fish avoided his makeshift hook, but he managed to catch a crab and a number of other small sea creatures that he couldn't name, but they made a meal, scant as it was.

On the eighth day, David spotted a second vessel, but it was too far away for anyone to be able to see him. Long days gave him time to read Scripture, and nights offered hours to think and pray. He had the assurance that God loved him. It was enough to give him peace in his heart, but he continued to struggle over how to escape his island prison.

The morning brought a different threat. Sitting on the beach, David studied the sky. The dark clouds that charged across the darkening dome multiplied his distress. The wind velocity rose. Waves slapped angrily on the beach.

He clasped his hands in prayer. "God, protect me through the storm." A verse he'd read from Psalm 91 that morning came to his mind. *He that dwelleth in the secret place of the most High shall abide under the shadow of the Almighty.*

Even in his present circumstances, David trusted God, yet he longed to have his questions answered. Where was he, and why was he here? Were there people on the land of the distant treetops? He frowned. He wished he could remember what had happened. Had he been traveling? If so, to where? Had he been fishing? If so, with whom? Surely his friends would be searching for him.

He rubbed his whiskered chin in thought. His faith was strong in the midst of trouble, and he thanked God for his oasis, yet he yearned for an end to this desolation.

He opened his book. His focus fell on Psalm 34. He scanned, then paused to read verse fifteen. "The eyes of the Lord are upon the righteous, and his ears are open unto their cry." Skipping a few lines, he read, "The Lord heareth and delivereth them out of all their troubles."

The sky turned gray. Angry clouds charged across the darkening dome. The wind whipped his hair and battered the palm fronds. Vibrating fingers of lightning seared from the heavens as though reaching for an object on which to avenge its rage. Thunder boomed, the sound creating a vibration in the rocks under David's feet. Soon, waves began to crash on the beach, sending spray and foam several feet into the air. Huge drops of rain spattered David's face. He wrapped his book of Psalms in the oilcloth, but what could he do to protect himself from the deluge? Even on the lee side, the wind ripped at his clothing and whipped his hair. One gust seized his shirt, ripped it out of his hand, and hurled it nearly over the edge. Scrambling after it, he put it on.

To protect his driftwood, he dragged the log to the highest point on the island. The cave would shield him from rain, but if he sat inside and there was a tidal wave, he wouldn't see it coming. He would be whisk out to sea again.

An hour later, the storm still raged. Lightning vibrated another set of fiery tentacles before the previous explosive sound of thunder rumbled into the distance. Waves grew larger and pounded the beach as though determined to force it into submission. Before long, they were breaking over the rocks at the edge of the slope to the ocean. David trusted God, but his heart pounded. Would he be struck by a bolt of lightning or whisk out to sea by a giant wave?

The storm's deafening! he thought as another wave whooshed in with a mighty force and crashed on the rocks near the crest, sending a swish of ankle-deep water over his feet. Rain lashed him with huge drops.

My bottle, David thought. It would be worthless elsewhere, but here it was his only possession. *And the only way I have to start a fire.* Squeezing between two waist-high rocks, he retrieved the bottle, thankful that the last wave hadn't stolen it. He dug under the rock that would afford the most protection, shoved the bottle in, buried it and rolled a rock over the top.

Standing, he leaned against a palm tree and glanced across the ocean. His eyes widened. A mountain of water rose from the raging surface and was approaching fast. It was difficult to gage its height, but the way the foam curled at the top made it look fierce. "Lord Jesus," David prayed, "I am in your hands." He assumed he was about to be ushered into glory on the crest of a tempestuous wave. The peace of Christ comforted him as he watched the approach of possible death. Jesus words, *"Into thy hands I commend my spirit,"* flooded his mind, yet he knew he should do what he could to protect himself.

A palm grew between two waist-high boulders. David had lost enough weight that his belt could encircle both his waist and the palm. He had just enough time to fasten his buckle and fill his lungs with air. The wave slammed him with a power that David thought might dislodge the rocks. Even between them, the mass of water struck with enough force to knock the air from him. He felt crushed. As the wave retreated, it yanked him as though determined to drag him from the island. His arms felt numb. Had he lost his grip? Had his belt failed to hold? Was he now a captive of the sea? His lungs burned and lights exploded behind his eyes. How much longer could he hold his breath?

A fist banged against the partition that separated the cabin into two rooms. "Hey, Dave?" Hunter's voice boomed. "What's going on over there?"

Shocked awake, David gasped for air. "Thanks for waking me."

"You were thrashing around as though you were wrestling a bear." Hunter yawned. "Maybe you should see a doctor."

"I probably need a psychiatrist!"

"Well, try to get back to sleep so we can both get a little rest." Hunter groaned. "If building the house doesn't kill me, the attackers will." He muffled a chuckle in his pillow. "If I don't have a heart attack from lack of sleep!"

Mumbling an apology, David closed his eyes. He couldn't take much more of this either. His dreams weren't all bad. It's just that so much of the time he relived his weeks on the deserted island, and his dreams forced him to go back. He hated it. During his isolation, he'd read Psalms, tried to concentrate on the positive, and thanked God for sustaining him. Eventually his prayers had been answered when someone on a fishing boat saw him and sailed to the island to rescue him. His needs had been supplied, but the loneliness had nearly driven him crazy.

Fatigued, he suffocated a groan. If his dreams didn't stop, he would ask Jonas to help him build a place in the shed. It wasn't right for him to continue to disturb Hunter's rest. Of course the horses had to work during the day, too. Would his dreams keep the animals awake?

Drawing a deep breath, he thought about Alaina. That was one dream that he wished he could relive every night. Their relationship was impossible, but thinking about her, he drifted into a deep sleep.

The sound of ocean waves whooshed against the beach. David looked out across the sea. A huge wave humped like a living thing and rushed toward him. Gripping the palm tree, he took a deep breath and held it. The wave hit, and he battled not to suck in water.

Just before unconsciousness claimed him, a breeze blew against his face. He gulped air, then choked. His arms were bruised and scraped, but otherwise, he thought he was all right. Unfastening his belt, he searched the ocean. He didn't have enough strength to fight another wave of that size and velocity. Being between the two boulders had saved his life.

*No!* God had spared him. *There must be a purpose for my existence.* Several minutes apart, two more waves crashed across the island, but they weren't as powerful as the first one had been. He wondered how wet his book of Psalms had become. Reaching to his pocket, he gasped. The giant wave had snatched it from him. Overwhelmed with loss, he knelt and gripped the gold cross still fastened around the palm.

It seemed like hours before the lightning ceased and the thunder hushed. Eventually the wind gave up its relentless siege, and the sea calmed. The clouds departed, permitting the sun to caress the island. The storm had taken some of the fronds from the palms, and there was scarcely enough left to afford a shelter. Exhausted, he flopped belly-down on the sand, dropped his head on his soaked shirt, and slept.

Gnawing hunger woke him. His tongue seemed thick and his lips burned. Sitting up, he surveyed the damage to his refuge. The large piece of driftwood was gone, but the end of the storm had deposited several smaller chunks along the beach. They would dry in the sun, something the log hadn't had time to do.

Going to the spring, he bent to drink, but spit the water on the sand. The waves that had crashed over the island had deposited salt in the pool. He tasted the trickle that issued from the rocks, found it sweet, and drank. Pressing his cheek against the rock, he permitted the pure water to splash over his face.

The storm had addled his brain. How long had he been here? He counted the nicks he'd made in the tree. "Three weeks," he mumbled. He thanked God for every mouthful of water, then prayed for an answer to his hunger.

Turning, he saw a snake coiled on a rock in the sun. God must've had a wave snatch it from another island and wash it ashore here. After killing and cleaning the serpent, David used the thick bottom of his bottle to concentrate the sun's rays and started a piece of driftwood on fire. Before this venture, the thought of eating snake would've repulsed him.

He thought about how he'd carved a wooden hook that had caught fish. His meals had been supplied for several days, then a shark had seized the hook and snapped his string. The nourishment had been enough to sustain him, but he was continuing to lose weight.

After his reptilian meal, he continued his trek around the island. On the far side, he found the remains of an old raft that had washed ashore. Was it the one the sea had stolen from him? If so, it had been returned unusable as a raft.

He'd learned not to waste anything. "If I lean it against a rock or palm, it will make a shelter." He gathered the few pieces of driftwood and placed them on stones to dry, then he sat to ponder and pray.

When the driftwood dried, David arranged it for a fire and chuckled. "You'll have to provide the lamb, God." Visions of roast turkey and duck, sizzling chops, and baked potatoes crowded into his thoughts and his stomach growled. He wasn't as hungry now as he had been the first few days, still he longed for a filling meal.

Three times a day, David circled his island. On one trek, he found a fish marooned in a small pool behind some rocks. *I will provide for you,* drifted through his soul like a soothing melody. Thanking God, he cleaned the fish with his pocket knife, then washed it in the waves. The remainder of the tongue depressor in his pocket stabbed him as he bent over, but he was reluctant to dispose of anything that might have some use. He wrapped the fish in wet fronds, covered it with small rocks, then built a fire on top. That evening he ate slowly, savoring each tender morsel.

Every two to three days another fish would get trapped in the pool on the beach, but even though David used his wood sparingly, his supply was nearly exhausted. After being marooned for a month, he was beginning to give up hope of a rescue, and he wondered why God was keeping him alive. His skin had been darkened by exposure; calluses padded the bottoms of his feet and had toughened his hands. A short beard that made his face itch, now covered the bottom half of his face, and his hair had grown enough to flop annoyingly over his ears. His shirt had worn into holes and was bleached white by salty mist and sun. The pants he wore kept fraying and had shortened to expose his knees. "I look like a wild man!" If someone on a ship saw him, the crew would probably be too frightened of him to offer a rescue.

He'd given up searching the sea for a glimpse of a sailing vessel, but something compelled him to lift his eyes. Leaping to his feet, he squinted. Was that a fishing boat?

"Hey!" David shouted, waving his arms feverishly. "Ho!"

"What's the matter with you now, Fisher?" Hunter's voice boomed from the other side of the divider.

David woke with a start, his breath coming in gasps. "Sorry." He sat up and put his bare feet on the floor. This had been going on for months. How much longer could he endure? If he explained things to Alaina, would the nightmares cease?

Rifle fire brought Hunter to his feet. "Not again!" He grabbed his clothes.

"Bret's out there." David rapidly donned his shirt and shoved his legs into jeans. Seizing his boots, he rammed his feet into them, grabbed his revolver and raced through the door. Hunter, rifle in hand, followed at his heels. Both men took cover behind a tree. The sound of galloping horses faded in the distance.

David glanced around. "Where's Bret?"

## Twenty-Five

"I don't know." Hunter peered into the darkness. "I don't see him. Was he on watch?"

"Yes." David's eyes scanned the new house, then searched the tree line. "Bret! Where are you?"

Silence.

Hunter scratched his beard. "I pray he's all right."

"So do I." David shook his head. "This is the fourth attack! Why does someone have it out for Bret and his family?"

"I wish I knew."

David combed his hair with his fingers. "Well, it's something we'd better find out. I know Bret wants us working on the house, but today, I'm going to investigate the tracks left by last night's horses and try to find out who was firing on us this morning."

"Right. But we'd better locate Bret right now."

David squinted and looked toward the pine. "From what direction were those bullets fired?"

Hunter pointed. "I think they came from that grove of trees. We could go over there, but whoever shot at Bret could be expecting that and waiting to ambush us."

David shook his head. "They act like a band of cowards. We heard their horses, so I suspect they got their tails out of here. All we would do is mess up the tracks and destroy any clues that might be present."

"That's true, but I'd don't want them to get too far away."

"At first light, we'll head out." David waved an arm. "I'll search to the left. You go right, and keep your head down! They could do the unexpected." David slipped into the darkness. If he crept through the brush, Bret was likely to shoot him. If he called out, and one of the raiders happened to be hiding in the bushes, they could pinpoint his location. Slipping from one shrub to another, he squinted to see into the shadows. He tripped over something and nearly fell.

"Hold it," a husky voice said, "or I'll blow a hole in you."

The voice was distorted, but it sounded familiar. "Bret?"

"Dave. Thank God. I'm behind the rock to your right."

"Hunter! Over here!" David called, quickly making his way to Bret's side. "You all right?"

"I was shot."

"Where!" The change in Bret's voice, David now realized, was because of the man's pain.

"My shoulder."

"Oh no. Your only arm will now be out of commission."

"It's my . . . left." Bret chuckled, but the sound was garbled by pain. "I'm fortunate . . . not to have a left arm. If I had, I . . . would've got it shot off again!"

"I'll help you back to the cabin."

Hunter crashed through the brush. David quickly explained. "Let's get him inside." He glanced at Bret. "I know you don't feel like talking right now, but you must confide in us. Who might want you dead and why? If we don't get to the bottom of this, we could be burying you."

"Can't figure this out. War's over. Don't have enemies."

David helped Bret up the porch step. The man seemed to be getting weaker. "Don't try to talk now. When it's light, I'm going to look around." He noticed that the left side of Bret's shirt was soaked. "Hunter, go in and tell Alaina what happened. If Jo sees this blood, she might faint. Have Alaina tell her that Bret's all right, but he needs care."

Hunter lit the oil lamp on the table.

Ellie, wearing a faded robe, came from her room. "What you be doin' shootin' off guns before daylight?" She noticed Bret, and her dark eyes widened. "You be shot!"

"Ellie, get some clean cloths and heat water." David pulled a kitchen chair out for Bret.

The man slumped onto it. "This is going to delay our building project."

A sudden thought streaked through David's brain. Was that the reason for the attacks? "Bret, can you think of anyone who might be trying to keep you from rebuilding the house?"

He looked bewildered. "Why would anyone want to stop me?"

"That's what I intend to find out."

Alaina floated into the room in a pink dress. It looked like a Sunday frock. Was she going to try a new tactic to get him to talk? It didn't matter what she wore or what she said, he had to discuss his past with her as soon as possible.

"Bret!" Jo squealed and ran to her husband. "Oh my darling!" The tears that had pooled in her gray eyes, spilled over and rolled down her pale cheeks.

"You be gettin' hold of you nerves, girl." Ellie flopped the remains of a white sheet onto the table. "You be gettin' that shirt off him so Ah can sees his injury."

As usual, the black woman was taking charge. Jo's fingers trembled and she had difficulty unbuttoning Bret's shirt. Stepping forward, David unfastened the garment, peeled it from the man and dropped it into the bucket Ellie offered. Jo's eyes widened when she saw her husband's bloody stump, and more color drained from her already ashen face.

David jerked another chair from under the table. "Jo, sit."

Apparently realizing she was about to faint, she obliged. Gripping the edge of the table, she breathed in short gasps. Hunter got her a glass of water.

"Miss Alaina, you be gettin' water in the basin." Ellie tore the white cloth into strips and rolled them up. "This be makin' the bandages easier for you to use."

Alaina looked at Jo. "You nursed wounded soldiers during the war. You must have seen much worse than this."

Jo stared blankly at her sister, then blinked. "I suppose nursing strangers would be a lot different than seeing the man you love all bloody."

Alaina hugged her. "I'm so sorry, Jo. I keep forgetting."

David was confused, but there wasn't time to ponder.

Jay appeared in the doorway of the bedroom he shared with Ellie. He grasped the door frame for support. "Looks like yo men are still fightin' the war."

Hunter set a chair by the old man and encouraged him to sit. "You didn't need to get up, Jay. Why don't you go back to bed."

The old man shook his head. "Ah gots to plant more garden today." He chuckled. "Besides, with all the shootin' and yellin' around here, Ah can't get no sleep."

Ellie glanced at him, her concern evident. "You don't needs to be messin' with no garden today. You needs rest."

"Now Ellie. Ah have the rest of my life to rest." He grinned at her. "Ah could use a pancake or two."

"You's gonna be waitin' for that." She took the basin of bloody water out the back door. When she returned, she refilled it with fresh water and brought it to Alaina. "You gots the bleedin' stopped. Don't look as bad now as Ah thought it was gonna be." She eyed Bret. "You better be restin' today."

He sighed. "Maybe. For awhile."

The first rays of dawn filtered through the worn curtains in Ellie's cabin as the women finished tending to Bret. Jo looked worried. Alaina chewed her lower lip. David was proud of her the way she'd taken over and dressed Bret's wound. Oh how he loved her. His arms ached to embrace her. His lips burned to experience another kiss. She looked at him, her brown eyes brimming with emotion. He knew that she, too, was thinking of the stolen moments they'd shared while he was on guard duty. Sighing, he turned to the door. *I don't need to wait for sunrise to scout around.* Going out, he headed across the yard.

Alaina hurried onto the porch, her skirt swishing. "David?"

Pausing, he turned.

One of her hands hovered in the air in front of her, the other fumbled with her lace collar. "Where are you going?"

"To see if I can discover any clues that would explain these attacks."

Her hand dropped to her side, then she grinned. "I'll change and come with you. Two sets of eyes can see twice as much."

"Not necessarily." There was no way he would put her in danger. "I want you to stay here. Your sister may need you."

"But, David, I want to help."

He shook his head. "If anyone else comes along, the tracks may be distorted."

Her mouth opened in an apparent denial, then she sighed. "Whatever you want." She blinked, then turned and went inside.

Protecting her had been foremost in his thoughts, but his good intentions had hurt her. Heart heavy, he plodded around the foundation and toward the stand of pine. Stopping some distance away, he examined the ground. There were no tracks. At the edge of the trees, he looked carefully with each step. He hadn't gone far when he spotted empty cartridges on the ground. There were footprints in the dirt, too. Kneeling, he measured the prints. By the length and depth, he could tell that the man had been large and probably heavy. *Harry Bunsen?*

He shook his head. There were no indentations made by the man's peg leg. The prints were made by a man with two feet, and they were too deep to have been made by Jud Horner. As skinny as that man was, he might not leave any prints!

On further examination, David discovered that there had probably been three individuals who had taken part in the attack. When he discovered where they had tied their horses, he followed the direction of their departure and nodded. Three horses. Now all he had to do was figure out who had been riding the animals. If he intended to track them, he would welcome Hunter's company. The sound of hammering told him that the man had begun work on the house. Today, carpentry was going to wait.

As he approached, Hunter looked up. "Find anything?"

"Tracks. We'll follow them."

Hunter nodded. "We'll need our horses." He stood. "I'm glad I brought my mount. I almost didn't."

"I'll saddle our animals. You go inside and tell Bret what we're going to do."

Hunter strode toward the cabin, David toward the shed. By the time he had two horses saddled, Hunter had joined him. David mounted his white stallion and headed out.

Hunter leaped to his chestnut gelding's back and kicked the animal into motion. "Which way did they go?"

"South. Now that the sun is up, we'll be able to see more. We'll start at the spot where they tied their animals. Maybe you can discover some clue I missed."

"We have to solve this before someone gets killed." Hunter sighed. "I had to argue with Bret to keep him from joining us."

"Knowing him, I understand that." David frowned. "He's the last one who should be investigating. Whoever's behind this, seems to be out to get him."

"I wish I could figure out why."

"We're going to try to." David showed Hunter the tracks. After studying them, the two headed south, their eyes to the ground. David straightened to search the area. "It might be wise for one of us to study the tracks and the other one to watch out for a possible ambush."

Hunter's eyes flashed to David's face. "You're right. I'll take a turn tracking. You watch out for my head."

Alaina chided herself as she removed her good pink dress. What had gotten into her? Did she think David could be softened by what she wore? Disgusted, she donned a slightly faded purple dress with short sleeves and a straight skirt. Before the war, Jo had embroidered white magnolias around the bottom ruffle, but she didn't remember having done it.

Moving to a window, she stared in the direction that she'd last seen Hunter and David. A feeling of desertion gripped her. She wished David would've permitted her to go along. *How?* She hadn't brought her horse. She'd tried to convince Hunter to leave his behind, but he'd argued that he needed a mount. She was glad that she'd agreed. If Hunter hadn't brought his animal, David would have had to track the culprits alone. Concern for the safety of her brother and the man she loved made her stomach tighten.

Sitting on the couch, she bowed her head and closed her eyes. *Oh, God, go with the men. Protect them, and help them find out who is after Breton and why.*

Lacy seemed to understand the earlier fracas. She had stayed out of their way, although she kept a close watch on Bret. Maybe it was the smell of blood that had her worried. She had followed Bret to the bedroom and taken up a vigil beside his bed.

Jonathan started to fuss. The pain in Bret's arm had kept him awake, and he'd just gone to sleep. Alaina didn't want the baby to waken her brother-in-law. She hurried to the cradle and picked Jonathan up. He was wet and probably hungry. Well, she could take care of the wet part.

In the living room, she changed the infant's clothing and sponged him. Powdered, dressed, and smelling good, he laid on his back, kicked his tiny feet and cooed up at her. Smiling, she tickled his chin, then picked him up and went to the kitchen. It must be wonderful to have a baby of your own. She pictured David. He was the one she wanted to be the father of all her babies. First, they would have to solve the problem that kept David from her.

She chewed her lower lip. What could be so bad? Could Jo have been right? Is David a convict? Had he killed someone, other than in the war? Had he robbed a bank? He seemed genuine now. Had he turned from a life of vice and corruption, but still wallowed in the guilt from the actions of his past? *Or is he hiding out from the law?*

Hunter had said that David was plagued by recurring dreams and nightmares. Were they caused by an earlier wild way of life? Her head swimming, she rocked Jonathan and tried to calm her frenzied thoughts.

Jo came from the bedroom. "Thanks for taking care of the baby. I didn't want to leave Bret just then."

"It's good you're here now. Jonathan's been sucking his fist. He would've been screaming in another minute." Surrendering the infant, Alaina called Lacy and went to the front porch. How long would it be before the men returned?

The puppy raced into the yard, then turned to yip. Grabbing a stick, Alaina tossed it. Lacy raced after it, but refused to give it back.

After several minutes of chasing around the foundation, Lacy, panting, flopped to her stomach. Alaina went to the swing. Since the men wouldn't witness her, she pushed with her feet until she was flying high, her skirt billowing dangerously. The exercise was good for her body, but her mind was on the men following the derelicts' tracks. Closing her eyes, she prayed for their safety.

"I wish we would've thought to bring something to eat." David looked up from the tracks. "We've gone several miles. How far do you suppose those men went?"

"Hard to tell." Hunter rubbed the morning stubble on his chin. "They've attacked four times, so I expected them to be camped closer than this."

David thought of the women who were alone with only a wounded man to protect them. Of course, there was Jonas. "Do you suppose they circled and are now within striking distance of Sunny Horizon?"

"I pray not. They usually wait until dark to strike."

"That proves they're cowards." David spied a berry bush and dismounted. "I guess this is dinner."

Hunter joined him. "The horses need water."

"So did the one's we're following. I assume there's a stream not far away." David popped a handful of berries into his mouth and crunched them. Juice trickled down his throat. After his time on the island, fresh fruit was a delicacy.

By early afternoon Hunter and David were three miles from Sunny Horizon. "You were right, Dave. Those men did circle back." He pointed. "Is that smoke?"

David nodded. "It looks like they may have a camp. We'll dismount and hide our horses. I want to sneak close enough to hear their conversation. Maybe we can discover their motive and what they're planning."

"Sounds good. Before we leave, we can swipe their mounts and foil their plans."

"Stealing their mounts wouldn't be a good idea. We could get hung as horse thieves." David grinned. "We'll chase their animals off, though. That will hinder them for a time."

Hunter remained a short distance away as a lookout. Flat on his belly, David inched his way toward the ruffians' camp. A skinny man strode around a campfire, kicking at the flaming logs. He looked a bit like Jud Horner, but he had dark hair and wasn't as tall. David grinned. The man's narrow nose was pointed and resembled a bird's beak.

A fat man slept under a nearby tree, his shirt unbuttoned, exposing his rounded belly. His protruding navel resembled a dirt-encrusted hickory nut, signifying that a bath was long past due. His snoring rumbled through the forest like an approaching freight wagon.

Using the noise as cover, David crept closer to the camp. As he studied the two, he nodded to himself. They looked like they could have been part of the threesome who had attacked the lumber wagon.

Another man flipped the tent flap aside and stepped out. He had a large frame and was somewhat muscular. That fit the description of the third man. He jerked a bandana from his hip pocket and blew his nose. The sound trumpeted, then echoed from the surrounding hills. A stained shirt hung limply over his worn pants. He scratched his head, then examined his fingernails. "Okay, Bones, you've had plenty of time to plan our next move. What will it be?"

David gritted his teeth as he watched. The skinny man's pointed nose twitched and he laughed. It sounded more like a cackle. He was enjoying his attacks. David wanted to wrestle him to the ground, tie him up, and deliver him to Bret. But he still didn't know the why of the attacks, and he needed proof that these were the culprits responsible.

"We gonna ride again tonight, Bones?"

## Twenty-Six

Bones grinned, exposing a gap between his front teeth.

David shifted slightly to get more comfortable. It looked like he was going to be here for a time. The men's appearance disgusted him. A small stream gurgled over rocks just behind their tent. There was no reason for them to skip bathing. Even at fifty feet, David thought he could almost smell them.

The tall man scowled. "Bones! I asked you a question! Are you deaf?"

"Nope."

"What's the plan? Do we use rifles, shoot arrows or start a forest fire?"

David's blood ran cold. These men had to be stopped before they set fires. As much timber as there was, it could end up looking like Sheridan made another march. According to Bret and Hunter, the general devastated the Shenandoah. They didn't need that again—even in part.

Bones scratched his greasy head, bouncing his soiled cap. "Relax, Radford. I'm gonna wait for Moose to wake up."

Radford bent and picked up a stone. Aiming, he hurled it at the fat man's exposed skin. The stone struck him just above his grimy navel.

Yelping, he sat up and looked around. "What stung me!"

Hunkering beside the fire, Radford picked up a stick.

Moose examined his belly. "Don't look like a sting." He glared at the other two men as though wondering which one to blame. Cursing, he rolled over, and with clumsy movements, got to his feet and lumbered across the small clearing. He sneered at Bones, then glared at Radford. "Blast you, you slimy maggots!"

"You plan on snoring you're life away?" Bones jerked his head. "We're gonna strike Harris again tonight."

David nodded to himself. Evidently the men didn't know that one of them had shot Bret. Had a random bullet accidentally hit him? If their actions were scare tactics, why? Did they just want to torment Bret? What could they have against the man? A new thought gripped him. *Could it be Jo they're meaning to heckle*? That thought only generated more questions. Puzzled, David watched.

A twig snapped about a hundred feet to his right. He wondered if Hunter was sneaking closer. David prayed they wouldn't draw the attention of one of the gang. He pondered the three. They had been responsible for the raid last night, but were there more members of this gang? Could they be planning to join forces tonight before the attack? Hearing their plan was crucial to planning a surprise preemptive strike.

Sitting on a log, Bones picked his teeth with his index finger. "One of you gotta hunt this afternoon, or swipe a couple of chickens. One rabbit hain't enough to keep a bird alive."

A snort that sounded animal-like issued from Radford. "It's your turn, Bones."

"You say?" Hyena-like laughter crackled through the trees. Bones snatched a stick from the fire. The end glowed red, then turning gray, it sent a coil of smoke upward. "If Moose didn't eat like a rhinoceros, we wouldn't have to hunt as often." He wiggled his smoldering stick at the fat man. "You're gonna supply supper."

The heavy man clenched his massive fists. For a moment, David thought there might be a fight. Instead, Moose only huffed and snorted. "Git on with your plan, Bones."

The skinny man seemed to enjoy agitating his men. He was also creating stress in David. *Could Bones have detected my presence?* Was that the reason the man was delaying giving the details of his plan? David drew a long slow breath. If Bones knew he was there, there was going to be a fight.

*With guns?* If so, David would be at a disadvantage. He had his revolver, but he didn't want to kill one of these men. He wanted to help to put them behind bars.

"I got some oil." Bones leaped to his feet, danced around the fire, and let out a screech that sounded like a wild bird of prey. "We're gonna soak rags and light them."

"Yeah? Then what?" Moose wheezed as he changed his position.

"We're gonna use flaming arrows and burn Sunny Horizon, again!" He cackled and rubbed his hands together. "I can't wait to see it go up in flames. Too bad it won't make as big a smoke as it did the first time we burned it."

Stunned, David swallowed. So! They were trying to keep the house from rising. They could be jailed for burning it. *If I can find proof.* Now if he could discover why. Barely breathing, he listened.

Radford dug a finger into one ear, then cleaning his fingernail with his pocketknife, he flipped a small yellowish gob into the flames. "What if we catch one of the cabin's on fire?"

"Just make a bigger blaze!" Bones jerked his shoulders. "I hain't gonna allow Sunny Horizon to rise again. We're gonna keep Jake's memory alive! It's the least we can do for old Jake." He grinned. "Besides, that niger woman stuck me in the ribs with a knife, and one of the Harris bitches shot me in the shoulder."

David crept away. He would question Bret about Jake. He had the nicknames of these three. With the added information, Bret might be able to solve this puzzle. He mounted, praying his stallion wouldn't whinny.

Hunter slipped from the thicket to his left. "Let's go." He mounted and nudged his horse forward. "What about chasing off their animals?"

David shook his head. "I don't want them to discover that we overheard their plans. Tonight, we're going to surprise them and catch them in their act of destruction."

"Good. I didn't get close enough to hear what they were saying. What are they going to do?"

"They plan to attack. And now I know why. I'll give you the details on the way home."

Alaina went to a window for the twentieth time. When she saw David and Hunter, her heart rejoiced. "Here they come! Ellie, set the ham on to heat." She was tempted to change her purple dress, but shook her head and went to the door. Should she race out like a ninny or remain in the house like a lady?

*Like a ninny.* Flinging the door wide, she went to the porch. The men were at the shed. They dismounted and Jonas took their horses inside. When they headed for the cabin, Alaina raced to meet them. "Did you find the men? What did you discover? Did you take care of the ruffians? Did they run or will they be back?"

"Whoa." David chuckled. "We're too hungry to discuss war strategy."

She hugged Hunter. "You did track those criminals, didn't you, Brother?"

"Sure did." He kissed her cheek. "But you're going to have to wait until we tell everyone. I don't want to go over our discovery more than one more time."

She glanced sideways at David. He was watching her. Heat crept up her neck and lodged on her cheekbones. His smile nearly sent her heart into the next county. If the mysterious attacks were uncovered and solved, and the culprits arrested, David would have to tell her what was in his past that kept him bound. She would tell him it didn't matter. They could marry and have lots of babies. The thought intensified the spots of heat on her cheeks.

David noticed Alaina's pink cheeks and wondered what she was thinking. He knew what was on his own mind. But that would have to wait. Putting off confiding in her had been necessary, now he despised the thought of revealing his past. He knew the truth was going to devastate her. How could he hurt this delightful creature? But how could he go on leaving her in the dark concerning his situation?

Jo and Bret sat at the kitchen table sipping coffee. Bret looked a bit pale, but his smile was back. "Let's hear about your venture."

"They's gots to eat." Ellie clunked a platter of ham onto the table and took baked potatoes out of the oven. "You needs meat and potatoes to put flesh on them bones, Misa David."

"That sounds good to me." Sitting, he bowed his head.

Bret said grace, then passed David the platter of ham.

David helped himself to a slice. "Anyone here ever heard of a man called Bones?"

Ellie's eyes widened and she dropped the carving knife. "You see Bones?"

Both David and Hunter dropped their fork. David stared at her. "You know him?"

The black woman nodded. David studied her expression and figured, had she been a white woman, there would be no color in her face. "Who is he?"

"He be the one who burned Sunny Horizon!"

Jo looked bewildered. Bret's mouth dropped open.

David had heard the raiders version, now he wanted to hear Ellie's. "Why did they burn the place?"

Ellie seemed to regain her composure. "Bummers came durin' the war. Ah was tryin' to get the ladies to hide. The bummers starts raidin' the big house. Miss Tiffany gits a pistol. Cassie be screamin'. Her children be cryin'. Bones be cacklin' likes he be crazy. Ah sees Miss Tiffany shoots Bones in the shoulder."

Alaina gasped. "She shot him!"

"Yes-um. Bones be gonna hang Jonas. Miss Tiffany be stoppin' him." The old woman took a breath and placed a hand on her chest. "That be one day Ah be wantin' to forget."

David watched her. "I'm sorry, Ellie, but we need to know what happened. Who's Jake?"

Jake be the leader! He be rippin' Priscilla's clothes off. Miss Tiffany shoots him in the leg. They all gits on their horses and starts gallopin' away. Old Ellie thinks it be over." She shuddered. "Then Miss Elizabeth Ann shoots Jake. Miss Tiffany fires at more and kills another one. Bones git away. A man be drivin' a wagon away that be filled with Harris furniture." Ellie gasped. "Miss Jo shoots him. He falls and be dead."

Jo covered her pale face with her trembling fingers. Alaina moved quickly to her. Hunter's mouth had opened a bit further with each sentence.

Ellie continued. "There be bummers layin' in the yard likes dead pigs. Jake be dead, too."

"Bones was wounded," David said. "I assume he got away. When did they burn the house?"

"Five men come gallopin' back when old Ellie be in the big house alone. Jonas be out in a far field. Cassie takes her children and hides in the woods. Bones say he be torchin' Sunny Horizon to be gettin' even for the ladies killin' Jake."

David took a drink of coffee and set his cup on his saucer. "That's the reason for the attacks now, Bret. Bones said he had to keep Jake's memory alive. He's also angry over Ellie's stabbing him and Tiffany's putting a bullet into him."

"It's a case of revenge. They plan to attack tonight." Hunter chewed a bit of ham and swallowed. "We're going to surprise them." He took a drink of coffee. "By morning, we'll be taking them to the sheriff."

David put butter on his potato. "We'll discuss strategy this afternoon. By sundown, we'll be ready and waiting."

Alaina hung on every word. A slight frown wrinkled her smooth forehead. "Why didn't you just grab them when you had the chance?"

"We have to catch them in the act in order to have a sentence stick. I want them to be behind bars."

"Catching them in the act will be dangerous!"

David smiled. Alaina's innocence made her look angelic. He fought an overpowering urge to kiss her right here in front of the family. Did they realize how much he loved her? There was one thing from his past that anguished him. The fact would crush Alaina, too. Nevertheless, he had to tell her.

Hunter pushed his plate away and tried to camouflage a burp. "Where's the best place to discuss our plans?"

David glanced at the anxiety on the ladies faces and realized it would be better if they weren't subjected to this discussion. "Maybe we should go to the building site and point out the different things Bones said." He looked at Bret. "Are you able?"

"I'm a bit shaky on my feet, but I'll make it." He chuckled. "This is nothing compared to the battlefield."

Jo stood. "I'm going with you. If I shot one once, I can do it again."

"I know how to shoot, too." Alaina jumped up and shoved her chair under the table.

Bret lifted his hand. "You ladies will remain inside tonight. And stay away from the windows." He eyed his wife. "There won't be any shooting. We want these culprits alive."

Jo sweetly argued, but Bret convinced her that her responsibility was to take care of Jonathan. Alaina grew silent and peered at the floor, but David knew she wasn't interested in the braided rug under her feet. He wondered why she'd given up so easily. Or had she. Could she be waiting until tonight to join them when she thought it would be too late for them to reject her doing so? Well, that wouldn't work. He'd make sure she was safe inside.

"Ah fought in the war, too." Propped on his cane, Jay grinned. "Ah can join the fight with yo men."

"You hain't gonna be doin' no such thing!" Ellie huffed. "You's gonna be asleep where you belongs."

"Yo still fussin at me, woman?" He chuckled. "Ah brought my rifle, and Ah still knows how to use it."

"Ah's gonna hide your walkin' stick." She grinned. "Or maybe Ah be beatin you with it."

The old man laughed, his voice cracking. "I believe yo might." He gazed admiringly at her. "Ah don't thinks yo's ever gonna change."

"Humph. Ah can't. You needs watchin'."

David smiled. He couldn't help enjoying the couple.

The men went outside to discuss different strategies, taking into account what Bones had said. Jonas joined them. John said he would hide and give them signals. He demonstrated his owl hoot and a couple other bird calls. Jonas agreed. The men discussed other signals, so they could notify each other without Bones and his cohorts becoming wise.

When their plans were discussed and their tactics mapped out, David took a deep breath. "I think that takes care of it. We need to be in position before the sun sets. If the gang comes early, I don't want them to catch sight of any of us."

All agreed. Bret yawned. "I'm going to take a nap so I'll be ready. I'll tell Ellie to prepare an early supper."

When the sun slipped behind the mountains to the west, David stood and stretched. Hunter seemed nervous. David was a bit anxious, too.

Bret came to their cabin. "Let's take our places and make sure we're camouflaged."

"We must be synchronized." David checked the pocket watch Bret had loaned him, then buttoned his dark blue shirt. "Don't either of you fellows make your move until I give the signal. That way, we can all act at once."

Jonas joined them and they headed for their designated places.

Alaina rested her book in her lap and sighed. It hadn't been just David who had told her she couldn't join them. Bret had underscored it. Hunter had tweaked her nose and said she was too young to play soldier. Her lips tightened.

Shadows crept into the kitchen, making it difficult for her to read. She lit a lamp and squinted at the pages.

Ellie bustled from her room and turned the lamp down. "We's been told not to light a lamp, girl."

Sighing, she tossed her book to the table. Jonathan began to whimper. Alaina joined Jo in the bedroom. "Do you think he knows there's danger?"

"No. But he can tell I'm tense, and that probably bothers him." She picked up the baby and took him to the rocker.

Alaina sat on the edge of her sister's bed. "I wish the men wouldn't be so . . . so stubborn."

"About keeping us safe?"

Standing, Alaina began to pace.

"Stay away from the windows," Jo reminded around a yawn.

"Why don't you feed Jonathan, then go to bed. I'll rock him if he gets fussy."

"That's an offer I can't turn down."

Alaina still paced, but to please Jo, she stayed away from the windows. Several ideas whirled through her mind. Eventually, one began to blossom.

Jo finally handed her the baby and stretched out on the bed. "I won't be able to sleep, but at least I'll rest."

"I'll rock the baby in the kitchen." Alaina didn't want the creaking rockers to keep her sister awake.

Finally, Jonathan was sleeping. Alaina took him to his cradle. She studied Jo to verify that she was also asleep. Tiptoeing from the room, she knelt to dig in her trunk. When she touched what she was searching for, she grinned.

David peered through the leaves to watch the sky turn from yellow and scarlet to burnt-orange and magenta. Soon, deep purple hues darkened the horizon, and shadows crawled from under saplings and rocks like determined demons. Darkness descended rapidly, like a glove had been slipped over the forest. Alert, David drew a long breath. His ears were attune to the slightest sound. An owl hooted. Another answered. *Jonas and John have spotted Bones and his men.*

Minutes ticked by. David heard a horse's snort to his right. He tensed. *Here they come!*

## Twenty-Seven

David's heart pounded. *Dear Lord, please don't let anyone get hurt.*

After what he'd discussed with Bret and Hunter, he knew making the first move was up to him.

Bones and his men approached the bush that was camouflaging him. Holding his breath, he peered through the leaves. He counted three horses. These men had to be the ruffians he'd watched that afternoon.

"Git off your animals behind these pine," Bones said. "We're gonna go closer on foot so we can git a clear shot."

David's pulse points throbbed. This was like being in a war. The men were close. Too close?

"Don't forget your bow, Moose." Bones swore. "I wish I had men I could depend on."

Radford's curse sounded like a growl. "If you were a better leader, you might get more men to follow you."

"Watch your mouth." Bones spit. The gob splatted on a rock near David. "I'll have you shot for insubordination."

"Yeah?" Radford's hoarse laugh grated on David's nerves. The man gave Bones a shove. Bones swung, and his fist thudded against the side of Radford's head. The bigger man dropped to one knee. A string of oaths issued from between his gritted teeth. Clenching his fists, he stood and stepped toward Bones.

Moose swore. "Stupid! If we're going to ruin Harris, let's do it and get out of here."

"Shut up," Bones growled. "I'll bash out your brains if you don't take orders

Radford snarled. "Hit *me* again, and you're dead meat."

Bones snorted. "Take your places."

The men's voices were easy for David to distinguish, since he'd listened to them on two previous occasions. If they stayed close together, it would be easier to get the drop on all three at the same time. He prayed they wouldn't separate and head in different directions.

Perfect timing was the key. In order to catch them in a criminal act, he had to wait until they'd lit their arrows, but he would have to stop them before they let their flaming torches fly. Were these men expert archers? If they were, the arrows would hit their target and the new house could be reduced to smoldering timbers. If their aim was off, one or more of the cabins could burn.

*Are the women aware of the danger?* David shuddered. *We don't have enough man power to extinguish the fires!*

Bones walked so close to David's hiding place that he could have seized the man's pant leg and tripped him. The temptation was strong, but it was too early to play his hand.

"Where's that oil, Moose?" Radford asked.

"You were supposed to bring it."

Radford swore. "Bones told *you* to get it just before we broke camp."

"Yeah? Well, I grabbed it when you mounted up without it." Moose wheezed as he lumbered toward his horse. "You take care of your job, Rat-face, I'll do mine."

"You call me that again, and I'll douse you with the oil and light you to torch the house."

A string of oaths poured from Bones. "Stop it! You two git your mind on what your supposed to be doin'!"

"Keep your voice down." Radford's words sounded like a growl. "You'll wake someone in one of the cabins."

A snort issued from Moose.

"Rags are soaked." Bones snapped his bowstring. "Get ready. We'll all light our torches and let our arrows fly at the same time."

An owl hooted to David's left. One answered to his right. He wondered if Hunter and Bret understood Jonas and

John's signals. How far away were they? He was too close to the raiders to answer the signal with a night bird's call. Would his silence confuse Hunter and Bret? He mouthed a prayer.

Bones lit his rag, then held it where the other two could light theirs with the flame. The smell of hot oil and smoke reached David. *This is it.* Whether or not Bret and Hunter were close, he had to make a move, and soon. He was thankful this was a rocky area. He didn't want the woods to burn. "Drop your weapons, and put your hands up!"

Bones whirled and let his arrow fly toward David's bush.

Leaping aside, David kept his revolver trained on the raiders as he kicked the arrow onto the rocks. He stomped the smoldering leaves under the bush before they began to blaze and thanked God it had rained the night before. Bones headed for his horse, David yelled. "Stop or I'll shoot."

Moose dropped his burning arrow on the stones and lumbered toward David. "I'll crush your stinkin' skull."

David had his revolver trained on Bones. If he swung it in Moose's direction, Bones could grab him.

"Halt!" Hunter called.

Moose whirled to stare into the trees. "What the . . ."

Radford pulled back on his bowstring and took aim, the rag on the end of his arrow blazing. Just before he released it, a pistol cracked. Radford yelped. Dropping his bow, he grabbed his arm. Bret rushed forward, stamped out the flames, and swung his rifle to cover the man.

David sighed with relief. "Good work, men. Let's get these culprits bound."

Bones began to screech. Moose grumbled. Radford cussed.

Hunter stepped toward the tall man. "And gagged." He pulled a rope from his pocket. "Bret, keep them covered. David and I will tie them up."

"Here's more rope." Jonas stepped foreword and glared at Bones.

"Git away from me, you rotten niger! I almost hung you once. Next time, I'll finish the job!"

David zipped a handkerchief from his back pocket and gagged Bones. He made muffled sounds, his eyes flashing in the light from Jonas's lantern.

When the three were tied and gagged, David glanced around the darkened clearing. "We'll take turns guarding them tonight."

Hunter nodded. "Bret and I will take first watch. You and Jonas take second."

"Jo and I will take third."

David whirled. "Alaina! Where were you?"

She waved a delicate hand. "Over behind that rock."

He was furious. "You could've been shot." He could barely see her in the moonlight, but there was no denying the grin on her face.

"You should be glad I was here. You were busy with Bones. Hunter was occupied with the fat one. And Bret was in the wrong position to stop Radford. If it weren't for me, you fellows would be fighting a fire."

David stared. "You mean . . . you shot Radford?"

"I was the only one in the right position." She tilted her chin, sweetly defying him.

She looked so lovely, it took his breath, yet he wanted to shake her. "You could've killed him!"

She laughed. "I'm a better shot than that!" She stood, her stance sweetly daring him to accuse her. She wore a dark dress with a high collar and long sleeves. All that was visible in the dim moonlight were her face and her right hand, in which the barrel of a revolver glistened. "I missed the battles during the war, and I was determined not to miss this one."

He sighed. "Go back to Ellie's cabin, Lainy. I'll stop in to see you when we get these men taken care of."

Bret looked about ready to fall over. "Can we put our prisoners in your cabin, Hunter?"

"That's a good idea. Dave and I can take turns watching them. You look like you need rest."

"I'll join the men on second watch." Gripping a tree limb, Bret yawned.

"You go back to your cabin." David smiled. "You've done enough tonight."

Alaina stepped forward. "Come on Bret. You can lean on me."

He chuckled. "I'll make it. But thanks for the company."

David watched them go, then turned to Bones. "On your feet."

Radford got up, but Moose remained sitting. Hunter warned him to get on his feet, but with his hands tied, the obese man couldn't get off his backside.

Hunter chuckled, then aided him. "We won't have to watch this one much. We just need to make sure his bonds are tight."

They took the three to Hunter's cabin and secured each to a separate leg of a bed.

David dressed the wound on Radford's arm where Alaina's bullet had creased him, then turned to Hunter. "Watch these men. I'll go back for their horses."

Jonas was waiting for him on the porch. They slipped through the night to collect the raiders' animals. They each mounted one and led the third back to the corral.

Jonas stopped near the gate. "There isn't room in the shed. I'll hobble them and let them graze."

"Good." David grinned. "Just make sure they don't get into Cassie's garden."

"Oh, Mama, Ah'd sure be in trouble."

David chuckled. This was the first time he'd relaxed all day. But conflict with the three raiders might not be over yet. He waved a hand toward Jonas. "See you in the morning."

Jonas shook his head. "I'll be coming over about three o'clock to take a turn watching them. You and Hunter will need to get a little sleep." He rubbed the back of his neck. "I don't think Mr. Harris should take a turn."

"I agree. With your help, Hunter and I will manage." David sighed. "Thank God there will be no more attacks." He strode toward Ellie's cabin. Alaina would be waiting up to talk with him. He wished he wouldn't have promised to stop in, but she'd refused to agree to anything else.

As he neared Ellie's cabin, the door opened and Alaina came out and joined him in a deep shadow. "I was watching for you. Bret is fatigued, and Jo is feeding the baby. I thought it would be better if we talked out here."

"Lainy, I know I promised to talk, but I'm exhausted, too." He rubbed his face. "And your brother is over there alone with the prisoners."

She touched her lips with her fingertips. "I know, David, but I had to see you a few minutes." She moved toward him.

"Lainy, wait." He yearned for her touch, but he was tired and his resistance low. If he took her in his arms, he wouldn't want to let her go. "I love you with all my heart, but until we talk, we have to wait. Besides, like I said, I need to get back to Hunter."

"I understand." She stepped toward him and lifted one hand.

He told his body to move away, instead he stepped forward. "Lainy." She was in his arms. He clung to her, then kissed her gently. "Good night." He pulled her arms from around his neck. It was the most difficult thing he'd ever done. "Go inside, so I know you're safe."

"I love you, David," she whispered. She brushed her lips across his cheek, then kissed the side of his mouth.

She was in his arms again, his lips on hers. He wanted to spend the rest of his life with this adorable woman, but it couldn't be. He had to explain his situation. He had to pull away. Yet he had to hold her. He had to kiss her. "I love you Alaina, but we have a problem."

"The biggest problem is getting you to talk about it." Her eyes were misty in the moonlight as she gazed up at him.

"Alaina, You don't understand."

"I will, darling." A shadow of a smile flitted across her lips, then she turned and entered the cabin.

He scarcely remembered walking across the yard, but he found himself on Hunter's porch. It had been several days since he'd had a good night's rest. Tonight was guard duty.

Tomorrow was escorting the prisoners to Staunton. He needed rest before he spoke with Alaina. He dreaded the confrontation, yet he looked forward to it. At last, things between them would be resolved. *And our heartache will be relentless!*

Opening the door, he entered Hunter's cabin. "Everything under control?"

"As much as can be expected." Hunter pursed his lips. "You suppose we should make our guests more comfortable?"

David's first reaction was to make them as miserable as possible. That wasn't the Lord's way. *It isn't mine, either, God.* "Well, we have to make sure they don't escape." He massaged his temples as he thought. "What if I bring in a heavy beam. We could secure them in a way that they could stretch out." The floor wouldn't be comfortable, and he supposed they could use a pillow, but the way these men reeked, he wasn't going to offer one of them his. *Under other circumstances, God.*

He hoped his selfishness was excusable. Usually, he was ready to give anything he had. Tonight, he was more than fatigued, and tomorrow was going to be daunting. Folding towels, he offered each man one to use as a pillow.

When the men were securely fastened to a beam, David sat on the edge of his bed and stretched his long legs. "What a day!" A muffled sound drew his attention to Radford. The man met his gaze, glanced at the water pail, then back. David's thirst on the island seared through his recall. "These men need a drink."

"If we remove their gags, no one will sleep all night!"

Stepping toward Radford, David eyed him. "If you promise to remain silent, we'll take off your gag."

"The man nodded. David untied the handkerchief. Radford licked his dry lips as David approached with a glass of water. He held it so the man could drink. Bones was next. In spite of his glare, David knelt beside him.

"If you curse, grumble or argue, the gag goes back on and stays until you're in the sheriff's custody. Understood?"

Bones nodded. David didn't like being a jailer. He hoped he wouldn't have to be again.

Hunter looked bleary-eyed. "I hope I don't fall asleep on guard duty."

"Jonas is coming over about three. I can keep an eye on these fellows if you want to sleep."

"You need rest, too." Hunter laughed. "Probably more than I do, considering the way you dream."

David shrugged. "If I went to sleep, I'd probably just have another nightmare." He chuckled. "I'm good for two hours or so. If I get sleepy, I'll waken you."

Hunter flopped onto his back. "That's a deal I can't resist." He closed his eyes. Within minutes, he was dozing.

David looked at Bones. The man seethed. His gaze moved to Radford, but the man turned away. Moose was snoring. David wondered if that was how he'd gotten his name. How could anyone sleep with the racket?

Moving to the water pail, he took a drink. Should they feed the prisoners breakfast? He frowned. It would be the right thing to do. Ellie wouldn't mind frying a few more pancakes. Bones didn't look like he ate much. Moose would probably make up the difference and then some.

As the night wore on, David had to struggle to stay awake. At three o'clock, Jonas came in. Hunter was still asleep. So were the raiders.

Jonas eyed David and grinned. "You get some rest. I'll keep an eye on these men."

"Thanks." David went to bed fully clothed and prayed that no nightmares would disturb his rest. Tomorrow, explaining his heartrending dilemma to Lainy would be nightmare enough! He tried to plan how to tell her what she had to know, but sleep reached out and pulled him into its depths.

A piercing scream shocked David awake. Jonas, his eyes wide, sat straight on a kitchen chair, a rifle across his lap. David leaped from his bed, jerked the door open, and raced outside before the man could get to his feet.

Another scream jangled his nerves. "Lainy? Where are you? Alaina!"

## Twenty-Eight

"Alaina!" David's heart thudded against his ribs and he could feel his pulse in his throat. He squinted to see into the night. "Where are you?"

Something growled to his left. He jerked his head in that direction. A dark shape moved, but it was far enough away that he couldn't tell what it was.

A rifle cracked. The shadow jerked, then lay still.

An icy chill gripped David's spine. "Alaina?"

"I'm . . . here." A tremor vibrated her words.

He whirled to face the shadow made by the cabin. "You all right?"

"No." She began to sob. "It attacked me. I think it was after Lacy."

He raced to her and took her in his arms. She was clinging to the puppy, but her body shook.

"It bit me!"

"What did?"

"I don't know. A wolf. Maybe a bear. It growled. Oh, David, it hurts!"

Ellie's cabin door opened. Bret stepped onto the porch. "Dave! What's going on?"

"I'm not sure. Something bit Alaina." He took the wiggling puppy and put his other arm around her.

Jo, wearing her robe, joined Bret. "I heard a rifle shot. Did someone shoot my sister?"

"No." He urged Alaina toward the porch. She took a step and stopped.

Hunter hurried to join them. "What happened?"

Jonas's form took shape in the darkness. "That was a wild dog. It's been snooping around here for a month. It growled at Cassie and Naomi several times, trapped Lettie in the henhouse for over an hour one day, and twice, it chased the boys into the shed. Ah tried to shoot it, but it always dashed into cover." He glanced around. "It won't again."

"Alaina said she thought it wanted Lacy."

"Ah don't know. That pup hain't old enough to breed. Ah'm thankful Ah got a direct shot this time."

"So am I, but I wish I'd known about it."

"Ah'm sorry. There's been so much happenin' around here, Ah haven't been thinkin' about wild dogs."

"It's all right, Jonas." Alaina leaned against David. "With all the chaos, it's easy to forget things."

"She gonna be all right?"

"I'm taking her inside where I can examine the bite."

"You want me to get Cassie?"

"Let her sleep. I can handle this."

Jonas scratched his frizzy head. "Ah better be goin' back to guard the prisoners." He vanished into the night. A moment later, his footsteps crossed Hunter's porch.

Alaina took one step and stopped.

David continued to hold her. "What were you doing out here alone in the dark?"

"Lacy had to come out to do her thing." Tears rilled down her face. "I didn't want to wake anyone."

"Well, she'd better learn to go before it gets so late."

"I'm so sorry, Alaina." Jo hurried to take the puppy from David.

He handed her the frightened animal, then brushed a strand of hair from Alaina's cheek. "Let's go inside."

"It hurts to walk."

Sweeping her off her feet, he carried her into Ellie's kitchen, sat her on a chair, and looked at her leg. Blood soaked her ripped stocking, ran down her calf and oozed into her slipper.

Ellie bustled around the kitchen, her faded blue robe flapping against her ankles. She huffed. "If you keeps runnin' around in the middle of the night, girl, you gonna be the death of old Ellie." Again, she brought bandages and thumped them onto the table.

Jay tottered from the bedroom. "Which one of yo men got wounded?"

"Humph." Ellie twitched her nose. "Hain't no man what's bloody."

"Oh my achin bones!" Eyes wide, he stared at Alaina. "Yo be fightin', too?"

"Yes! But I wasn't wounded in battle." She peered at her leg and cringed.

"When you gonna stay put like a lady?"

"A lady doesn't have to be helpless, Ellie. Just your knowing Tiffany, Elizabeth Ann and Jo should have taught you that."

"Ah hain't the one who needs learnin', girl." She grabbed the kettle and poured water into a basin.

David figured he should let one of the ladies attend to Alaina's injury, but unless Jo complained, he wasn't going to give up his position. He gently swabbed the blood from around the bite and struggled to suppress a shudder. "This is nasty. That canine not only sunk his teeth into your calf, it looks like he twisted his bottom jaw."

Alaina wiped tears from her cheeks. "I think he was trying to make me fall."

"There isn't any flesh missing, but you'll need sutures."

"Oh no!"

"I'll do it as gently as possible, Lainy."

"But I'll have scars!"

He strangled a chuckle. "It will be on the back of your leg. Your stocking will cover it."

"But I don't want a scar." She glanced at Bret's empty sleeve. "Oh." The syllable came out in a tiny rush of air. "I'm so sorry. A bite is really nothing."

She was right, unless it didn't heal properly. David shivered. *Or if the dog had rabies!* In that case, there would be nothing anyone could do. He looked at Ellie. "You have any whisky?"

She gaped. "You gone mad?"

"I want it for Alaina."

Her eyes widened. "You *is* mad!" She huffed. "You hain't givin' that poor girl no poison."

Bret chuckled. "He wants it for the dog bite, Ellie."

"Well, Ah hain't got no whisky."

"I do. I'll be back." Hunter went out.

Jo looked puzzled. "Does our brother drink?"

Alaina sighed. "He claims not, but he keeps a fifth around. He says it's for emergencies."

Hunter returned, bottle in hand. "Use this sparingly. It's all we have."

Alaina studied the container. Her lips tightened. "It was full when you packed it."

His brows raised. "It's still almost full!"

David knew the direction of her thoughts. He chuckled. We use it when we scratch our skin on a nail or get a splinter. Tipping the bottle, he dribbled some on her wound.

She jumped and squealed.

Holding her ankle, he gave the wound another douse. "Ellie, please get me a saucer."

Appearing puzzled, she turned to the cupboard, retrieved one of her chipped dishes, and clattered it onto the oak tabletop.

He poured a few drops into it, then rammed the cork back into place and handed the bottle back to Hunter. "I need a needle and thread."

Ellie vanished into her bedroom.

"You know how to sew me up?" Alaina's eyes were pools of burnished bronze with gold flecks.

"Someone has to." He smiled to put her at ease. "I guess I can do as good a job as anyone else." That statement didn't sound comforting, even to himself, but he wasn't going to trust anyone else to ram a needle into her flesh. This was his Alaina.

Ellie returned with a needle threaded. Accepting it, David dropped it in the saucer of whisky, then picked it up and eyed Hunter. "You'd better give her your hand. She may need something to grip."

Alaina swallowed. "That sounds like you're going to hurt me."

He wished he could promise that she wasn't going to feel it, but that wouldn't be realistic. "It won't be as bad as you might be imagining."

"Yes it will! I've stuck myself when I'm sewing!"

"The sooner we get this over with, the quicker you can get back to bed." Refusing to look at her again, he bent to work. The gash would take at least five stitches. "Try to keep your leg still, Alaina."

"I'm trying. Get this over with," she said through clenched teeth, as though she were already feeling pain.

When he jabbed her, he heard her sudden intake of air. Her leg jerked and pulled the needle from his fingers. This wouldn't do. "Hunter, kneel down here and hold her ankle tight." He eyed Bret. "Hold her hand."

"I'm such a baby," Alaina whimpered. "I'll be brave." Gritting her teeth, she closed her eyes.

David stabbed the needle through again, then twice more. He glanced at Alaina. She sat straight, her eyes closed tight. He took two carefully spaced stitches. "Just one more."

"Hurry." Her facial muscles were drawn taut.

He glanced at her pale complexion, then took a quick stitch and tied the knot. "Done."

She giggled. "It still hurts, but I guess I'm going to live."

"I'd say your prognosis is good." He grinned at her, then soaked up the whisky with a corner of the cloth and dabbed the injury again. He supposed he should let Ellie or Jo bandage the wound, but he wanted to do it.

"Will I be able to walk?"

He chuckled. "You'll be fine. Walk when you have to, but it would be wise to baby your leg for a few days." He stood. "What time is it?"

Ellie huffed. "It be time to be gettin' up." Lifting the lid of the cookstove, she rammed in kindling and lit it. "Ah's gonna be gettin' breakfast. Nobody hain't gettin' no sleep around here no more. Humph! Beds hain't gettin' no use." She pointed to David. "You never be in yours long enough to be gettin' the sheets warm!" She glared at Alaina. "And you better be stoppin' the night jaunts." She huffed. What this world be comin' to." She clattered the iron skillet onto the stove and continued to mumble under her breath.

Jay sat rocking and grinning. "That be my Ellie."

"You better be watchin' your talk, old man. Ah's gonna be sendin' you to the garden without breakfast."

"Ah hain't gonna worry 'bout that." He picked up the newspaper beside the rocker and rolled it up. When Ellie hustled by, he gave her a playful swat.

"You be pressin' your luck, old man."

He chortled. "Where yo be hidin' the coffee?"

"Humph. You be needin' coffee likes you be needin' a lump on the head." Pouring him a cup, she handed it to him.

"Aaah, that's my Ellie."

"Ah gots to feed you. Jonas been workin' the land and has a spot ready for plantin'. Come sunup, Ah's gonna chase you out of here with my washin' stick."

Jay laughed and splashed coffee on his pants.

David wanted to remain just to listen to the old couple banter, but there were too many other things demanding his time. Standing, he rested a hand on the back of Alaina's chair. Later, he intended to question her. Why hadn't she taken the puppy outside before she went to bed? The next time the dog insisted on going out after dark, one of the men should do it.

She was still wearing her navy dress! Why? Had Lacy really begged to go out, or had Alaina planned her night escapade. Why? Did she assume he was on guard duty and intended to question him? Didn't she know there was no reason to guard the building site with the marauders under surveillance? Or did she think there could be more in the gang? If so, what did she intend to do about it?

She was avoiding his gaze. Surely she hadn't been planning to go on guard duty herself. He could hardly wait to get her alone to question her. But she wasn't the only one who better have answers. She was going to interrogate him, too! He touched her shoulder to get her attention. She looked up. He smiled to put her at ease. "You try to get some sleep."

"I won't be able to now." She sighed. "I'm so sorry to have awakened you."

He shrugged. "It was almost time for me to get up. I'll watch the prisoners so Hunter and Bret can eat."

"You have to eat, too."

"I wouldn't miss Ellie's pancakes." He glanced at the old woman. "And that sizzling bacon smells wonderful."

"We're making a big dint in the smokehouse supplies." Bret yawned. "As soon as things settle down around here, I'm goin hunting."

"Humph." Ellie cracked eggs in a bowl. "You wait 'til things be settlin' down to be huntin', we's all gonna starve!"

Smiling, David headed for the door.

"You be waitin' to take a cup of coffee with you." Ellie splashed some of the steaming black brew into a cup and proffered it.

"Thank you." Gripping the handle, David took a sip.

Ellie clattered a plate of crisp bacon on the table, then smiled as she shoved it toward him.

"Thanks again." Taking two slices, he bit off a bite and chewed. "Perfect, Ellie." Still munching, he went out. The air was fresh, and the grass wet with dew. Faint light kissed the eastern horizon and a pink hue tinted the sky. He yawned. Last night he hadn't been plagued with nightmares. He was thankful for that, although he hadn't slept much. He pictured the ride to Staunton with the ruffians. That was a trip he wasn't going to enjoy. Gripping his cup, he stretched, flexed his muscles and headed for Hunter's cabin.

Limping to a window, Alaina watched David. *My hero.* How she adored that man. What was his problem? Why did he think she wouldn't understand? Why was something always happening to keep him from confiding in her? *How long will I have to wait?* If she had her way, it wouldn't be long. When he came back from Staunton, she intended to corner him where he couldn't get away. Her questions were ready. *And his answers better be!*

"You dreaming again, Alaina?"

There was humor in her sister's voice. Alaina faced her. Jo was wearing the blue and green calico dress Alaina loved. Jo had always admired it. When she'd learned that Jo couldn't remember anything, she'd let out the seams and given her the dress, hoping it would jog her memory. "It looks like I'll be getting out of work for a few days, Sister." A giggle vibrated her throat. "Since I can't flit around the kitchen, you'll have to help Ellie with the cooking."

"I don't mind. Actually, I like to cook." She frowned. "I must have had favorite recipes, but I can't remember them."

"Ellie knows plenty." A shrug lifted Alaina's right shoulder. "I noticed last night that Jonathan's nightgowns were getting a bit tight. The baby has to be able to move his arms freely. Since I should be off my leg, I'll make him a couple new ones today." She put a finger beside her mouth. "Mama packed several pieces of flannel." She grinned. "You think he'd like pink?"

Jo laughed. "His papa would take a look at him and faint!" Jo shook her head. "He's already explaining the building project to him. And he told him he was going to give him a ride on a horse."

Alaina giggled. "We didn't know the baby had arrived. Mama was hoping for a boy, so she figured you'd have a girl."

"That pink material would make a nice winter blouse."

"Wonderful! I'll make it for you. It will look nice with either your navy skirt or your brown one."

Jo looked heavenward. "Just make sure there's enough room in front to let me button it!"

"You ladies stop gabbin' and get busy. Missy Jo, you can be settin' the table." She eyed Alaina. "And you don't needs to walk to be fryin' pancakes."

Alaina grinned at the old black woman and hobbled around the table. Ellie was harmless, and she gave her life for the betterment of all around her. Everyone loved her and seemed to enjoy her bossy ways. Alaina figured that most of the time, the woman's use of her sharp tongue was her sense of humor. Besides, she was always right.

When Bret and Hunter came in, Alaina had a stack of pancakes several inches high. Hunter eyed them. "I'll take these, Bret. You can wait for the next pile." Chuckling, he forked four, slapped them onto his plate, and passed the platter.

Bret helped himself and dribbled syrup on his stack. "The prisoners will need something to eat, too."

Ellie sighed. "Ah's been thinkin' that. Ah mixed double." She looked at Alaina. "You all right fryin', or you needs to sit?"

"I'm fine." Her leg was aching, but she wasn't going to admit it. David would be coming in soon, and she wanted to fry his pancakes.

Ellie studied Bret. "Hows you gonna feed the men when they's tied up?"

He groaned. "Like they were two years old. We'll fork them a bite at a time."

"We aren't going to untie them." Hunter rammed another big bite into his mouth and chewed, then washed it down with coffee. "Great pancakes, Ellie." He cleaned his plate and took three more, along with two more sausage patties.

Bret ate two more pancakes and another helping of bacon. He stood. "If you get three plates ready, Hunter and I will take them to the prisoners. Jonas will feed one of them, and that will free David to come to eat.

Alaina's pulse quickened. She poured batter in the pan in the shape of hearts and grinned. Would he notice?

The door opened. David came in. He glanced at Alaina. "I see you're taking my advice and staying off your leg."

"I'm not walking." She smiled at him. "Bret can build a house with one arm. Don't you think I should be able to cook standing on one leg?"

The warmth of his chuckle seemed to fill the room and wrap her in a cocoon of delight.

Ellie picked up the plate of freshly fried pancakes, looked at them and laughed, apparently not missing their shape or the significance. "I guess you gonna be enjoyin' breakfast, Misa David." She crossed the room, but watched him from the corner of her eye.

He glanced at the pancakes, and a grin stretched his lips. His eyes found Alaina's. He winked. She felt a rush of warmth to her face and knew he hadn't missed her blush. It would be wonderful to be married to this man. Oh, what was the matter with him?

David took his time at the breakfast table. It might be the only time all day that he would be able to relax. Besides, he reveled in Alaina's nearness. She poured herself a cup of coffee and took a place at the end of the table. Her toe touched his foot. She pulled it back, but the contact made his heart skip a beat. As she sipped her coffee, she peered at him over the rim of the cup. Their eyes met. His love for her welled up within him until swallowing his food became difficult.

Draining his coffee cup, he stood and gripped the back of his chair. "Bret and Hunter will probably be about ready to go. I'll see you when I get back."

She made a move to get up. He rested a hand on her slender shoulder. "Stay put."

"Tell Bret to stop for the mail before you start home."

"You seem anxious." He tugged on a curly strand of her hair. "You expecting correspondence from a lover?"

She grinned. "From at least two."

"Then by all means, we must forget." He couldn't miss the taunting gleam in her eyes.

Jay had eaten and gone to the back porch. Ellie stood by the dishpan. David wished she would go outside with her husband. Would the old woman keep her back turned long enough? What was life without taking a chance at times. He looked down at Alaina. Their eyes met. Bending, he touched his lips on hers. He'd meant to give her a quick kiss, but her arms went around his neck and she pulled him closer. All thoughts of Ellie vanished. It was just the two of them, alone in a world of bliss and passion.

"Humph!"

David straightened. Ellie stood six feet away, hands on hips. He cleared his throat. It was as though he were standing in front of a general, awaiting a pronouncement of a court-martial. Her expression said, *You's gonna be shot at sunrise.*

"I . . . was just saying good bye."

The old woman's stare didn't waver. "Well, you said it. Humph."

Feeling like a recalcitrant schoolboy, he departed. Outside, he laughed. There wasn't a sorry fiber in his being. Alaina's kiss still felt warm on his lips.

He wondered how large the wild dog was that bit her. He looked around. There was blood on the grass, but no animal. The black man had saddled the horses and had tied them to the hitching post.

"Jonas, where's that dog you shot? Did it get away?"

"Not this time. Ah buried 'im."

"Was it large?"

The black man shrugged. "About seventy pounds. That's big enough to give a nasty bite." He shook his frizzy head. "Ah been afraid it would attack someone. I'm glad it's dead."

So was David. Bret and Hunter were ready. Within minutes, they were on their way. Bret rode ahead as scout. David made the three prisoners ride three-abreast. He and Hunter rode rear where they could keep their eyes on them. Everyone was tense. Stress was in the air so thick one could nearly smell it. What if one or more of these culprits tried to escape?

Suddenly, Bones yelled, kicked his mount and galloped into a nearby stand of pine.

"Halt!" Hunter yelled.

Bones cackled, yipped, and vanished behind the trees.

## Twenty-Nine

"Plan A!" Determination tightened David's jaw. Wheeling his stallion, he kneed him into a gallop. Bones wasn't going to get away. The attacks on Sunny Horizon had to cease.

Bret twisted in his saddle and held a revolver on the remaining two prisoners. Hunter, his features set, circled them, his revolver drawn.

David rounded the stand of pine. Bones yanked on the rope that tied him to his horse. If he toppled, the mare would either drag or trample him. Awkwardness slowed his progress. He cursed and spit.

David's stallion seemed to enjoy the chase. In moments, David grasped the mare's reins and brought both horses to a stop. "This is the end of this trail."

Bones gritted his teeth. "Wait until I get out." With the warning, spit exploded between his teeth and sprinkled his mare's neck. His tongue resembled a snake's. He licked slobber from his bottom lip. Glaring, he cursed.

"You've lost more of your privileges, Bones." A tug on the mare's reins set the animal in motion.

The man's oaths bombarded David's back until they reached the road. David jerked a handkerchief from his pocket and blindfolded Bones.

He swore and spit.

"You want a gag, too?" He waited. When Bones didn't reply, he nodded to Bret to move out. "If there's any more trouble, the one starting it will be blindfolded and gagged."

Snorts issued from Radford's hooked nose. Moose grunted and wheezed. Bones gritted his teeth, his expression a sneer.

Tense, David took up the rear. Bret's taut muscles portrayed his alertness. Hunter rode in front for a time, then joined David at the rear. His eyes searched the underbrush at the sides of the road. David was on guard, too. There could be more to Bones' gang, and he didn't want any surprises.

"This light blue flannel with bunnies is cute. There's enough to make the baby two nightgowns." Alaina unfolded the material on the bed.

"I like this plain blue, too." Jo held Jonathan with one arm while he nursed and flipped pieces of fabric with the other. "While we're cutting, it would be easy to cut out four. We can sew up one of each color today."

"Good idea. I'll cut them on the table." Grabbing the material and scissors, Alaina limped toward the kitchen.

Clutching the pins and a nightgown to use as a pattern, Jo followed. Lacy scrambled around her as though she were hoping something would drop that she could seize and run. "We can't play this morning."

The puppy yipped, her tail in continuous motion and her eyes shining. *"Want to bet?"* her actions told her mistress.

A piece of scrap material slipped from the edge of the table. Lacy pounced, grabbed it, and raced to the oak rocker where old man Jay snoozed. Bumping his leg, she woke him.

"You sweet little nuisance." A chuckle created a tremor in Jay's throat. Bending, he grabbed the end of the scrap. The two began a tug-of-war. Lacy growled. Jay laughed, his voice cracking.

Jo smiled as she lifted the baby to her shoulder and rubbed his back.

The afternoon wore on. Alaina changed into her favorite yellow dress and brushed her long hair. She glanced out a window every few minutes. "How long does it take to go to Staunton and back?"

Jo joined her and stared down the lane. "The men should have been back by now. I pray they didn't have trouble with their prisoners."

"So do I." Her focus fell on the blood spattered grass not far from the porch, and she relived the dog attack. She couldn't remember a time when she'd been more frightened, even when the Yankees had pounded on her parent's door. Now she was concerned for David. What would she do if one of the prisoners killed him?

"They'll be all right, Alaina."

"They have to be."

"We've been praying, dear sister. This is a test of our faith."

Ellie glanced out a back window and grinned. "That old man just be sittin' in the sun."

"Oh, Ellie. He planted three rows of peas and one of beans this afternoon."

Don't you be makin' excuses for him, Miss Alaina. Ah's gotta keep that old man on his toes."

Jo laughed. "You're good at keeping everyone busy."

"Ah's gonna start supper." Ellie grabbed a pan and headed for the back room. "Ah needs potatoes."

"Wait!" Alaina looked at her, then at Jo. "I've been climbing down the ladder into Ellie's root cellar, but I don't know if I should try it with my injured leg. She's too old to wrestle with that rickety old thing."

Ellie waggled a finger. "You watch you' tongue, Missy."

Jo chuckled. "I'll get the potatoes, Ellie." She handed Jonathan to Alaina and reached for the pan.

Alaina watched her go, then looked at the baby in her arms. Gazing up at her, he blew a bubble. His little arms waved in the air and he cooed. "Jo's so lucky to have you."

The trapdoor squeaked open in Ellie's bedroom. Ellie warned Jo to watch her step. Alaina turned to look out a window. There was a cracking sound. Jo screamed. The pan clattered on stones that littered the floor of the root cellar. Gasping, Alaina hobbled to Ellie's bedroom.

The old woman sidestepped beside the opening, her hands fluttering. "Oh Lordie! She done fall!"

Handing the baby to her, Alaina knelt and peered down into the darkness. "Jo?" There was no answer. Fright bubbled into Alaina's throat like bile. "Jo!"

"Ah thinks a rung broke. Ah was waitin' to hand her the lantern."

"Pray my leg doesn't buckle."

Horror replaced the old woman's fright. "You can't be goin' down there, girl. You has trouble just walkin'!"

"Pray, Ellie." Cautious, Alaina turned and began her descent. She gasped. "The second rung is missing. It must have snapped when Jo stepped on it." Finally, she felt earth under her feet. She reached up. "Give me the lantern." The light revealed Jo's crumpled body. Alaina knelt and reached to touch her sister. "She's breathing. Put Jonathan in his cradle and get Jonas."

The next few seconds seemed like hours. How badly was Jo hurt? *Oh please, Lord, don't let her be injured badly.* "Jo," she called again.

Cassie rushed in with Jonas. He lowered another ladder and climbed down. Cassie followed. The woman knelt on the other side of Jo. "Ah can tell her arms and legs aren't broken, but Ah don't know about her back. We won't be able to move her until the men return."

"Oh, dear Lordie," Ellie said for the fifth time. "Ah gits her a blanket. You be coverin' her. That cellar be damp. Ah don't wants her to be catchin' her death."

The word *death* ricocheted through Alaina until every nerve in her body jangled. She knew her sister would be in heaven. But what about poor Bret and sweet little Jonathan? Tears spilled over and ran down her face. *And me. I can't give her up.*

"I can't wait to get home."

David looked at Bret and understood the man's longing. He wanted to get home, too. Alaina would be waiting. He grinned. "Can't these horses run?"

With a yip, Bret kicked his mount into a gallop. Hunter and David followed suit. When they reined up by Ellie's cabin, Jonas flung open the door and ran across the porch toward them. Instead of his usual cheerful greeting, worry lined his black face.

David leaped to the ground. "Is something wrong?"

"Jo. She fell in the root cellar."

"No!" A guttural sound rumbled in Bret's throat. Apparently Jonas's expression had alarmed him, too.

The men raced to the cabin. Bret entered first. David followed, Hunter close behind.

"She be in here," Ellie said.

Bret hurried to the old woman's bedroom, dropped to his knees, and stared into the hole. "How badly is she hurt?"

When David saw Alaina's face, his heart sank. Bret gripped the ladder and climbed down. Kneeling, he reached out. "Jo?"

David followed. "Excuse me." He touched Bret's shoulder. *What must it be like for a man with one arm when his wife needs someone to pick her up?* Compassion nearly swamped him, but he had to keep his head and do what he could for the woman. "Let me examine her."

Hunter's bearded face appeared over the opening. "What can I do to help?"

David dropped to his knees beside Jo and reached for a pulse. The way she was sprawled, he was surprised to find one. Relief flooded him. "She's alive." He rapidly examined her arms and legs. Her neck was all right too. That was what had worried him. "Her head must have struck the edge of the potato bin." He ran a hand down her spine. "I think her back is all right, but we should use a stretcher to move her."

"I'll get the cot." Hunter hurried away.

Bret knelt on the other side of Jo, holding her hand and speaking softly. Worry lines creased his face.

David glanced at Alaina. Tears brimmed in her eyes as her focus lingered on her sister. His throat tightened. He heard Hunter coming with the cot and turned to grasp one end of it.

Climbing down, Hunter tested the cot's stability on the earthen floor, then gently lifted his sister.

Jonas waited in the bedroom above, his black head hovering over the opening. "Hunter, pass me one end of the cot." He gripped his end and slowly backed as David hoisted the other end. During the entire ordeal, Jo didn't move.

Bret paced as Hunter placed her on the bed. Her face was so pale, she looked like death. "Her lips have color." David rested his hand on her forehead, then lifted her eyelids to check her eyes. "She's still unconscious."

Moisture collected in Bret's eyes. David felt his pain, but didn't know how to comfort him.

Jonathan began to cry. Cassie lifted the baby and hushed him. "Ellie, make some gruel. It will have to do for this afternoon."

Bret frowned. "What about tonight?"

A slight smile curved Cassie's mouth. "A woman doesn't need to be conscious to nurse an infant. We'll push these men out and let Jonathan eat."

The afternoon was long. Bret paced. Hunter wrung his hands. Alaina fussed. David prayed. He supposed they all did.

Toward evening, Jo moved and moaned. Bret rushed to her side. "Darling?"

She blinked and tried to sit up. "I have to get the potatoes."

Bret laughed. "They can wait. How do you feel?"

She smiled. "I've felt better." She rubbed her arm. "I must have bumped my arm. It feels stiff." She laughed. "I haven't felt like this since I took the tumble down the steps at Sunny Horizon."

"What?" Bret's eyes widened. "You remember?"

"Silly. How could one forget something like that? You were away in the war."

Now the tears did rush down Bret's face. "Jo! You're remembering! You're really remembering!"

"Oh." She covered her lips with her fingers. "I forgot. I mean I didn't remember that I forgot! Oh, Bret. I can remember!" She giggled. "I remember everything!"

He hugged her.

Ellie chuckled. "Ah's gonna bake a cake. We's gonna have a party!"

Hunter chuckled. It must have been the second bump to her head. Alaina clasped her hand, her eyes bright and a big smile on her face. Cassie was praising the Lord. Jay looked confused. David was confused, too.

"Where's Jonathan?" Jo looked around. "I thought I heard him crying."

"You did, dear Sister." Alaina waved her arm. "You males clear out of here. Master Jonathan is going to have his supper."

Dazed by all the fracas, David went to the porch. He absently strolled around the cabin to Cassie's flower bed and wished he could figure out what had just happened. The door banged. He turned to see Alaina. She looked like sunshine in her yellow dress, and her smile was even brighter.

After glancing around, and apparently not seeing him, she limped to the swing that hung from a limb of an old oak. Sitting, she pushed with her good foot and gazed into the sky.

Circling, he approached from behind her. "Need someone to push?"

"Thanks."

He gave her a gentle shove that set the swing into motion. "I take it that everyone in the cabin is happy."

"Jo's fine and Bret's ecstatic. Jay is rocking and watching Ellie. She's singing and whipping up a cake. Hunter is just walking around with a big grin on his face." She sighed.

David watched her waist-length hair flow out behind her and reached to touch a sun-kissed wave. "Then all is well?"

"Not quite, Mr. David Fisher."

Her tone jolted him. "What's the trouble?"

She stopped her swinging motion. "We have some serious talking to do."

He rubbed his chin. He was too tired to think straight, and enlightening Alaina was going to take concentration. Delaying again was the only answer. He grinned at her. "I thought you were looking for correspondence from your lovers."

She looked mystified, then giggled. "You brought mail?"

"There were two letters."

"Don't just stand there. Get them!"

Thankful for the reprieve, he went to his saddlebags and retrieved the envelopes. "I'm so sorry. There are none from lovers." He glanced at the return addresses. "The first one's from Tiffany Lynn James. The second is from Elizabeth Ann Sherwood."

"Wonderful. They're Bret's sisters. I'll take them in." Eyes sparkling, she limped to the porch and pulled herself up the step. He opened the door and she stepped inside.

"Jo, here are a couple letters from your family."

Jo was slumped against the back of the couch cradling Jonathan. Bret lounged beside her. Hunter sat backwards on a straight-backed chair. Jay rocked and grinned. Ellie joined them. Bret reached for the envelopes as Alaina entered.

David's stomach twisted. A stranger couldn't expect to be part of this family group. Turning, he headed for the door.

Alaina whirled to seize his sleeve, lost her balance, and took a quick sidestep. "Come in and sit."

"But, Lainy . . ." The look she gave him melted him. What could he do but oblige. Nodding, he sat on a nearby kitchen chair. She took a seat beside her sister.

Jo picked up the first envelope, broke the seal, removed the sheets of paper and handed them to Bret. This one's from Tiffany.

As Bret read, David listened and tried to figure out names and relationships.

"The twins are healthy and gaining weight. They are awake more now, but they don't cry much. Adam has begun to rock each little sister for a few minutes before he goes to bed. He says he thinks he'll let them stay.

"Constance is getting stronger. She's so grateful to Mama for insisting she see a doctor in Richmond. She's decided to stay on and help out with the twins."

Bret chuckled. "I think Joe Billings has something to do with her wanting a job at Castle Crest." He held his grin. "Constance seemed to be fond of the man."

He looked back to the letter. "Adam and Alexandra are usually well-behaved, but occasionally one or the other is a mischievous instigator that gets them both in trouble.

"Nathan says he'll be shipping another load of lumber by next week. I can't wait to see Sunny Horizon in all her glory again! I have another bit of news, but I promised to let Elizabeth Ann tell you.

"Andrea Sue is beginning to fuss, and Cassandra Jo will be awake and hungry, too, so I'll say so long for now.

"Love Tiffany."

Alaina clasped her hands. "I can't wait to see those twins! What must it be like to have two baby Jonathans?"

David felt like an intruder and longed to flee, but he knew Alaina would be after him. It would be different if he hoped to someday be part of this family. That couldn't happen. *No amount of wishing can change the facts.* His heart ached.

Alaina bounced on the cushion. "Well, Bret, lets hear what Elizabeth Ann has to tell us."

Again Jo unsealed the envelope and handed Bret the letter.

"Let me see if I can make this out." He squinted and looked closely at the paper.

"Don't you dare." Giggling, Jo poked him. "Elizabeth Ann has perfect penmanship!" She leaned to see over his shoulder.

He flipped the pages and grinned, then began. "Dear Bret and Jo, Wait until you hear my news! I know Tiffany's writing, so there won't be a lot more to say, except that

Joshua has finally proposed to Emily Rose. The wedding is to be the week before Thanksgiving.

"Bret, you promised to bring Jo to Saxon Oaks for a visit before winter. This is perfect! I pray you'll come for the wedding and stay for Thanksgiving.

"Uncle Zachary hired a new man. He has his eye on sweet Ruthie Ann, but I think his attentions are futile, because there's something else in the wind. Of course, Ruthie's still grieving, and she will be for a time. However, Amos has been spending a lot of time at Saxon Oaks and seems more than anxious to help her. He's twelve years older, but that shouldn't matter. He makes Ruthie Ann smile, and her four children adore him. I've never seen him play games and tease. Will wonders never cease?"

David heard a noise and turned to see Ellie. Tears brimmed in the old woman's eyes, but a smile brightened her withered face. "Now Ah won't have to worry 'bout who be takin' care of my dear boy when Ah's gone."

Bret continued. "Uncle Zachary says to say hello. He's anxious to see wee Jonathan again.

"Now for the most wonderful news of all. There's going to be an addition to the Sherwood household! I'm ecstatic, and so is Trenton. Darcy Mae hums and rolls her eyes. Uncle Zachary just smiles."

The letter went on to thank Jo for her prayers and encouragement, but David's mind wandered. He had to plan how to confess to Alaina. She wasn't going to let him procrastinate much longer. After that, he would probably be leaving. The thought pinched his heart. Another prayer whispered between his lips, but his hope was gone.

When the letters were back in their envelopes, David's heart thudded against his ribs. He wanted to run, but that wouldn't help. He knew Alaina was determined enough that, even with her injured leg, she would probably catch him. The time had come! He slowly made his way to the porch.

Alaina's footsteps resounded softly behind him. He strolled to the swing, knowing she liked to sit there, but telling her here would make her hate her favorite spot.

She eyed him. "Well, I'm waiting, Sir David."

"I wanted to take you to the arbor for our . . . discussion."

Her eyes widened. "That old arbor is still standing?"

"It's not in very good shape. I was going to repair it."

"Oh no you don't. You're not putting our talk off that easy. You want to talk in the arbor, we'll go to the arbor."

"You shouldn't be on your leg."

She propped a fist on her hip. "Let's go. If I crumple to the ground in agony, you can carry me the rest of the way."

He chuckled. "I can do that anyway."

"And suffer Ellie's tongue?" Her yellow skirt swished as she turned and headed toward the path.

The old wooden bench might soil her dress. He took a slight detour to swipe the white towel that Ellie had boiled and draped over the back of a porch chair in the sun. He was glad it was dry. After covering the bench, it would no longer be white. The old woman would probably be furious.

He approached Alaina's left side and offered the support of his right arm. She seemed glad to hold on to him.

The going was slow, but he could tell she was determined. His heart pounded. He swallowed. *This is it.* The revelation he'd been dreading.

Finally, they reached the arbor. He spread the towel on the seat and waited for her to get settled. Taking a seat beside her, he tried to draw a deep breath. His chest felt tight.

"Well, I'm listening." Her tone was soft, but demanding.

"I've been trying to figure out how to tell you things, but confusion has made it difficult."

"You can't be any more confused than I am."

He swallowed. "I don't know where to start."

"Just begin anywhere, David, and go from there."

"Well . . . I . . ." He hesitated.

"That's established. Go on Mr. Fisher."

He shuddered. "To begin with, I'm not Mr. Fisher."

"What do you mean?" Alarm made her voice resonate at a higher pitch. "David?"

# Thirty

The way Alaina said his name, her voice small and pleading, tore at David's heart. "Oh, Lainy, I'm so sorry."

"That you're not Mr. Fisher?"

"Yes."

Her eyes bore into him. "Why did you say you were?"

He shrugged to camouflage a grimace. "I did a lot of fishing for a month and just chose that name."

"Why?" She looked stunned. "Who are you?"

His gaze met hers. "I don't know." He sighed. "How can you understand someone not knowing who they are?"

"David . . ." She hesitated. "You're not David?"

"I am, but that's all I know." He swallowed. "I regained consciousness facedown on an uninhabited island. I don't remember anything previous to that time."

"Jo was like that. She just remembered the past when she came to after bumping her head in Ellie's root cellar."

He gasped. "So *that's* what your family and Ellie were so elated about!" His mind flashed back over the scene. It made sense now. "What happened that caused her memory loss?"

"A buggy accident in March. She gave birth before she regained consciousness. She wouldn't accept that Jonathan was her baby, and at first, she refused to nurse him. She didn't even know Bret." Reaching out, she rested a hand on his arm. "We love each other, David. We can work this out. Your not remembering your past doesn't matter."

"I'm afraid it does, Lainy."

"Why? No mountain is too high to climb if two people really love each other."

"There's more than just a mountain."

"Any crisis can be solved if we work at it."

"You don't understand."

"I'm trying to."

Skirting the main issue, he explained how he'd struggled to climb to the island's crest as the tide was rolling in. Hesitating, he rubbed his temples. "I was marooned on that desert island for a month before I was rescued."

"How were you rescued?"

"I'd been signaling ships by glancing rays of the sun from the thick bottom of a glass bottle. Finally, a man on a fishing boat noticed me. They told me I was on an island in the Caribbean." He sighed. "They had no idea who I was or where I was from." The misery in his heart continued to intensify. Frustration knotted his stomach. He clenched his fingers into fists. "I don't even know my family!"

"I'll be your family, David. I love you."

Her voice was so soft, he hardly heard her. "I can't love you, Lainy."

"But . . . I thought you did."

"I do, more than you know, but there's more. I'm trying to tell you, but the words get stuck in my throat."

Anxiety created creases in her otherwise smooth forehead. "I'm trying to be patient."

Skirting the main issue, he described the desolation, confusion, and the emotional torment he'd suffered.

"Were you sick?"

"I was weak. I didn't have any idea how long I'd been on the water. I peered at my hands. They looked like they belonged to a stranger. Panic wrenched my stomach."

"What did you do?"

"I existed. And I prayed a lot."

"You would've had to swim from where the ship sank."

"I was on a small life raft." He tried to express how isolated he'd felt and how much he'd depended on the small book of Psalms he'd found in his pocket.

"Didn't it get wet?"

"It was wrapped tightly in oilcloth, so it didn't get saturated. I tediously dried pages in the sun." One side of his mouth jerked in a half-grin. "I didn't have much else to do."

"After all that work, the book must mean a lot to you."

"It did." He suffocated a groan. "A huge wave stole that, too." This conversation was painful, and he wanted to get it over with. But that would mean that he'd lost Alaina forever. "My biggest problem was finding food. I caught some sea creatures, and God provided by depositing a fish in a pool behind some rocks every day or so. I longed to get back to civilization, but unless rescued, that was impossible."

Alaina blinked. Astonishment made her eyes lustrous. "I can't imagine how confused, frustrated and isolated you must have felt." Her hand hovered between them.

He gripped her fingers. She flung herself into his arms. He told himself to turn away, but his arms wouldn't listen. She looked up to meet his gaze. Overwhelmed, he tightened his embrace and his lips covered hers. Her warm and genuine response swept him from reality with as much force as the tidal wave that had nearly swept him out to sea.

Finally, struggling to regain his senses, he straightened. "You have to hear it all."

Her face was flushed and passion smoldered in her brown eyes. "You can take as much time as you want."

"No. I must tell you before I lose my courage." He tore his focus from her face. "I yearn to unlock the secrets in my mind." He struck the bench with a fist. "Yet I long to forget what I don't want to remember." A shudder raked his length. Sucking in air, he continued. "I was so thirsty. Sand gritted between my teeth. My lips were dry and cracked. Salt from the ocean coated my skin and made my cuts and scrapes burn. I suppose that was God's way of helping them to heal." He ran his fingers through his hair. "I realized I'd nearly drown. At first I was thankful, then I thought maybe it would've been better if the sea had claimed my body as well as my past."

"Oh, David. Don't say that." She clasped her hands in her lap and studied his face.

"When I circled the island, I discovered a small freshwater spring trickling from a crack in a rock."

"Like the children of Israel in the wilderness."

"Yes, but other than the presence of God, I was alone. The water ran in a tiny stream into a hollow in a rock that formed a natural basin. I lowered my face to the pool for a drink, then stared in amazement at my reflection. Indigo eyes stared back at me. They looked friendly, but unfamiliar." He shivered. "I touched the black stubble on my cheek. It was my face, my eyes, yet the features were those of a stranger!"

"Jo told me the same thing." She smiled. "I understand. Probably because Jo told me so much about how she felt. We have to be patient. In time your memory will come back."

"When it does, there will be more problems."

"Jo said the first time she looked in a mirror, she thought she was going to faint."

"I know how she felt. After I drank my fill, I tried to study my reflection, hoping to remember something. Anything! I looked at my forehead. It was unlined, denoting that I wasn't a worrier. Laugh lines told me I must have a jovial personality. I stared at my cheekbones. They seemed slightly prominent, and a strong jaw hinted of strength and determination, but I couldn't be sure."

"You were right."

He shrugged. "Am I what I seem? Or am I really something else?"

"Jo's personality didn't change. She was still the same sweet, wonderful sister that she'd always been, whether she remembered me or not." A smile relaxed her features. "It will be the same for you. She said she pictured herself a blond like Trisha, and when she saw her black curls she had to suppress a scream."

"I didn't have any reaction. I felt numb. I ran my fingers through my hair. It was stiff. I knew it was because it had been saturated by salt water, cooked by the scorching sun, and whipped by the ocean breeze . When I discovered it was more curly than I'd surmised, I didn't care."

"That's because you're a man. You probably still don't care."

"There are more important things to be concerned about." Picturing the circle of metal in his pocket, he cringed and withdrew into silence.

"I can tell there's something really bothering you, David. Please don't keep me in the dark any longer."

He opened his mouth to speak, but his throat constricted. He choked and tried again. How could he put it into words? He rammed his hand deep into his pocket to touch the piece of metal that nestled there. It felt hot against his fingers. "This might explain my situation." Slowly withdrawing the circle of gold, he dropped it into her palm.

She stared at it. "A wedding ring?"

"What else could it be?"

Her soft lips parted. "Yours?"

He shrugged. "Who else would put their wedding ring in my pocket."

"How could you do this to me?" Tears filled her eyes and coursed down her cheeks.

"It's . . . engraved."

"Why should I care!"

"That's how I know my name is David." He withdrew into silence. Why had he told her this way? There had to have been a better way. What did it matter? Her anguish and his would be the same regardless.

Taking a deep breath, she held the ring up and peered at the engraving. "Two entwined hearts." Squinting, she read, "To David with love, from Emma." She glared at him through her tears. "Emma? Who's Emma?"

"I have no idea, Lainy."

"You don't know your own wife?" Her voice had risen with each new word.

"Did Jo know she was married to Bret?"

"No! But that's different!" She tossed the ring back. "Jo didn't pretend to be someone she wasn't, seduce someone, then crush their heart beyond repair!"

"I didn't mean to hurt you. I'm devastated, too, Lainy. I love you!" He lowered his voice when he realized he was shouting.

"Why didn't you wear your stupid ring? At least I would've known better than to fall in love with you."

He shoved it back into his pocket, wishing he'd never seen it. "It was too large. I lost a lot of weight on the island, and I couldn't keep it on my finger."

"And of course, since it's so precious, you wouldn't want to lose it." She gasped. Tears came. Her slender shoulders shook.

"It's the only link to my past."

"Keep your rotten past!" She gasped and a sob shook her frame. "You don't have any future. At least with me!" She leaped to her feet and took several steps. Her injured leg buckled, and she cried out as she went down on one knee.

He leaped up to help her.

"Don't touch me! I hate you! Understand? I hate you!" Covering her face, she sobbed.

David felt as though he died a little more with each tear she shed. He was weeping inside. His heart convulsed. This was his fault. What could he do to remedy the anguish now? How could he undo the damage he'd caused?

"Why did you wait . . . so long to tell me?"

"At first it didn't matter who I was. I remained to help Bret." He reached out to touch her, then drew back. "When I realized I was in love with you, I didn't know how to tell you."

"So you waited until the news would destroy me?" She grabbed a tree limb and pulled herself to her feet, then slowly limped down the path.

"Alaina, I didn't want to hurt you. I would rather die."

"But you didn't! You lived to make me wish *I* was dead!" She paused to catch her breath, then stumbled on.

He walked behind her, not daring to help. If Hunter didn't kill him, Bret would. Picturing Ellie's scorn, he shuddered. He deserved it and more. "I'll pack and leave in the morning."

She whirled and nearly fell. Her glare scorched him. "Oh no you won't! What sort of beast are you? Bret is counting on you, and so is Hunter. You'll stay and complete your job. Don't you dare even consider breaking your promise to Bret and my brother!"

"I'll remain as long as they want me to, Lainy, but I don't think we should see each other again."

She sniffed. "You don't have to worry about that!" Turning, she continued down the path.

"I only want you to remember one thing, Lainy. I love you with all my heart. I'll never love anyone else."

"Except Emma." The words hissed through her teeth.

"I don't even know her!"

"So? You don't know yourself either." She sniffed. "And I wish you didn't know *me*."

"Alaina, you are the only bright and wonderful thing in my life."

"And you crushed it!" She paused to blow her nose, then went on. At the cabin, she crossed the porch and went inside without looking back.

He felt as though he'd just been battered like a ship in a storm. He had no desire to stay afloat. His heart had already sunk to the bottom of the sea. He stepped onto Hunter's porch. It wasn't going to be easy to confess what he'd done. *If the man wants to rip me apart for hurting his sister, so be it.*

Alaina noticed Bret and Jo at the far side of the construction site, and was thankful they were preoccupied and didn't see her. She pushed Ellie's door open and stepped into the kitchen. She wished there was some place to hide. She didn't want anyone to see her blotched face and reddened eyes.

Ellie turned, took one look, and clucked her tongue. "You's been talkin' to Misa David?"

Alaina nodded.

"He do this to you, child?" The black woman hurried forward and took her in her arms. "Old Ellie be afraid this gonna happen."

"I don't want Jo to see me like this."

"You come to my room. Ah's gonna take care of you." She ushered Alaina into the bedroom and guided her to the bed. "You rest. Ah'll be fetchin' some tea."

Alaina flopped facedown across the newly laundered sheets and let more tears flow. She never wanted to see David again. *But how am I going to live without him?*

Within minutes, Ellie appeared with tea. "You drink this."

Alaina just wanted to die, but she sat up and accepted the cup.

"You's gonna be fine, honey."

The tea was hot. Alaina hiccupped as she took a tiny sip. "I won't ever be fine."

"You thinks that, but you be listenin' to old Ellie when Ah be sayin' that time gonna make you forget there ever be a Misa Fisher."

"There isn't any Mr. Fisher now. He lied!" She tried to take a long breath, but the air seemed to hurt her chest.

Ellie looked bewildered. "Then who he be, child?"

"David thinks he could've been shipwrecked. He lost his memory, just like Jo. He was alone. He doesn't know his family or who he really is." She hiccupped. "Except Emma."

"Who be Emma?"

"His wife."

"Oh, dear Lordie!" Ellie plopped to the chair beside the bed. "Why hain't he be with her?"

"He doesn't remember her. He has no idea who she is or where to look for her." She jerked her handkerchief from her pocket and blew her nose. "He found his wedding ring in his pocket. The names engraved on the inside were David and Emma." She sipped her tea. "I used to like Emma for a name. He ruined that for me, too." She looked at Ellie. "I wanted to call my first little girl Emma. Can you beat that!"

"Humph. If anything gets beat, it needs to be Mr. David."

After drinking the tea, Alaina felt exhausted. "I think I'd like to rest."

"You rest long as you likes. Ah be tellin' folks you don't want disturbed. And Ah be makin' old man Jay stay on the porch." She patted Alaina's shoulder, left the room, and closed the door behind her.

Alaina stared at the cracked panels. Ellie was usually right, but this time, Alaina doubted the old woman's words.

*How will I ever stop loving David?*

She thought about the crushes she'd had in her mid-teens. Compared to what she felt for David, her other courting had been just frivolous, but harmless flirting.

Her lips tightened. *I flirted a lot, but I never hurt anyone.*

Standing, she went to a window. Jo headed for the house with Jonathan in her arms. Hunter and Bret were busy pounding on the second floor. David stood on the third, staring into the sky. Was he praying?

"He'd better be." Watching him made more tears come. The scene blurred. She blinked. If only he hadn't promised to help Bret build the house, he'd go away, and she wouldn't have to look at him anymore.

Her heart cramped. *But what will I do when he's gone?*

As the days passed, Alaina continued to agonize over the misery David had created within her. The pain gouged a canyon in her heart that continued to widen. She would peer through the lace curtain at the men at the building site and yearn to feel David's embrace. He'd explained his predicament to the men. They understood better than she did. It was impossible to be in David's presence; yet it was torture not to be with him.

She considered his amnesia. *What were the chances of a member of my family suffering from memory loss, then meeting and falling in love with a man who had the same problem?* It seemed impossible. Yet this horrid situation was real. *Unless David's lying.* That would mean he had devastated her on purpose. *Could he be that cruel?*

Unable to control her desire to watch him, she went to peer through the lace curtain toward the building site.

Jo joined her. "Isn't the man Bret hired to build the fireplaces supposed to come today?"

"I think so." Alaina had explained her situation to Jo. Her sister was compassionate and understanding, thus she hadn't pressed the issue or said "I told you so."

Jo sighed. "The right half of the house is coming along great. I can't wait until next summer when we finish the other half. The two-story porches encircled three sides of the house. I loved to stroll the second-story one at night. Oh, Alaina, do you remember it?"

"I was only eleven when I saw it last, but I sort of remember. Wasn't there a small balcony on the third floor?"

"Yes. Jonathan finished the attic as a place for Tiffany to paint. He put in a large window, and built a balcony."

"Is Bret planning to do that, too?"

"He'll put in a smaller window, but I don't think we're adding a door or the balcony."

"The third floor will be a great place for little Jonathan to play when he's older."

Jo laughed. "Bret suggested that."

It was wonderful to talk to Jo about the past. She seemed to enjoy it as much as Alaina. She supposed losing one's memory made one value it more when it came back. She thought about David's torment and cringed. She was beginning to understand how much he was hurting, too.

The late afternoon sun streamed through a window and formed a streak of light on the wooden floor and brightened the yellow in Alaina's dress. It was the first time she'd worn it since David had broken her heart. Determined to get over her love for him, she'd gritted her teeth and donned the garment that morning.

The calico kitten meowed at Alaina's feet. She scooped it up. "This is Patches. She's mine."

Ellie shook her head. "I don't know where that one be comin' from. My old Susie never be havin' a calico cat."

Jo picked up the white kitten. "This one's mine." She grinned. "Lacy seems to like her best, too."

"Priscilla is taking the yellow spotted male home as soon as it's weaned."

The sound of an approaching horse and buggy drew Alaina to a window. The conveyance came into view. "Someone's coming."

Jo hurried to join her. "It's Jenna Leigh Cristen."

"She has a child with her."

"That's Robby, her adopted son. Her brother-in-law was killed in the war, then her sister died, leaving the little boy in Jenna's care. He must be about six years old."

"He's cute. They both have the same shade of strawberry-blond hair."

"Jenna's sister was a blond, too." Jo headed for the door. "Jenna's our first visitor." She paused to glance over her shoulder at Ellie. "Please put the kettle on for tea."

Alaina trailed Jo across the porch and past the new house. She watched Jenna gracefully alight and give her purple skirt a flip to insure that the folds fell into place. After adjusting her broad-brimmed hat, she turned to aid the boy's climb to the ground.

Robby's blue eyes roamed over the construction, and a big grin stretched his lips.

"Hello, Jenna." Jo called. "It's so good to see you." She hurried to hug the woman, then turned to introduce her to Alaina.

During the greeting, Alaina quickly calculated the woman's size. She couldn't be much over five feet tall, and her waist about twenty inches around. Alaina was surprised at Jenna's firm handshake, for her hands seemed small and delicate. Alaina smiled at Robby. He returned her greeting, but his attention never left the building.

"Mama, can I help build while we're here?"

"I think you should come into the cabin with me." Jenna retrieved her bag from the buggy seat, then reached for his hand. "I don't want you to get in the way."

"I won't. I wanna learn to build like Uncle Robert."

"Your Uncle Robert draws plans for buildings. He doesn't construct them."

Alaina read disappointment on the child's face. "Ellie baked cookies this morning. She was hoping a little boy would come to help us eat them."

The promise of a treat seemed to help convince Robby, but his focus lingered on the building as he accompanied the ladies toward the porch.

David came out of Hunter's cabin, looked up, and smiled. "Hello."

"David!" Jenna stopped mid-step. "You helping rebuild Sunny Horizon?"

"Yes. How's your mother's wrist?"

"Doing much better, thanks to you." Her smile was as warm as her greeting.

David spoke to Robby and invited him to get a closer look at the construction. The child gazed up at Jenna for permission. She nodded. Grinning, he ran to join David.

Alaina's heart cramped. Had David romanced Jenna before coming to help Bret? Refusing to look at him, she accompanied the ladies inside. Jenna removed her hat and tossed it to a chair. Blond curls dangled from a bun at her nape and adorned her oval face.

While sipping her tea, Alaina listened to Jo and Jenna catch up on what had happened since Jo had left the Valley. Alaina wondered if David had hurt this woman, too. Finally, she could no longer contain her quandary. "How long have you known David?"

Jenna lowered her cup. It clinked on the saucer. "I met him about three months ago in Staunton."

"Did he . . . Did you . . ." Alaina swallowed and tried again to phrase the question. "I mean, were the two of you involved"

"We were friends." Jenna smiled. "He aided my mother when she'd sprained her wrist." Jenna's smile slowly faded as she studied Alaina's face. "I take it that you and he have more than a friendship."

"No. We were . . . But not now." Alaina's breath caught, then she continued. "I didn't know he was married."

"Married? He never mentioned having a family."

The woman apparently didn't realize that David was suffering from memory loss. Jo quickly explained.

Without words, Jenna reached out to touch Alaina's hand. "I, too, loved and lost. My betrothed didn't return from the war. Had he been killed, it would have been easier to understand. I learned recently that, after the fighting, he left for Nevada territory without seeing me or his family."

"I suppose it would be easier for me if I didn't have to see David every day." Alaina shuddered. "But not to see him at all would be worse than I could imagine."

"In a way, I suppose." Jenna frowned as she thought. "Although, once I knew Kenneth wasn't coming home to marry me, I was able to put my life back together and go on without him." She patted Alaina's wrist. "God helped me. I know he'll give you courage, too."

Jonathan began to cry. Jenna's blue eyes shimmered as she faced Jo. "Tiffany wrote and told me about your having a son. That was one reason for my visit."

"I'll get him, Jo." Alaina hurried into the bedroom and scooped the baby into her arms. He stopped fussing and gazed up at her. She changed his wet clothing, then took him to the kitchen and handed him to Jenna.

"He's precious. Oh, Jo, you and Bret are so blessed." She reached into her bag and retrieved a wrapped parcel. "I brought something for the baby."

Jo unwrapped the gift and gasped. "It's lovely." She unfolded a blue crocheted baby blanket with a light-blue border. "This must have taken you many hours."

"I worked on it each evening." Jenna smiled. "I thought you could use it for a sofa throw once Jonathan doesn't need it any more."

"I'll use it for Jonathan, then I'll put it away for my other babies."

The sound of a horse galloping up the Valley drew Alaina's attention. Curiosity lured her to a window. A tall, broad-shouldered man in his thirties dismounted and ground-tied his bay mare at the new house. His shirt sleeves pulled taut around his biceps. He removed his hat, and the sun struck his blond hair.

Jo's blue skirt flipped as she stood and headed for the door. "I'm going to see who that is. I can eavesdrop better from the porch." Pausing, she glanced at Jenna.

"Go ahead, Jo. I'll stay with the baby."

"I'm coming, too." Alaina followed her sister through the portal. If the stranger had news, she wasn't going to miss hearing it.

"Mr. Harris!" The man glanced toward the building.

Bret poked his head out a window opening. "Yes?"

The man pointed. "Those chimneys you want examined?"

"Yes. You the man who's going to rebuild the fireplaces?"

"That's me. Ronald Franks at your service." He bowed humorously and chuckled. "Hunter in there with you?"

"Hey there!" Hunter jumped out a door opening and hurried toward the man. "Good to see you, Ron. It's been a long time."

"Sure has. I've been in a war, been shipwrecked, and got married since we've chewed the fat."

"Good for you!" Hunter chuckled. "I'm still single and loving every minute of it."

David took Robby's hand and headed for Ellie's cabin.

Ronald whooped. "Hey! You old renegade! Where have you been?"

David didn't break his stride. Hunter glanced at him. "Hey, Dave! Ron's talking to you."

Halting, David whirled to face the man, surprise registering on his face. He stared at the stranger and appeared bewildered.

Ron hurried toward him. "I thought you were dead!"

"You . . . know me?"

Ronald chortled. "Come off it, Doc!"

Robbie joined Jo on the porch. Bret and Hunter's full attention was on David. Hunter seemed to find his voice. "David is suffering from memory loss. He came to on an island and doesn't remember anything prior to that time."

Ronald looked astounded. "This bloke is Doc Jefferson."

Astonishment made a noise squeak in Alaina's throat. Blinking, she gripped a porch post, her eyes glued to David.

His knees seemed to buckle, and he sat on a beam. "You know . . . my family?"

"Sure. I attended your memorial service. It was real nice. Singing and crying and everything. The reverend read weepy poems, and we all felt rotten." Suddenly, Ronald grew serious. "Your folks have been grieving for months." He scratched his head, bouncing his golden locks. "Why haven't you notified them that you're all right?"

"I didn't know who they were or where to find them."

"Oh, yeah." Ronald slapped his thigh. "They're Dr. Harvest and Margaret Jefferson. Your entire family lives in Harper's Ferry."

Alaina left the porch and took a few steps into the yard, then paused to stare at Ronald Franks. Her attention clung to his every word. "You know David really well?"

"Of course. He's ten years younger than I am, and I watched him grow up." He chuckled. "I never understood why he preferred to help his father in the doctor's office rather than go hunting and fishing. It didn't surprise me when he became a medical doctor."

"A doctor?" Alaina whispered.

Bret gaped. "I wondered how he knew how to set bones and suture wounds. It just seemed to come to him naturally."

Ronald shrugged. "I guess there are some things a sawbones never forgets."

David sat in stunned silence. This revelation overwhelmed him. Since returning from the island, he'd prayed to run into someone who knew him. Now that it had happened, he felt tongue-tied. Waves of elation and shock surged over him, then collided to create a shower of both delight and remorse. So many controversial questions crashed into each other in his mind, that he failed to compose an intelligent inquiry. He would get to meet Emma. But he would have to say good-bye forever to Alaina. He yearned to know about his past. He had to know, yet knowing would destroy the life he'd made for himself the past few months.

*I'll have to get over my love for Alaina, but that's impossible!*

Anxiety swirled within him, creating a whirlpool that threatened to suck him under. Thoughts slammed him from all sides like chunks of debris. The joy of being recognized marbleized with the anguish of loss that both gave his heart wings and tortured his soul.

There were things he had to know. *And facts I don't want to find out.* Apprehension pounded him. Heart throbbing, he looked at Alaina.

Her eyes wide, she stared at Ronald. "How many in Dr. Jefferson's family?"

"He has a mother and father, one brother and two sisters."

She swallowed and blinked. "and . . . Emma?"

He wrinkled his broad nose and scratched above one ear. "Emma?"

"David's . . . wife."

A hooting laugh spouted from the man and he slapped his thigh with his hat. "I don't know about any David or if he has a wife named Emma. But Dr. Michael Aaron Jefferson isn't now or never was married." Ronald shrugged. "Unless he got hitched since we were shipwrecked."

Alaina staggered. "No . . . Emma?" The question issued out in a whisper.

*No Emma! No wife*! David leaped to his feet. *No David either. I'm Michael*! His eyes found Alaina's. He grinned.

*No Emma!* The words blasted his senses and ricocheted through his reeling brain. For a moment he felt suspended between the ability to comprehend and full realization.

Alaina took one step toward him. He took a step toward her, then hurried across the yard. Her yellow skirt billowed out behind her as she raced to meet him. They came together with a force that knocked the breath from them both.

"Oh, Michael! There's no Emma!"

"But there's my Lainy." He kissed her long and slow. An ecstasy *he knew* he'd never known filled his heart.

"Well!" Ronald chuckled. "Looks like Doc has finally succumbed."

"And it couldn't be more wonderful." Michael grinned at Alaina. "How would you like to be Mrs. Michael Aaron Jefferson?"

"I'd be delighted."

"We can get used to the name together."

She giggled. Maybe she would call her first little girl Emma after all. She pulled away enough to look up at Michael. "Who is David, and how did you get his ring?"

He glanced toward Ronald. "Do you know?"

The man looked contemplative, then he brightened. "You were in sick bay when a steamer collided with our ship. A man named David had cut the fingers on his left hand. On deck, you removed his ring so you could examine the wound." He shrugged. "You must have absently dropped it into your pocket. Later, not remembering the man or the incident, you assumed the ring was your own."

Michael faced Alaina, his heart soaring. "I thank God I accepted the job to deliver the lumber to Sunny Horizon."

She kissed his neck. "We were meant to be together. It was the Lord's plan." She giggled. "It was our destiny."

"Our gift from our heavenly Father." He held her close. "My darling. My wonderful Shenandoah destiny."

*The End*

# MORE NOVELS by Barbara Michel

## BLAZE SERIES
*Historical-Mystery-Romance*

### CASCADE FUGITIVE   Book I

To keep her baby out of the clutches of a wicked woman, Susanna takes the infant and flees into the Cascade Mountains. She is caught in many perilous situations. Because of her love for Maria, she becomes a fugitive, and her trust in God is tried.

Chased by bounty hunters, she's forced to go deeper into the mountains. Is the deserted cabin a sanctuary, or a trap?

Who killed her friend's husband? Is one of the men chasing her the murderer? A malefactor is injured. Susanna is the only one who can aid him. If she refuses, he'll die. If she helps, he'll report her to collect the reward. Will fear spur her to race into another unknown danger?

Adoration for Matthew Colt nestles in her heart, but when she meets Adam, love blossoms. Mystery surrounds him. Why is he hiding in the mountains? From whom? Can she trust him? Can she trust her heart?

### COLORADO BLAZE   Book II

Mike, a vivacious teen, follows her grandmother to Luke's ranch. Enigma surrounding the old man's disappearance suggests foul play. Mike resolves to investigate the murder.

Why are the ranch hands elusive? How many play a devious part? Because of Mike's flaming red hair, Tom, the foreman, dubs her Blaze.

Her delightful spontaneity keeps the family and the man she loves in a flux. She solves one dilemma only to leap headlong into another. She discovers a secret passageway, then finds trouble.

Blaze uncovers clues to the murder, but her curiosity and snooping invariably lures her into precarious situations.

Tom is arrested. Mike vows to find the killer. She snoops, gets lost, and discovers that the killer is on her trail!

# REBEL SERIES

*Historical-Romance-Sagas*

## FORTRESS OF A REBEL  Book I

The War Between the States rages. Tiffany Harris disguises herself as Victoria Patton, her deceased Northern cousin, in order to spy for the Confederacy. Resentment toward the Union blazes within her. She blames the conflict and permits her animosity to grow.

Nathan James, also a spy, is wounded wearing Federal blue. Tiffany nurses him. Against her will, love blossoms. She builds a fortress to protect her emotions, but her heart becomes a rebel, too.

Conflicts abound. Tiffany and Nathan are pulled in separate directions to serve their country. Nathan has her heart, but the Confederacy has a prior claim to her loyalty.

An arrogant Union Colonel discovers Tiffany's spying and vows to see her hang.

Tiffany nearly tells Nathan that she was the one he'd loved as Victoria, but she discovers another devastating secret that seals her lips. Can their love flourish, or has truthfulness been violated once too often and their trust forever destroyed?

## SHENANDOAH DESTINY  Book II

\* \* \*

## AWAKE TO VICTORY

Frightened, Shanna rejects her call to nurse in the Amazon jungle, but to comfort a friend, she's drawn to Brazil. Opposing spirits create havoc between her and Dr. Charles Powers and are determined to influence her to return to the States.

She's frightened by wild animals, pursued by Satan worshipers, and confronted with witchcraft. Angels battle the evil.

Charles adores Shanna and prays she will learn to love the jungle as he does. Loving him, she strives to win his approval. He misunderstands her humor and falsely accuses her. Their relationship deteriorates. Will she learn to take authority over the spiritual forces of darkness and fulfill her calling? Will it be too late to restore the doctor's love and faith in her?

# THE AMISH EDEN SERIES
*by*
## Barbara Michel

### SEARCH FOR EDEN **Book 1**

Rebecca, a Mennonite young woman, makes wrong choices and becomes innocently embroiled in trouble. Fear prods her to hide the truth. Doing so ensnares her in a web of deceit. She falls in love with Aaron King, but isn't he betrothed to Sarah, Rebecca's Amish friend? How can she permit his kisses? How can she betray sweet Sarah? What if Aaron discovers the truth? Will she ever find her Garden of Eden?

### RETURN TO EDEN **Book 2**

Elizabeth, a young Amish widow, finds love again. But how can she rip her infant daughter away from her family and her Lancaster church community to go to Mercer County to be with Elam? Through many trials, her faith in God remains steadfast. Then the buggy accident! Will the results crush her hope for fulfillment?

### DAWN OF EDEN **Book 3**

Rachel ponders Jonas' interest in her. Would learning to care for this man again bring ecstasy or another heartache? Rachel's faith is firm, but is her trust in der gut Man strong enough to sustain her when a disfiguring accident threatens her new found love?

### BEYOND EDEN **Book 4**

Lapp's carriage is stoned. Why? An intruder mysteriously enters their locked home. How? Leah's faith is strong, but her hope is sorely tried when S*hunning* overshadows Peter. What will she do if he refuses to conform?

*"As a native of Lancaster County, Pa, where Old Order Amish people abound, I can attest to the authenticity of Michel's books. Her characters are like the ones with whom I went to school and to whom we sold our family farm. Her writing is bright and creative and her plots superb."*

**Norman Rohrer, Former Director**
**The Christian Writers' Guild**

# JOY BOOKS

## REBEL SERIES
***FORTRESS OF A REBEL*** Book I (540 pages)
Retail: paperback $26.99   hard cover $33.99
***SPECIAL*** FROM **JOY BOOKS**: (subject to change)
Paperback $19.95   hard cover $25.95
***SHENANDOAH DESTINY*** Book II (325 pages)
Paperback $17.95

\* \* \*

## BLAZE SERIES
***CASCADE FUGITIVE*** Book I
***COLORADO BLAZE*** Book II
234 page paperbacks $14.95 each

\* \* \*

### *AWAKE TO VICTORY*
388 page paperback $17.95

\* \* \*

### *CROSSING PATHS TREASURY*
A compilation of 26 inspiring true-life stories, 6 by Michel
240 page paperback   $11.95

\* \* \*

## AMISH EDEN SERIES
***SEARCH FOR EDEN*** Book I   ***RETURN TO EDEN*** Book II
***DAWN OF EDEN*** Book III   ***BEYOND EDEN*** Book IV
$9.95 each   S/H 1 book, $3.50   Add $1. for each additional book.
**SPECIAL:** Set of 4: $35.95   S\H $4.00

\* \* \*

### MILLER FAMILY *AMISH COOKBOOK* $15.00
\* \* \*

ORDER INFORMATION
SHIPPING: 1 book, $3.50.  Add $1. for each additional book
Pa residents add 6% sales tax

Make checks payable to: JOY BOOKS
P.O. Box 3, Hawthorn Pa 16230

**NOVELS AVAILABLE ONLINE** *(online prices may vary)*
*www.joybooks1.com   website uses PayPal*